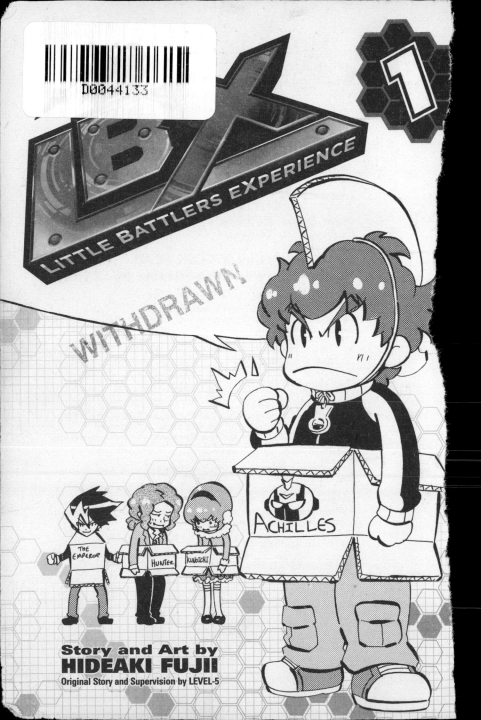

LBX Volume 1
New Dawn Raisers
Perfect Square Edition

Story and Art by Hideaki FUJII
Original Story and Supervision by LEVEL-5

Translation/Tetsuichiro Miyaki
English Adaptation/Aubrey Sitterson
Lettering/Annaliese Christman
Design/Izumi Evers
Editor/Joel Enos

DANBALL SENKI Vol.1
by Hideaki FUJII
© 2011 Hideaki FUJII
© LEVEL-5 Inc.
All rights reserved.
Original Japanese edition published by SHOGAKUKAN.
English translation rights in the United States of
America, Canada, the United Kingdom, Ireland, Australia
and New Zealand arranged with SHOGAKUKAN.

Printed in Canada

Published by VIZ Media, LLC
P.O. Box 77010
San Francisco, CA 94107

10 9 8 7 6 5 4 3 2 1
First printing, November 2014

www.perfectsquare.com   www.viz.com

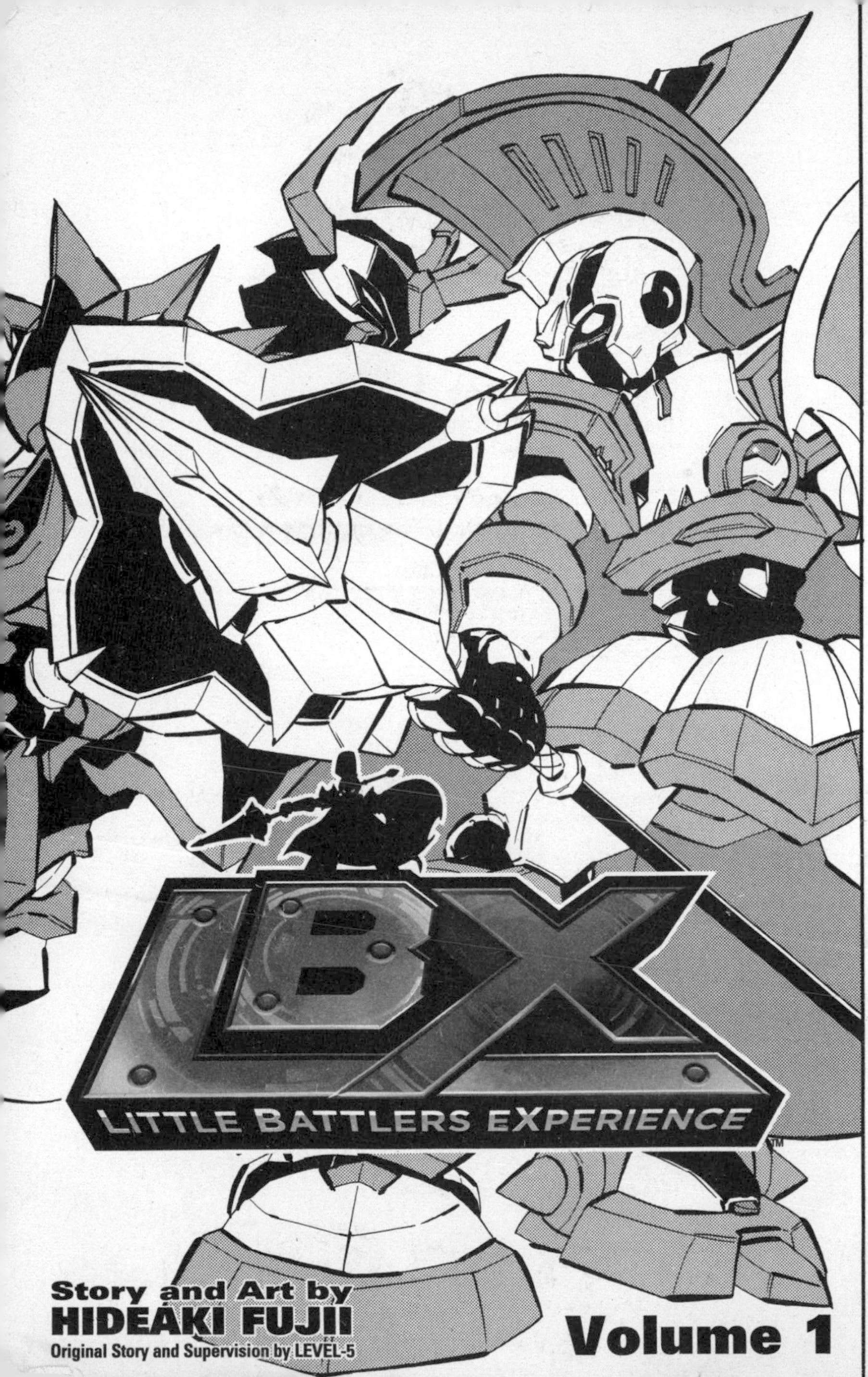

LBX
LITTLE BATTLERS EXPERIENCE™

Story and Art by
HIDEAKI FUJII
Original Story and Supervision by LEVEL-5

Volume 1

TABLE OF CONTENTS

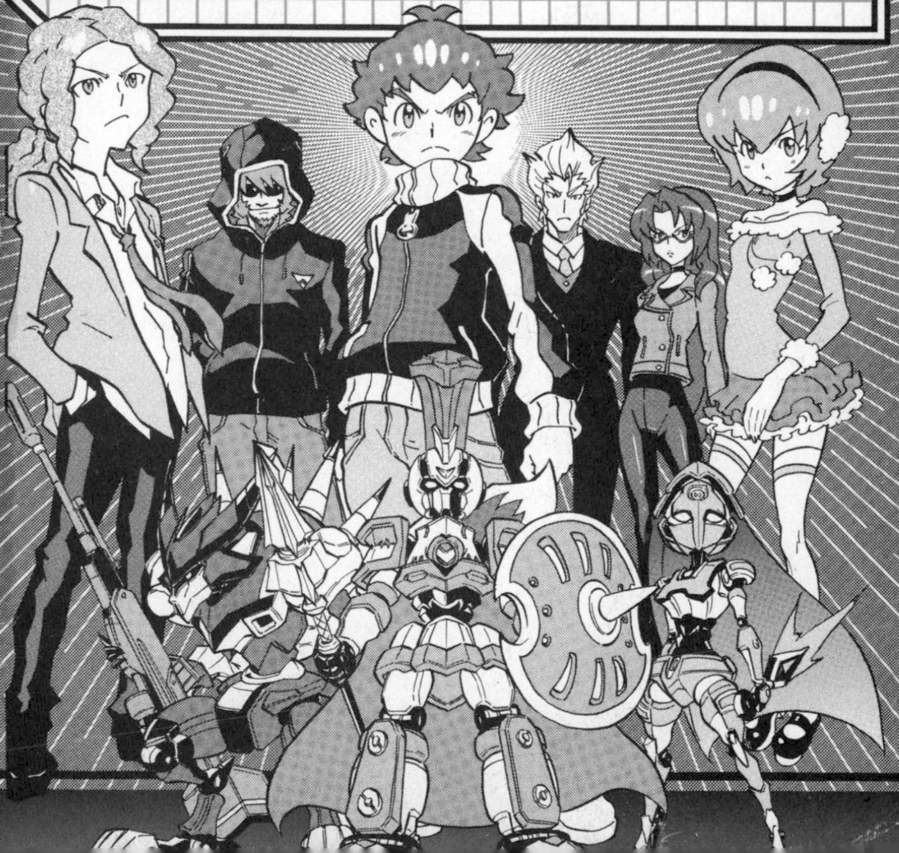

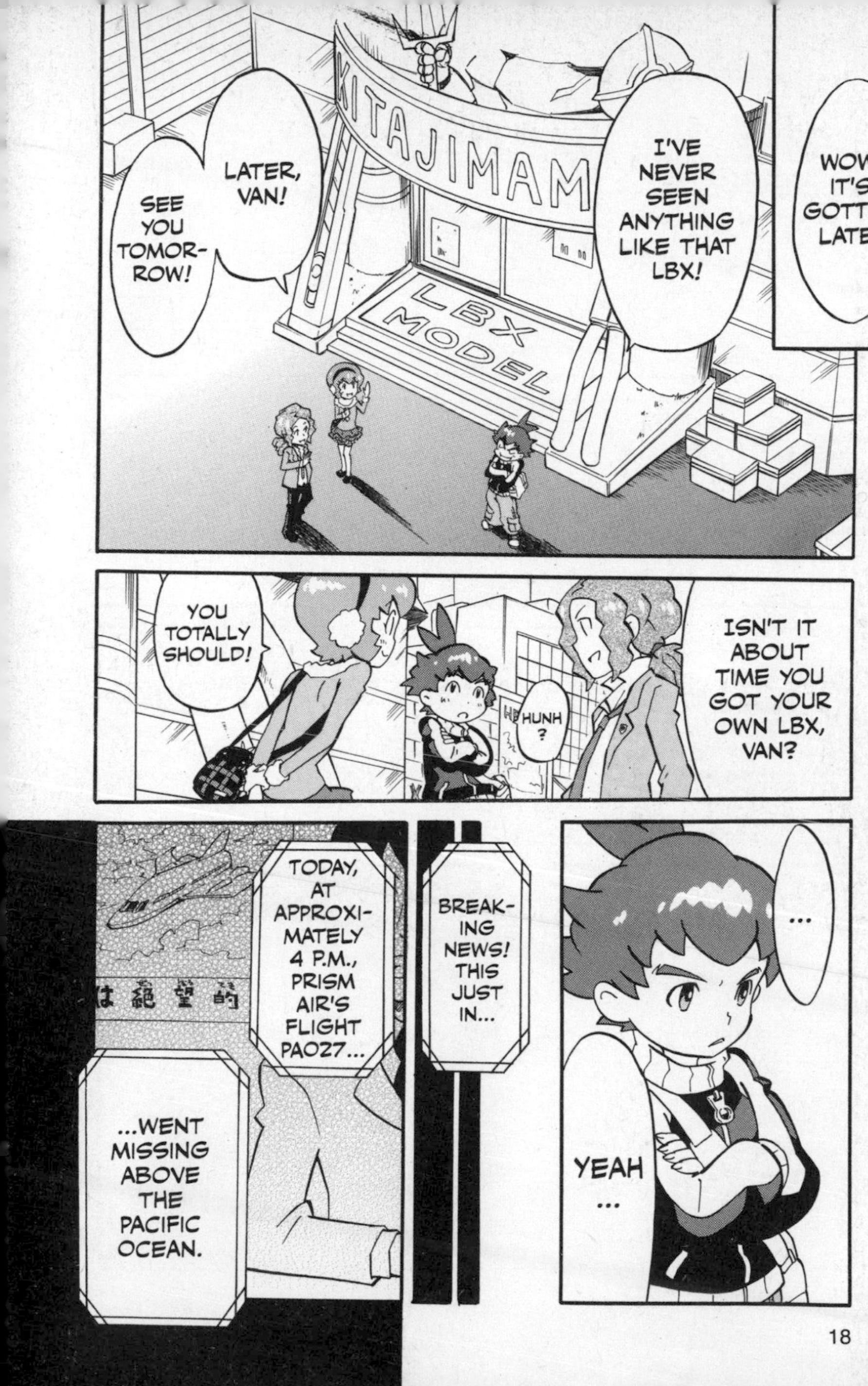

WOW, IT'S GOTTEN LATE!
I'VE NEVER SEEN ANYTHING LIKE THAT LBX!
LATER, VAN!
SEE YOU TOMOR-ROW!
KITAJIMAM
LBX MODEL
ISN'T IT ABOUT TIME YOU GOT YOUR OWN LBX, VAN?
HUNH?
YOU TOTALLY SHOULD!
...
YEAH ...
BREAK-ING NEWS! THIS JUST IN...
TODAY, AT APPROXI-MATELY 4 P.M., PRISM AIR'S FLIGHT PA027...
は絶望的
...WENT MISSING ABOVE THE PACIFIC OCEAN.

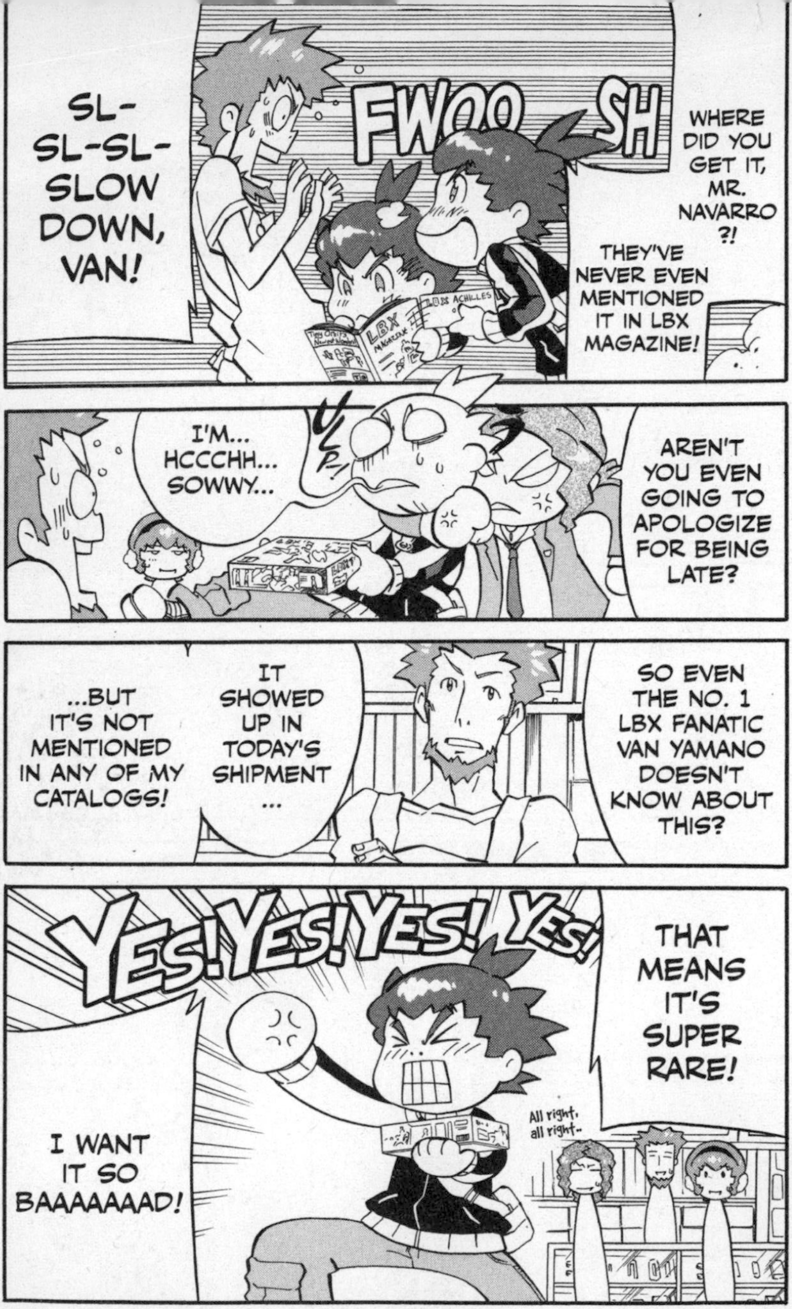

WHERE DID YOU GET IT, MR. NAVARRO?!
THEY'VE NEVER EVEN MENTIONED IT IN LBX MAGAZINE!
FWOOSH
SL-SL-SL-SLOW DOWN, VAN!
AREN'T YOU EVEN GOING TO APOLOGIZE FOR BEING LATE?
ULP!
I'M... HCCCHH... SOWWY...
SO EVEN THE NO. 1 LBX FANATIC VAN YAMANO DOESN'T KNOW ABOUT THIS?
IT SHOWED UP IN TODAY'S SHIPMENT...
...BUT IT'S NOT MENTIONED IN ANY OF MY CATALOGS!
THAT MEANS IT'S SUPER RARE!
YES! YES! YES! YES!
All right, all right..
I WANT IT SO BAAAAAAAD!

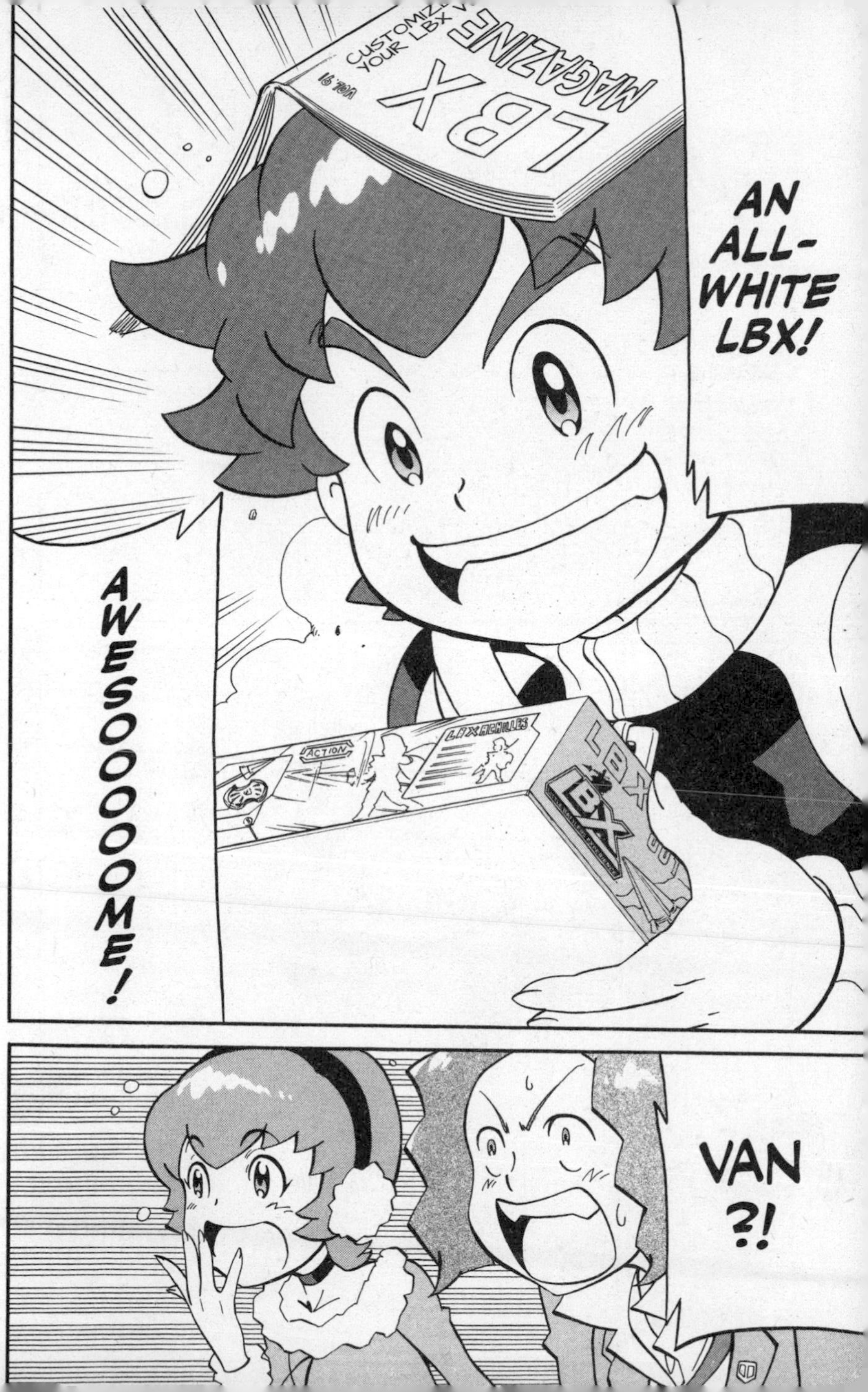
LBX MAGAZINE
VOL. 91
AN ALL-WHITE LBX!
AWESOOOOOME!
VAN ?!

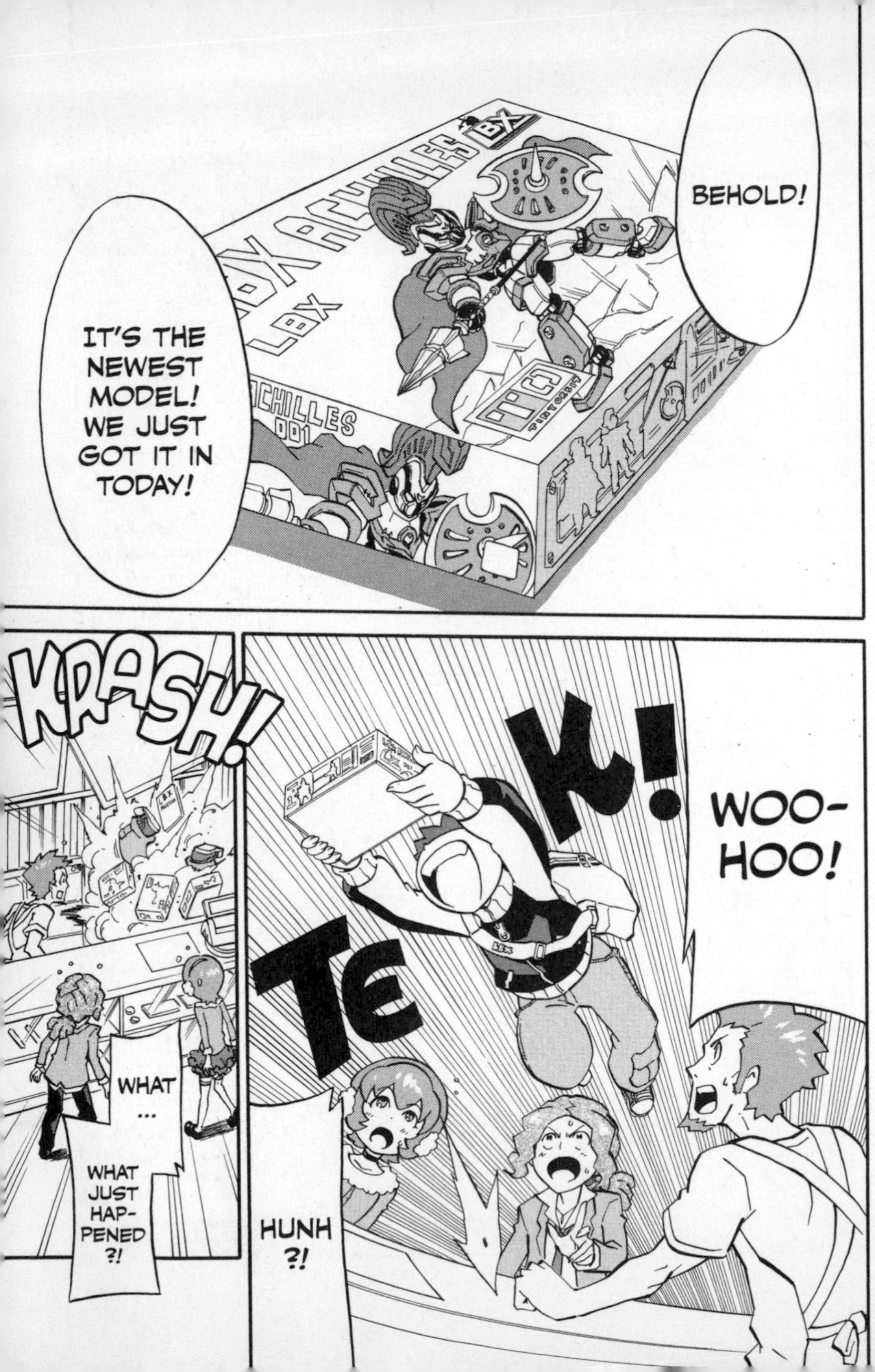
LBX ACHILLES
LBX
ACHILLES 001
TINY ORBIT
BEHOLD!
IT'S THE NEWEST MODEL! WE JUST GOT IT IN TODAY!
WOO-HOO!
K!
TE
HUNH ?!
KRASH!
WHAT ...
WHAT JUST HAP-PENED ?!

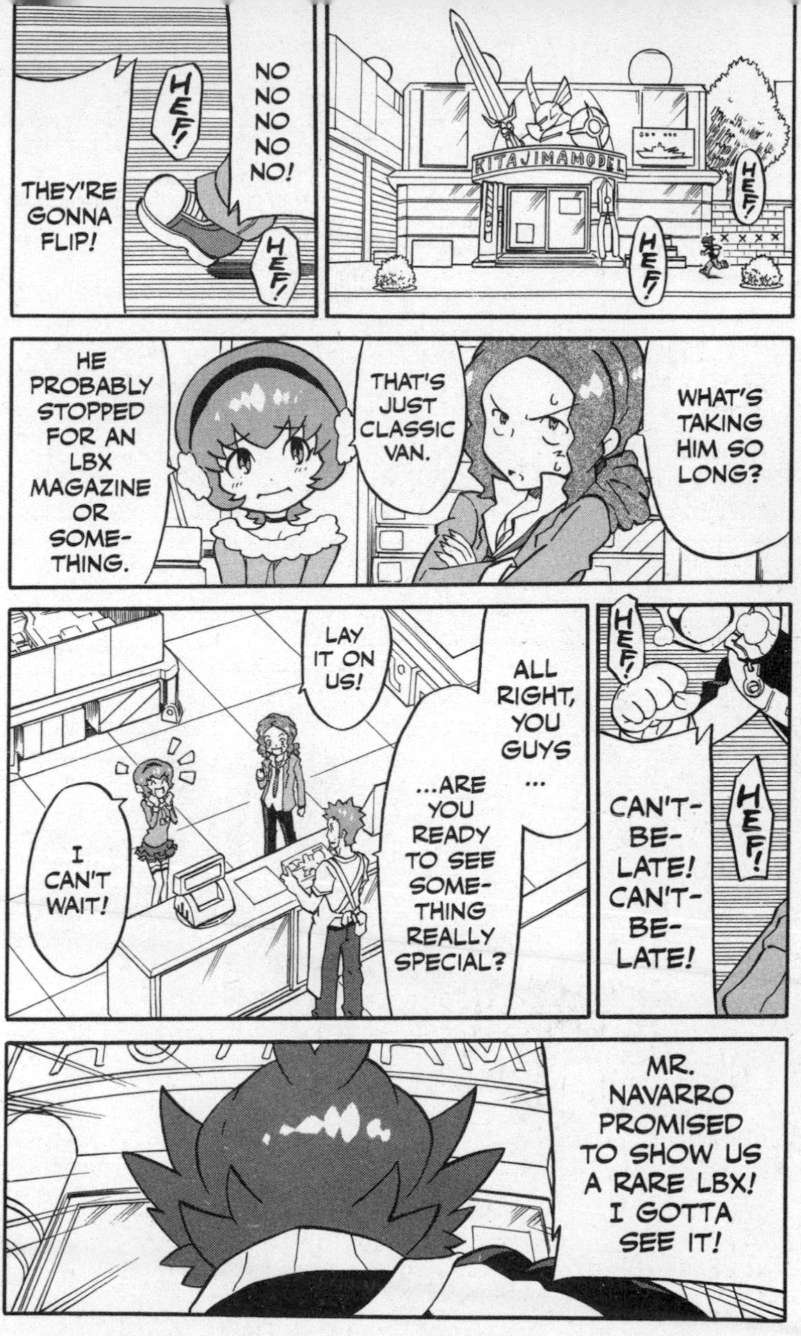
KITAJIMA MODEL
HEF!
HEF!
NO NO NO NO NO!
HEF!
THEY'RE GONNA FLIP!
HEF!
WHAT'S TAKING HIM SO LONG?
THAT'S JUST CLASSIC VAN.
HE PROBABLY STOPPED FOR AN LBX MAGAZINE OR SOME-THING.
HEF!
HEF!
CAN'T-BE-LATE! CAN'T-BE-LATE!
ALL RIGHT, YOU GUYS ...
...ARE YOU READY TO SEE SOME-THING REALLY SPECIAL?
LAY IT ON US!
I CAN'T WAIT!
MR. NAVARRO PROMISED TO SHOW US A RARE LBX! I GOTTA SEE IT!

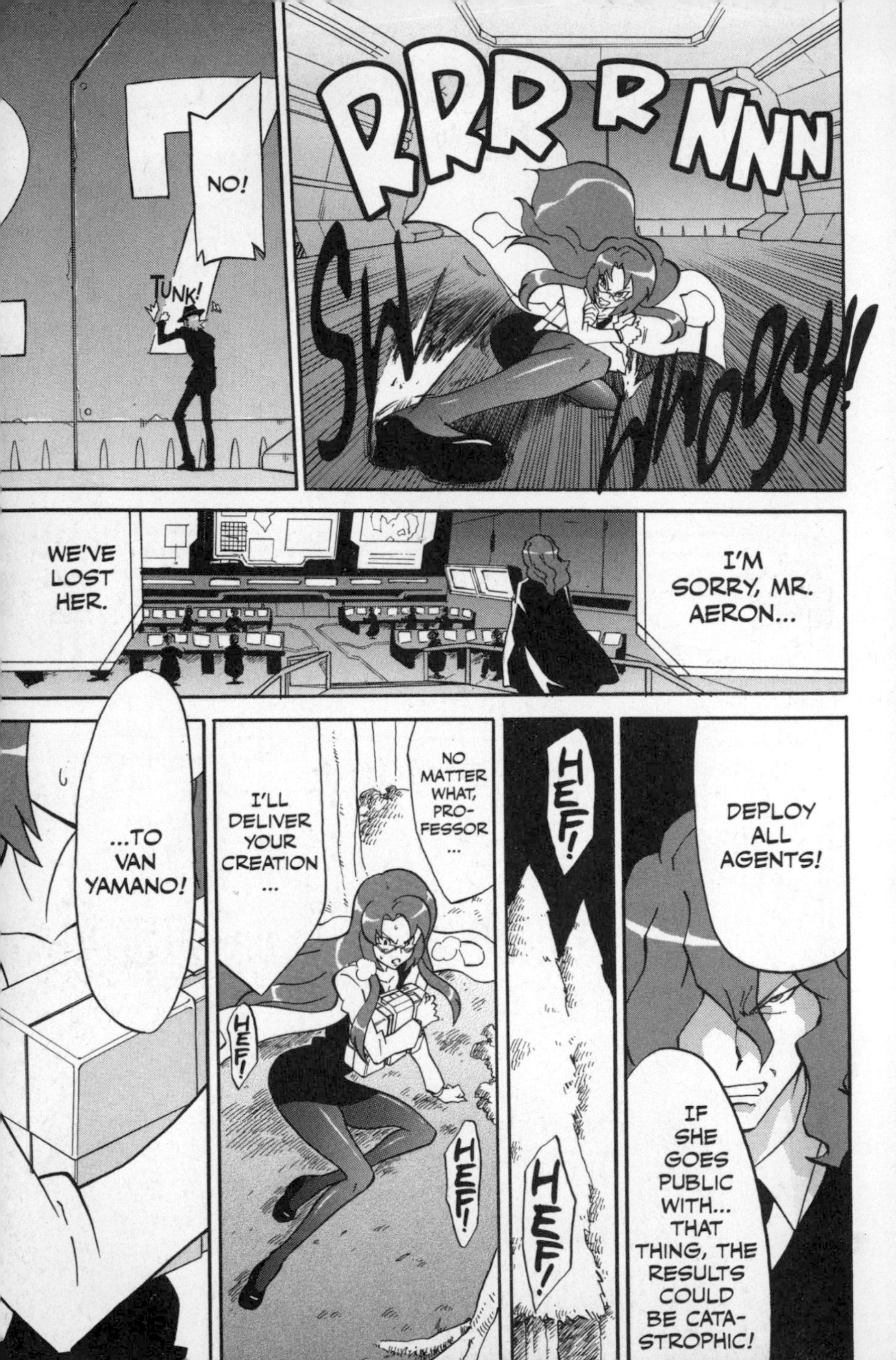
RRR R NNN
SH WHOOSH!
NO!
TUNK!
I'M SORRY, MR. AERON...
WE'VE LOST HER.
DEPLOY ALL AGENTS!
IF SHE GOES PUBLIC WITH... THAT THING, THE RESULTS COULD BE CATA-STROPHIC!
HEF!
HEF!
NO MATTER WHAT, PRO-FESSOR ...
I'LL DELIVER YOUR CREATION ...
HEF!
HEF!
...TO VAN YAMANO!

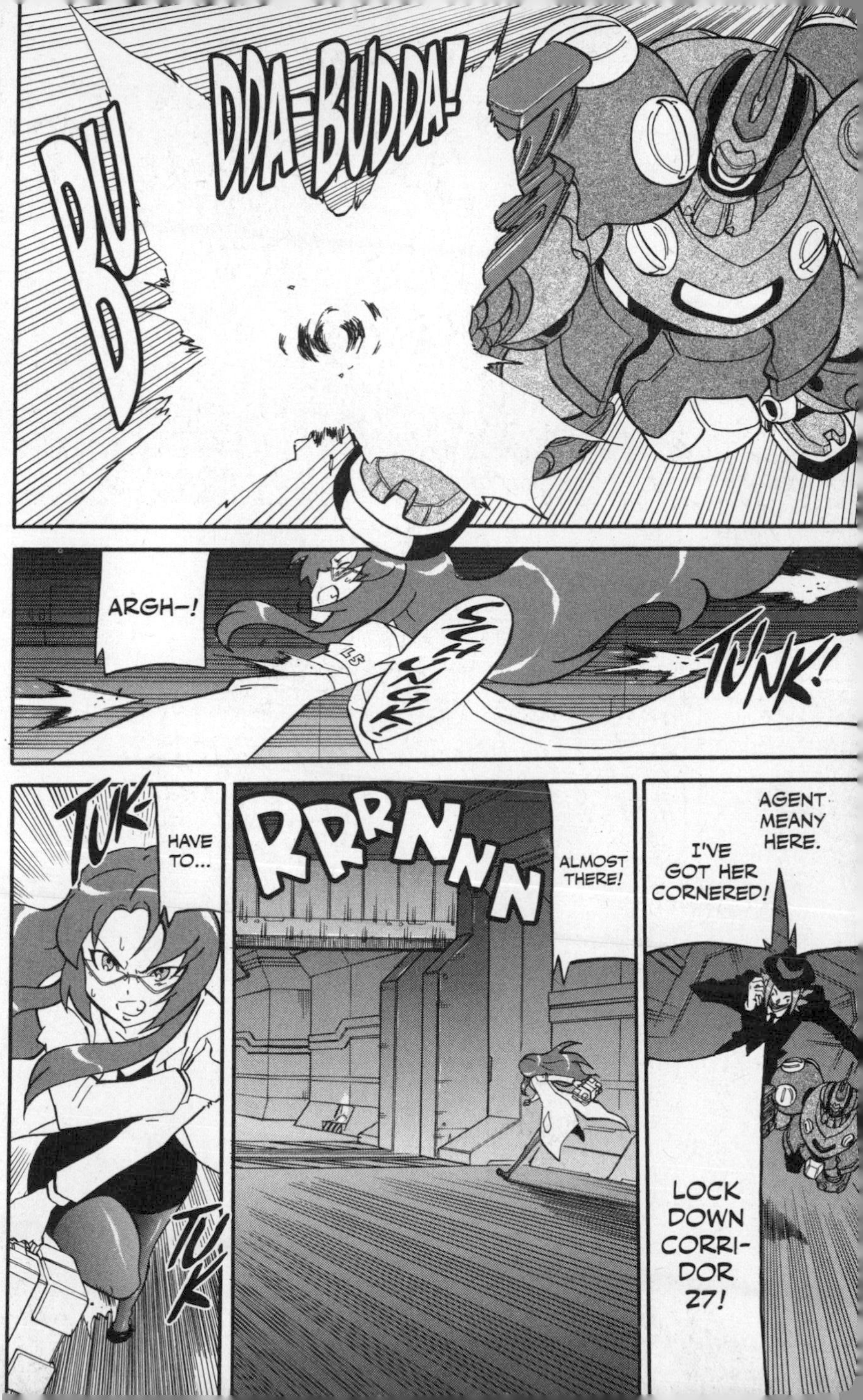
BUDDA-BUDDA!
TUNK!
WHUNGK!
ARGH–!
AGENT MEANY HERE.
I'VE GOT HER CORNERED!
LOCK DOWN CORRIDOR 27!
ALMOST THERE!
RRRNNNN
TUK-
HAVE TO...
TUK

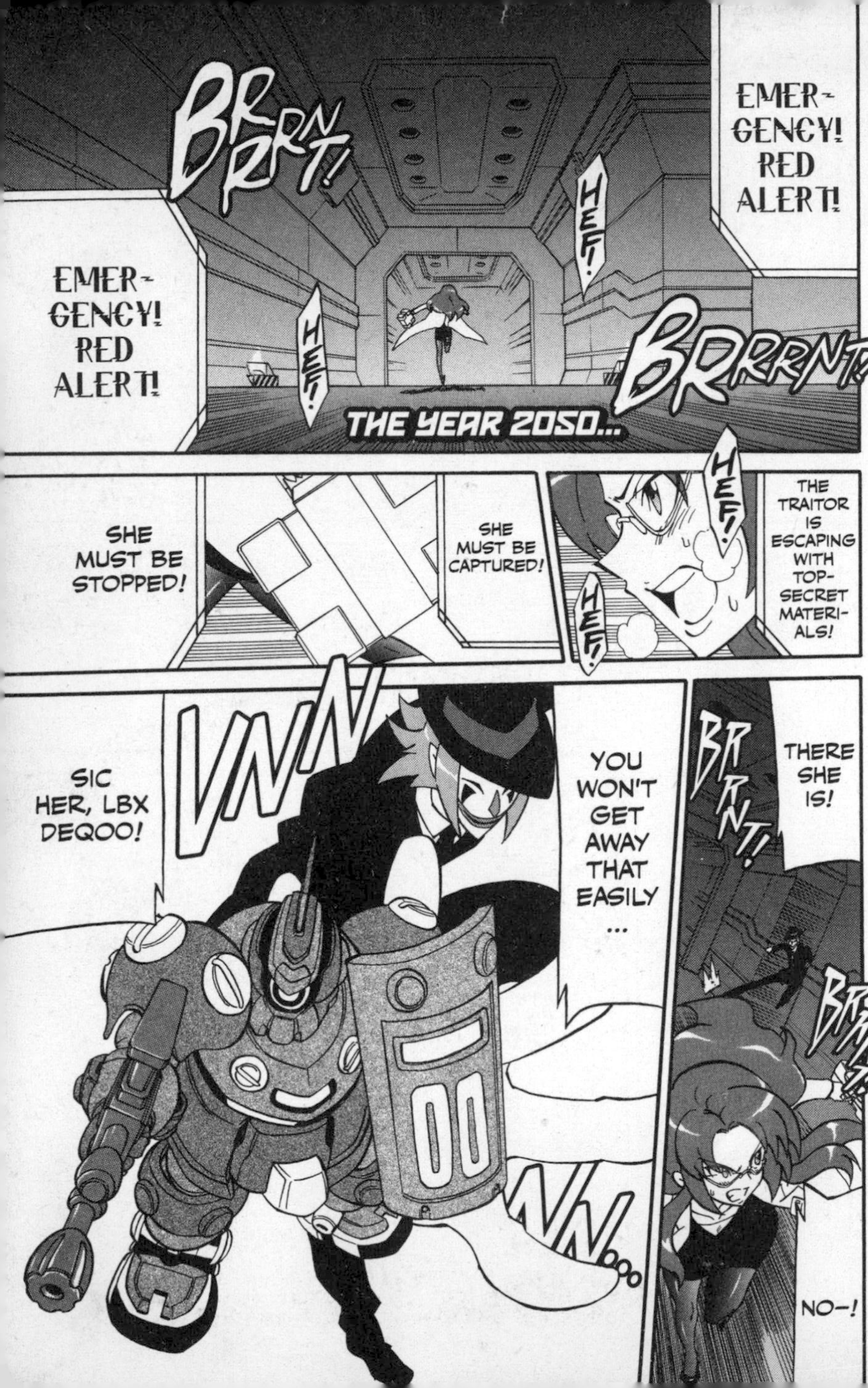
EMER-GENCY! RED ALERT!
HEF!
BRRRNT!
BRRRNT!
HEF!
EMER-GENCY! RED ALERT!
THE YEAR 2050...
THE TRAITOR IS ESCAPING WITH TOP-SECRET MATERI-ALS!
HEF!
HEF!
SHE MUST BE CAPTURED!
SHE MUST BE STOPPED!
THERE SHE IS!
BRRNT!
BRRNT!
NO—!
YOU WON'T GET AWAY THAT EASILY ...
VNN
SIC HER, LBX DEQOO!
NNN...

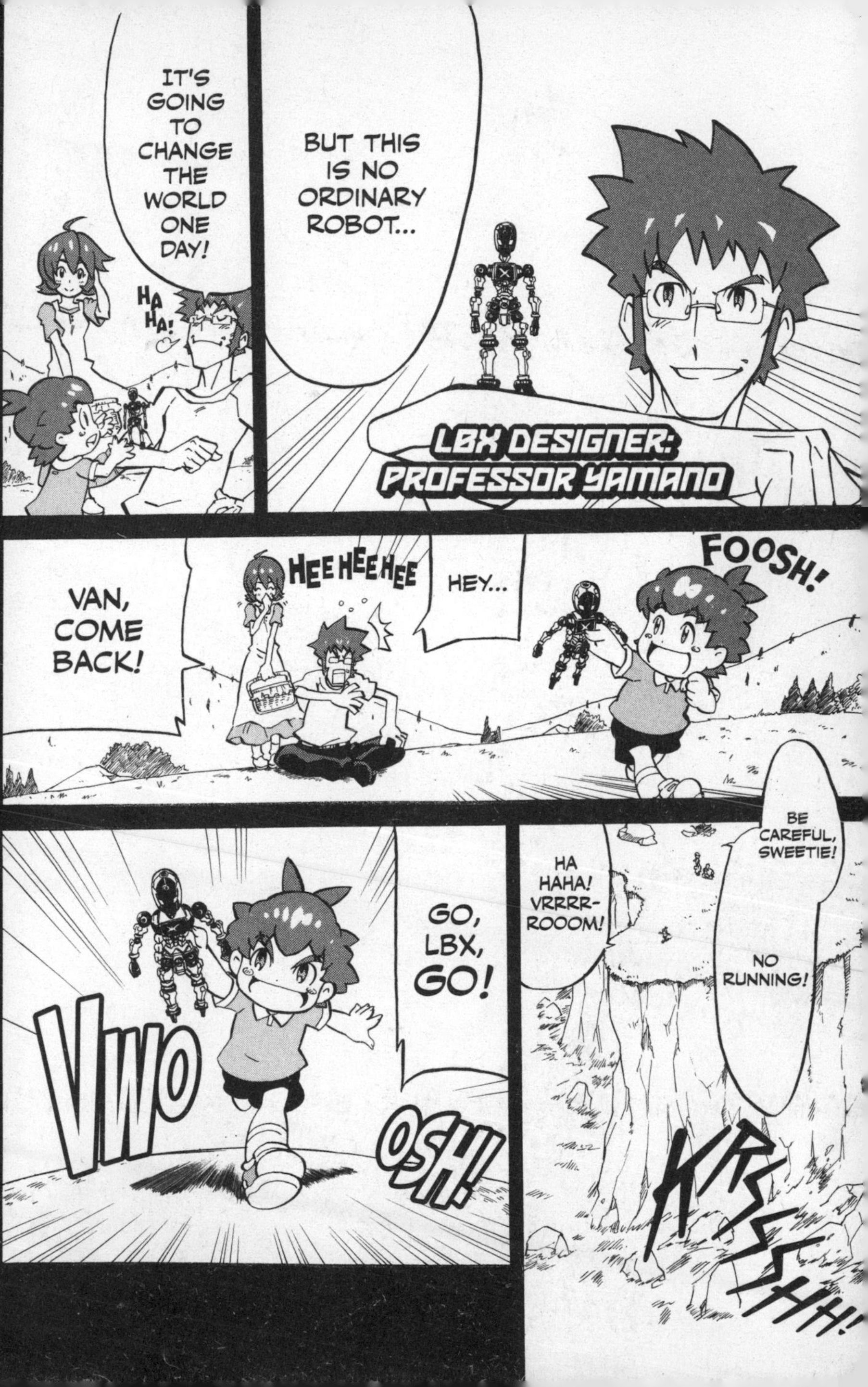
BUT THIS IS NO ORDINARY ROBOT...
LBX DESIGNER: PROFESSOR YAMANO
IT'S GOING TO CHANGE THE WORLD ONE DAY!
HA HA!
FOOSH!
HEY...
HEE HEE HEE
VAN, COME BACK!
BE CAREFUL, SWEETIE!
HA HAHA! VRRRR-ROOOM!
NO RUNNING!
KRSSHH!
GO, LBX, GO!
VWOOSH!

WOW!

A ROBOT!

THE YEAR 204X...

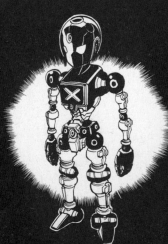

I CALL IT LITTLE BATTLERS EXPERIENCE...

LBX FOR SHORT!

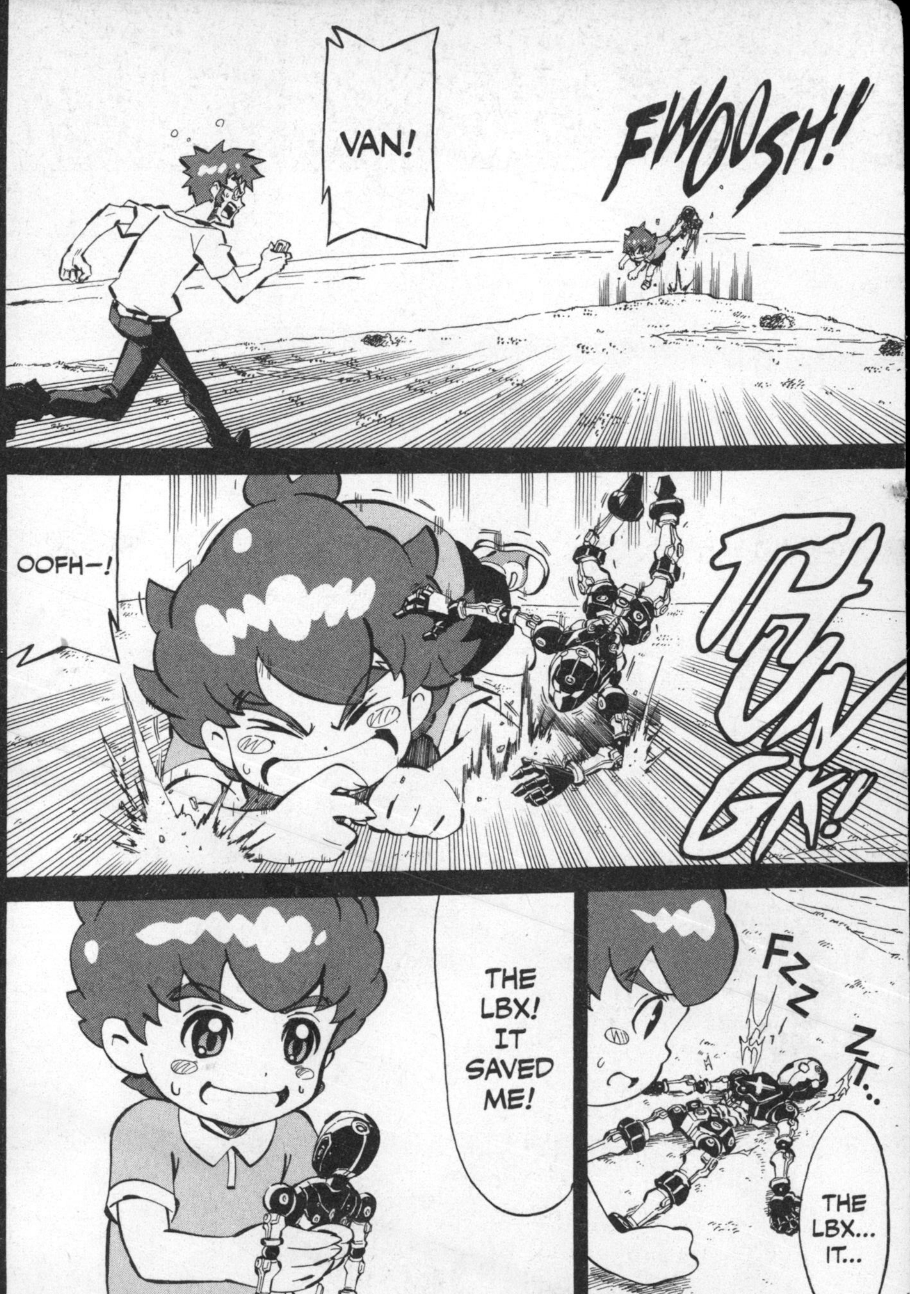
FWOOSH!
VAN!
THUNGK!
OOFH—!
FZZ ZT...
THE LBX... IT...
THE LBX! IT SAVED ME!

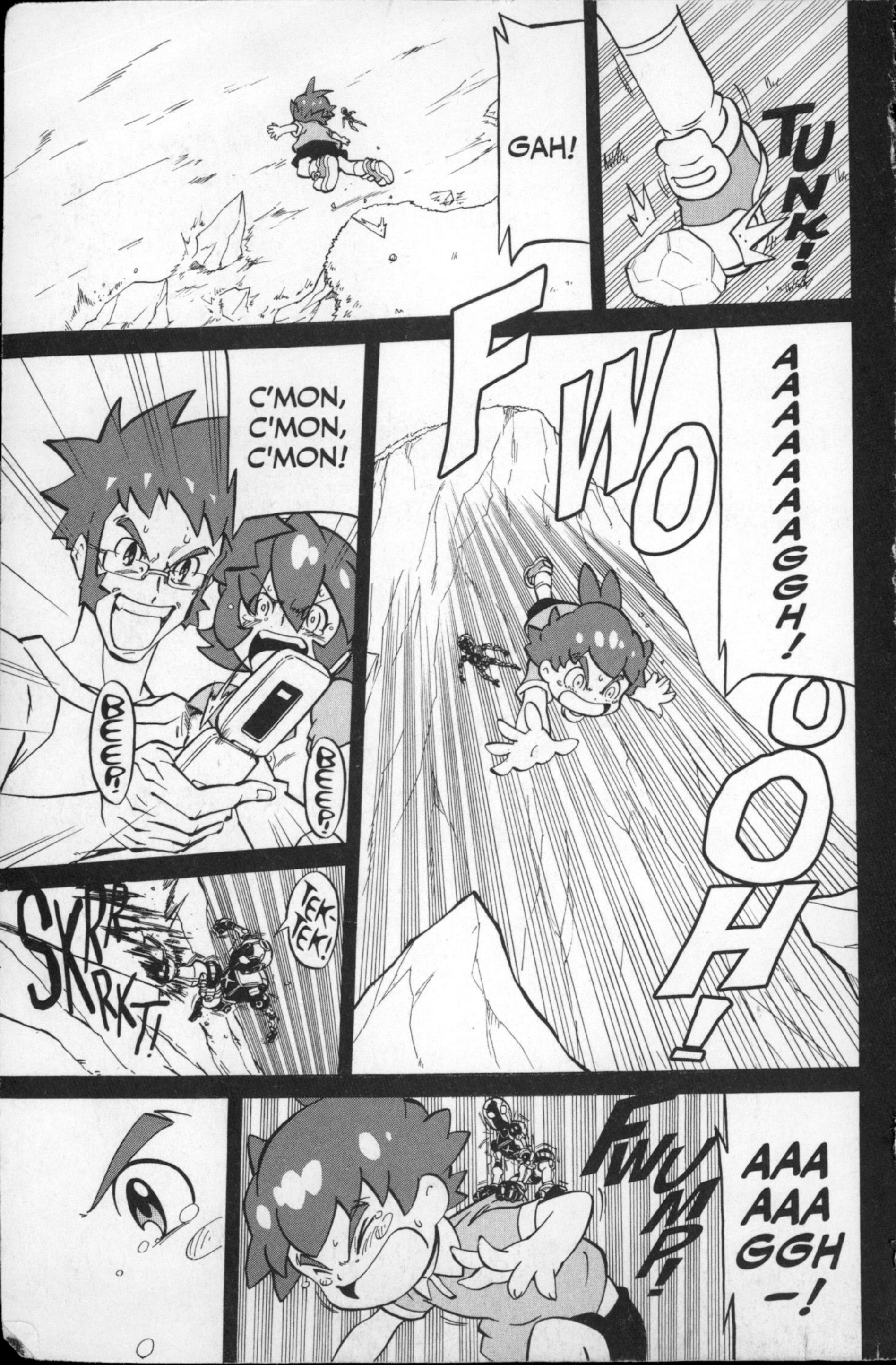
TUNK!
GAH!
AAAAAAAAAGH!
FWOOOOH!
C'MON, C'MON, C'MON!
BEEP!
BEEP!
TEK-TEK!
SKRRKRKT!
AAAAAAGGH—!
FWUMP!

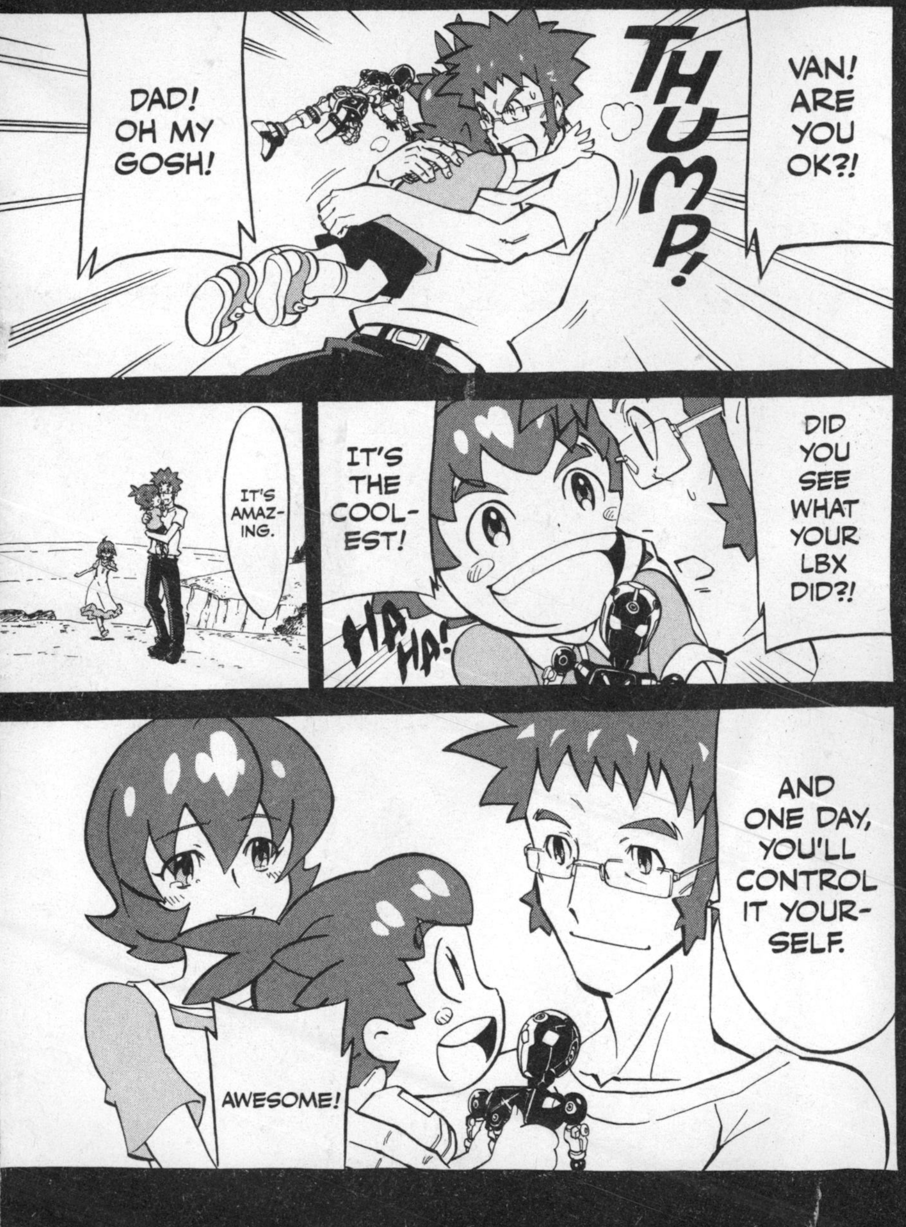
VAN! ARE YOU OK?!
THUMP!
DAD! OH MY GOSH!
DID YOU SEE WHAT YOUR LBX DID?!
IT'S THE COOL-EST!
HA HA!
IT'S AMAZ-ING.
AND ONE DAY, YOU'LL CONTROL IT YOUR-SELF.
AWESOME!

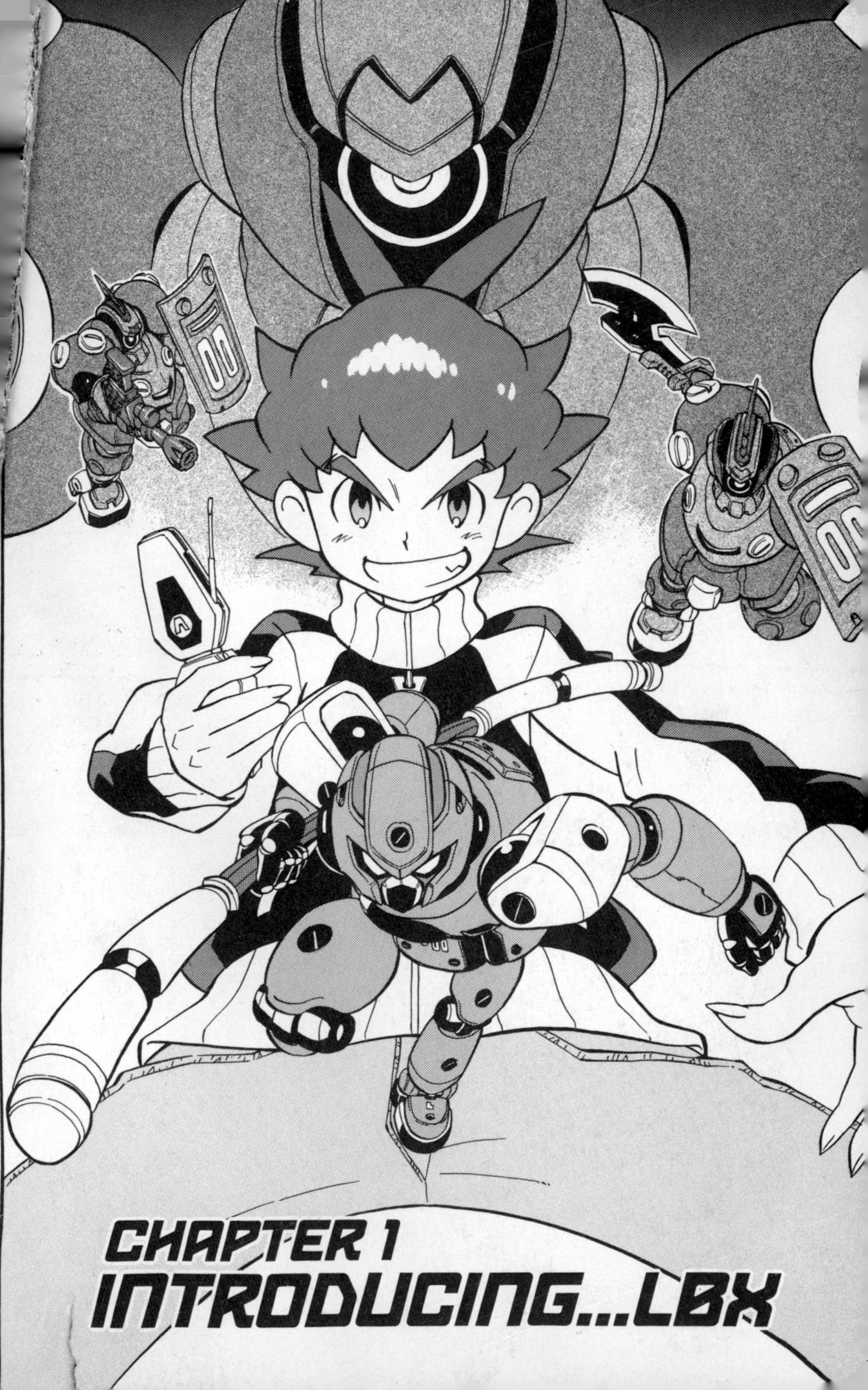

CHAPTER 1
INTRODUCING...LBX

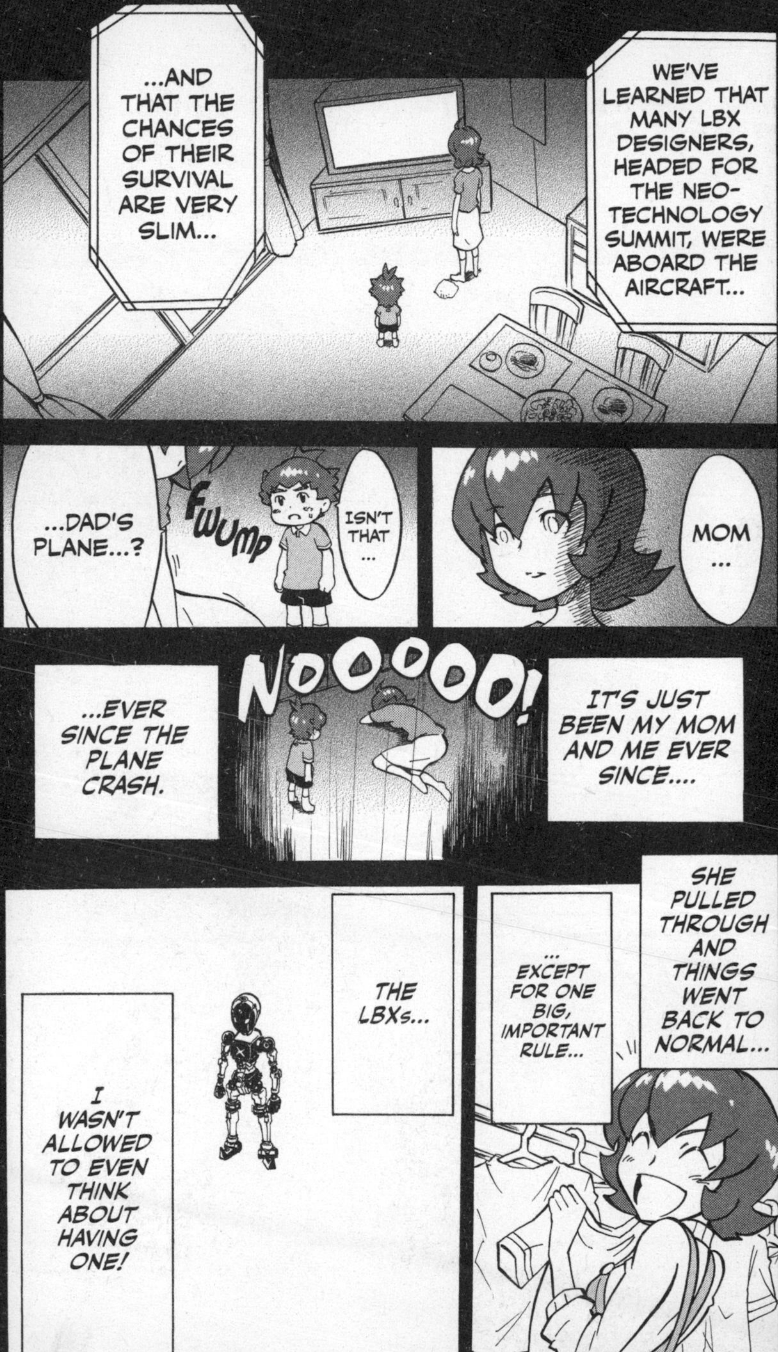
WE'VE LEARNED THAT MANY LBX DESIGNERS, HEADED FOR THE NEO-TECHNOLOGY SUMMIT, WERE ABOARD THE AIRCRAFT...
...AND THAT THE CHANCES OF THEIR SURVIVAL ARE VERY SLIM...
MOM ...
ISN'T THAT ...
FWUMP
...DAD'S PLANE...?
IT'S JUST BEEN MY MOM AND ME EVER SINCE....
NOOOOO!
...EVER SINCE THE PLANE CRASH.
SHE PULLED THROUGH AND THINGS WENT BACK TO NORMAL...
... EXCEPT FOR ONE BIG, IMPORTANT RULE...
THE LBXs...
I WASN'T ALLOWED TO EVEN THINK ABOUT HAVING ONE!

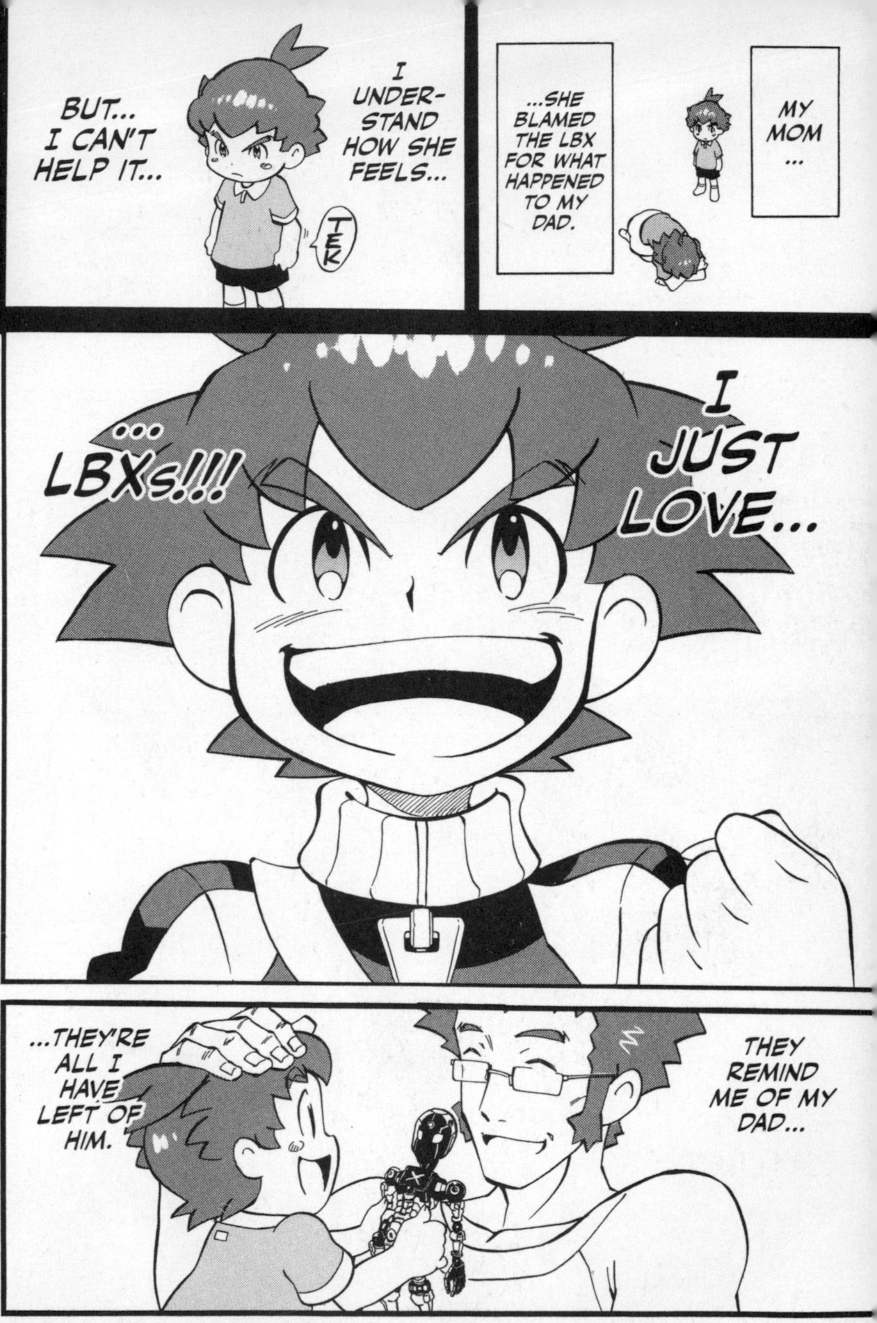
MY MOM ...
...SHE BLAMED THE LBX FOR WHAT HAPPENED TO MY DAD.
I UNDER-STAND HOW SHE FEELS...
TEK
BUT... I CAN'T HELP IT...
I JUST LOVE...
...LBXs!!!
THEY REMIND ME OF MY DAD...
...THEY'RE ALL I HAVE LEFT OF HIM.

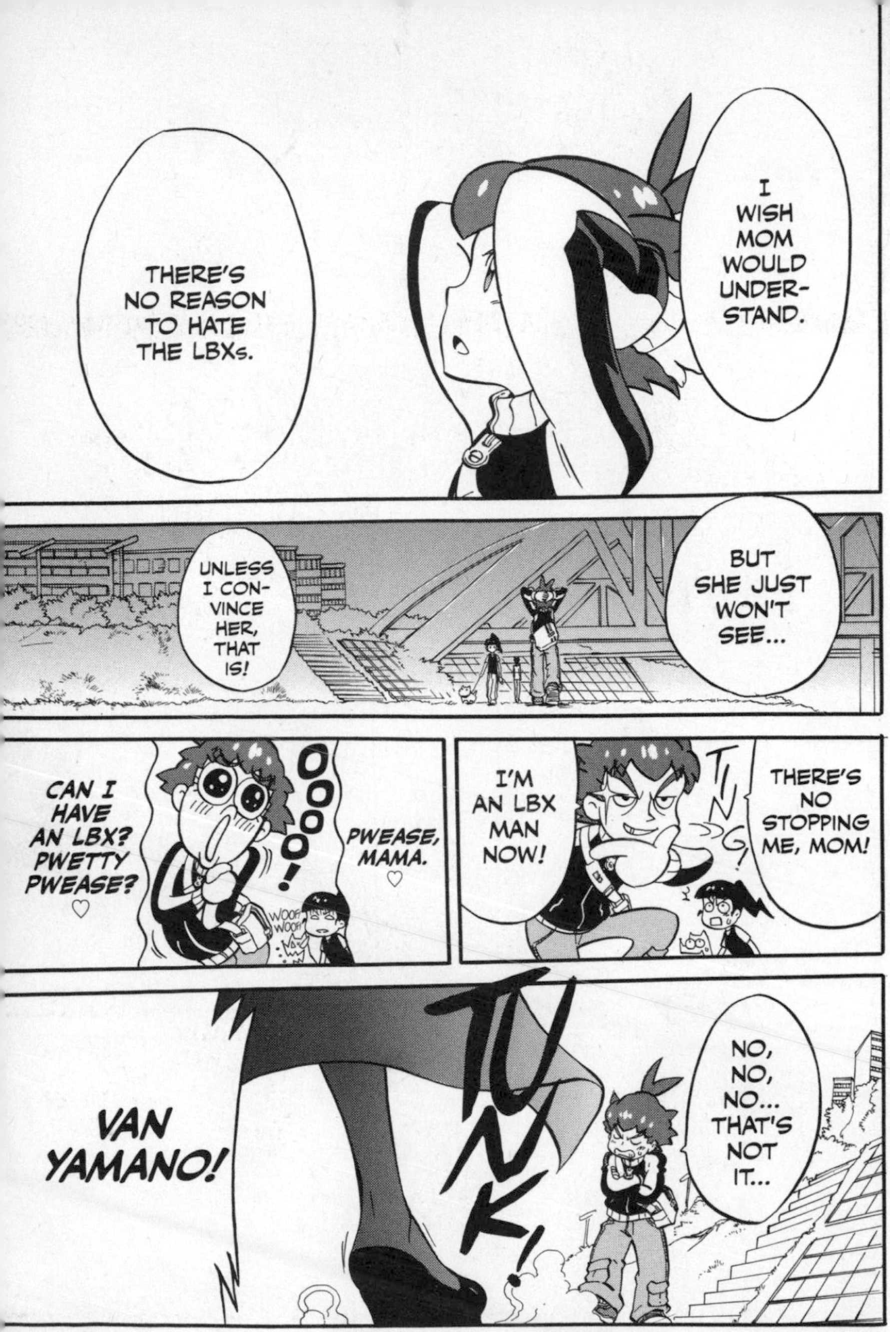
I WISH MOM WOULD UNDER-STAND.
THERE'S NO REASON TO HATE THE LBXs.
BUT SHE JUST WON'T SEE...
UNLESS I CON-VINCE HER, THAT IS!
THERE'S NO STOPPING ME, MOM!
TING!
I'M AN LBX MAN NOW!
PWEASE, MAMA. ♡
OOOOO!
WOOF! WOOF!
CAN I HAVE AN LBX? PWETTY PWEASE? ♡
NO, NO, NO... THAT'S NOT IT...
TUNK!
VAN YAMANO!

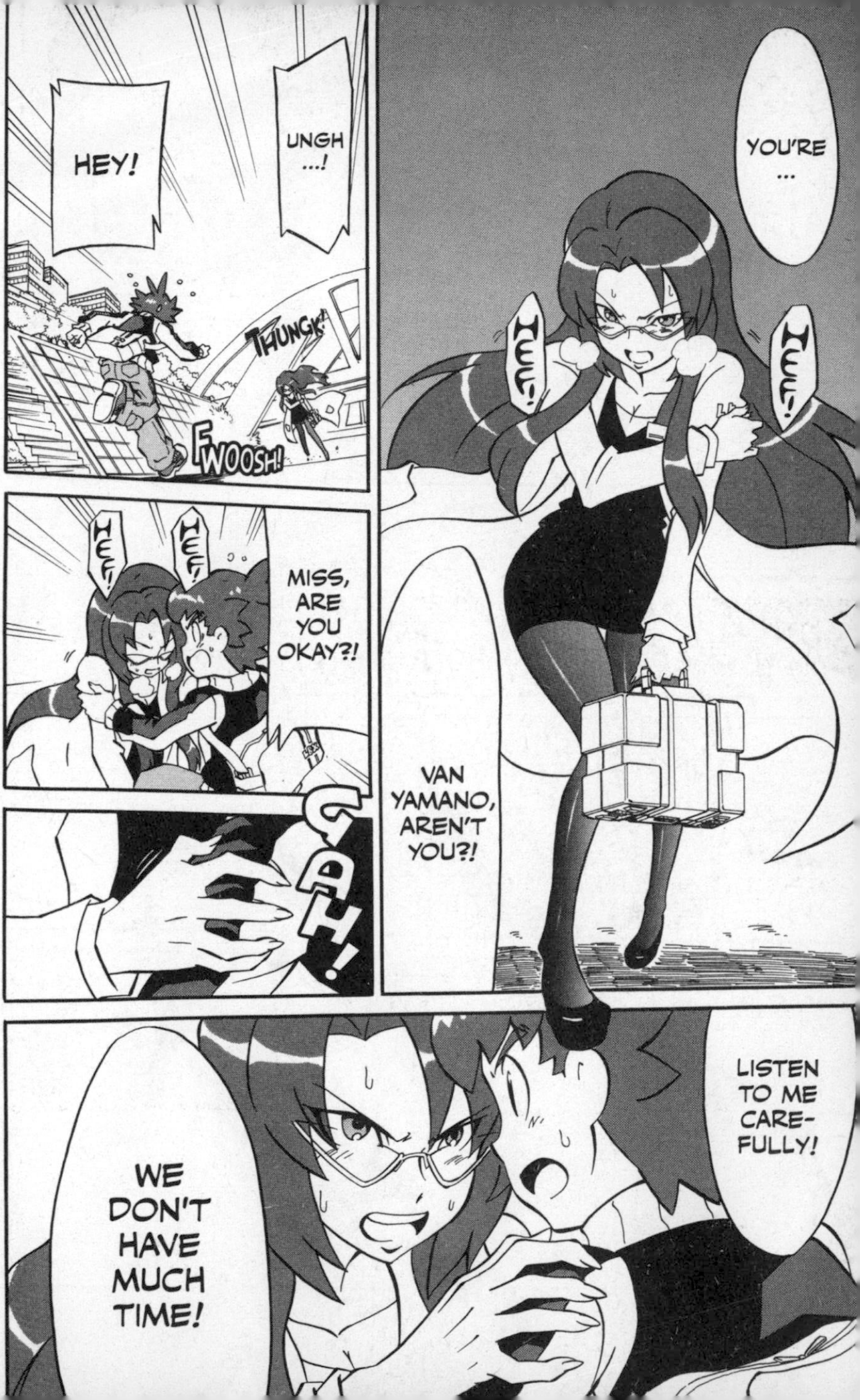
YOU'RE ...
HEF!
HEF!
VAN YAMANO, AREN'T YOU?!
UNGH ...!
HEY!
THUNGK!
FWOOSH!
HEF!
HEF!
MISS, ARE YOU OKAY?!
GAH!
LISTEN TO ME CARE-FULLY!
WE DON'T HAVE MUCH TIME!

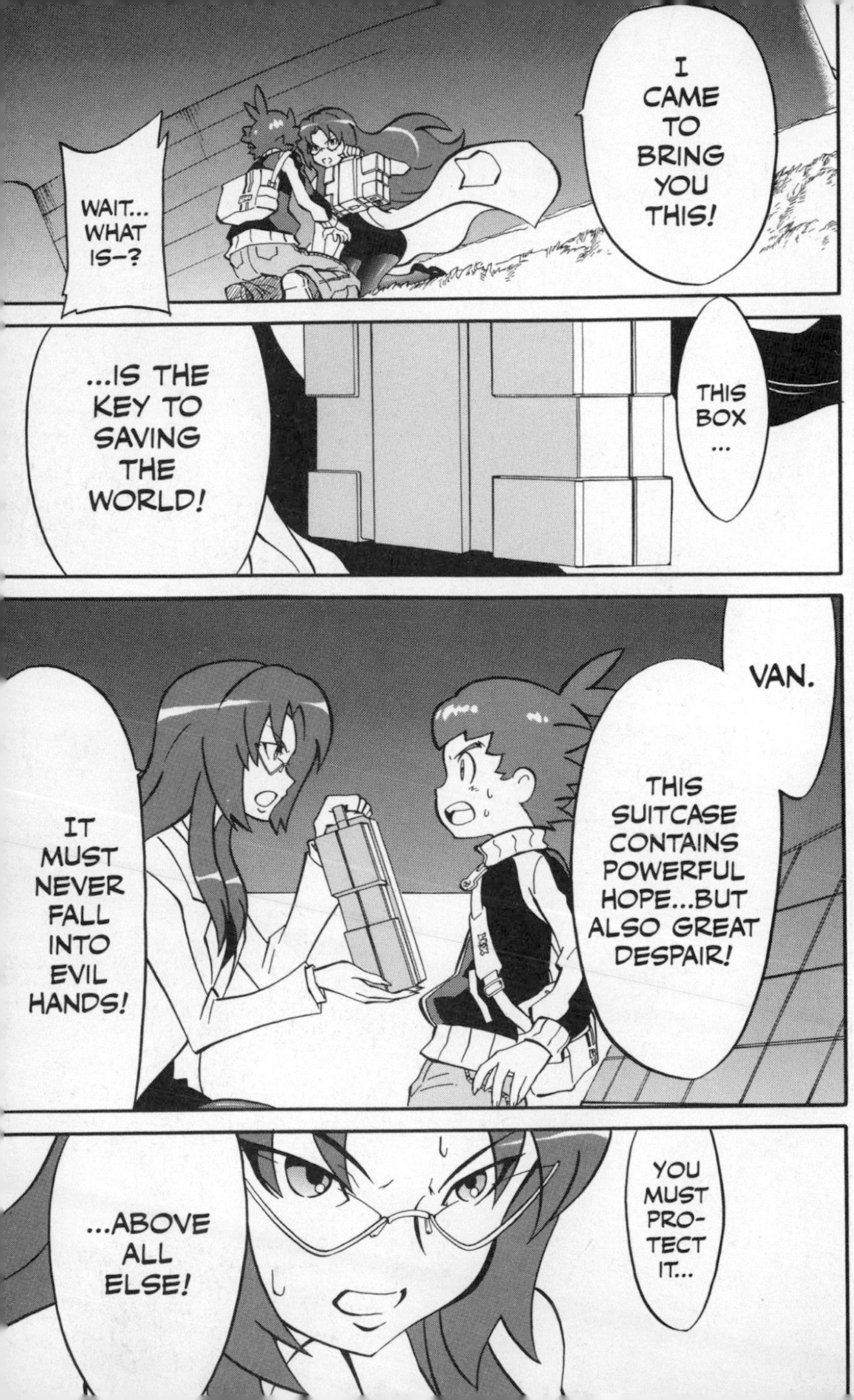
I CAME TO BRING YOU THIS!
WAIT... WHAT IS–?
THIS BOX...
...IS THE KEY TO SAVING THE WORLD!
VAN.
THIS SUITCASE CONTAINS POWERFUL HOPE...BUT ALSO GREAT DESPAIR!
IT MUST NEVER FALL INTO EVIL HANDS!
YOU MUST PRO-TECT IT...
...ABOVE ALL ELSE!

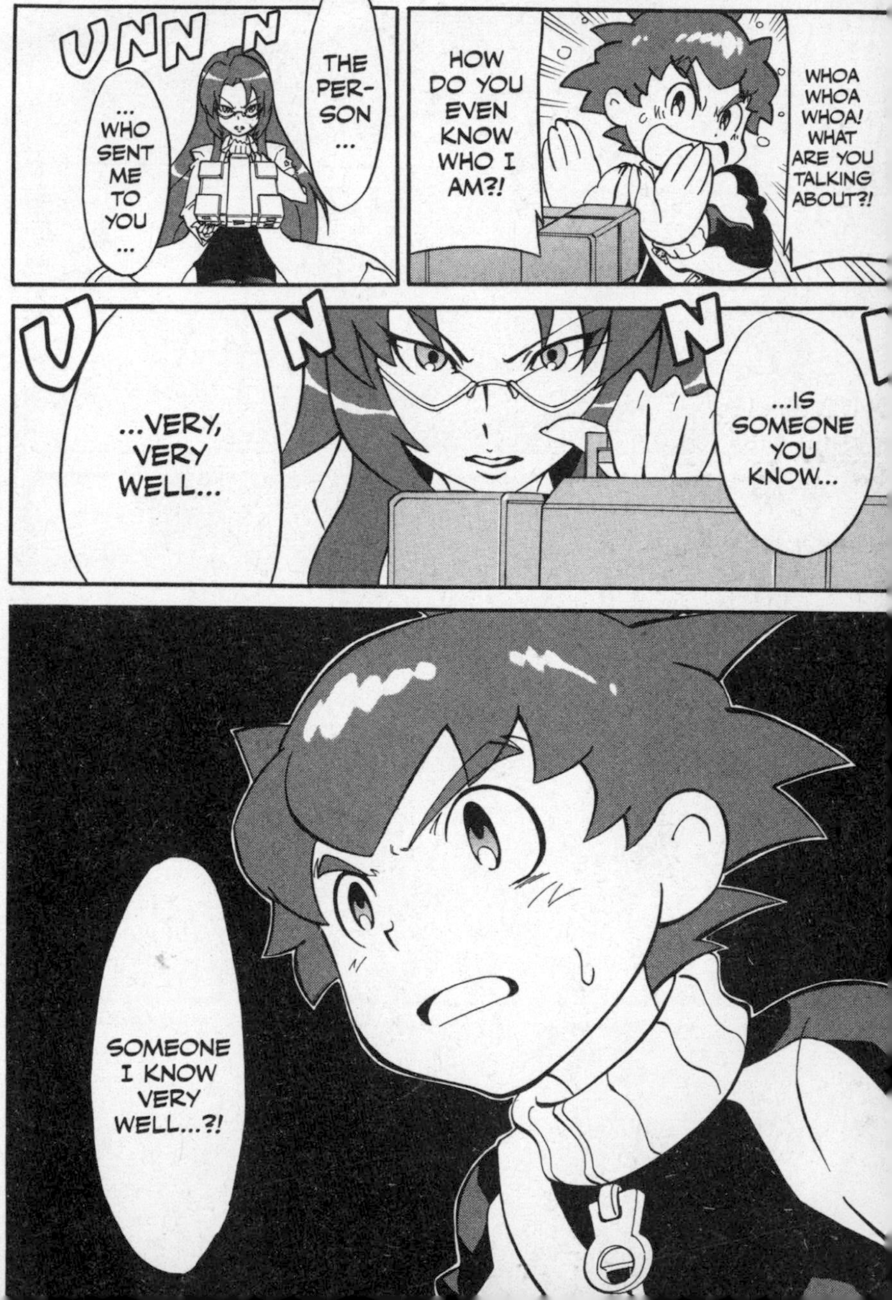
WHOA WHOA WHOA! WHAT ARE YOU TALKING ABOUT?!
HOW DO YOU EVEN KNOW WHO I AM?!
THE PER-SON...
...WHO SENT ME TO YOU...
UNN N
...IS SOMEONE YOU KNOW...
...VERY, VERY WELL...
SOMEONE I KNOW VERY WELL...?!

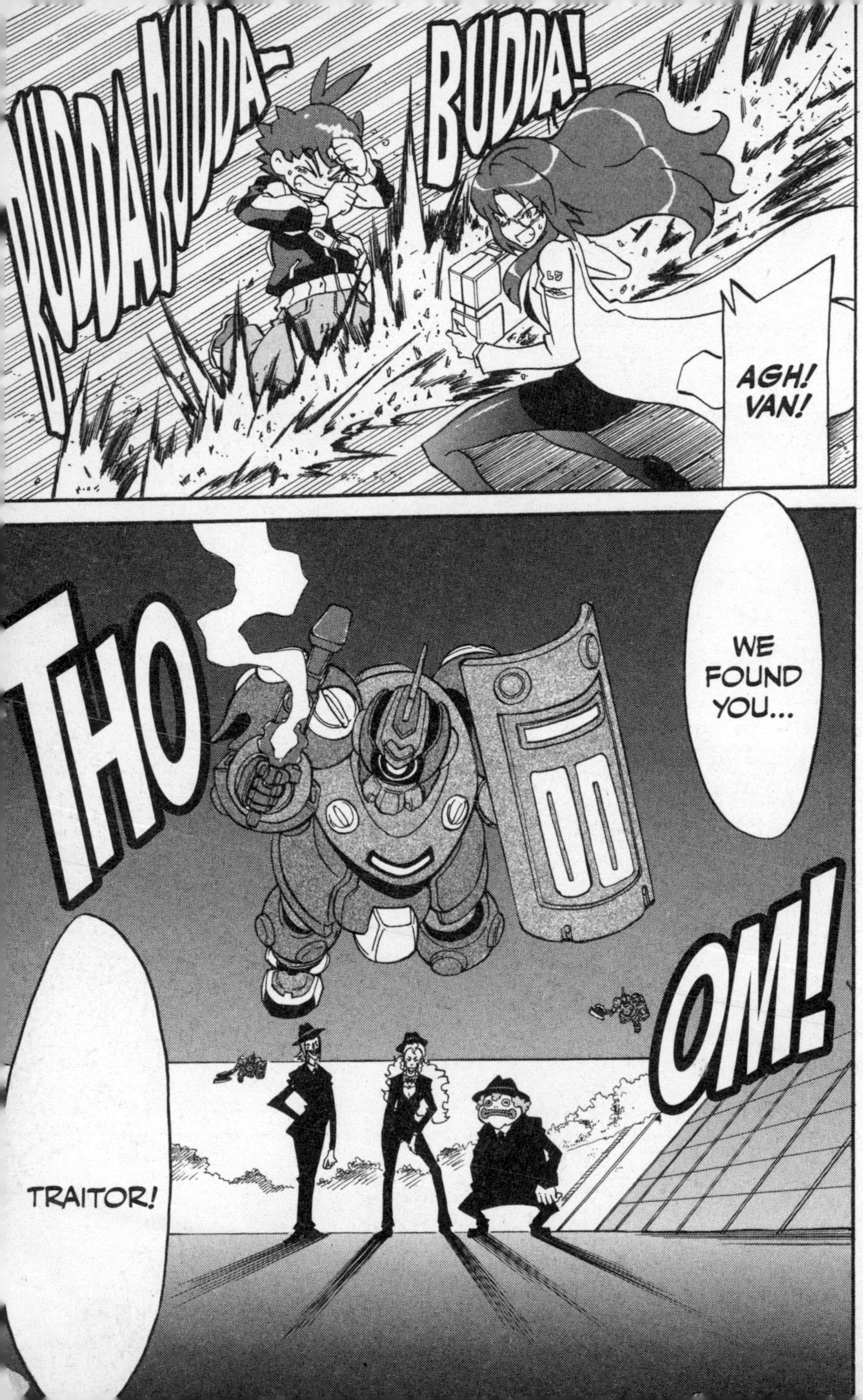
BUDDABUDDA-
BUDDA!
AGH! VAN!
WE FOUND YOU...
THO
OM!
TRAITOR!

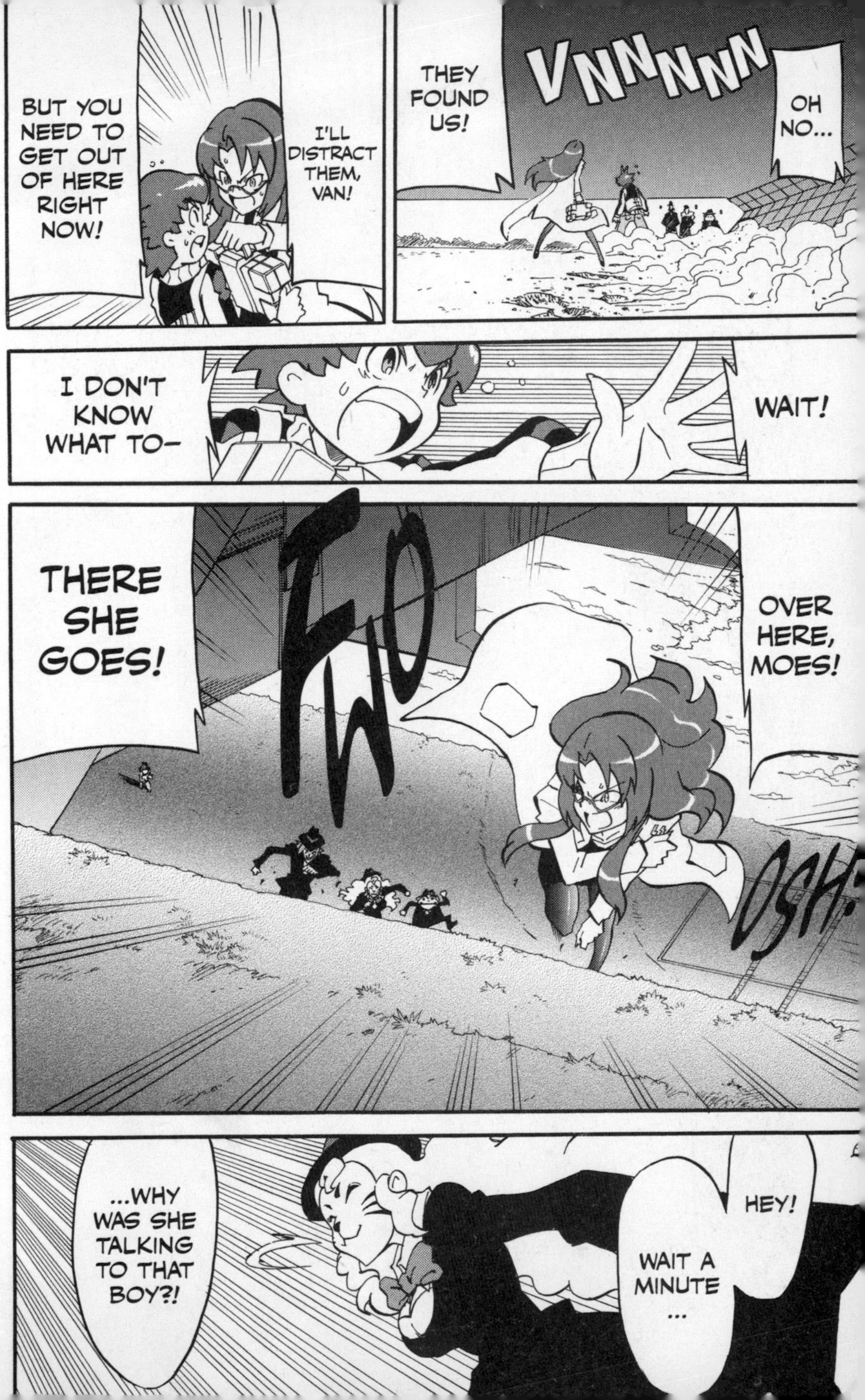
VNNNNNN
OH NO...
THEY FOUND US!
I'LL DISTRACT THEM, VAN!
BUT YOU NEED TO GET OUT OF HERE RIGHT NOW!
WAIT!
I DON'T KNOW WHAT TO–
OVER HERE, MOES!
OSH
FWO
THERE SHE GOES!
HEY!
WAIT A MINUTE ...
...WHY WAS SHE TALKING TO THAT BOY?!

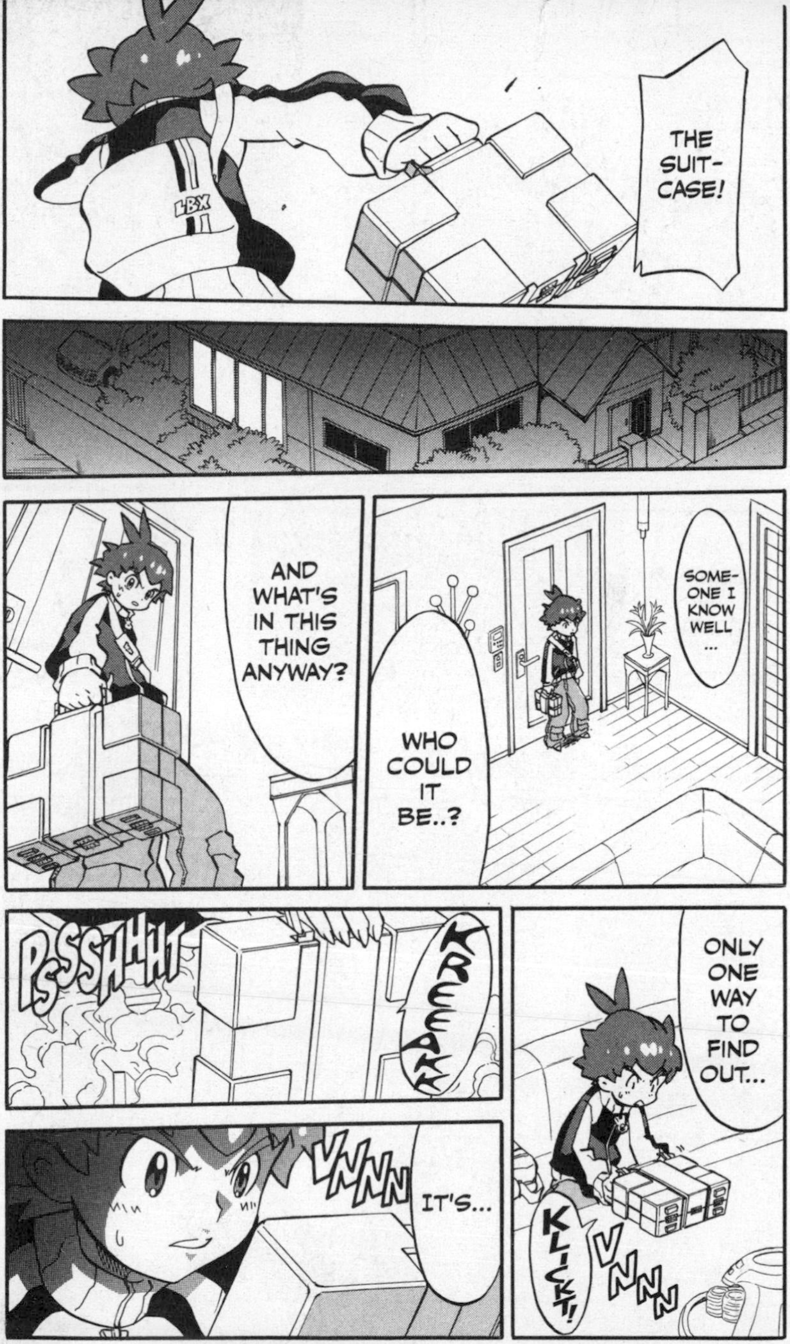
THE SUIT-CASE!
SOME-ONE I KNOW WELL ...
WHO COULD IT BE..?
AND WHAT'S IN THIS THING ANYWAY?
ONLY ONE WAY TO FIND OUT...
VNNN
KLICK!
KREEAKK
PSSHHHT
IT'S...
VNNN

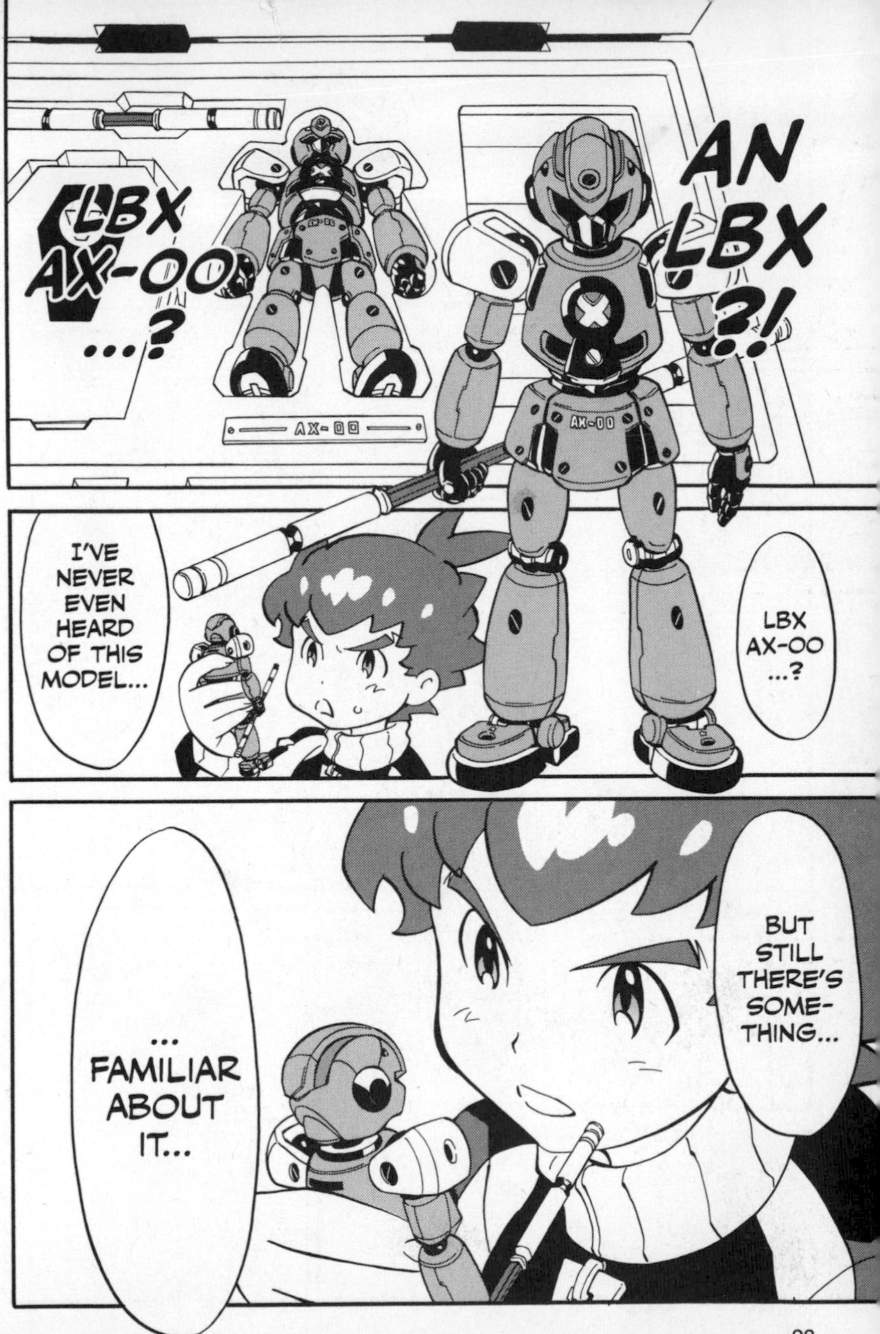
AN LBX ?!
LBX AX-OO ...?
LBX AX-OO ...?
I'VE NEVER EVEN HEARD OF THIS MODEL...
BUT STILL THERE'S SOME-THING...
... FAMILIAR ABOUT IT...

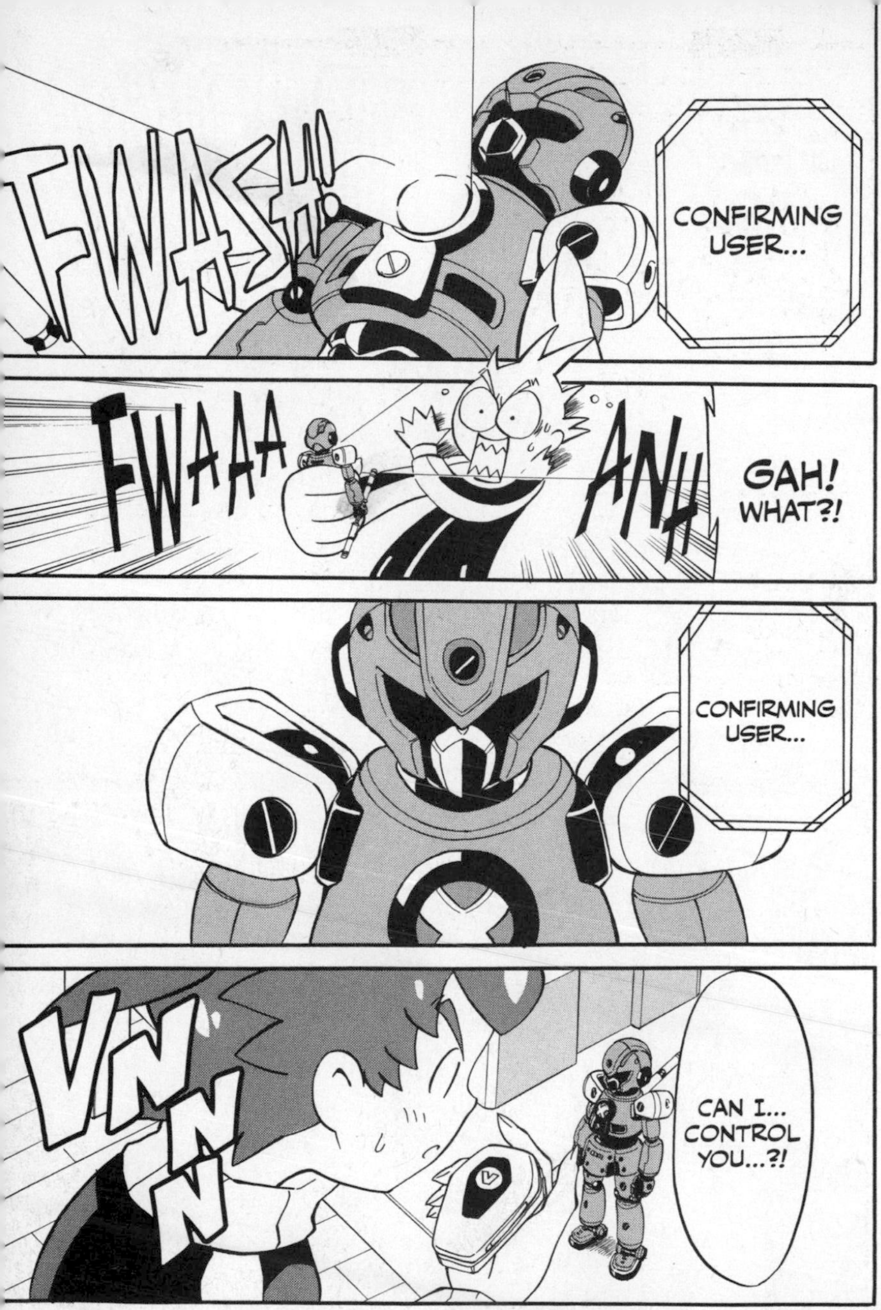
CONFIRMING USER...
FWASH!
GAH! WHAT?!
FWAAAANH
CONFIRMING USER...
CAN I... CONTROL YOU...?!
VNNN

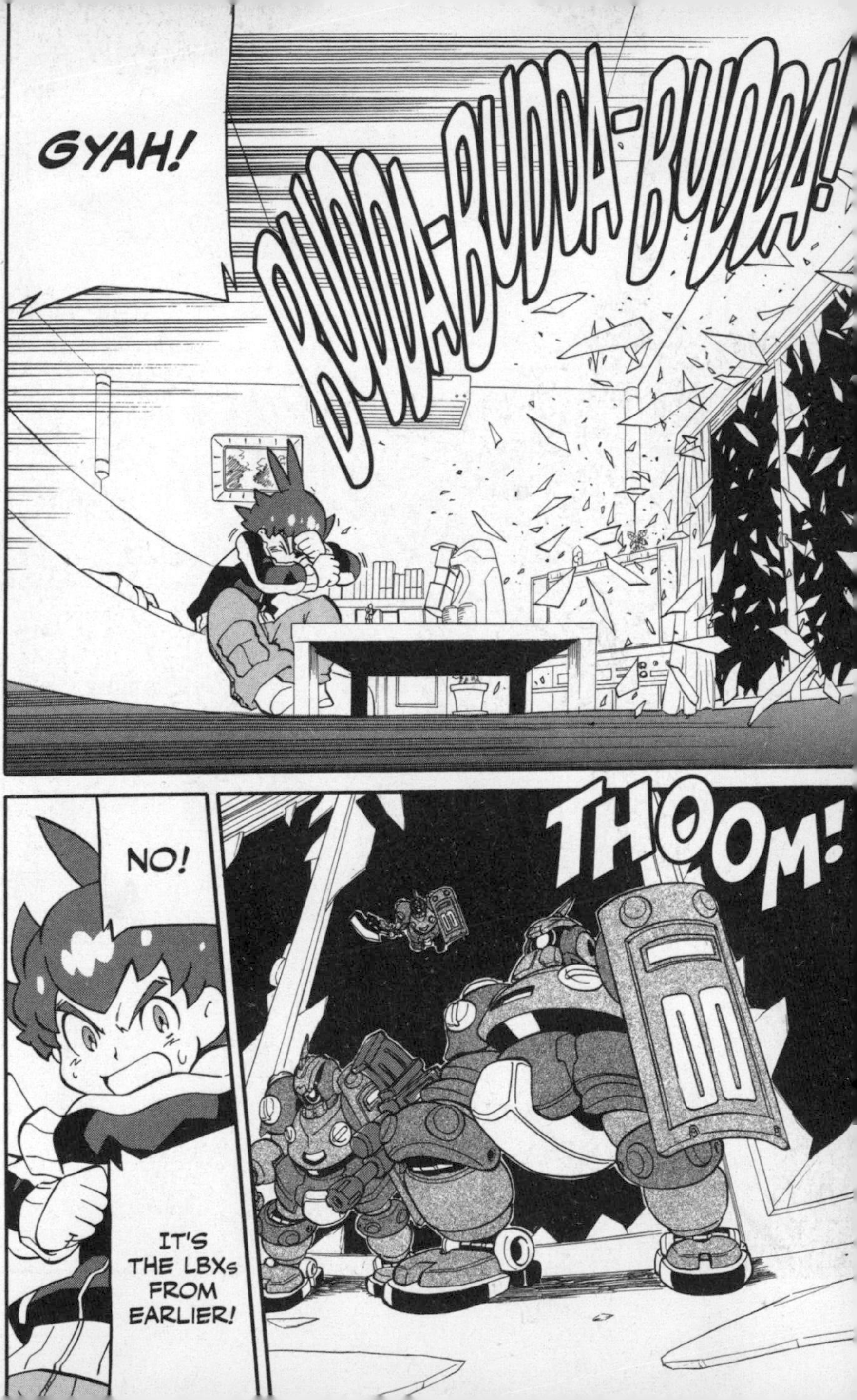
BUDDA-BUDDA-BUDDA!
GYAH!
THOOM!
NO!
IT'S THE LBXs FROM EARLIER!

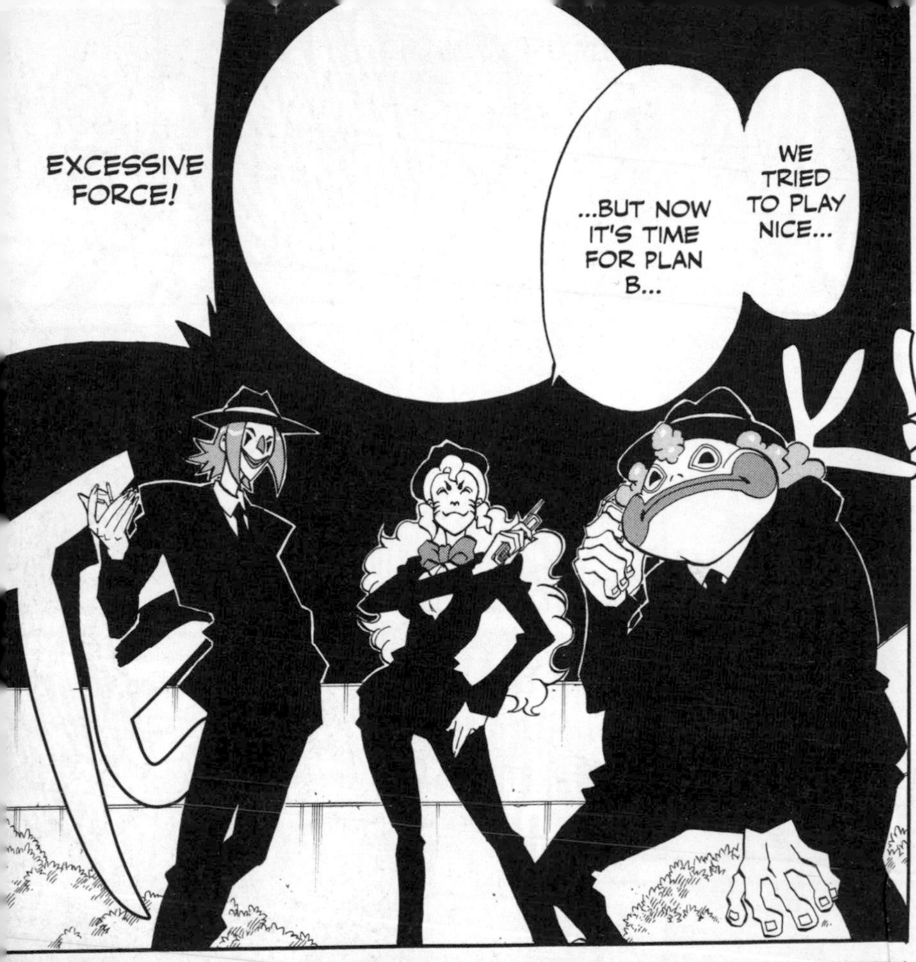
WE TRIED TO PLAY NICE...
...BUT NOW IT'S TIME FOR PLAN B...
EXCESSIVE FORCE!

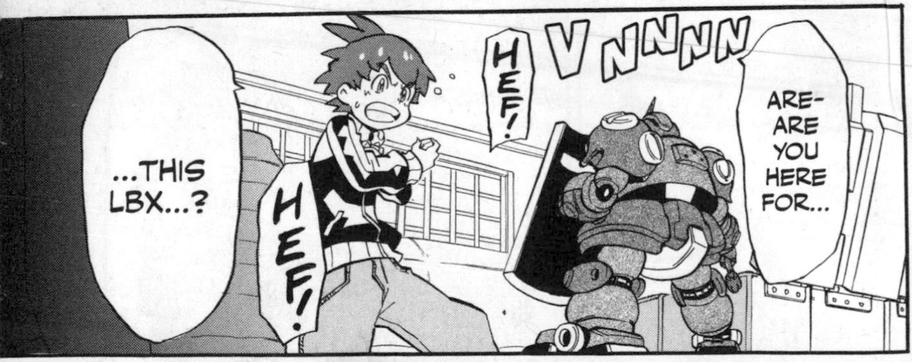
ARE-ARE YOU HERE FOR...
VNNNN
HEF!
HEF!
...THIS LBX...?

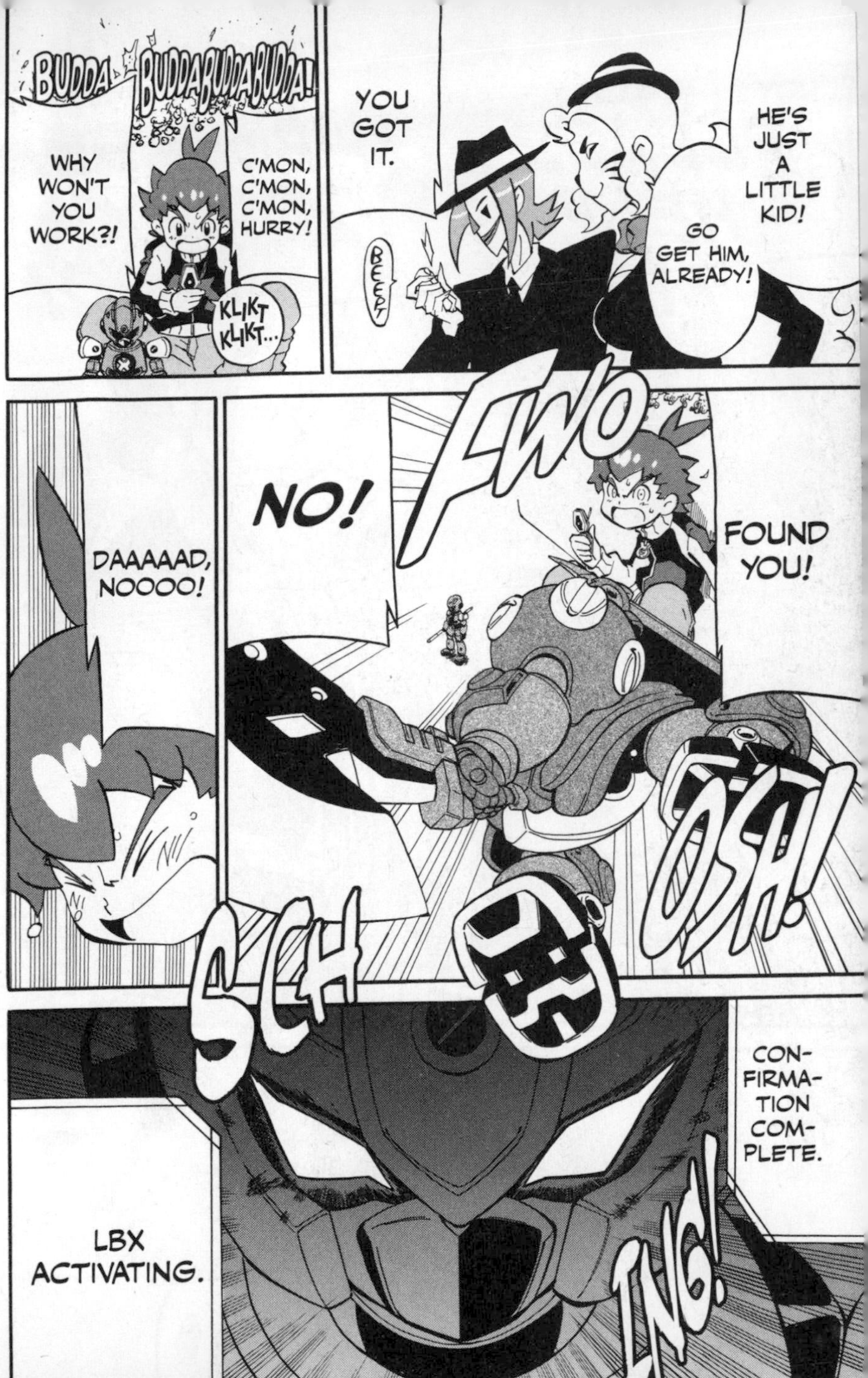
HE'S JUST A LITTLE KID!
GO GET HIM, ALREADY!
YOU GOT IT.
BEEP
BUDDA BUDDABUDDABUDDA!
C'MON, C'MON, C'MON, HURRY!
WHY WON'T YOU WORK?!
KLIKT KLIKT...
FWO
FOUND YOU!
NO!
OSH!
SCH
DAAAAAD, NOOOO!
CON-FIRMA-TION COM-PLETE.
TING!
LBX ACTIVATING.

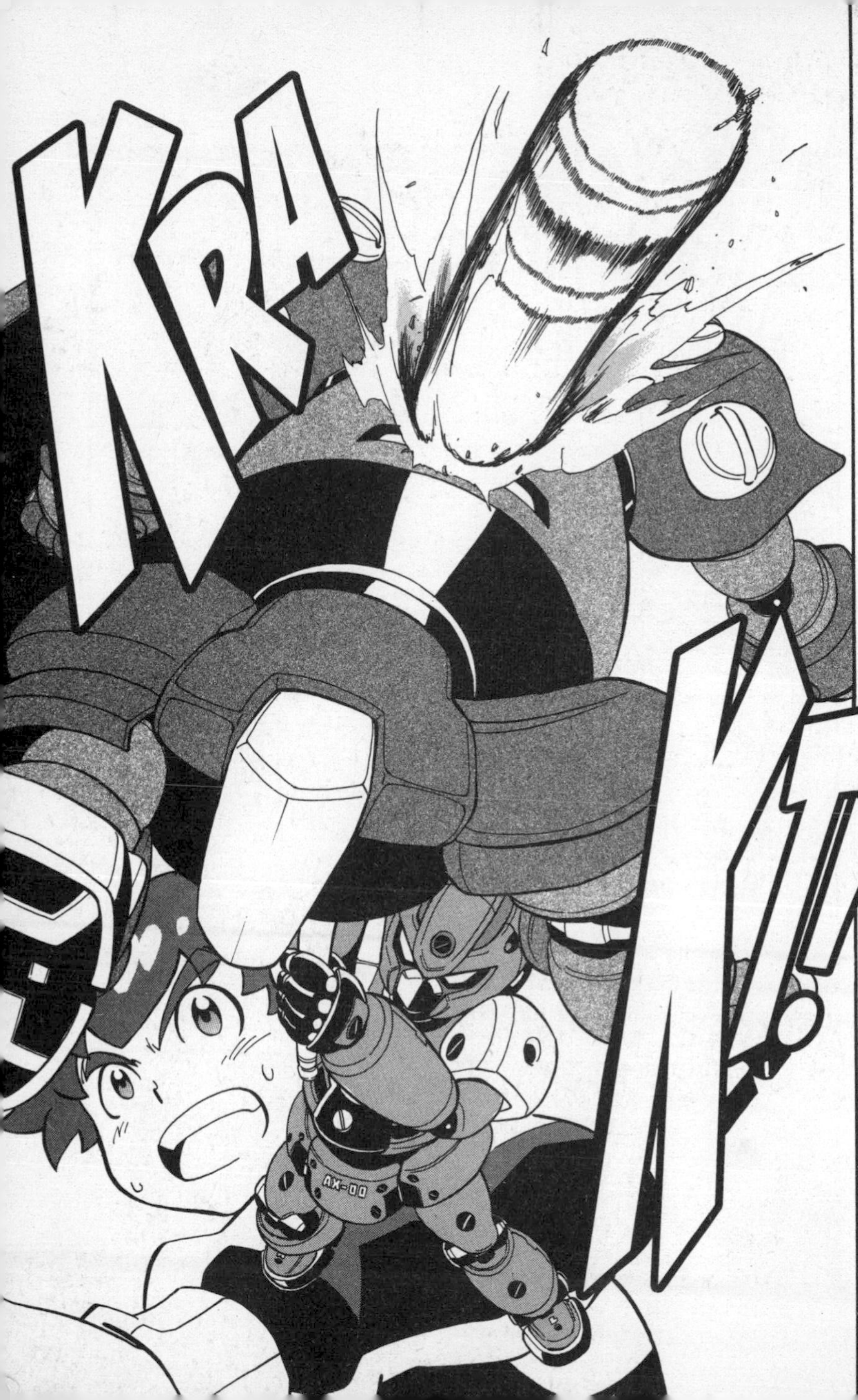
KRANK!

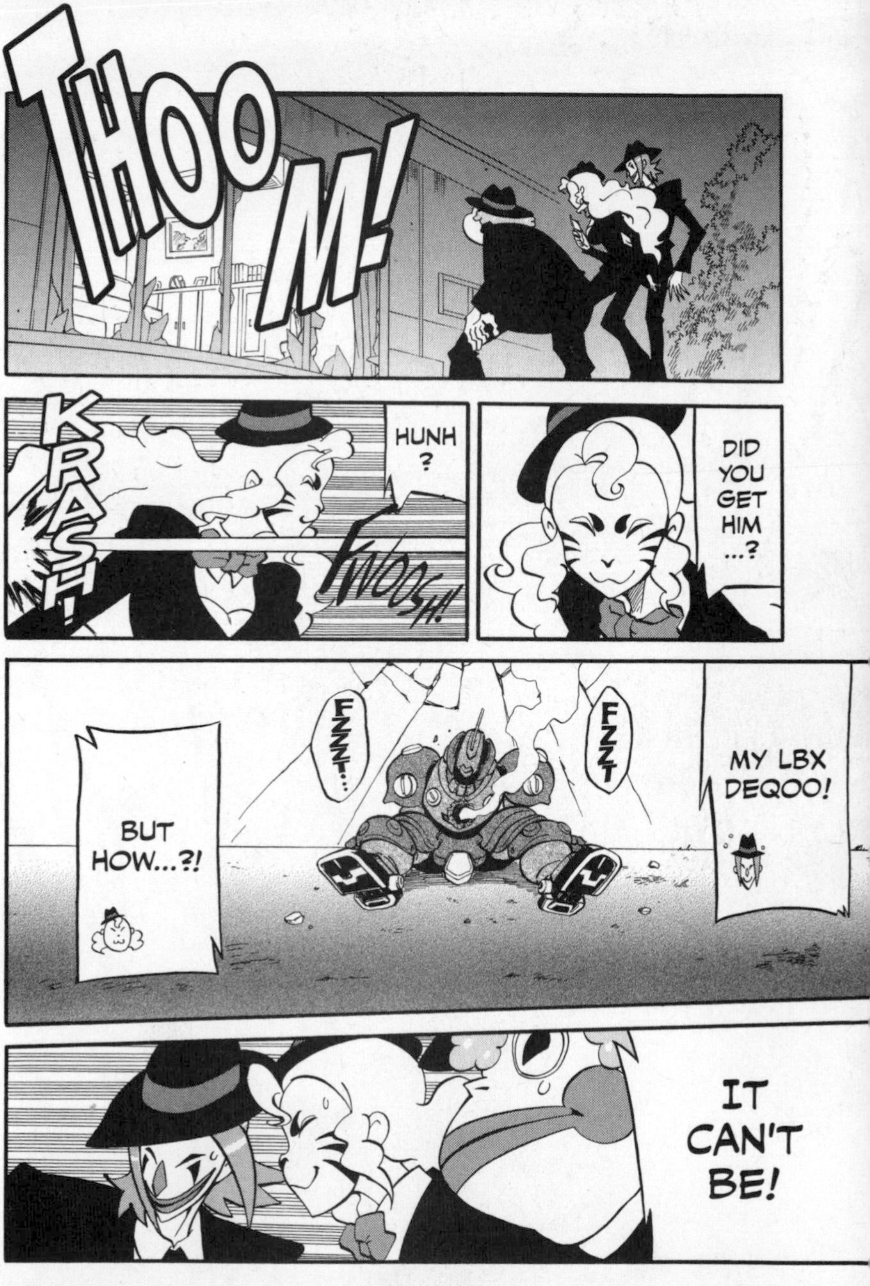
THOOM!
DID YOU GET HIM ...?
HUNH ?
KRASH!
FWOOSH!
MY LBX DEQOO!
FZZZT
FZZZT...
BUT HOW...?!
IT CAN'T BE!

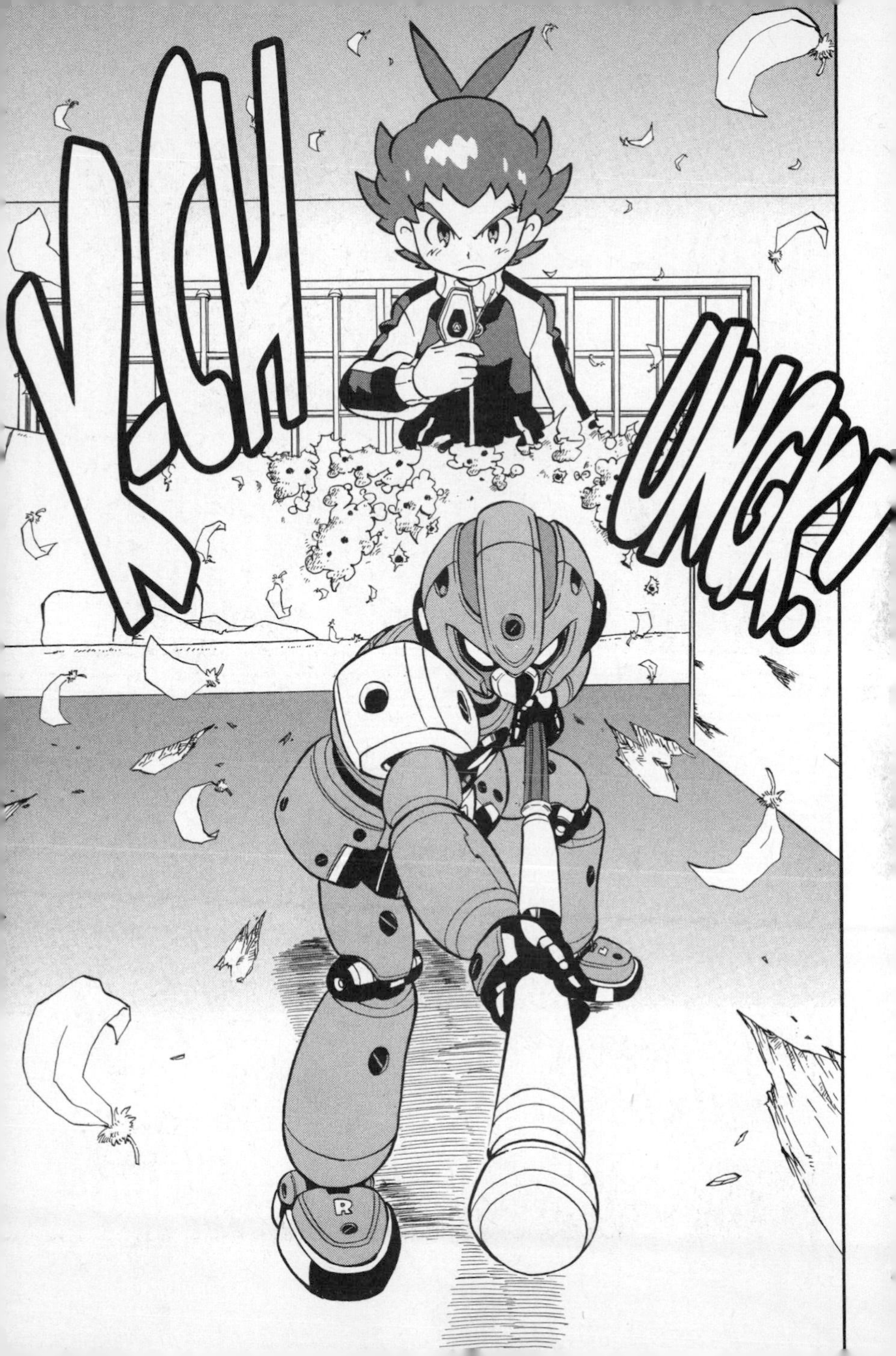
KACH
UNGK!

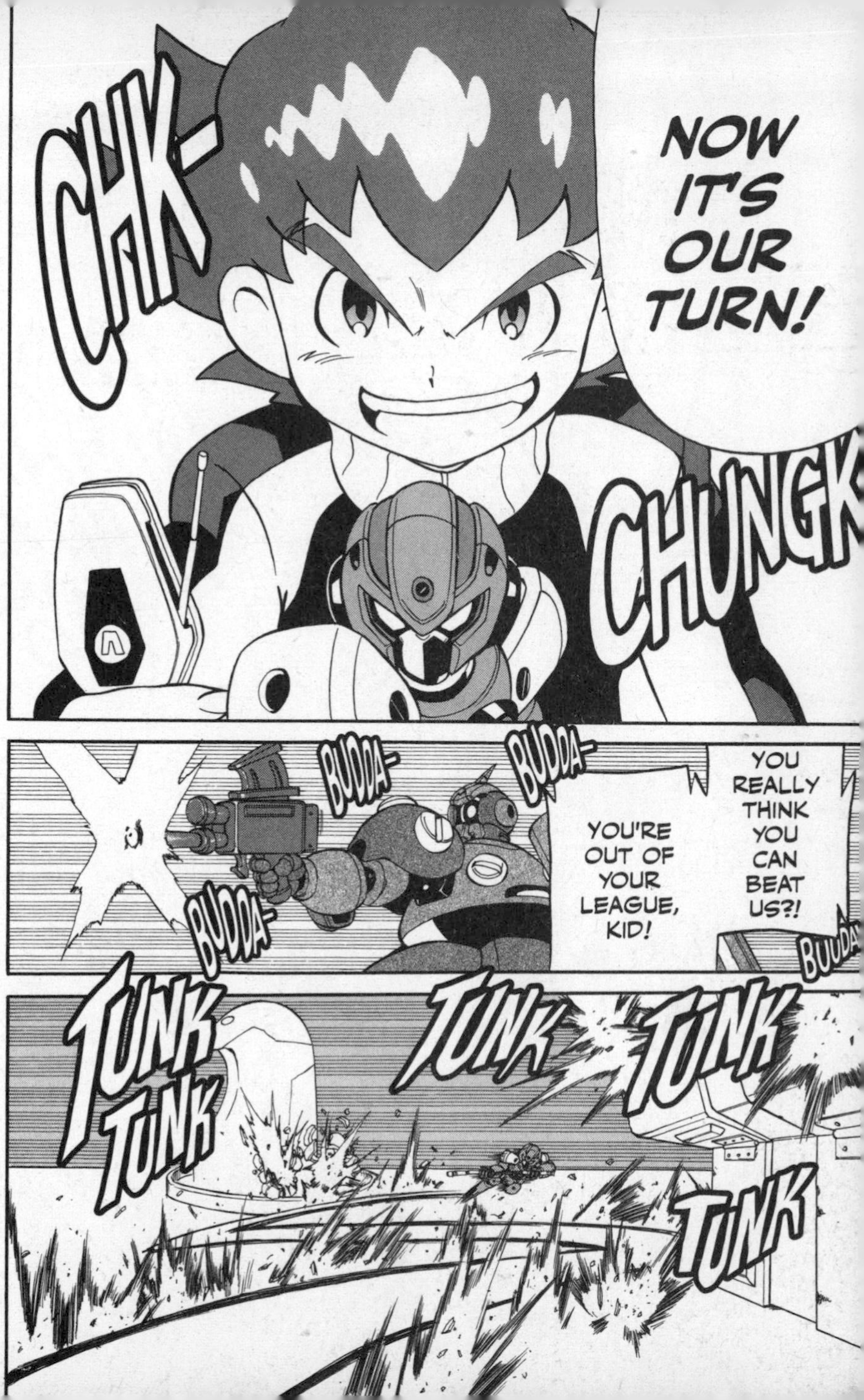

NOW IT'S OUR TURN!
CHUNGK
CHK-
BUDDA
YOU REALLY THINK YOU CAN BEAT US?!
YOU'RE OUT OF YOUR LEAGUE, KID!
BUDDA-
BUDDA-
BUDDA-
TUNK
TUNK
TUNK
TUNK TUNK
TUNK

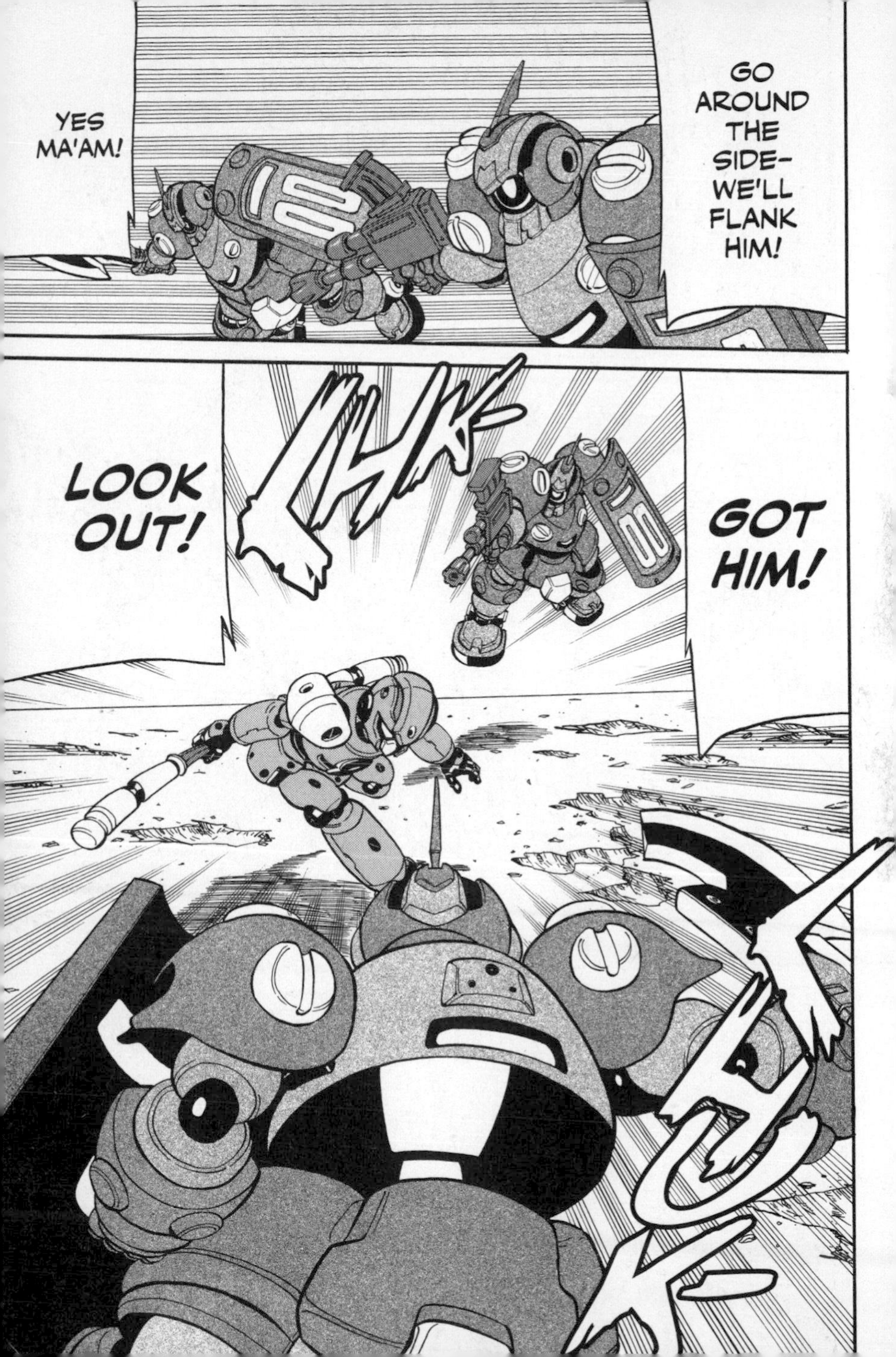
GO AROUND THE SIDE— WE'LL FLANK HIM!
YES MA'AM!
GOT HIM!
LOOK OUT!

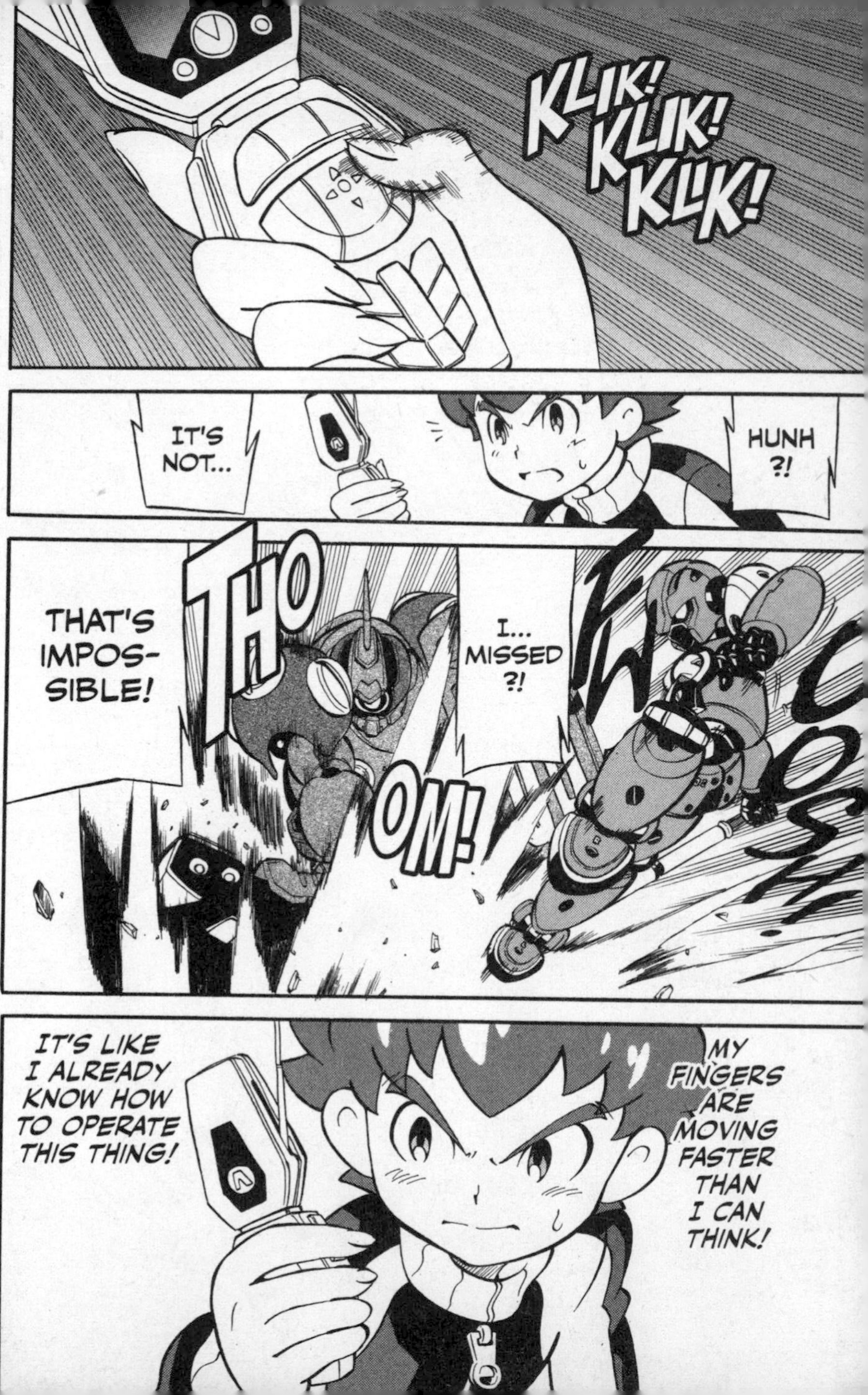
KLIK! KLIK! KLIK!
HUNH ?!
IT'S NOT...
I... MISSED ?!
THOOM!
THAT'S IMPOS-SIBLE!
MY FINGERS ARE MOVING FASTER THAN I CAN THINK!
IT'S LIKE I ALREADY KNOW HOW TO OPERATE THIS THING!

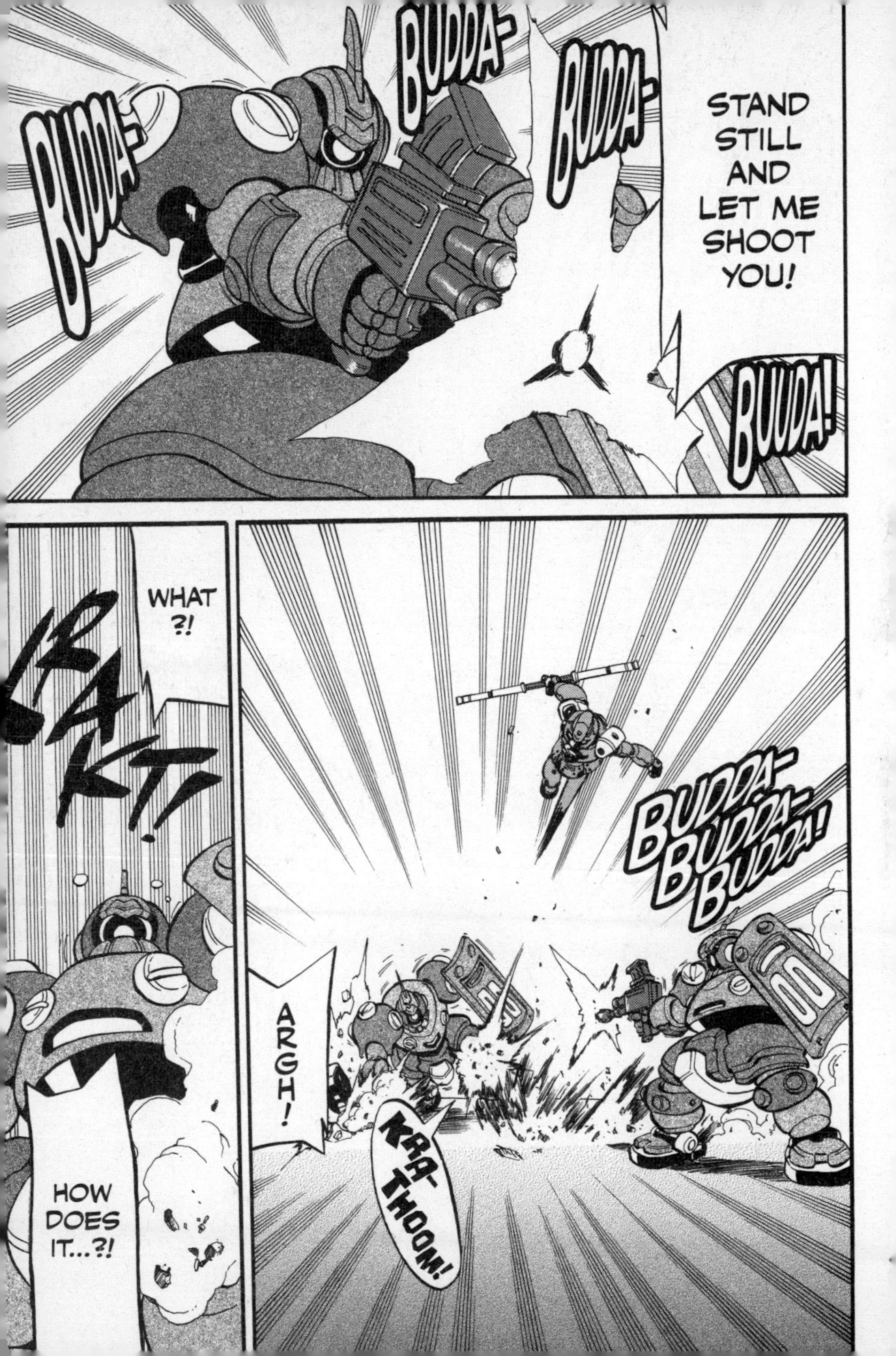
STAND STILL AND LET ME SHOOT YOU!
BUDDA-
BUDDA-
BUDDA-
BUUDA!
BUDDA-BUDDA-BUDDA!
ARGH!
KRA-THOOM!
WHAT?!
HOW DOES IT...?!

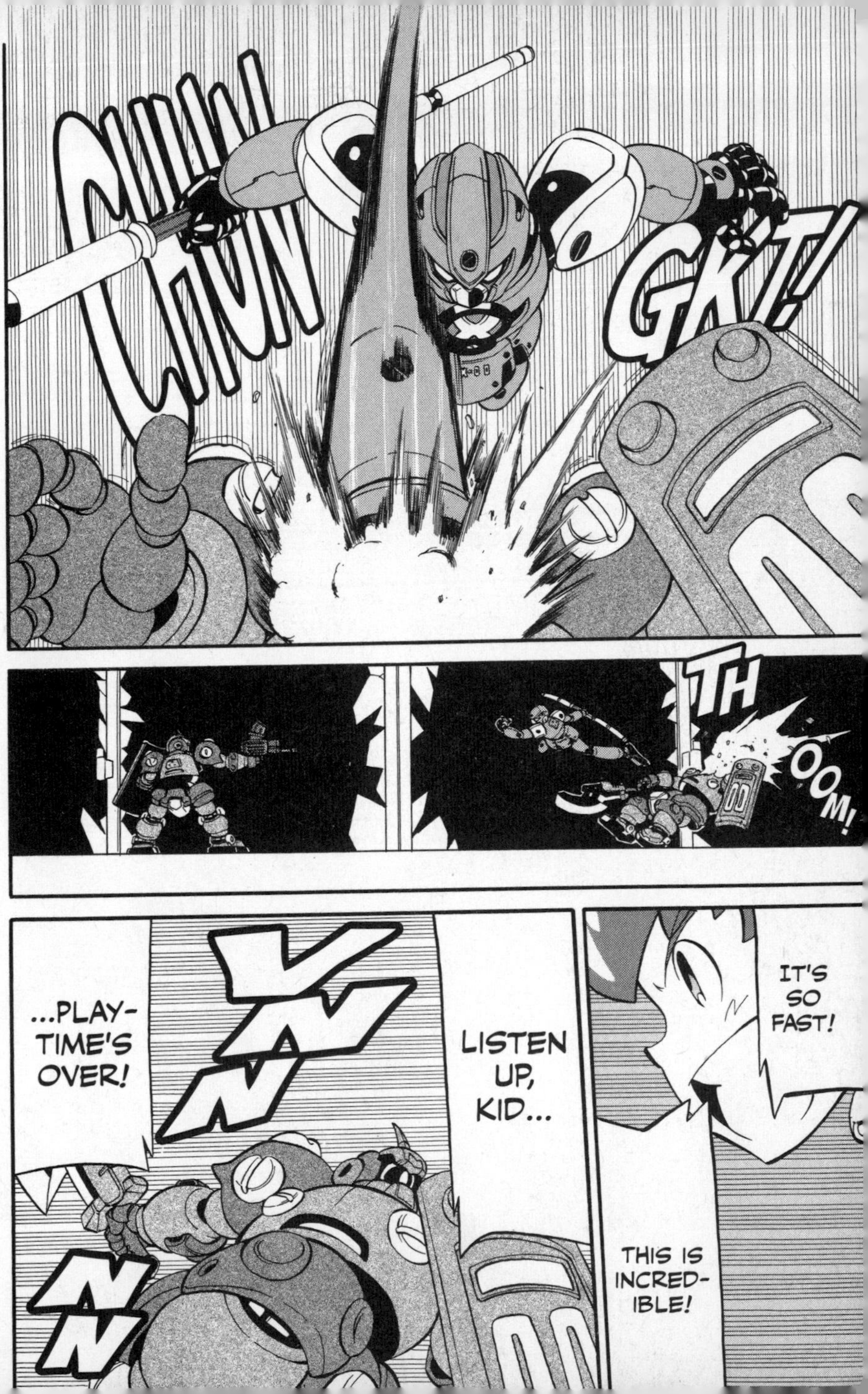
GK'T!
CHUN
THOOOM!
IT'S SO FAST!
THIS IS INCREDIBLE!
LISTEN UP, KID...
...PLAYTIME'S OVER!

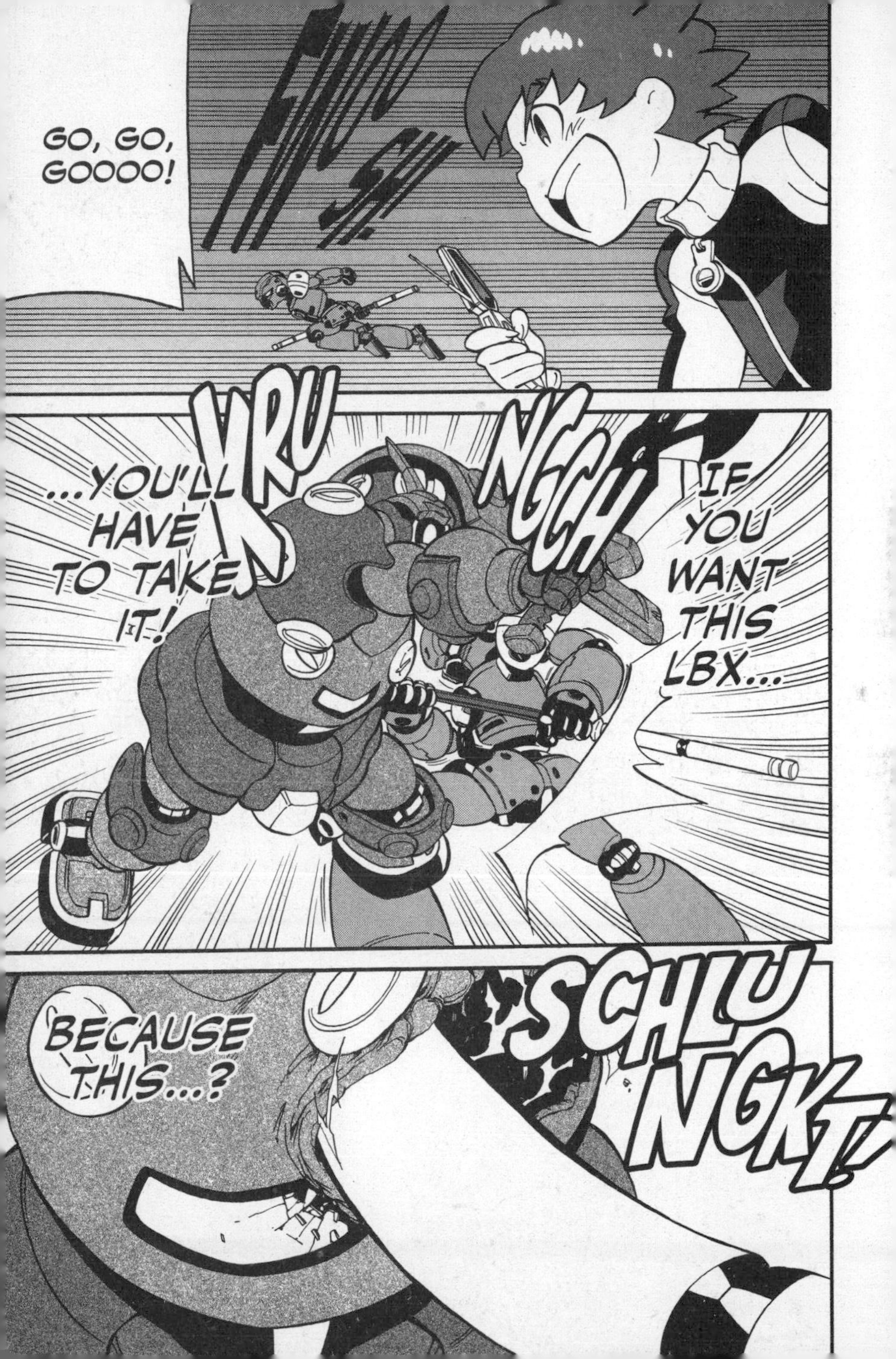
FWOOSH
GO, GO, GOOOO!
IF YOU WANT THIS LBX...
KRUNCH
...YOU'LL HAVE TO TAKE IT!
SCHLUNGK!
BECAUSE THIS...?

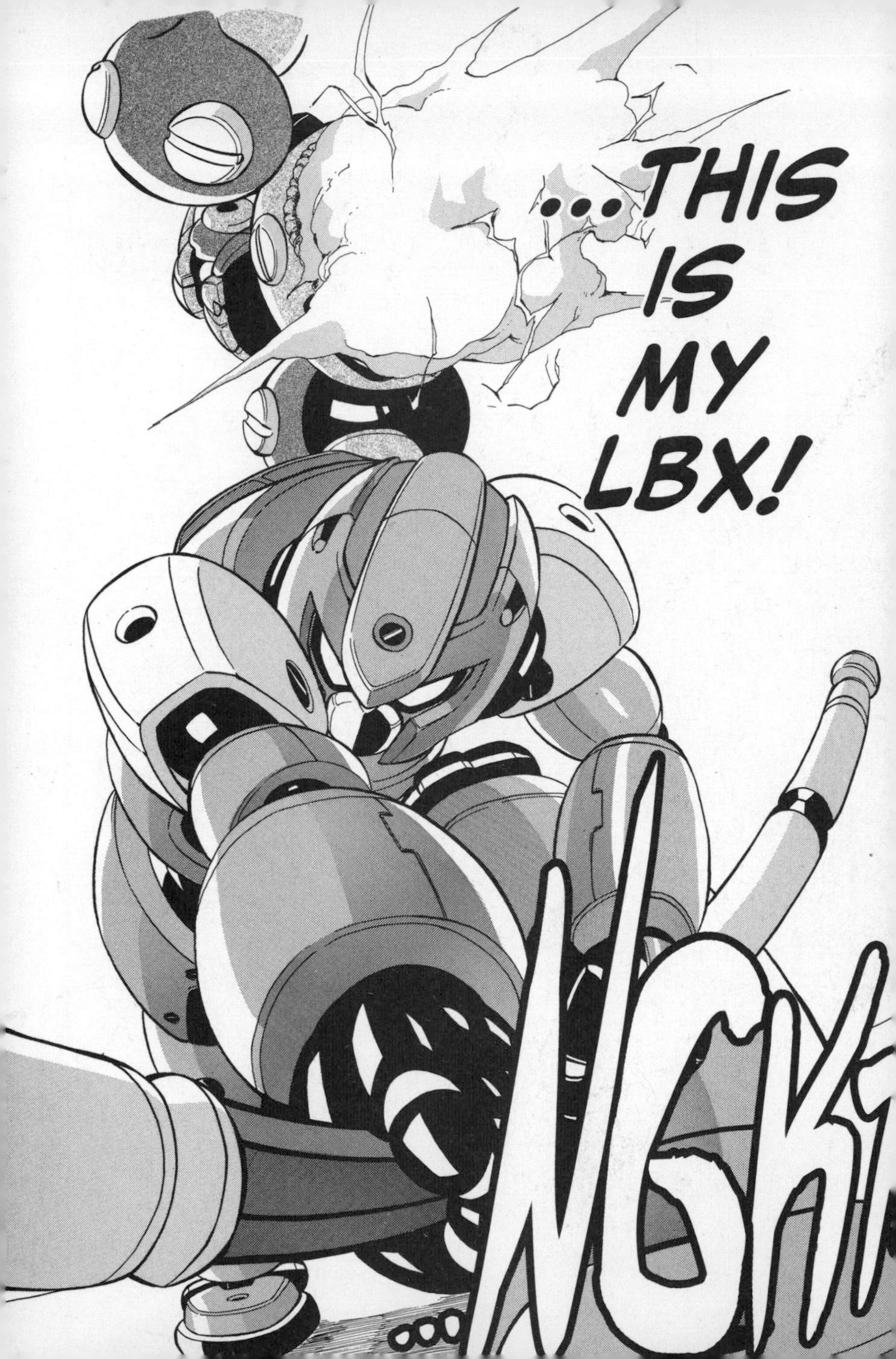
...THIS IS MY LBX!

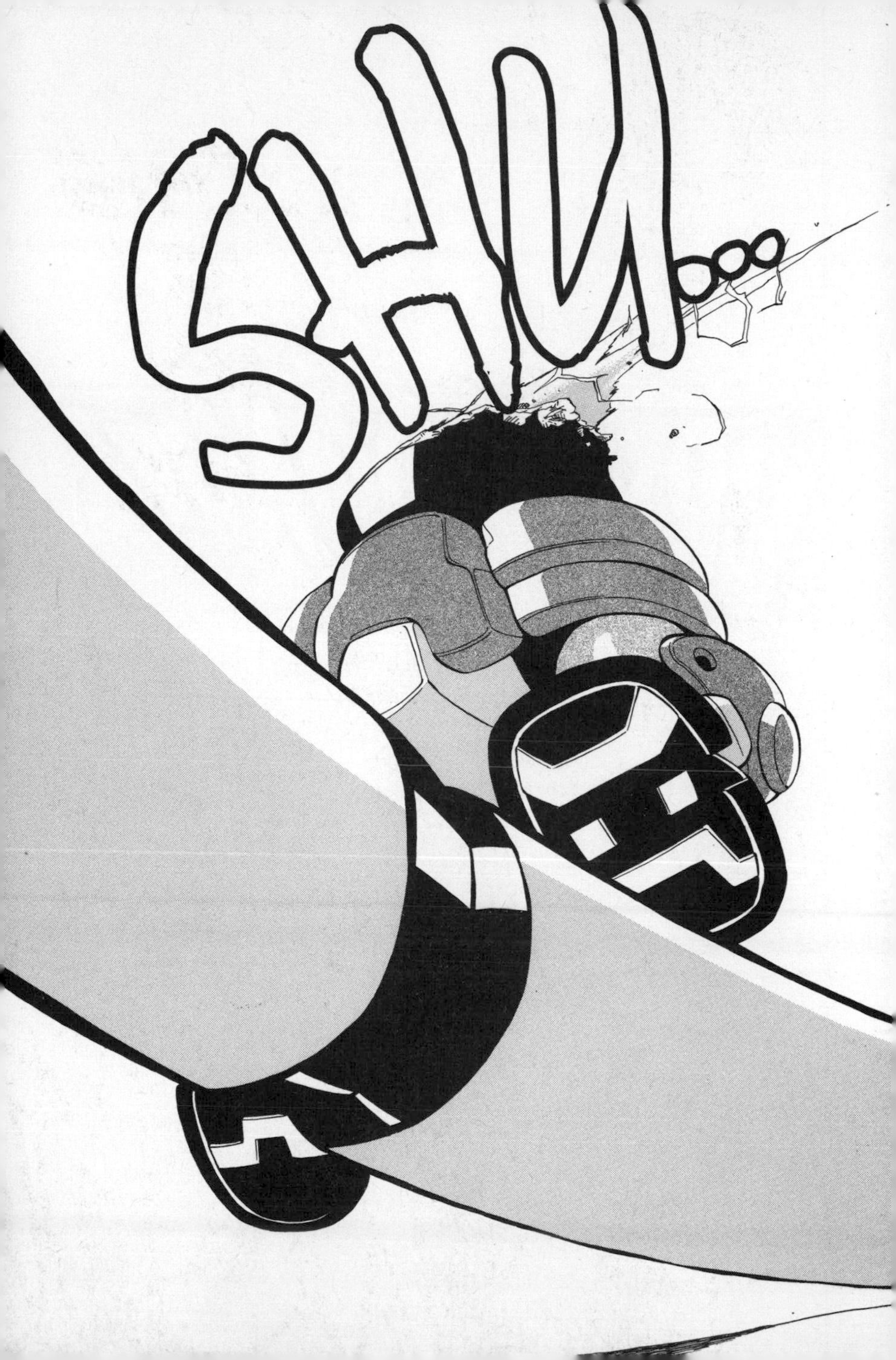
SHU...

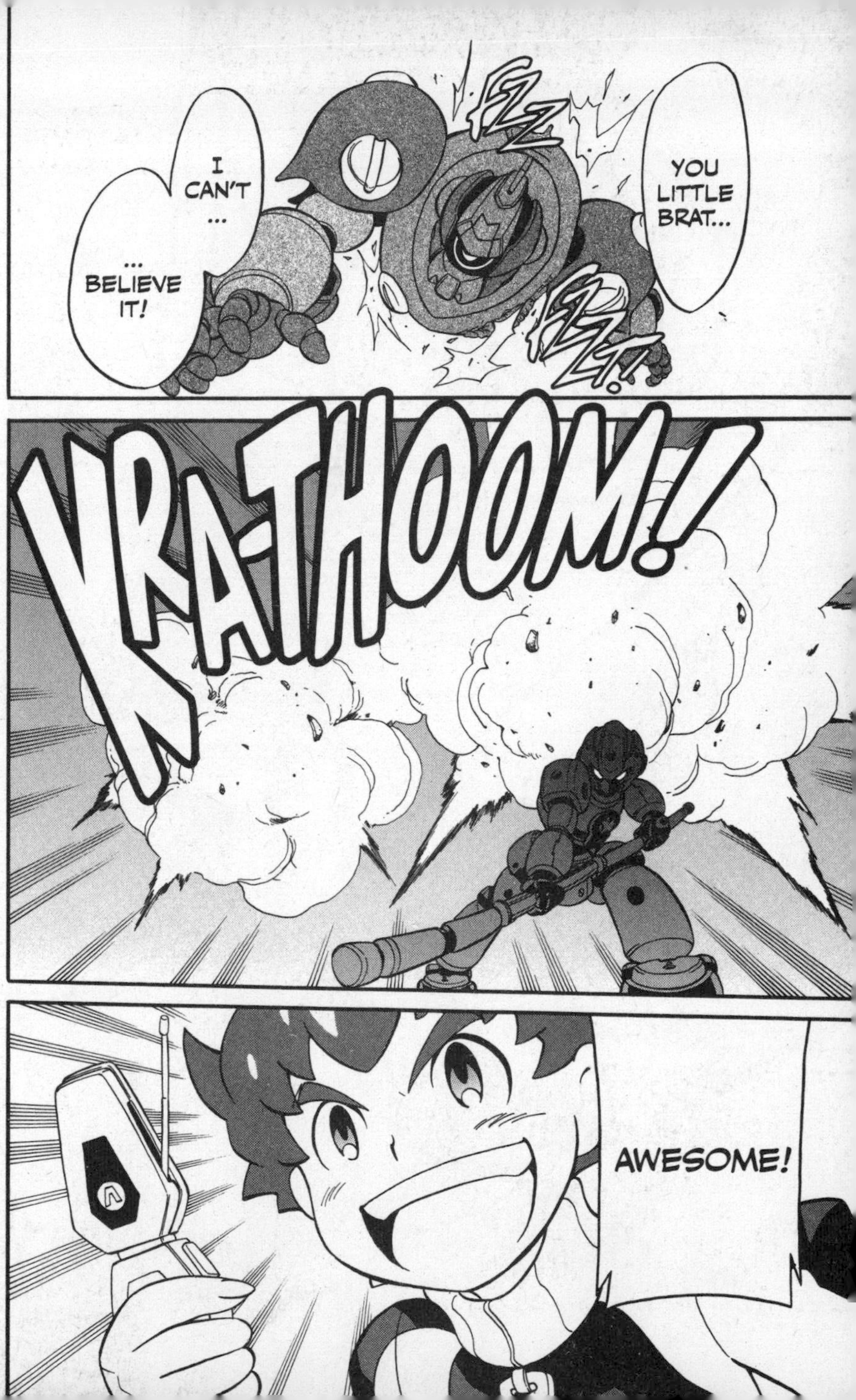
YOU LITTLE BRAT...
FZZ
FZZT!
I CAN'T ...
... BELIEVE IT!
KA-THOOM!
AWESOME!

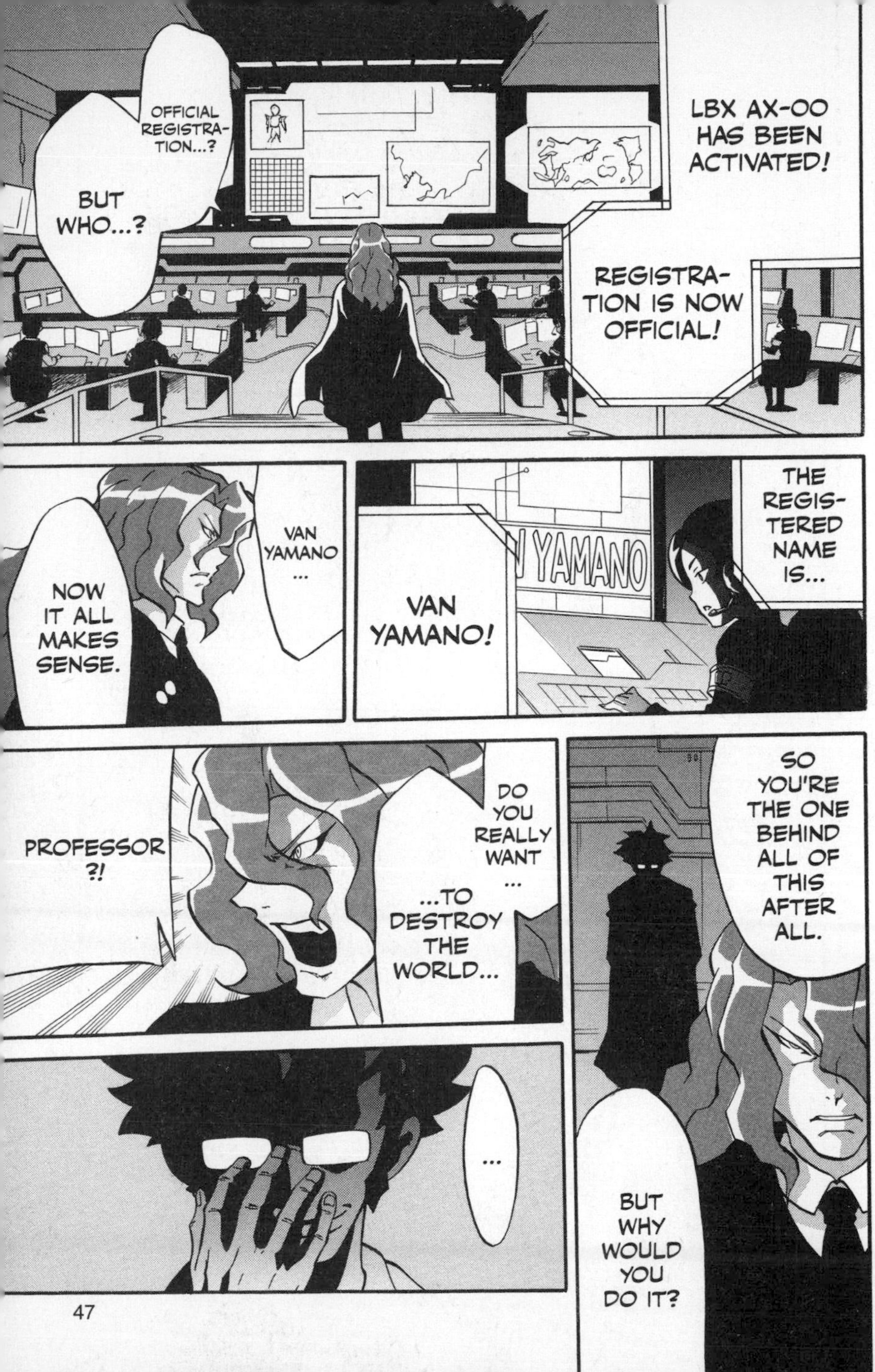
LBX AX-00 HAS BEEN ACTIVATED!
REGISTRATION IS NOW OFFICIAL!
OFFICIAL REGISTRATION...?
BUT WHO...?
THE REGISTERED NAME IS...
VAN YAMANO!
VAN YAMANO...
NOW IT ALL MAKES SENSE.
SO YOU'RE THE ONE BEHIND ALL OF THIS AFTER ALL.
BUT WHY WOULD YOU DO IT?
DO YOU REALLY WANT...
...TO DESTROY THE WORLD...
PROFESSOR?!
...

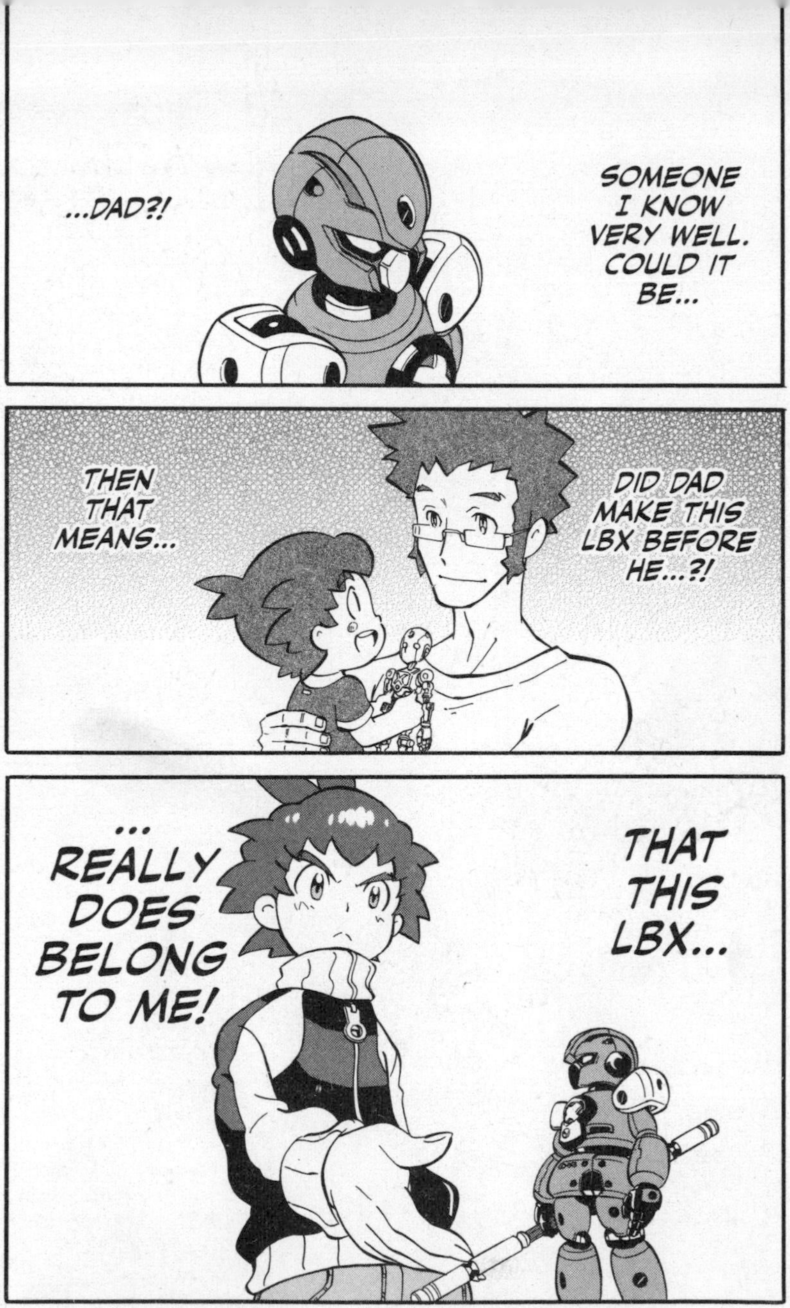
SOMEONE I KNOW VERY WELL. COULD IT BE...
...DAD?!
DID DAD MAKE THIS LBX BEFORE HE...?!
THEN THAT MEANS...
THAT THIS LBX...
...REALLY DOES BELONG TO ME!

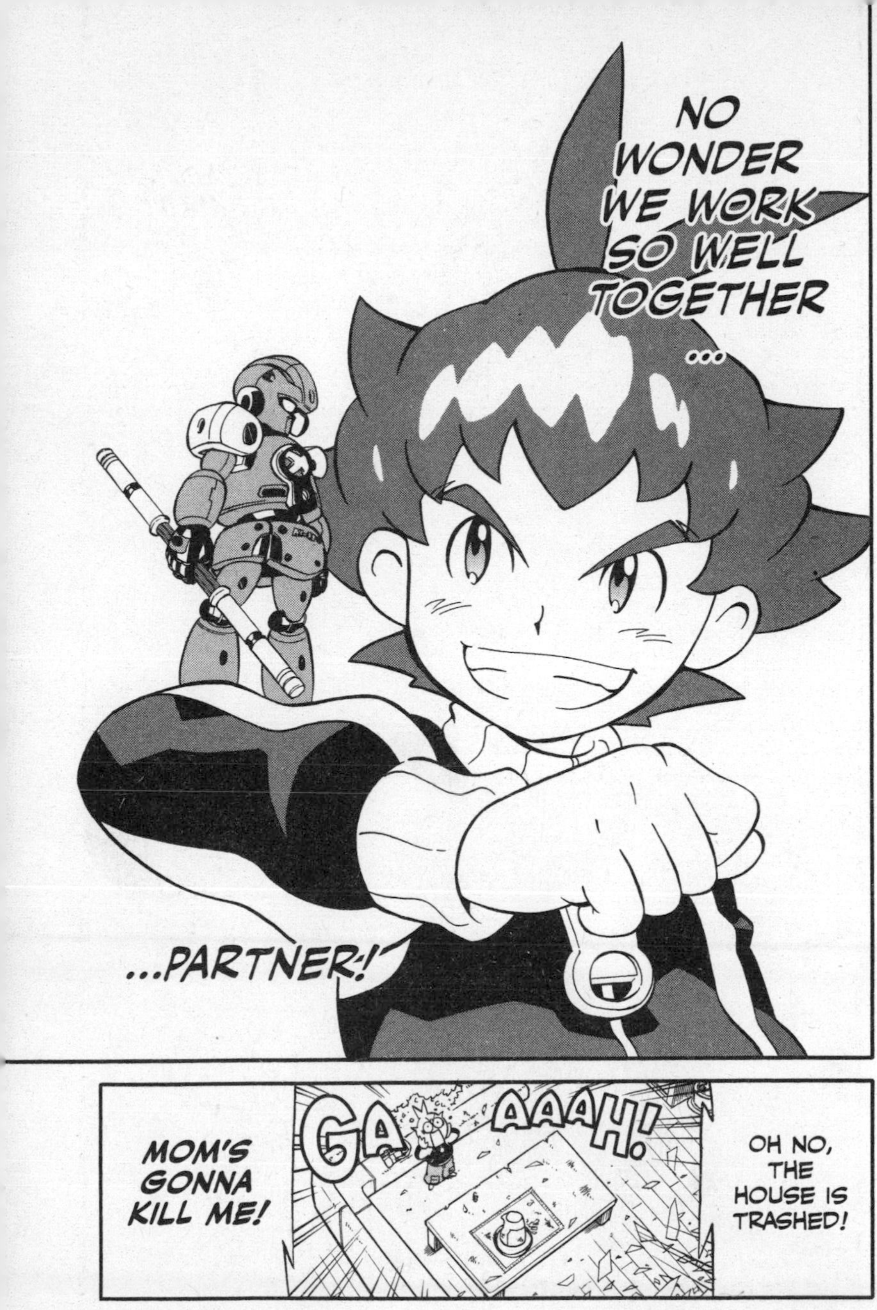
NO WONDER WE WORK SO WELL TOGETHER...
...PARTNER!
OH NO, THE HOUSE IS TRASHED!
GAAAAH!
MOM'S GONNA KILL ME!

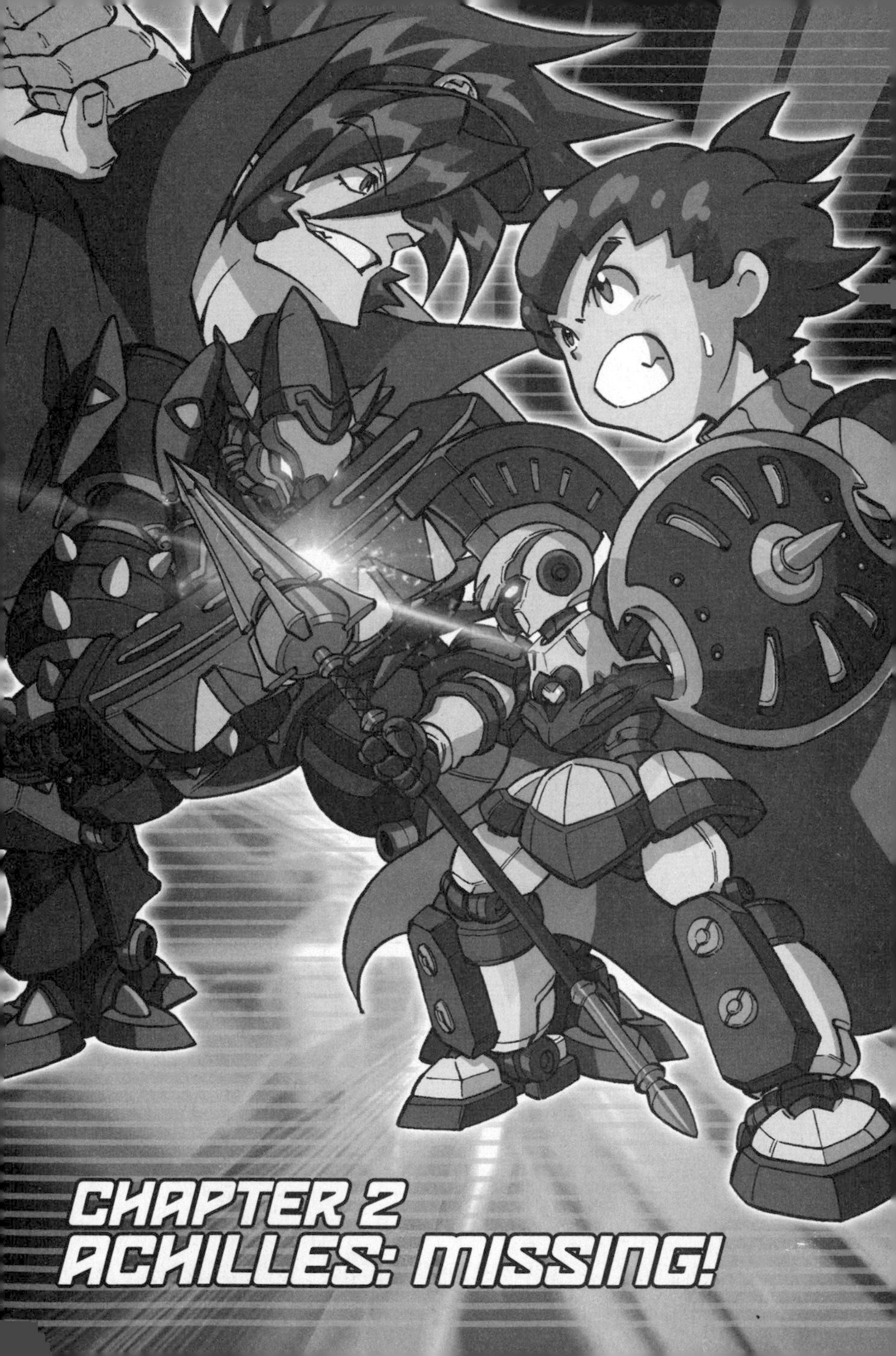
CHAPTER 2
ACHILLES: MISSING!

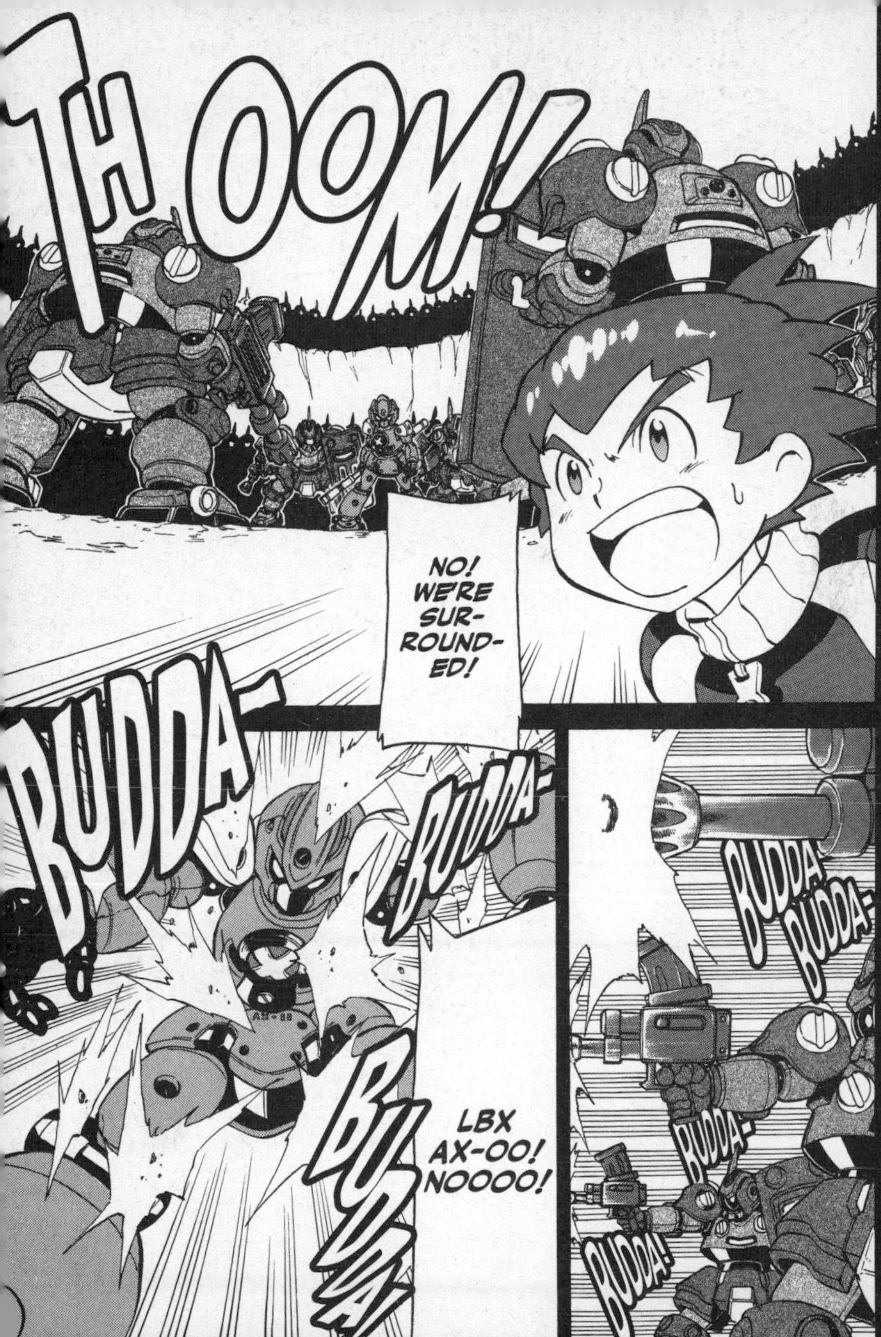
THOOM!
NO! WE'RE SUR-ROUND-ED!
BUDDA BUDDA-
BUDDA-
BUDDA!
BUDDA-
BUDDA-
LBX AX-00! NOOOO!
BUDDA!

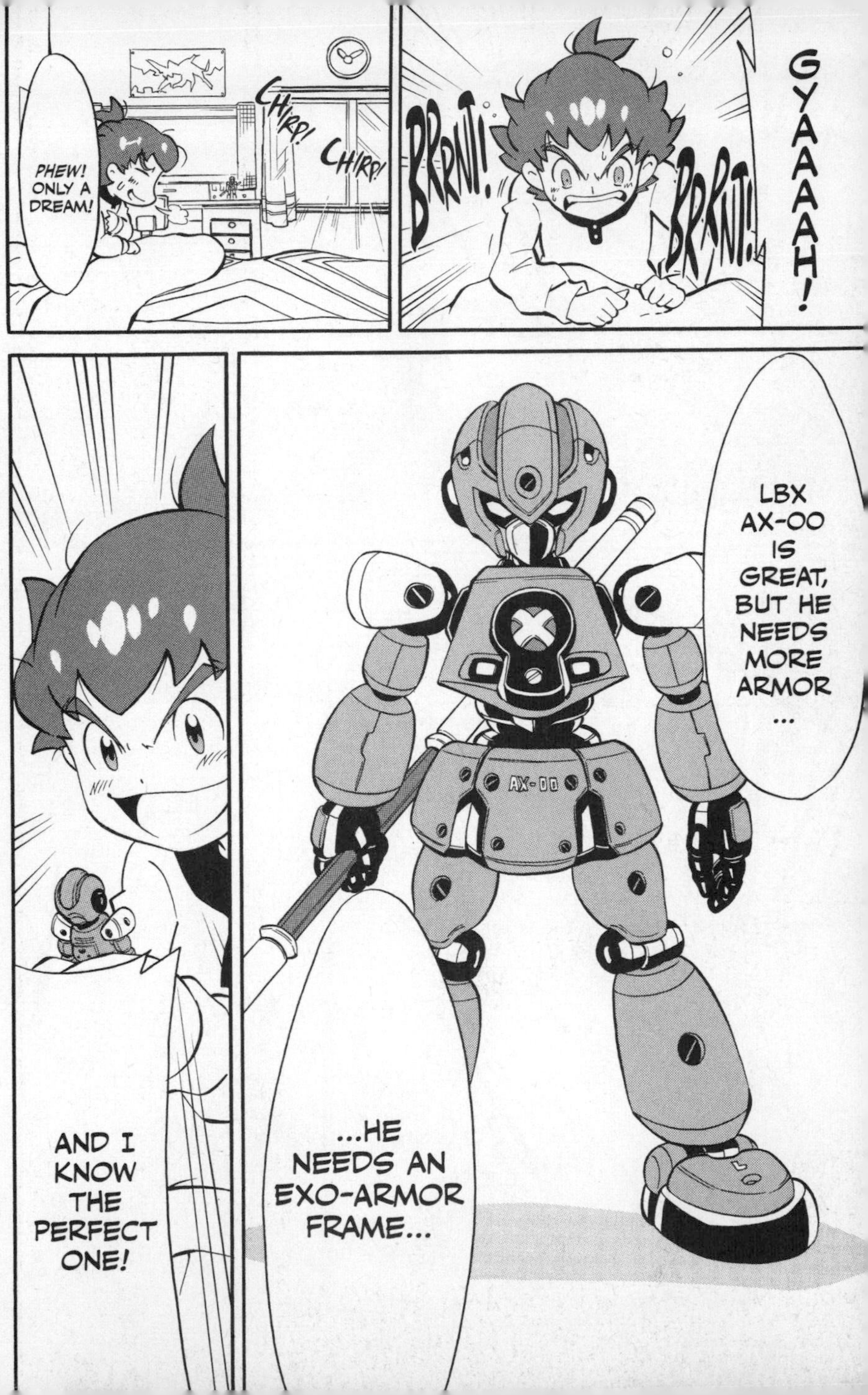
GYAAAAH!
BRRNT!
BRRNT!
PHEW! ONLY A DREAM!
CHIRP!
CHIRP!
LBX AX-00 IS GREAT, BUT HE NEEDS MORE ARMOR ...
AX-00
...HE NEEDS AN EXO-ARMOR FRAME...
AND I KNOW THE PERFECT ONE!

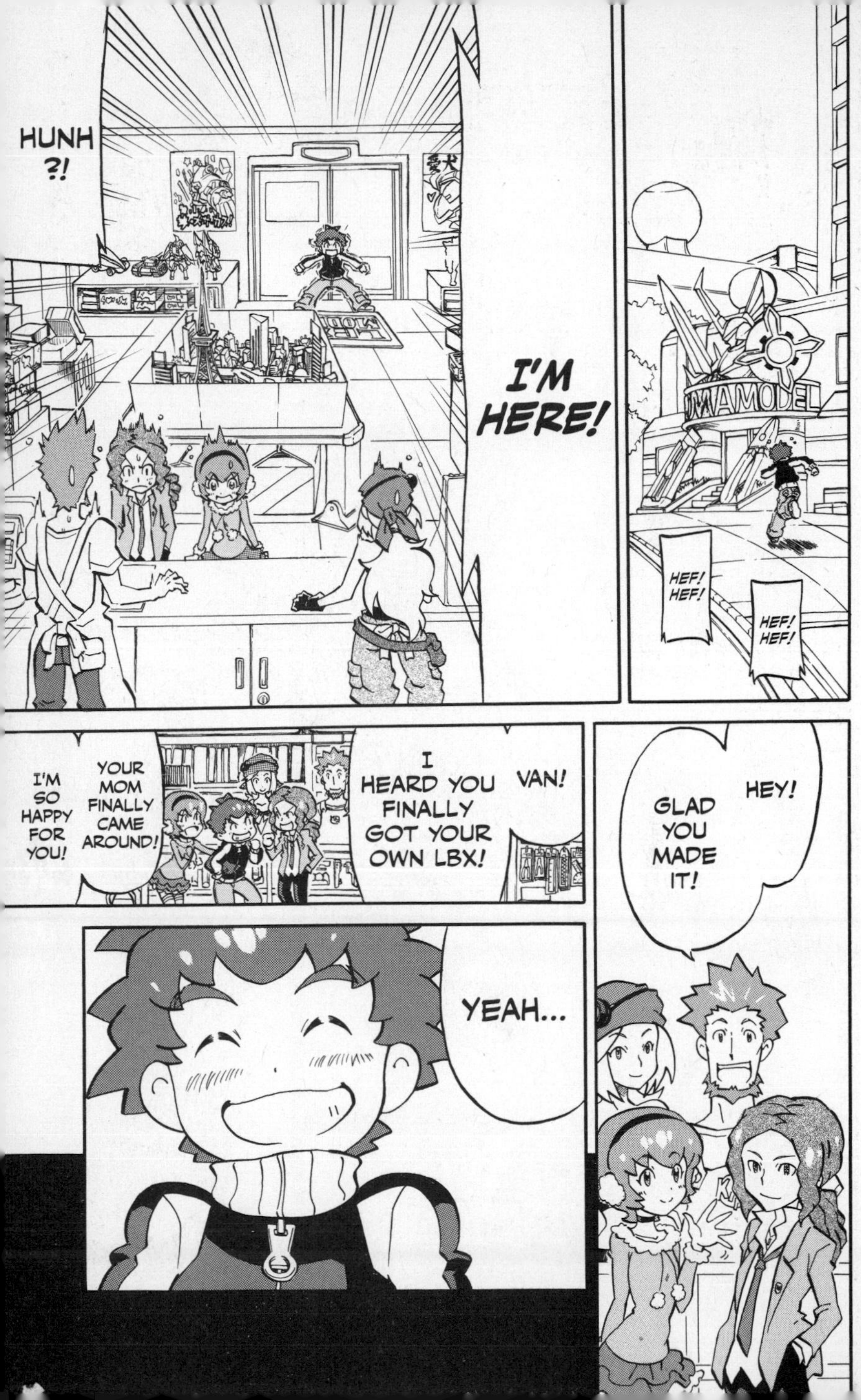
HEF! HEF!
HEF! HEF!
I'M HERE!
HUNH ?!
愛犬
HEY!
GLAD YOU MADE IT!
VAN!
I HEARD YOU FINALLY GOT YOUR OWN LBX!
YOUR MOM FINALLY CAME AROUND!
I'M SO HAPPY FOR YOU!
YEAH...

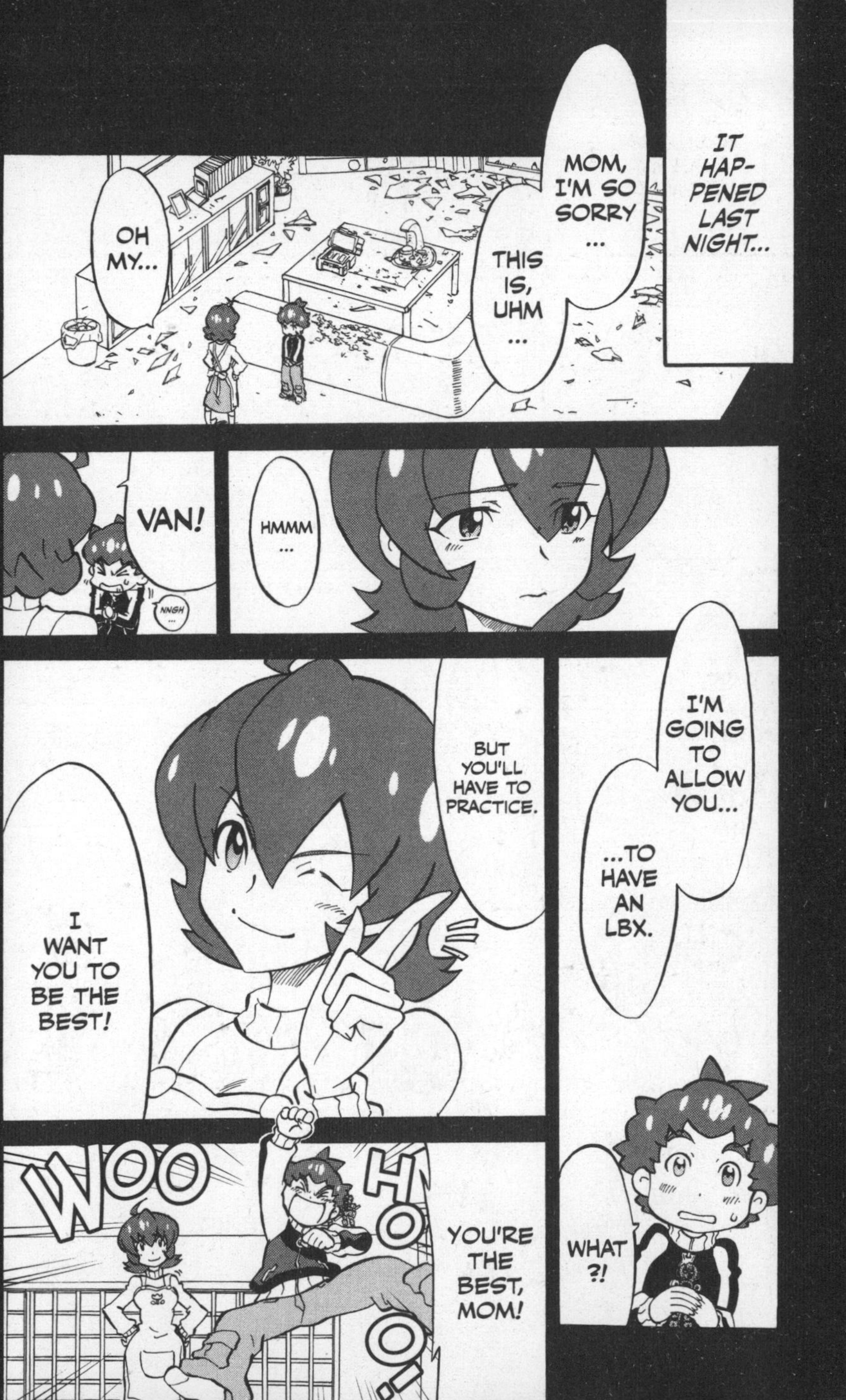
IT HAPPENED LAST NIGHT...
MOM, I'M SO SORRY...
THIS IS, UHM...
OH MY...
HMMM...
VAN!
NNGH...
I'M GOING TO ALLOW YOU...
...TO HAVE AN LBX.
WHAT?!
BUT YOU'LL HAVE TO PRACTICE.
I WANT YOU TO BE THE BEST!
WOOHOO!
YOU'RE THE BEST, MOM!

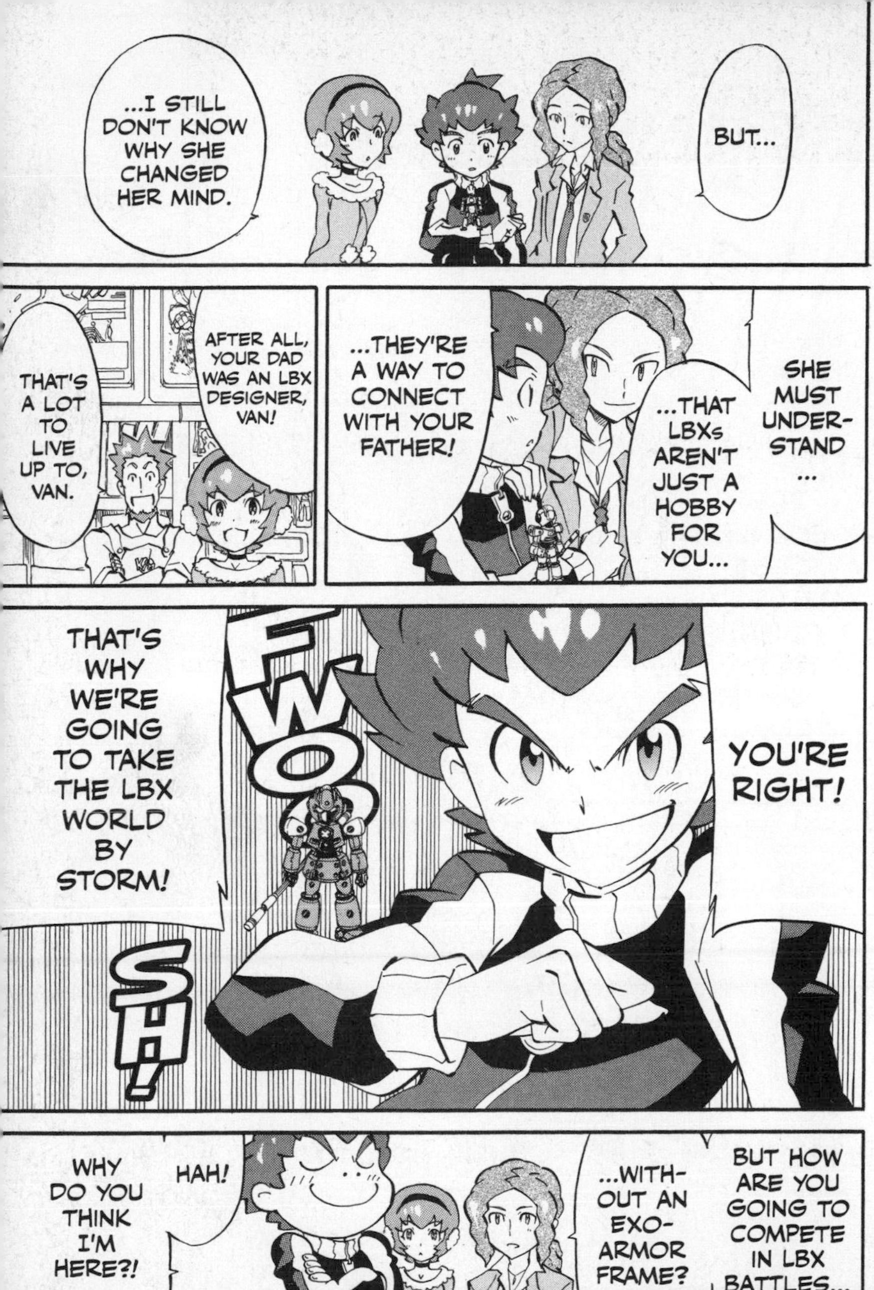
BUT...
...I STILL DON'T KNOW WHY SHE CHANGED HER MIND.
SHE MUST UNDER-STAND...
...THAT LBXs AREN'T JUST A HOBBY FOR YOU...
...THEY'RE A WAY TO CONNECT WITH YOUR FATHER!
AFTER ALL, YOUR DAD WAS AN LBX DESIGNER, VAN!
THAT'S A LOT TO LIVE UP TO, VAN.
YOU'RE RIGHT!
FWOSH!
THAT'S WHY WE'RE GOING TO TAKE THE LBX WORLD BY STORM!
BUT HOW ARE YOU GOING TO COMPETE IN LBX BATTLES...
...WITH-OUT AN EXO-ARMOR FRAME?
HAH!
WHY DO YOU THINK I'M HERE?!

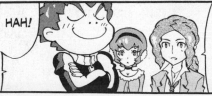

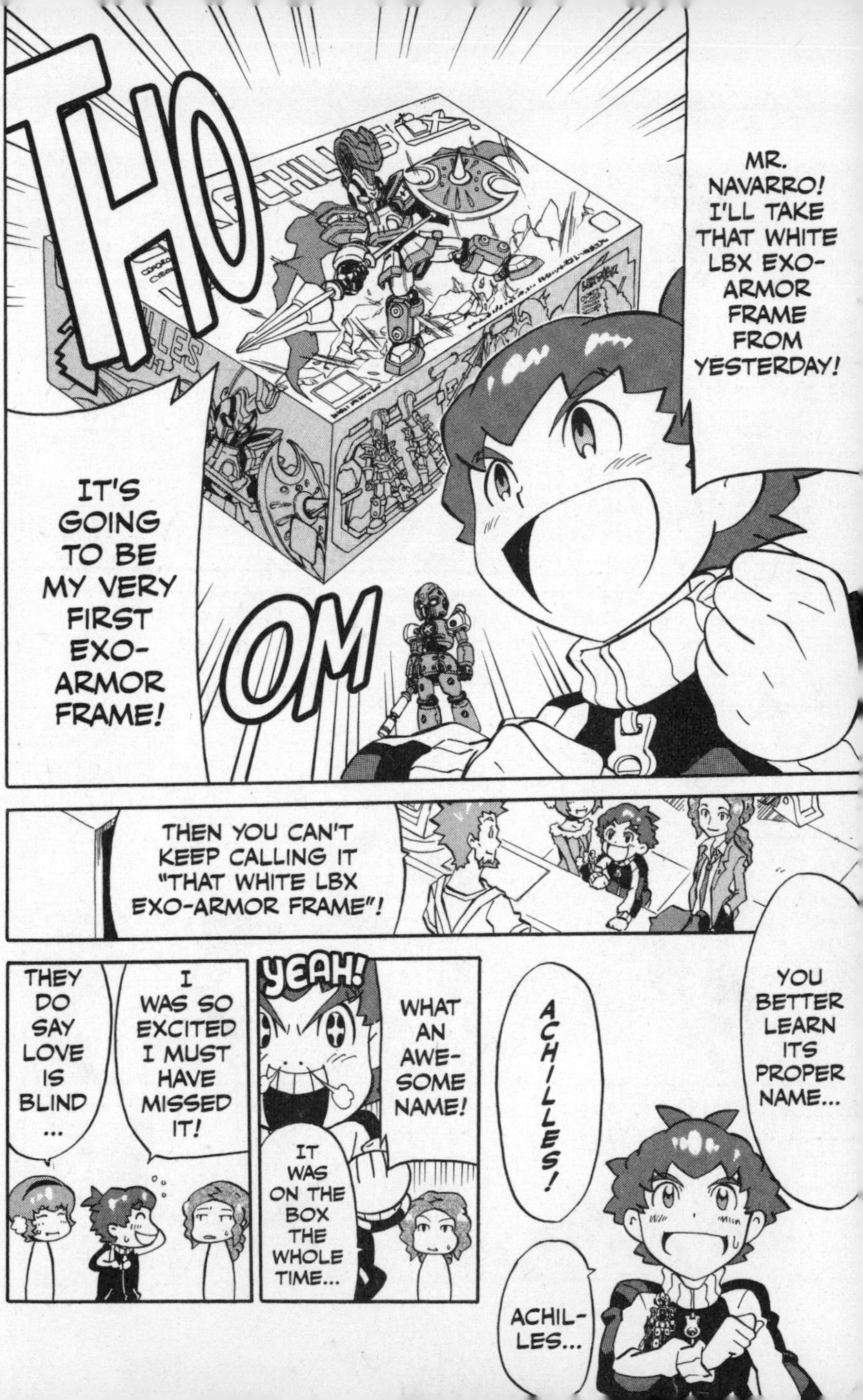
MR. NAVARRO! I'LL TAKE THAT WHITE LBX EXO-ARMOR FRAME FROM YESTERDAY!
THO
OM
IT'S GOING TO BE MY VERY FIRST EXO-ARMOR FRAME!
THEN YOU CAN'T KEEP CALLING IT "THAT WHITE LBX EXO-ARMOR FRAME"!
YOU BETTER LEARN ITS PROPER NAME...
ACHILLES!
ACHIL-LES...
WHAT AN AWE-SOME NAME!
YEAH!
IT WAS ON THE BOX THE WHOLE TIME...
I WAS SO EXCITED I MUST HAVE MISSED IT!
THEY DO SAY LOVE IS BLIND...

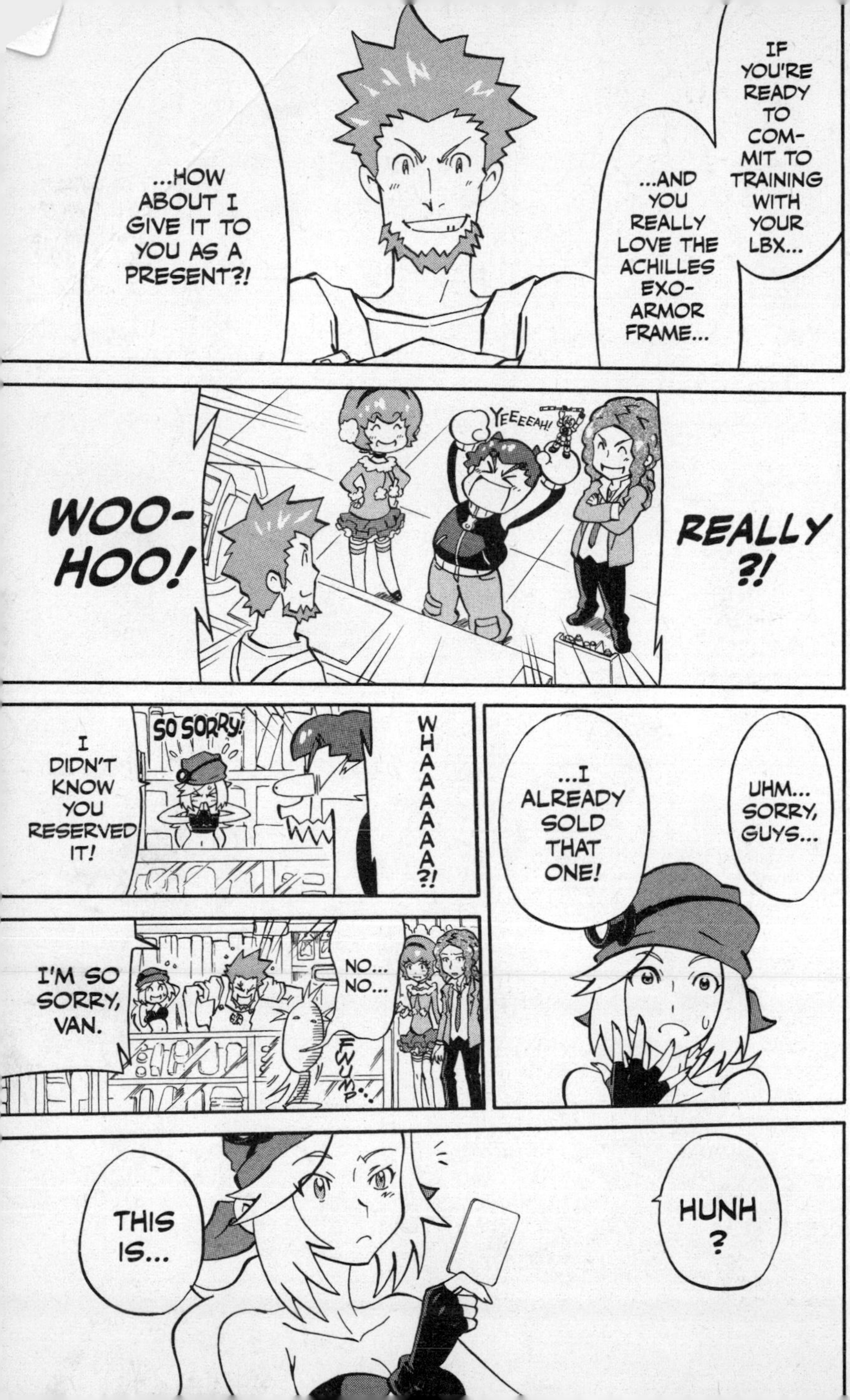
IF YOU'RE READY TO COMMIT TO TRAINING WITH YOUR LBX...
...AND YOU REALLY LOVE THE ACHILLES EXO-ARMOR FRAME...
...HOW ABOUT I GIVE IT TO YOU AS A PRESENT?!
REALLY?!
YEEEEAH!
WOO-HOO!
UHM... SORRY, GUYS...
...I ALREADY SOLD THAT ONE!
WHAAAAAAA?!
SO SORRY!
I DIDN'T KNOW YOU RESERVED IT!
NO... NO...
FWUMP...
I'M SO SORRY, VAN.
HUNH?
THIS IS...

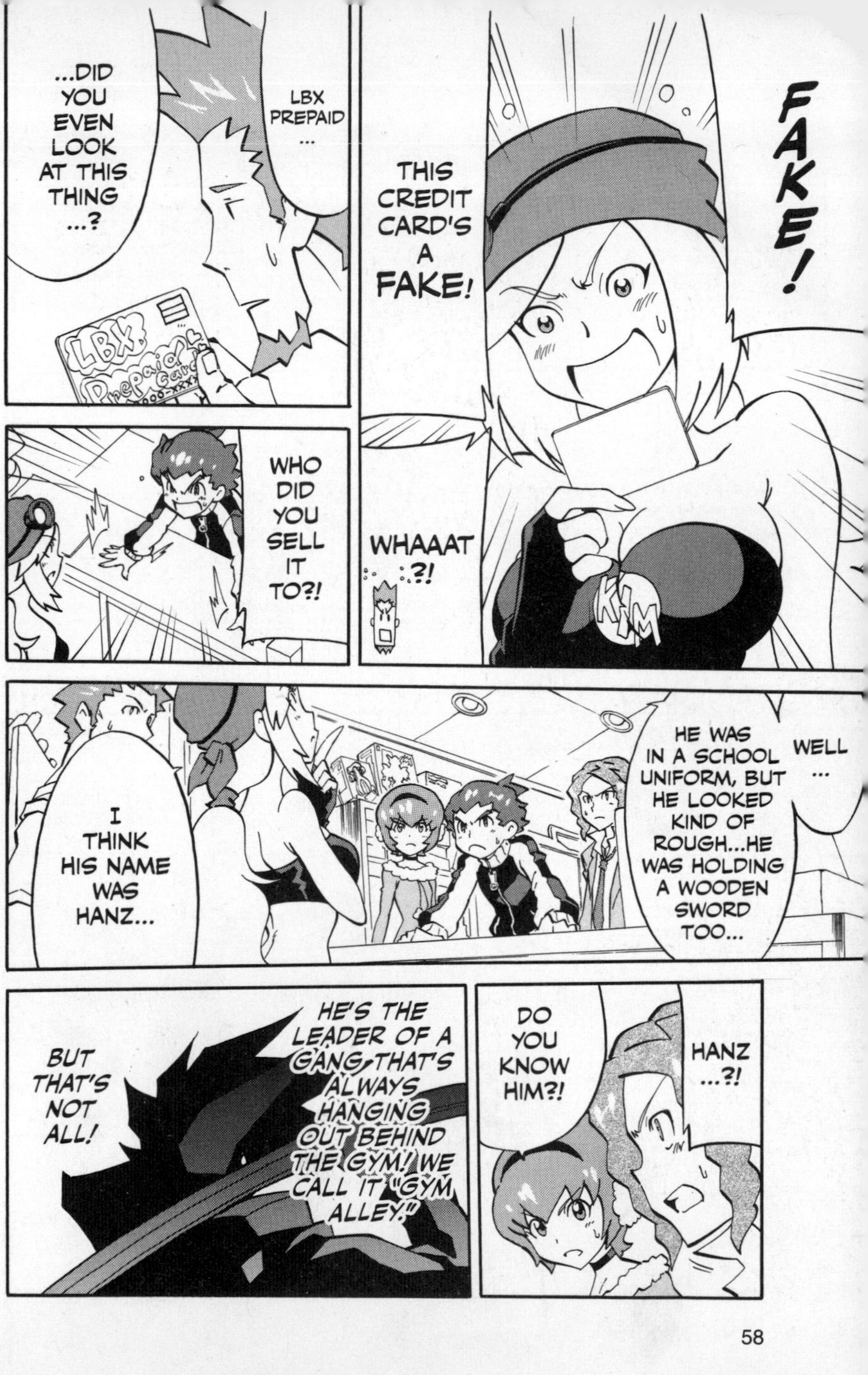
FAKE!
THIS CREDIT CARD'S A FAKE!
WHAAAT?!
KIM
LBX PREPAID...
...DID YOU EVEN LOOK AT THIS THING...?
LBX Prepaid Card
WHO DID YOU SELL IT TO?!
WELL...
HE WAS IN A SCHOOL UNIFORM, BUT HE LOOKED KIND OF ROUGH...HE WAS HOLDING A WOODEN SWORD TOO...
I THINK HIS NAME WAS HANZ...
HANZ...?!
DO YOU KNOW HIM?!
HE'S THE LEADER OF A GANG THAT'S ALWAYS HANGING OUT BEHIND THE GYM! WE CALL IT "GYM ALLEY."
BUT THAT'S NOT ALL!

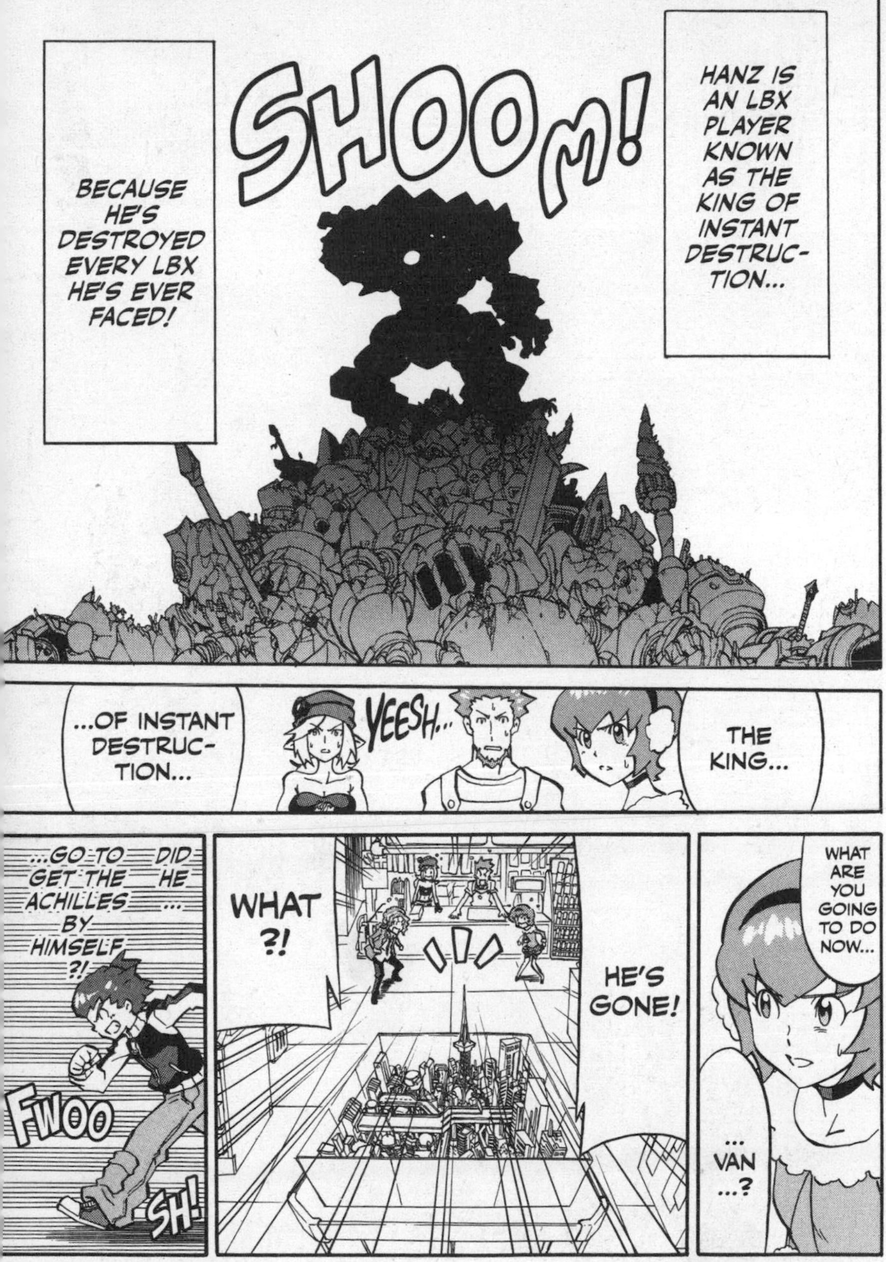
HANZ IS AN LBX PLAYER KNOWN AS THE KING OF INSTANT DESTRUCTION...
SHOOM!
BECAUSE HE'S DESTROYED EVERY LBX HE'S EVER FACED!
THE KING...
YEESH...
...OF INSTANT DESTRUCTION...
WHAT ARE YOU GOING TO DO NOW...
... VAN ...?
WHAT ?!
HE'S GONE!
DID HE ...
...GO TO GET THE ACHILLES BY HIMSELF ?!
FWOOSH!

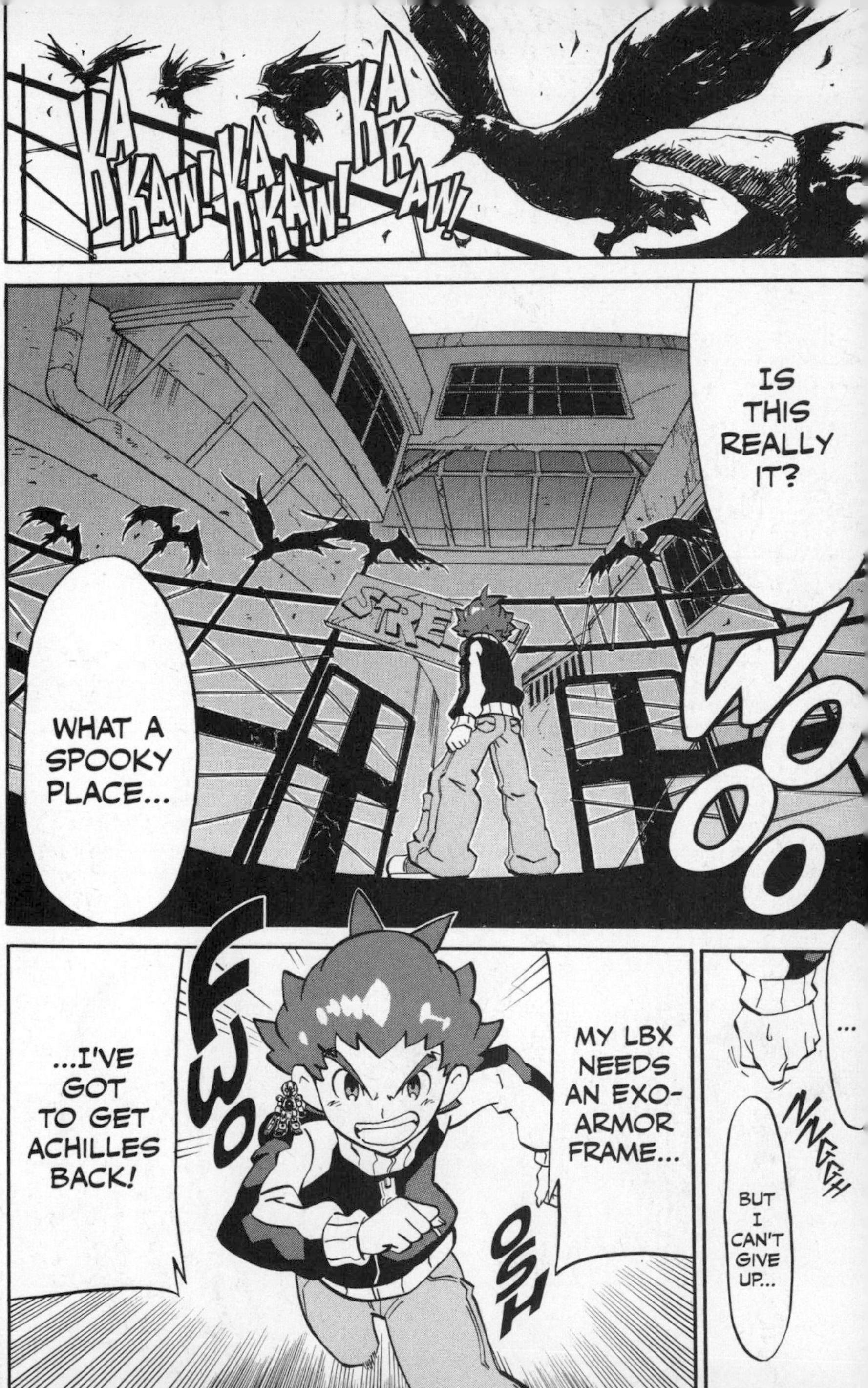
KA KAW!
KA KAW!
KA KAW!
IS THIS REALLY IT?
WOOO
STRE
WHAT A SPOOKY PLACE...
...
NNGGH
BUT I CAN'T GIVE UP...
MY LBX NEEDS AN EXO-ARMOR FRAME...
WOOSH
...I'VE GOT TO GET ACHILLES BACK!

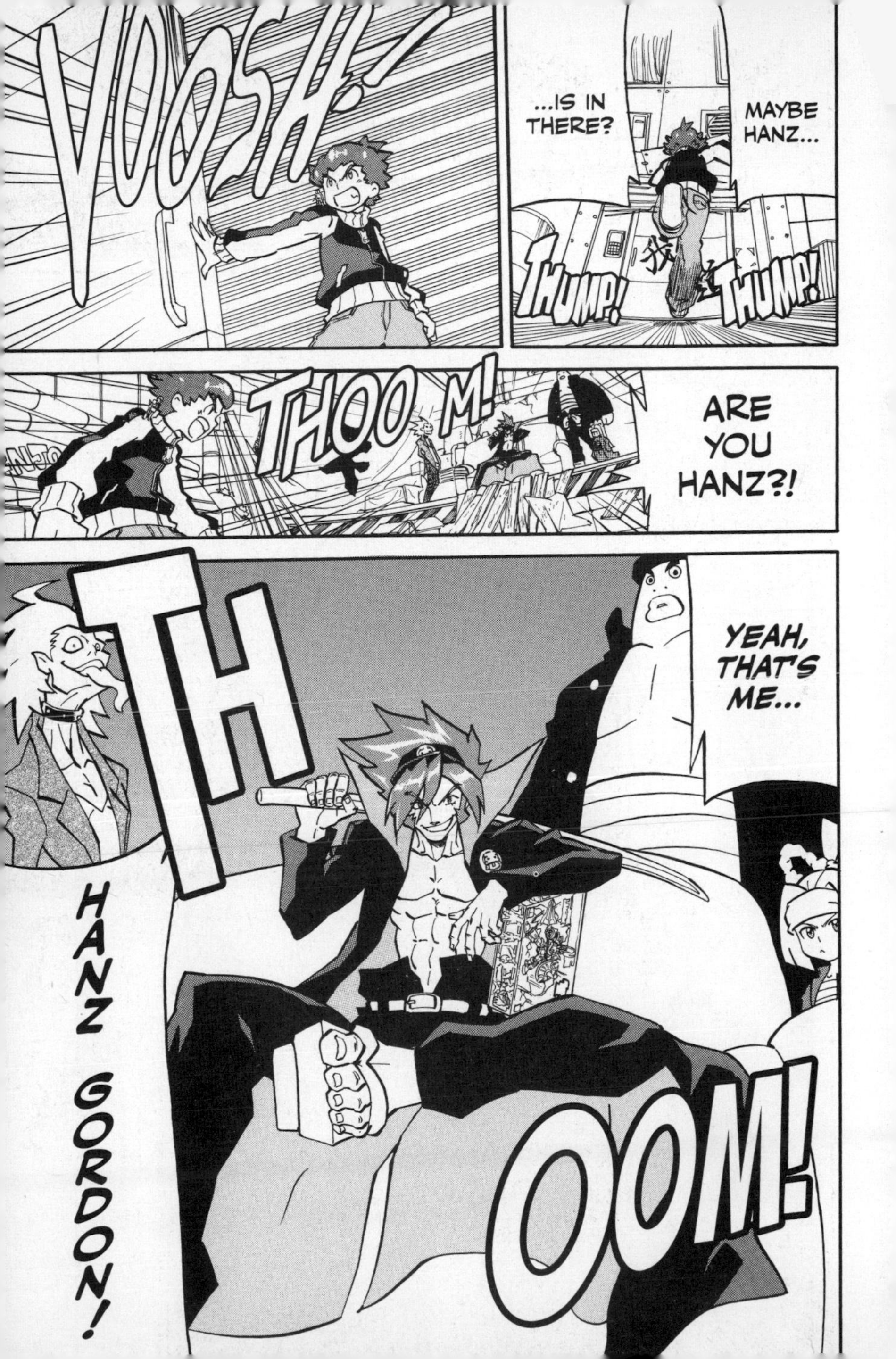
MAYBE HANZ...
...IS IN THERE?
THUMP!
THUMP!
VOOSH!
ARE YOU HANZ?!
THOO M!
YEAH, THAT'S ME...
TH
OOM!
HANZ GORDON!

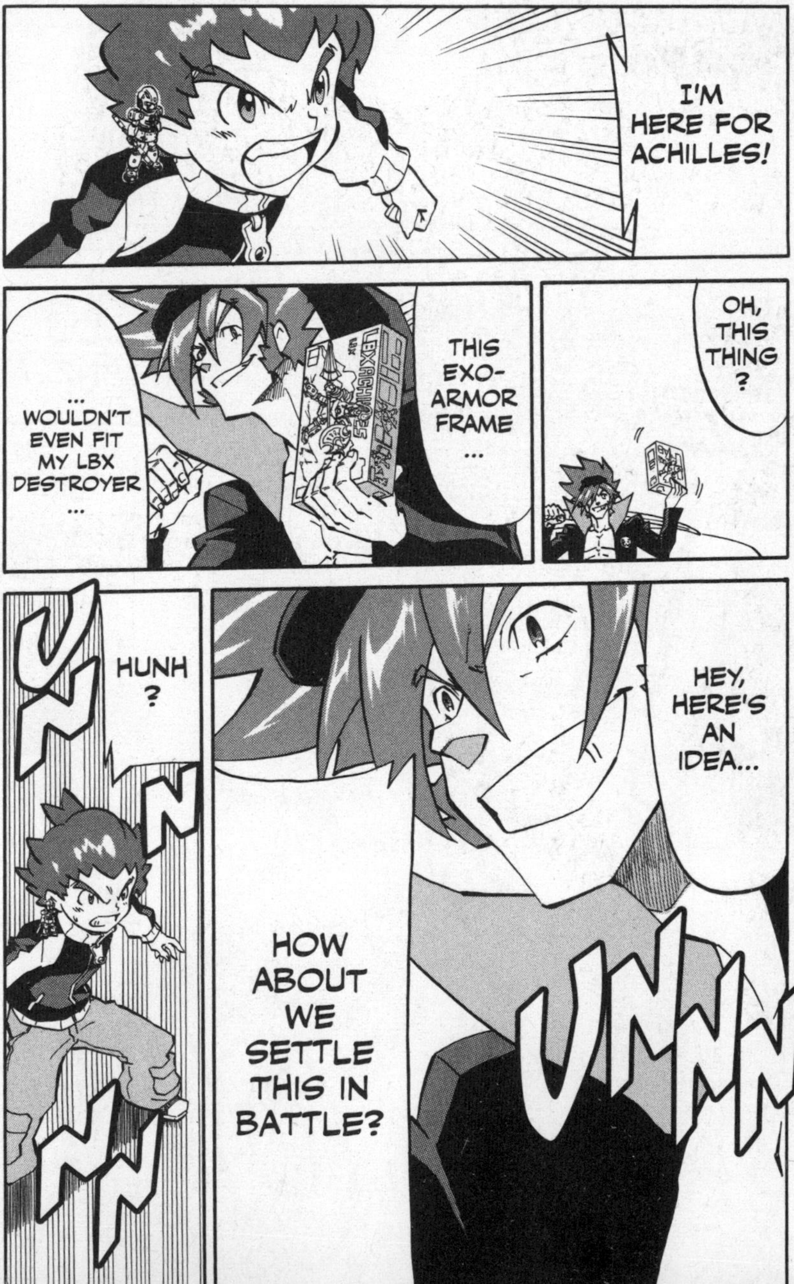
I'M HERE FOR ACHILLES!
OH, THIS THING?
THIS EXO-ARMOR FRAME...
...WOULDN'T EVEN FIT MY LBX DESTROYER...
HEY, HERE'S AN IDEA...
HOW ABOUT WE SETTLE THIS IN BATTLE?
UNNN
HUNH?

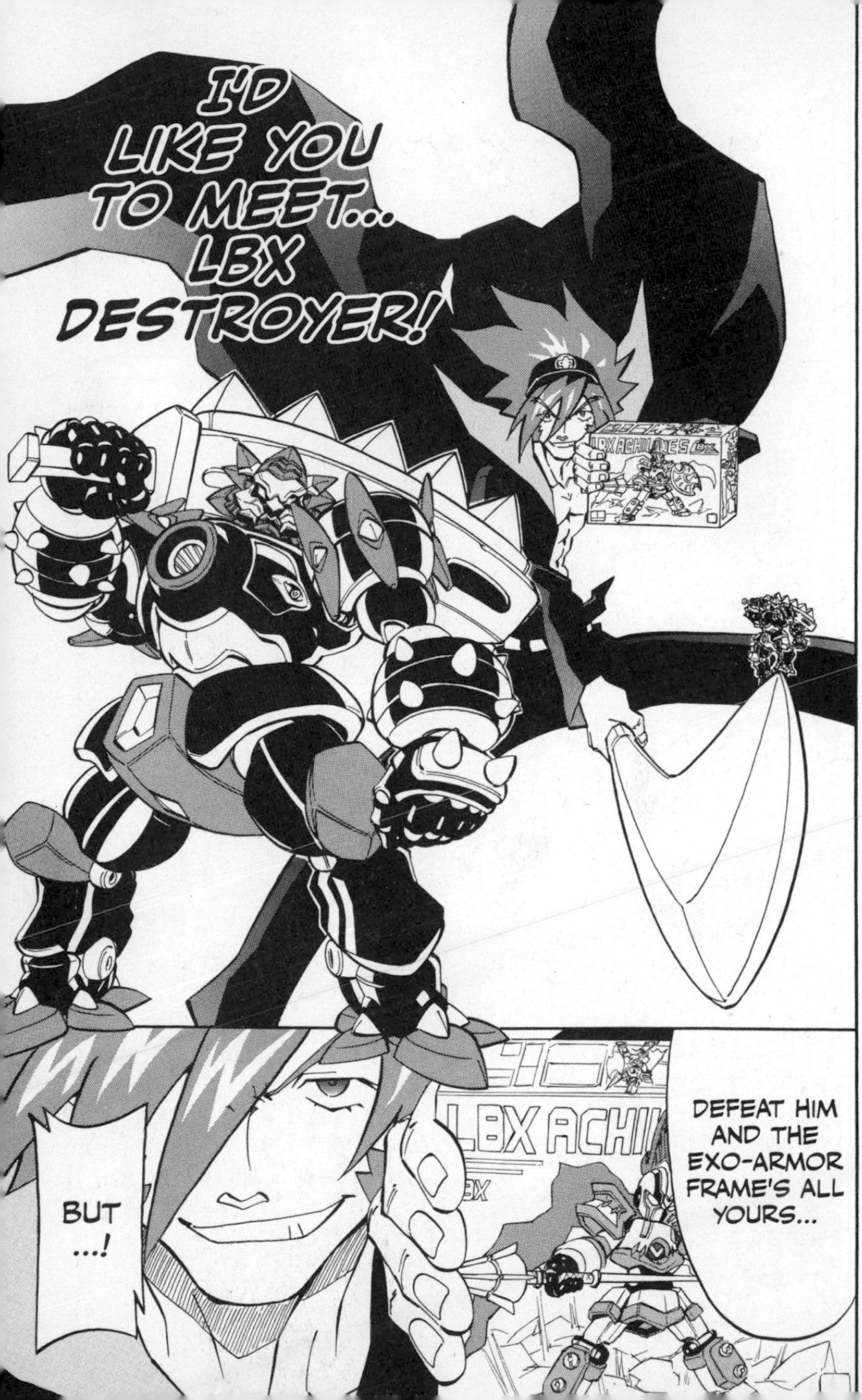
I'D LIKE YOU TO MEET... LBX DESTROYER!
DEFEAT HIM AND THE EXO-ARMOR FRAME'S ALL YOURS...
BUT ...!

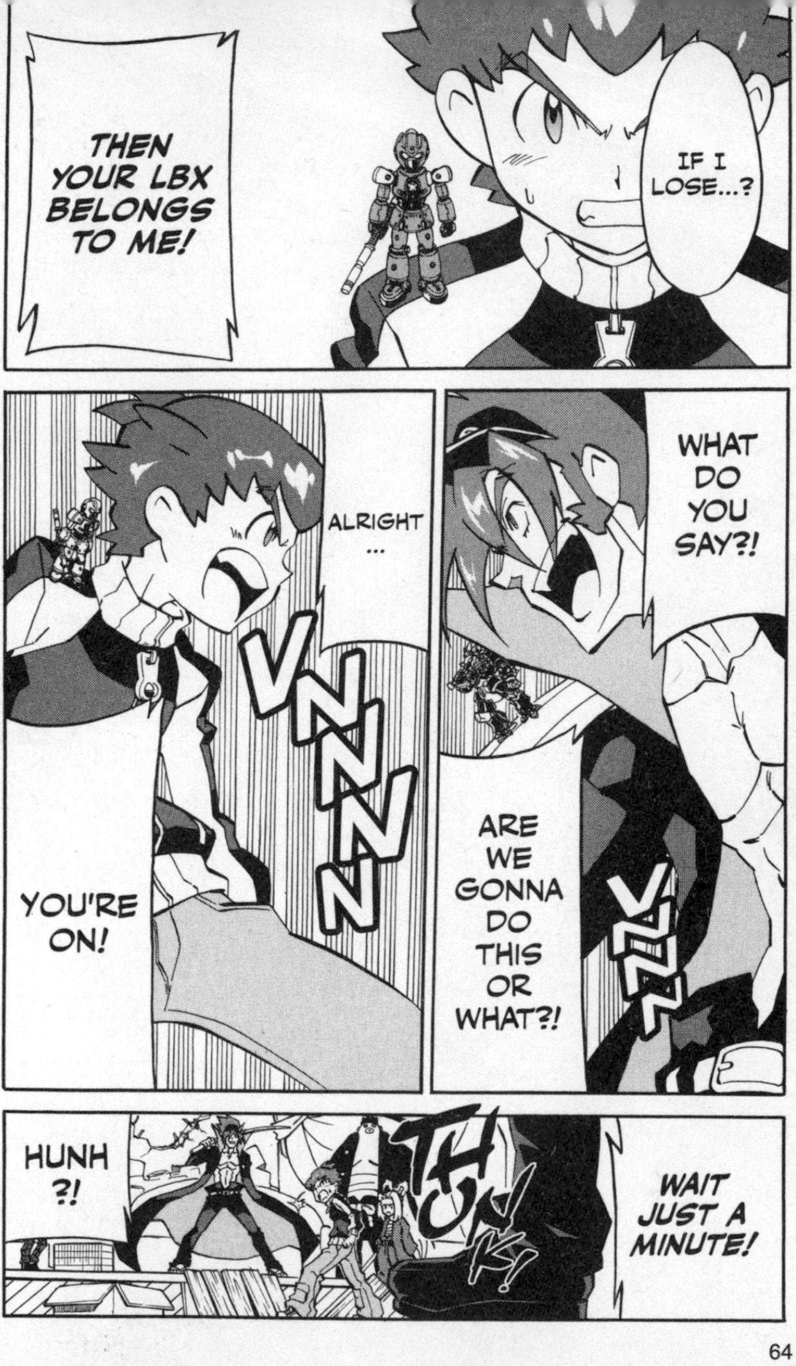
IF I LOSE...?
THEN YOUR LBX BELONGS TO ME!
WHAT DO YOU SAY?!
ARE WE GONNA DO THIS OR WHAT?!
VNNN
ALRIGHT ...
VNNNNN
YOU'RE ON!
WAIT JUST A MINUTE!
THUNK!
HUNH ?!

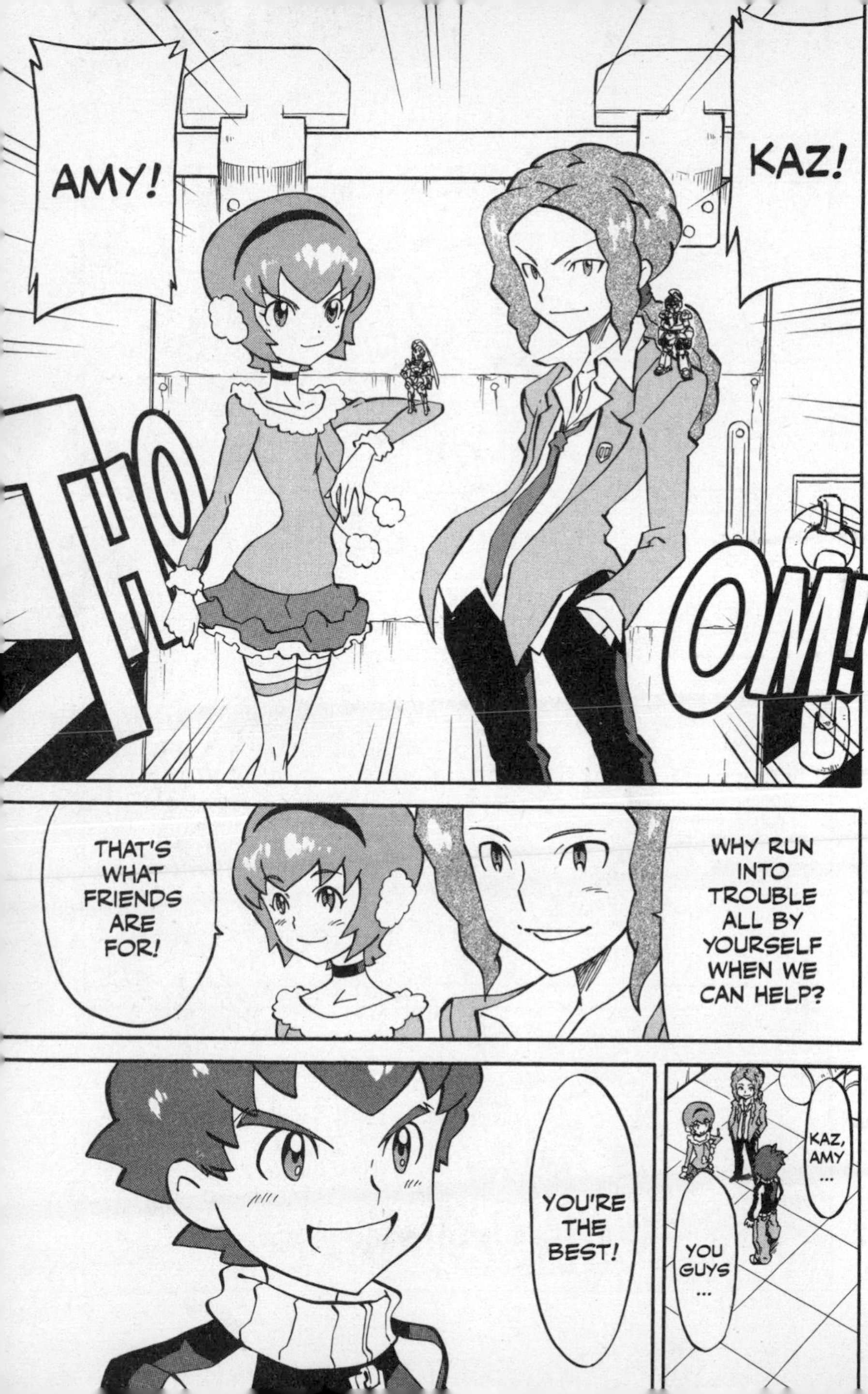
KAZ!
AMY!
THOOM!
WHY RUN INTO TROUBLE ALL BY YOURSELF WHEN WE CAN HELP?
THAT'S WHAT FRIENDS ARE FOR!
KAZ, AMY ...
YOU GUYS ...
YOU'RE THE BEST!

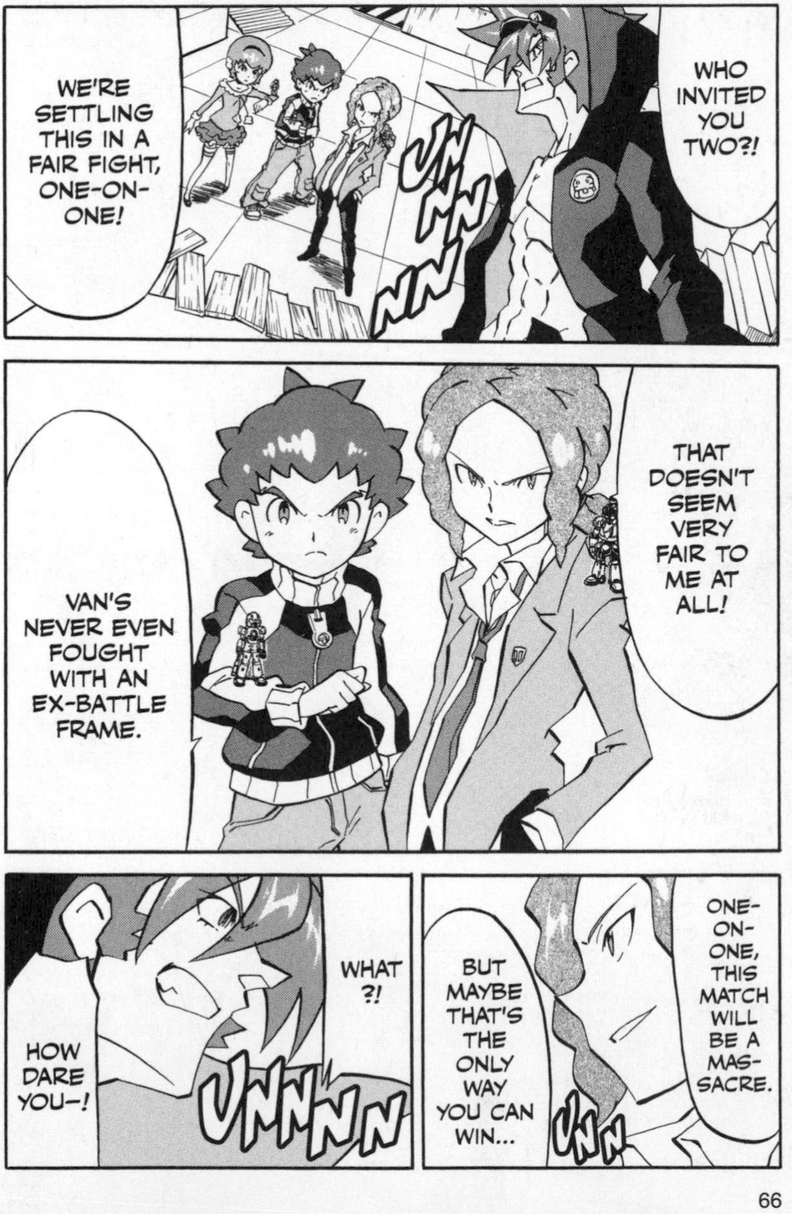
WHO INVITED YOU TWO?!
UNNNNNN
WE'RE SETTLING THIS IN A FAIR FIGHT, ONE-ON-ONE!
THAT DOESN'T SEEM VERY FAIR TO ME AT ALL!
VAN'S NEVER EVEN FOUGHT WITH AN EX-BATTLE FRAME.
ONE-ON-ONE, THIS MATCH WILL BE A MAS-SACRE.
BUT MAYBE THAT'S THE ONLY WAY YOU CAN WIN...
UNN
WHAT?!
HOW DARE YOU--!
UNNNNN

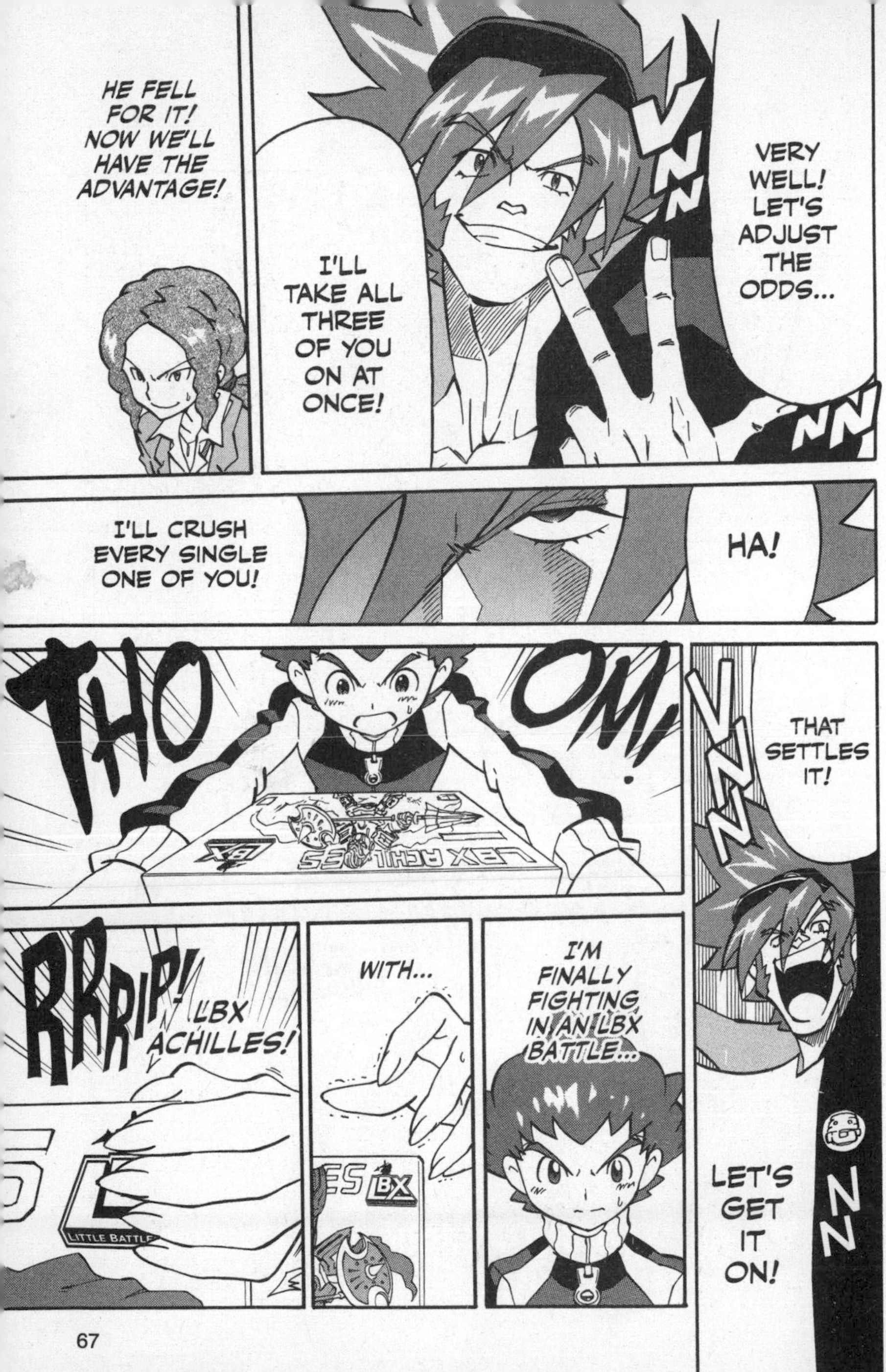
VERY WELL! LET'S ADJUST THE ODDS...
VNN
I'LL TAKE ALL THREE OF YOU ON AT ONCE!
NN
HE FELL FOR IT! NOW WE'LL HAVE THE ADVANTAGE!
HA!
I'LL CRUSH EVERY SINGLE ONE OF YOU!
THAT SETTLES IT!
VNN
LET'S GET IT ON!
NN
THOOM!
I'M FINALLY FIGHTING IN AN LBX BATTLE...
WITH...
RRRIP!
LBX ACHILLES!
LITTLE BATTLE

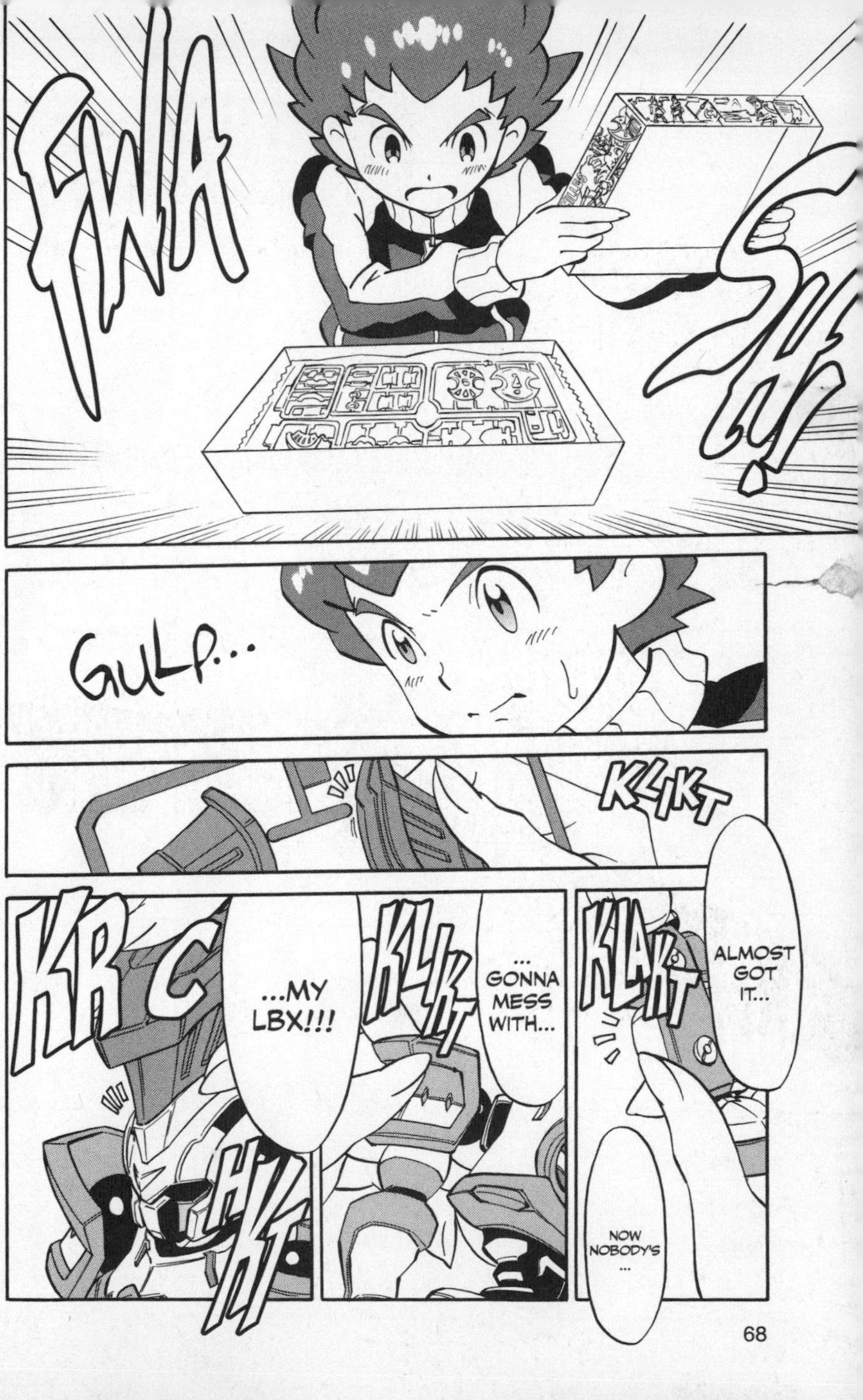
SHU!
FWA
GULP...
KLIKT
ALMOST GOT IT...
KLAKT
NOW NOBODY'S ...
... GONNA MESS WITH...
KLIKT
...MY LBX!!!
KRCHKT

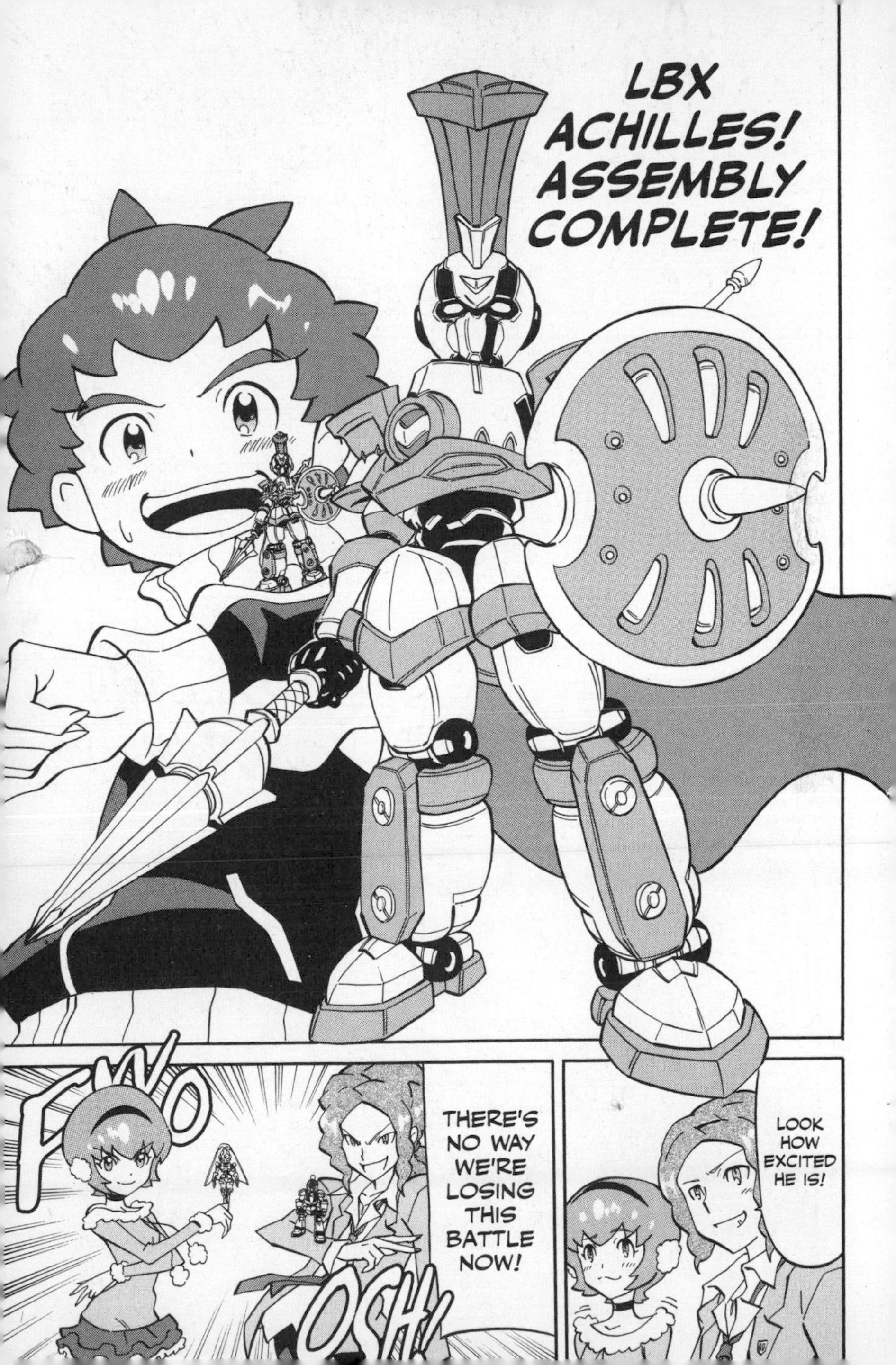
LBX ACHILLES! ASSEMBLY COMPLETE!
LOOK HOW EXCITED HE IS!
THERE'S NO WAY WE'RE LOSING THIS BATTLE NOW!
FWO
OSH!

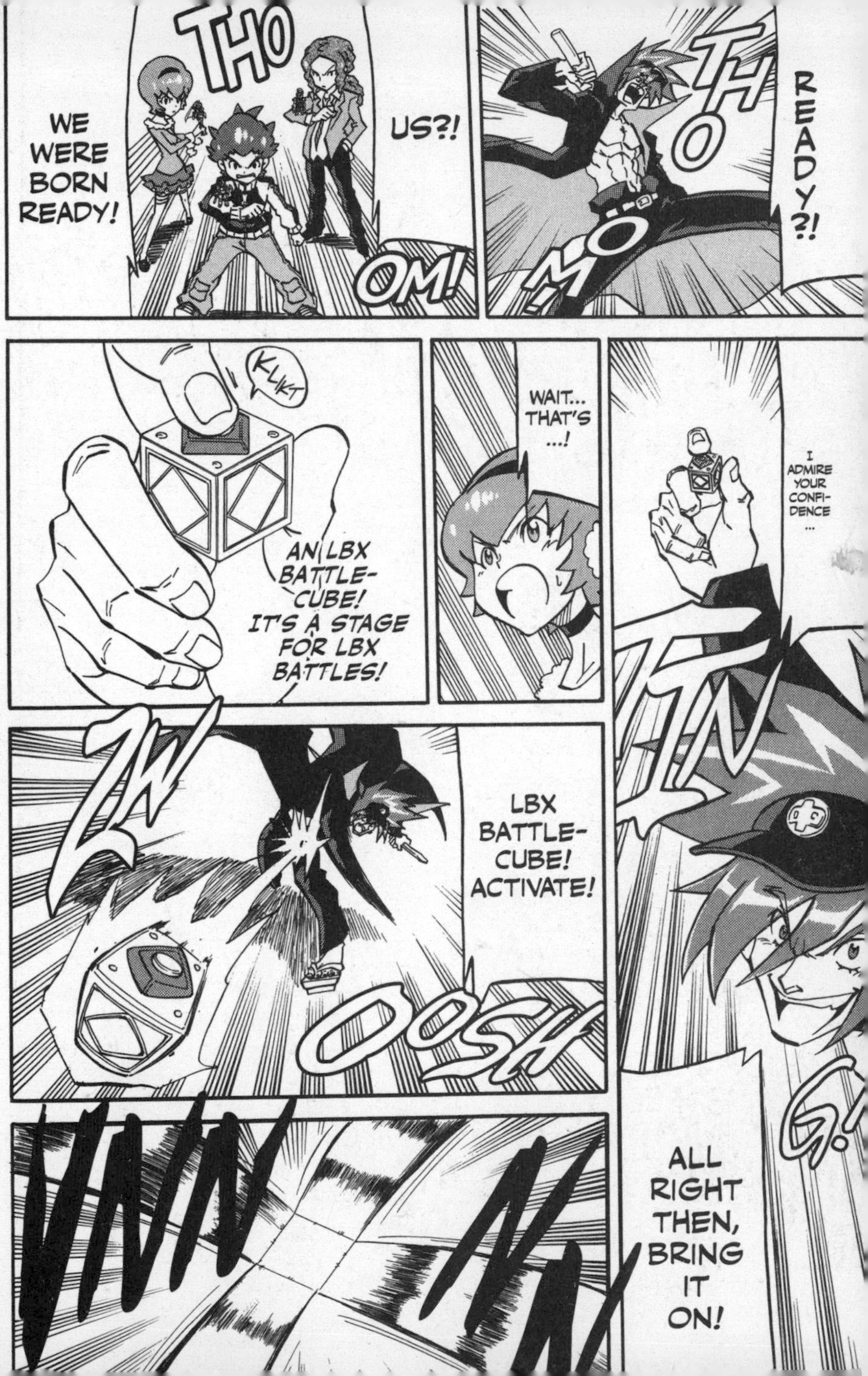
READY?!
THOMOOM!
US?!
WE WERE BORN READY!
THOOM!
I ADMIRE YOUR CONFIDENCE ...
ALL RIGHT THEN, BRING IT ON!
WAIT... THAT'S ...!
KLIKT
AN LBX BATTLE-CUBE! IT'S A STAGE FOR LBX BATTLES!
LBX BATTLE-CUBE! ACTIVATE!
ZWOOSH

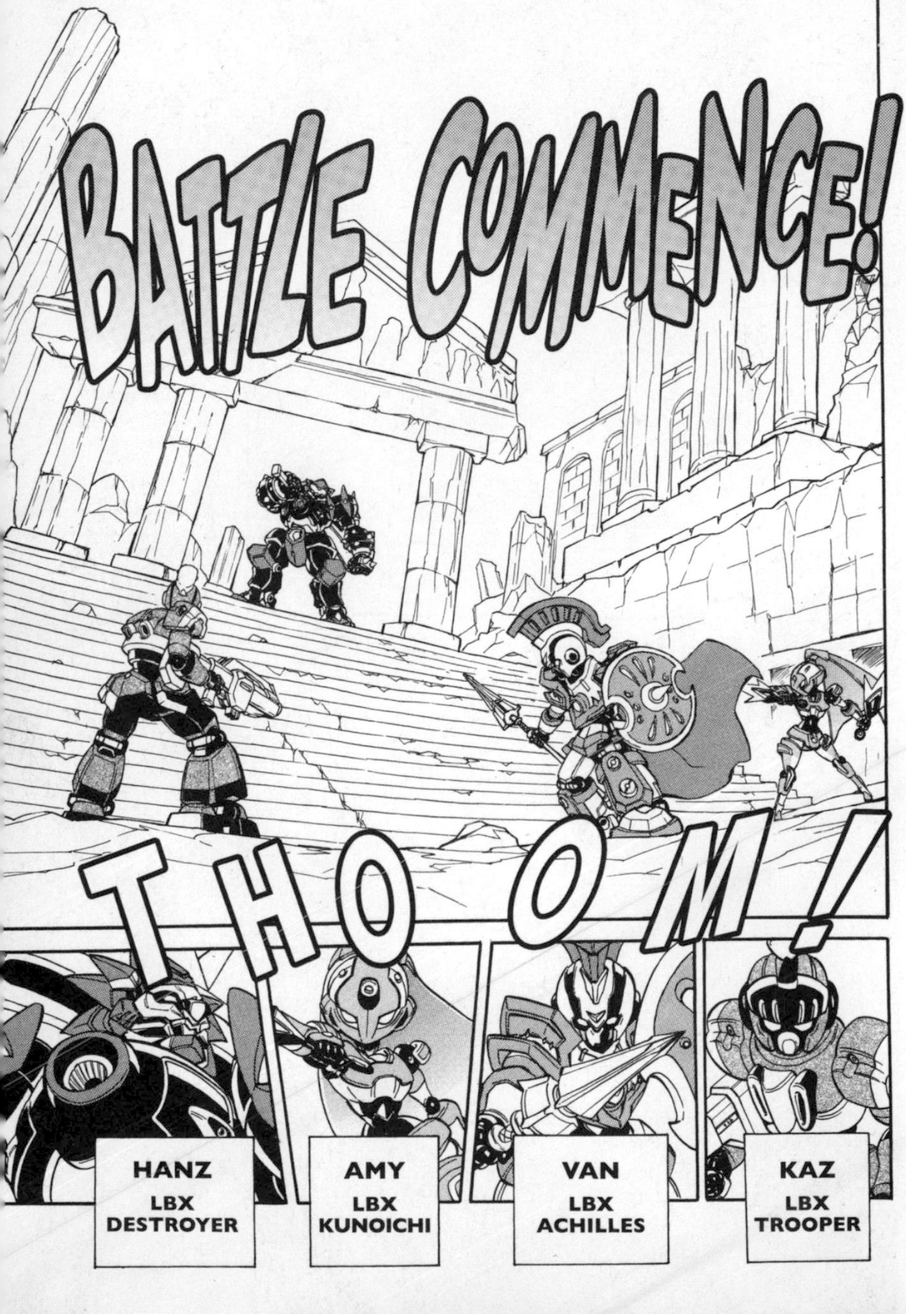
BATTLE COMMENCE!
THOOM!
KAZ
LBX TROOPER
VAN
LBX ACHILLES
AMY
LBX KUNOICHI
HANZ
LBX DESTROYER

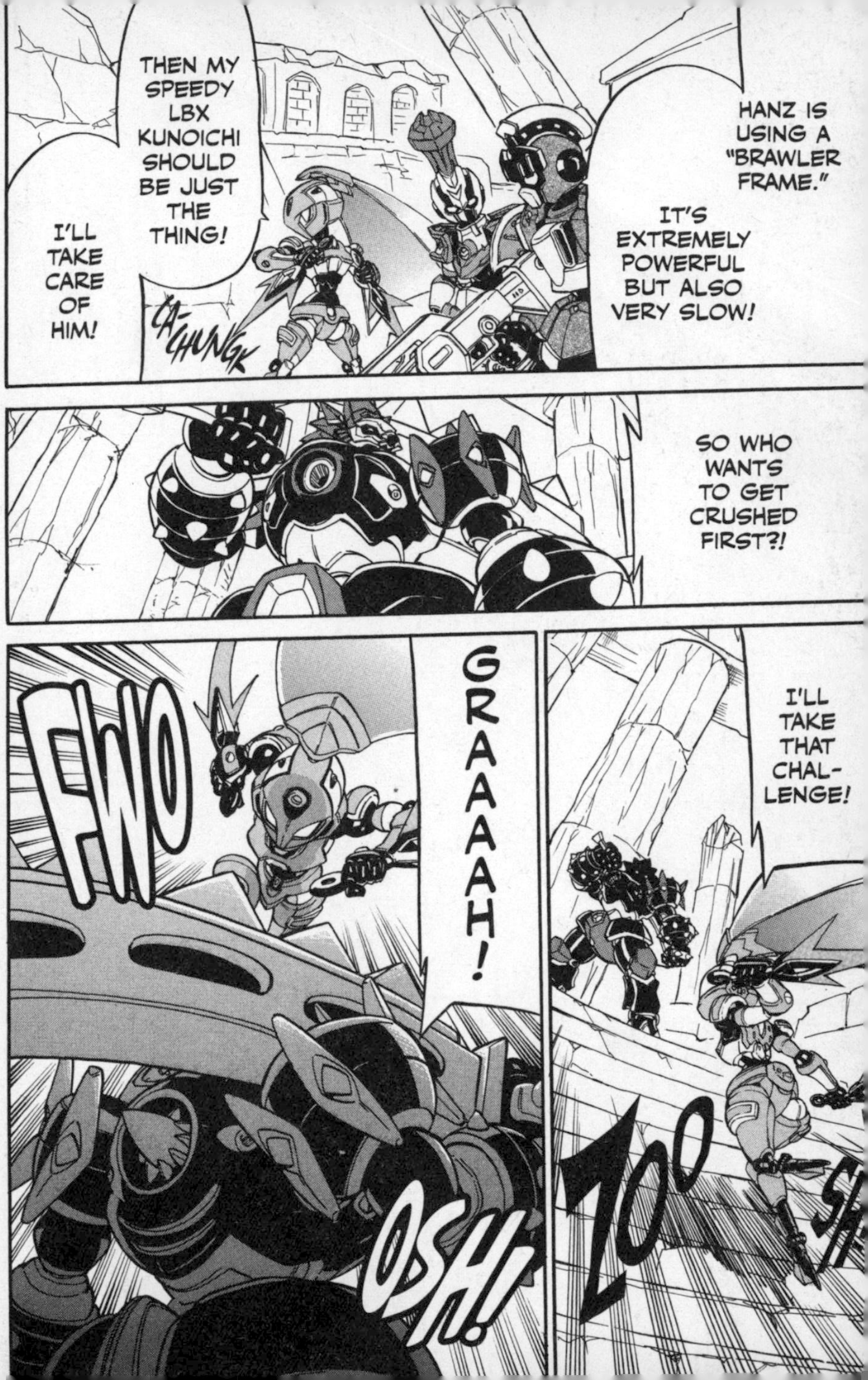
HANZ IS USING A "BRAWLER FRAME."
IT'S EXTREMELY POWERFUL BUT ALSO VERY SLOW!
THEN MY SPEEDY LBX KUNOICHI SHOULD BE JUST THE THING!
I'LL TAKE CARE OF HIM!
CA-CHUNGK
SO WHO WANTS TO GET CRUSHED FIRST?!
I'LL TAKE THAT CHAL-LENGE!
ZOOO
GRAAAAH!
FWO
OSH!

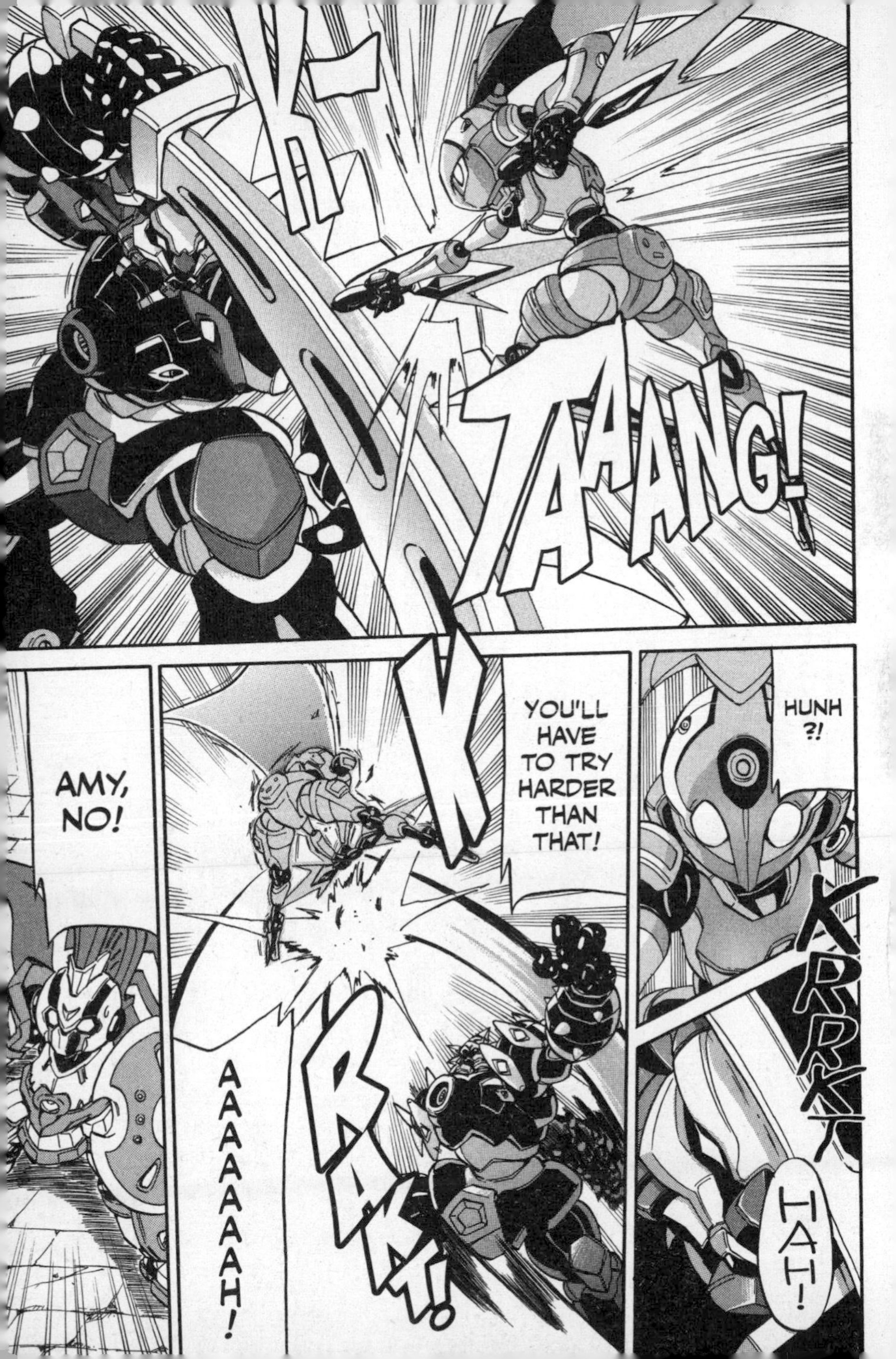
KA-
TAANG!
HUNH ?!
KRRRKT
HAH!
YOU'LL HAVE TO TRY HARDER THAN THAT!
K
RAK!
AAAAAAAAH!
AMY, NO!

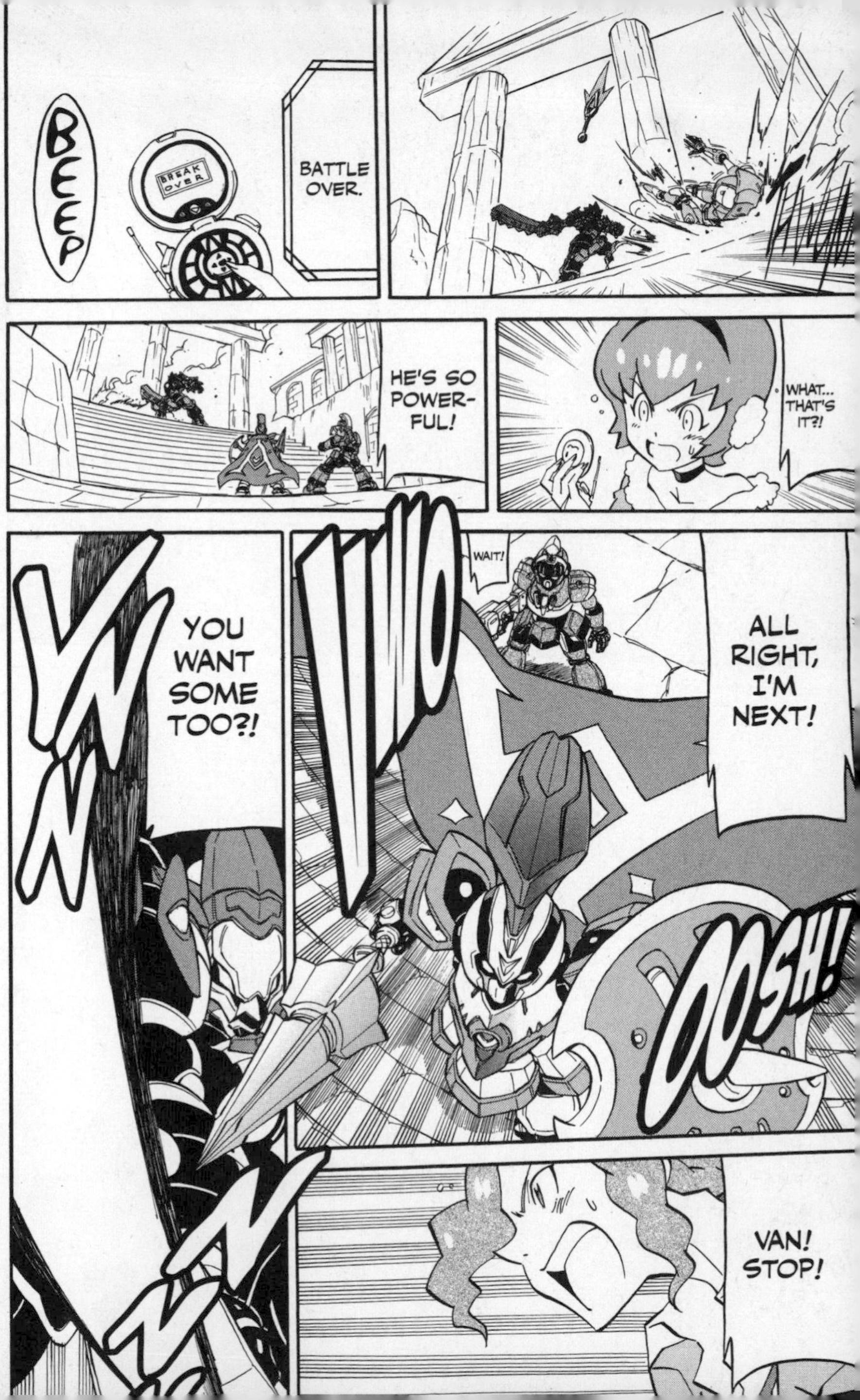
BATTLE OVER.
BREAK OVER
BEEP
WHAT... THAT'S IT?!
HE'S SO POWER-FUL!
WAIT!
ALL RIGHT, I'M NEXT!
YOU WANT SOME TOO?!
VAN! STOP!

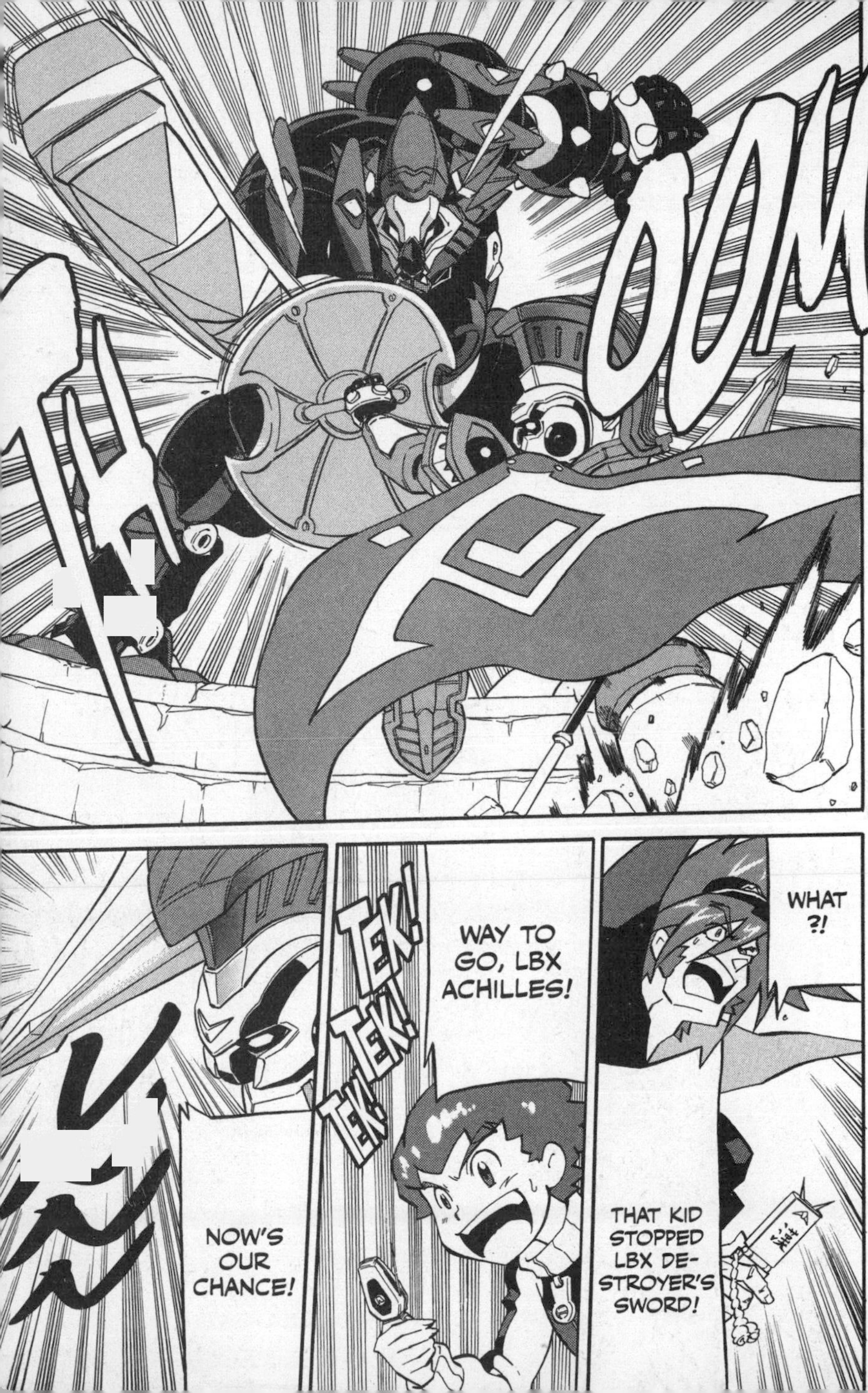
OOM!
WHAT ?!
THAT KID STOPPED LBX DE-STROYER'S SWORD!
WAY TO GO, LBX ACHILLES!
TEK! TEK! TEK!
NOW'S OUR CHANCE!

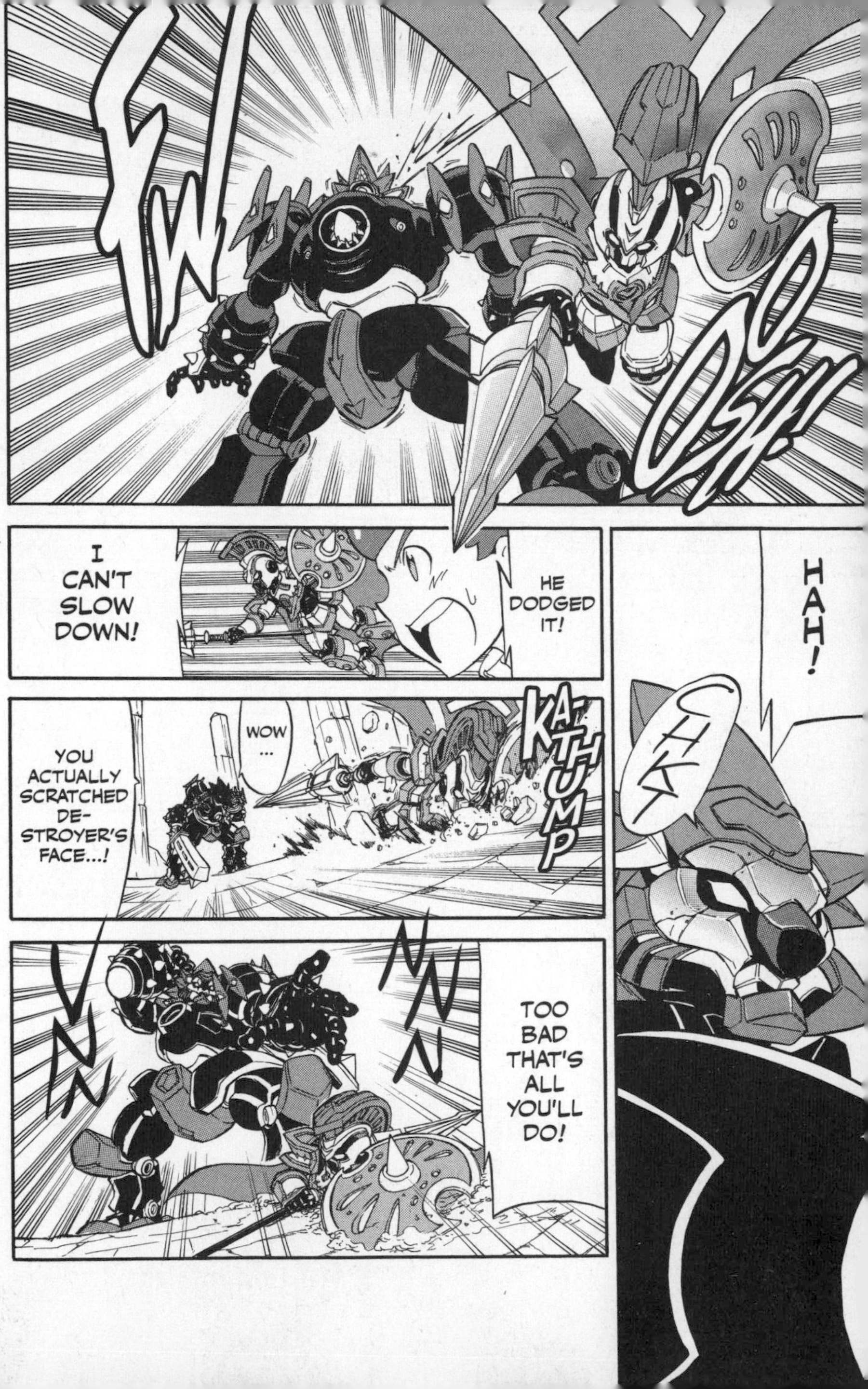
FWOOSH
HAH!
CHKT
HE DODGED IT!
I CAN'T SLOW DOWN!
KA-THUMP
WOW ...
YOU ACTUALLY SCRATCHED DE-STROYER'S FACE...!
NNN
TOO BAD THAT'S ALL YOU'LL DO!
VNNN

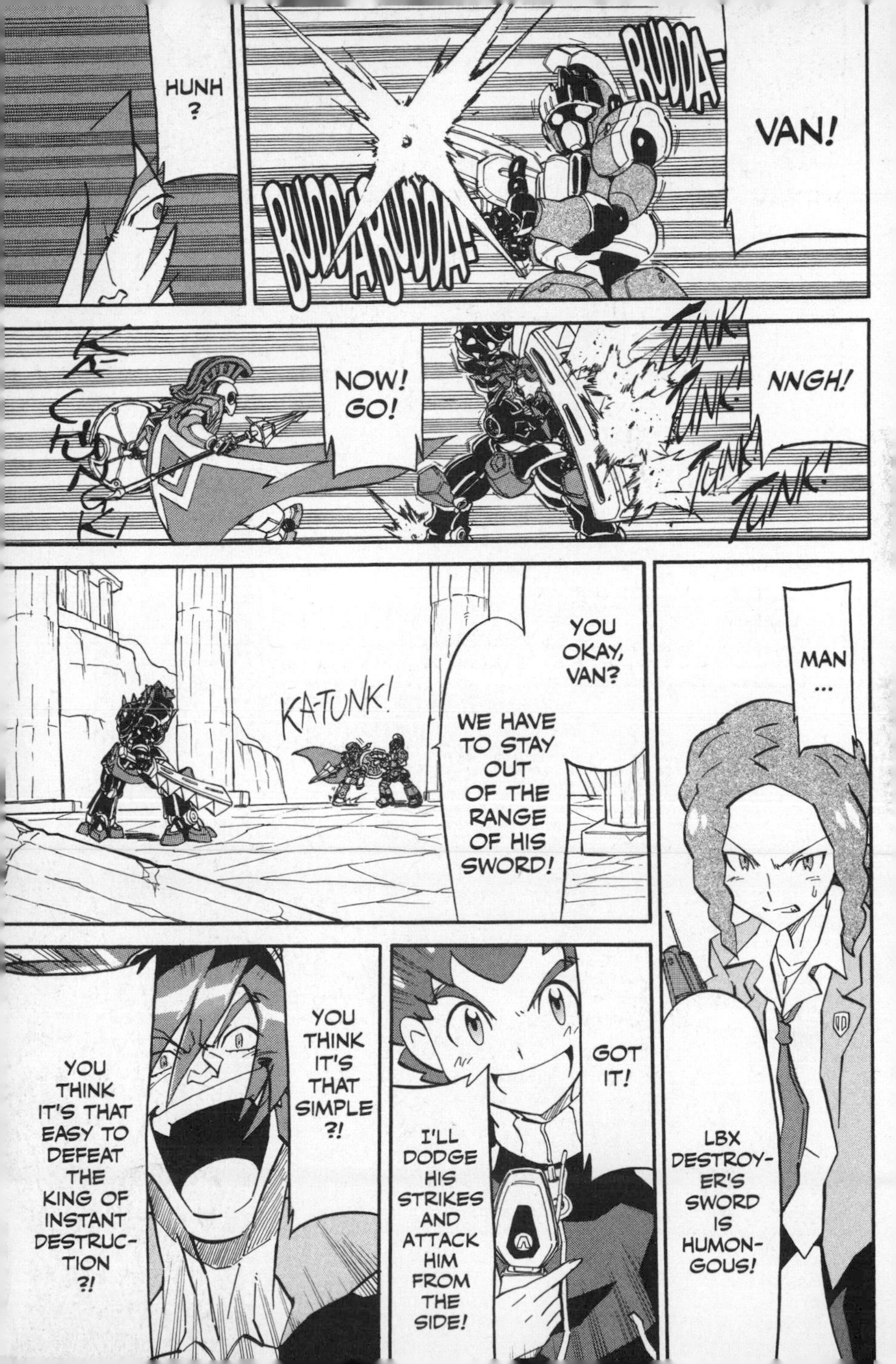
VAN!
BUDDA-
BUDDABUDDA!
HUNH ?
NNGH!
TUNK! TUNK! TUNK! TUNK!
NOW! GO!
KA-CHUNK!
MAN ...
LBX DESTROYER'S SWORD IS HUMONGOUS!
YOU OKAY, VAN?
WE HAVE TO STAY OUT OF THE RANGE OF HIS SWORD!
KA-TUNK!
GOT IT!
I'LL DODGE HIS STRIKES AND ATTACK HIM FROM THE SIDE!
YOU THINK IT'S THAT SIMPLE ?!
YOU THINK IT'S THAT EASY TO DEFEAT THE KING OF INSTANT DESTRUCTION ?!

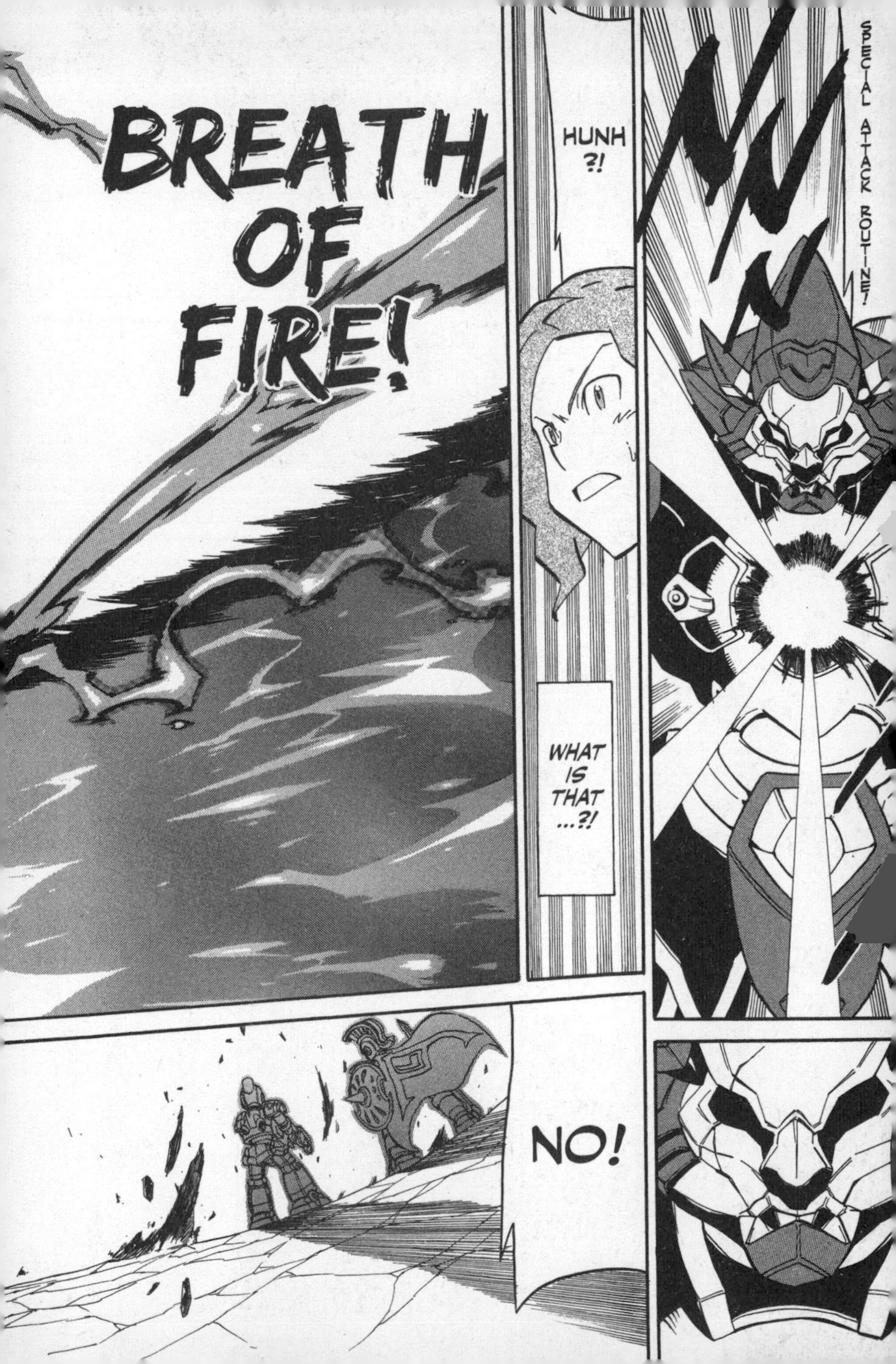
SPECIAL ATTACK ROUTINE!
HUNH ?!
WHAT IS THAT ...?!
BREATH OF FIRE!
NO!

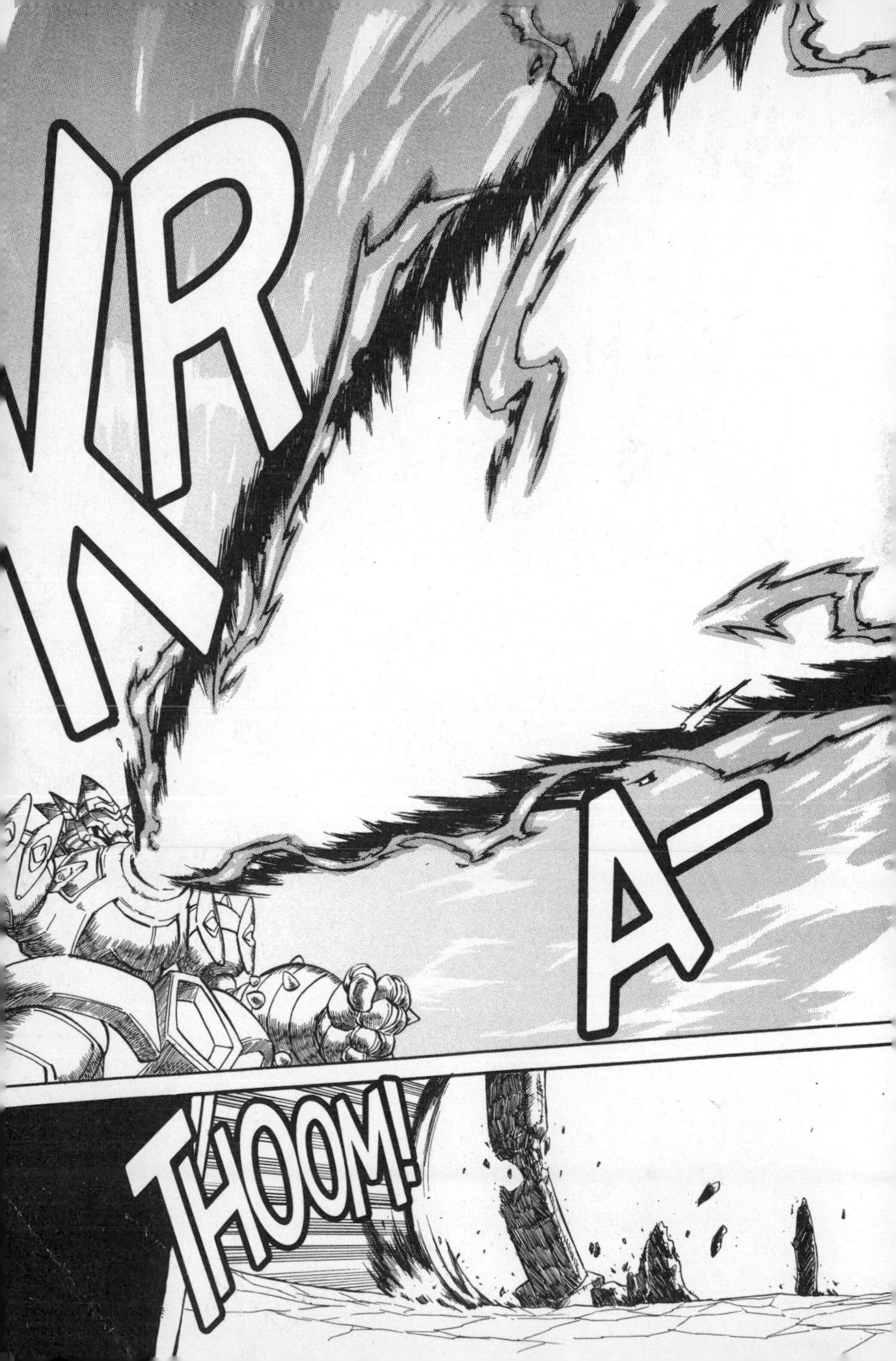
THOOM!

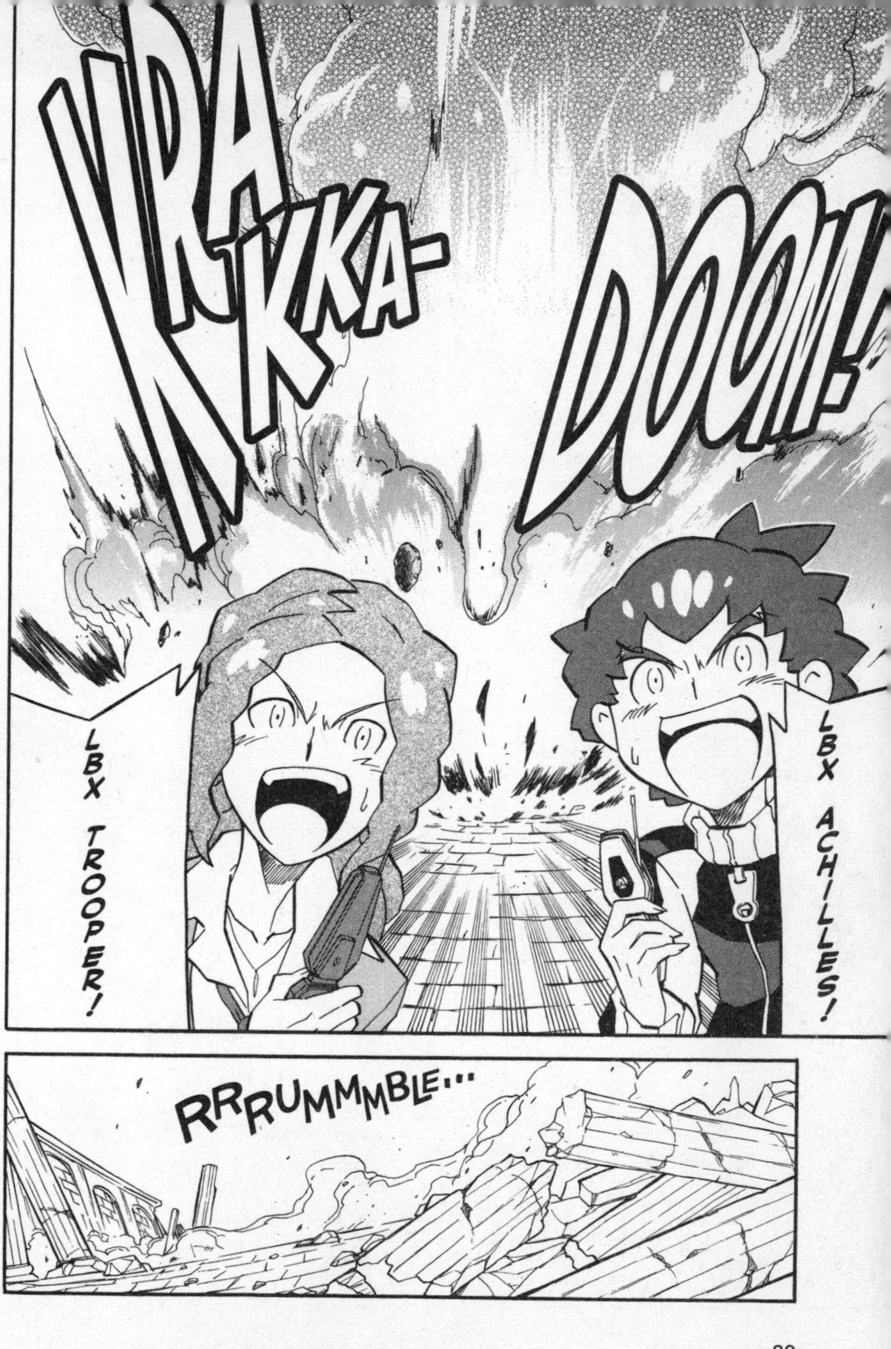
VRAKKA-DOOM!
LBX ACHILLES!
LBX TROOPER!
RRRUMMMBLE...

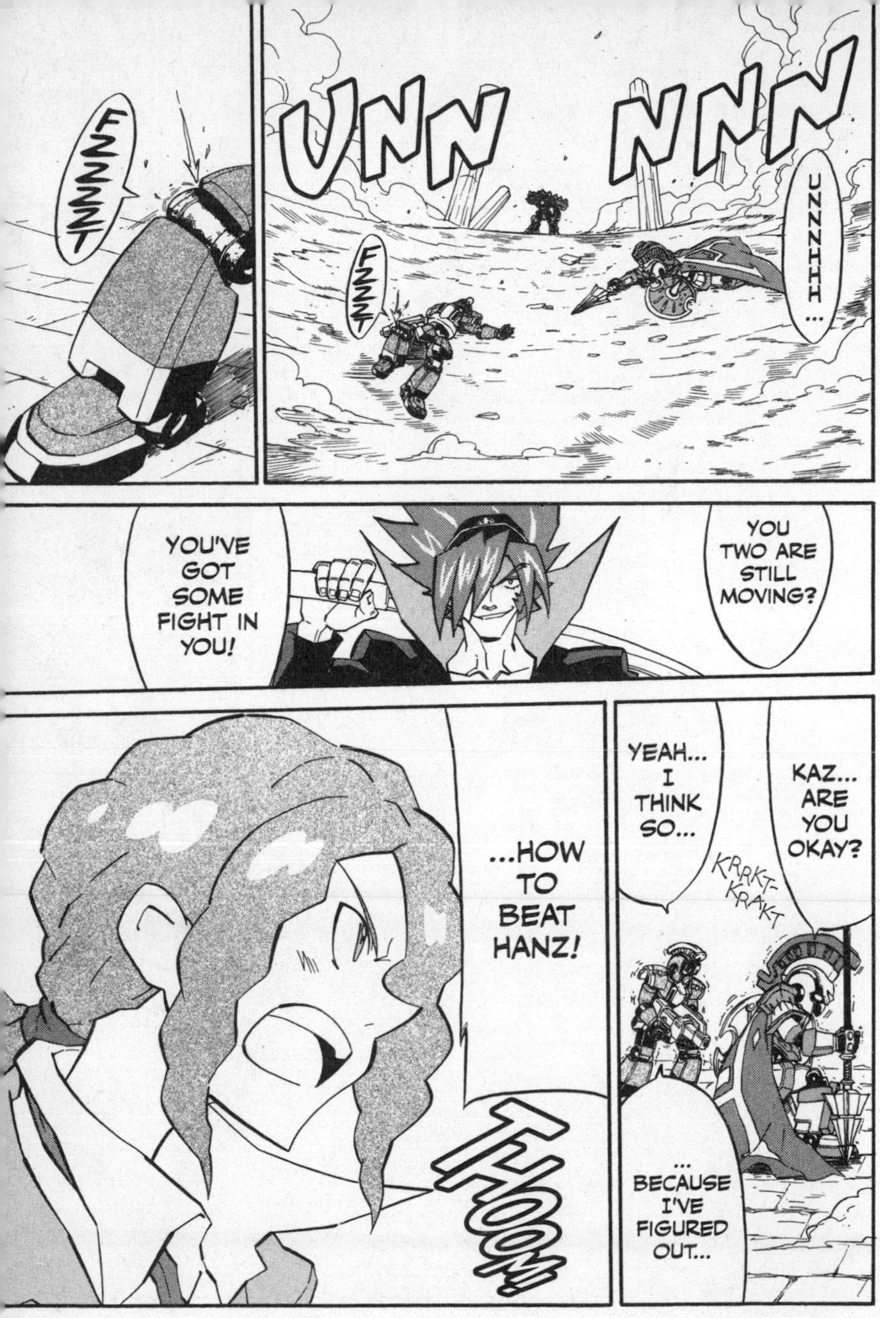
UNN NNN
UNNHHH...
FZZZT
FZZZZT
YOU TWO ARE STILL MOVING?
YOU'VE GOT SOME FIGHT IN YOU!
KAZ... ARE YOU OKAY?
KRRKT-KRAKT
YEAH... I THINK SO...
...BECAUSE I'VE FIGURED OUT...
...HOW TO BEAT HANZ!
THOOM!

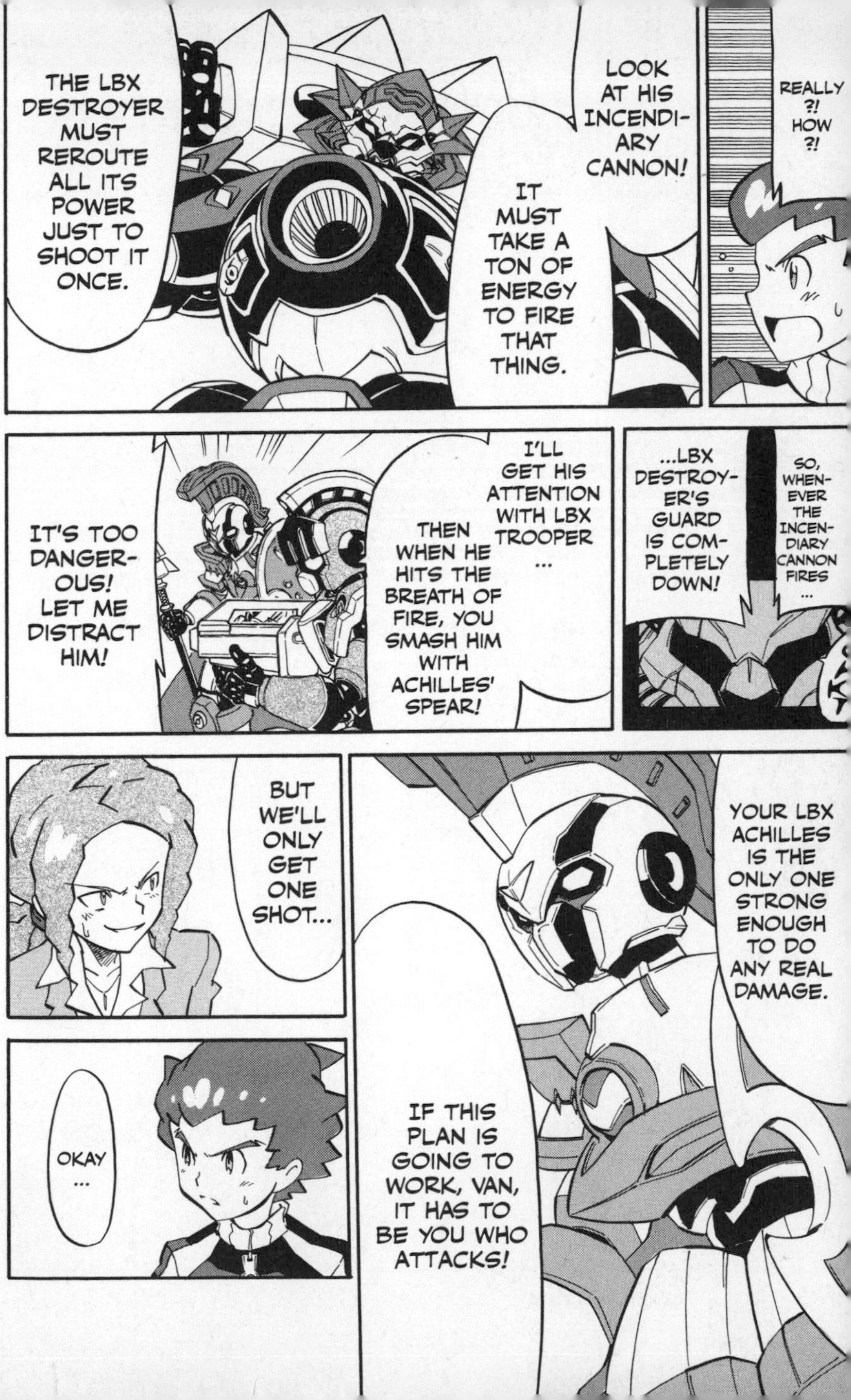
REALLY ?! HOW ?!
LOOK AT HIS INCENDIARY CANNON!
IT MUST TAKE A TON OF ENERGY TO FIRE THAT THING.
THE LBX DESTROYER MUST REROUTE ALL ITS POWER JUST TO SHOOT IT ONCE.
SO, WHENEVER THE INCENDIARY CANNON FIRES...
...LBX DESTROYER'S GUARD IS COMPLETELY DOWN!
I'LL GET HIS ATTENTION WITH LBX TROOPER...
THEN WHEN HE HITS THE BREATH OF FIRE, YOU SMASH HIM WITH ACHILLES' SPEAR!
IT'S TOO DANGEROUS! LET ME DISTRACT HIM!
YOUR LBX ACHILLES IS THE ONLY ONE STRONG ENOUGH TO DO ANY REAL DAMAGE.
IF THIS PLAN IS GOING TO WORK, VAN, IT HAS TO BE YOU WHO ATTACKS!
BUT WE'LL ONLY GET ONE SHOT...
OKAY...

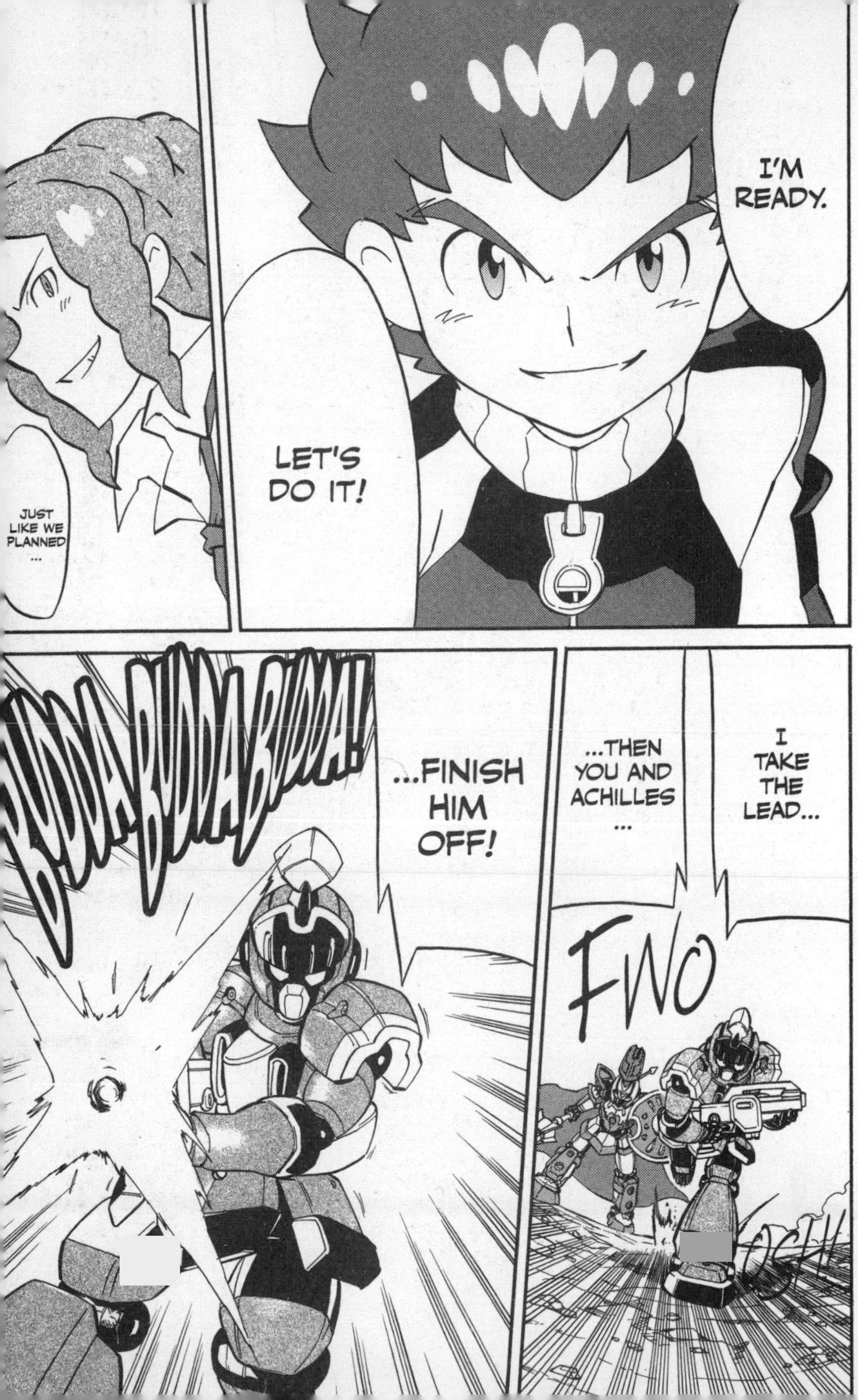
I'M READY.
LET'S DO IT!
JUST LIKE WE PLANNED...
I TAKE THE LEAD...
...THEN YOU AND ACHILLES...
FWO
OSH
...FINISH HIM OFF!
BUDDA BUDDA BUDDA!

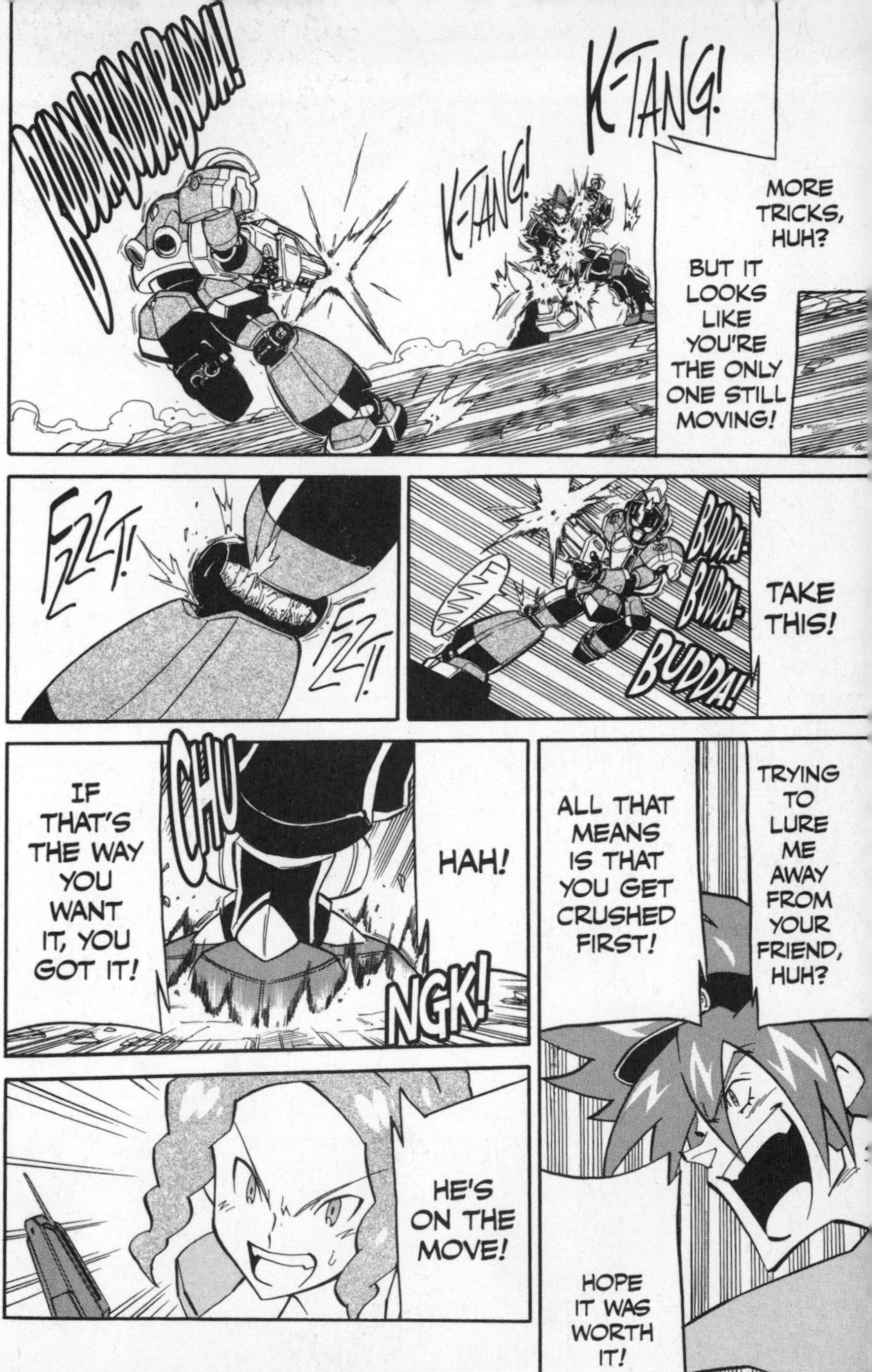
K-TANG!
MORE TRICKS, HUH?
BUT IT LOOKS LIKE YOU'RE THE ONLY ONE STILL MOVING!
K-TANG!
BUDDABUDDABUDDA!
TAKE THIS!
BUDDA-BUDDA-BUDDA!
FZZZT!
FZZT!
TRYING TO LURE ME AWAY FROM YOUR FRIEND, HUH?
ALL THAT MEANS IS THAT YOU GET CRUSHED FIRST!
HOPE IT WAS WORTH IT!
HAH!
CHU
NGK!
IF THAT'S THE WAY YOU WANT IT, YOU GOT IT!
HE'S ON THE MOVE!

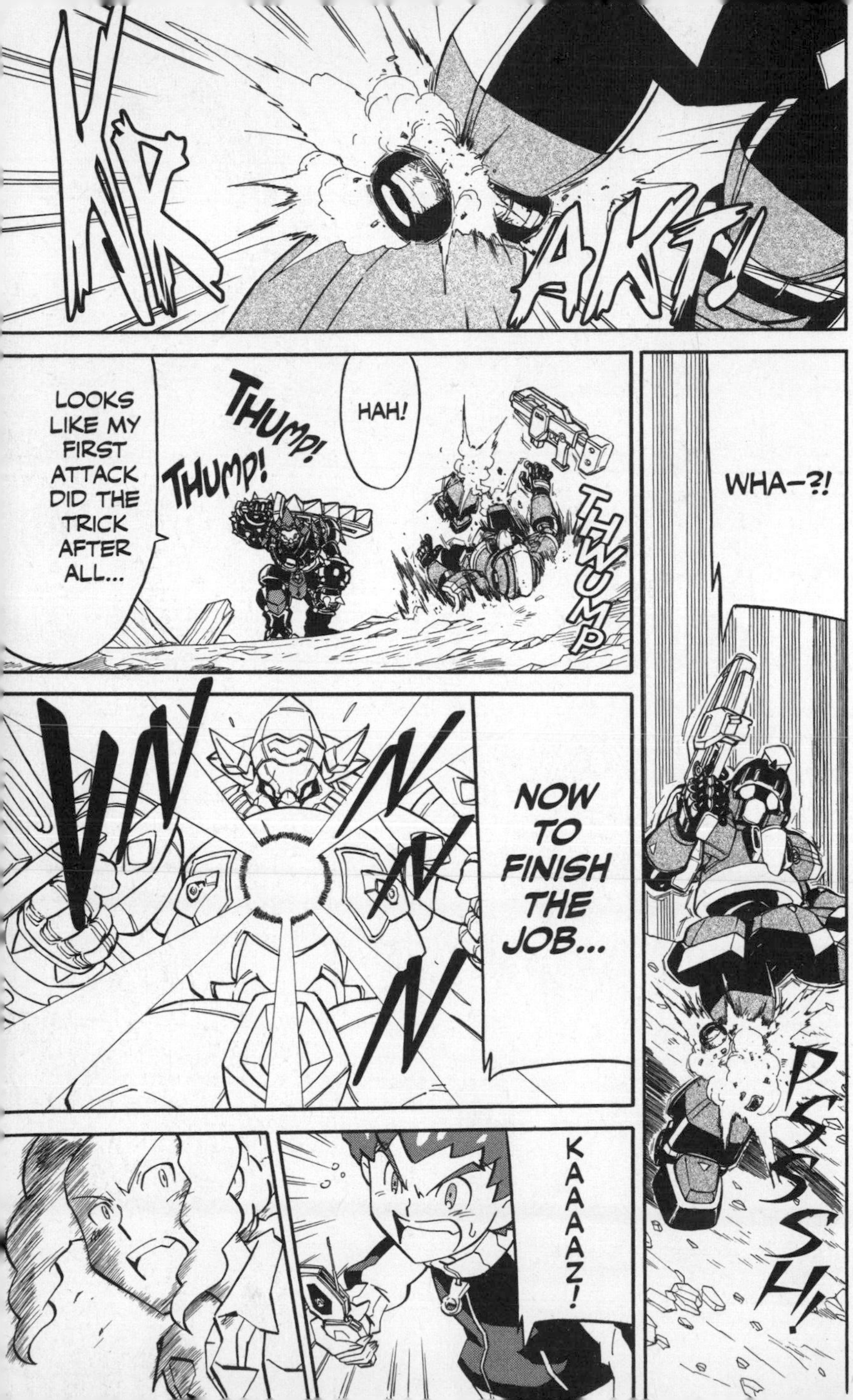
KRAKT!
WHA-?!
PSSSH!
HAH!
THWUMP
THUMP! THUMP!
LOOKS LIKE MY FIRST ATTACK DID THE TRICK AFTER ALL...
NOW TO FINISH THE JOB...
VWNNNN
KAAAAZ!

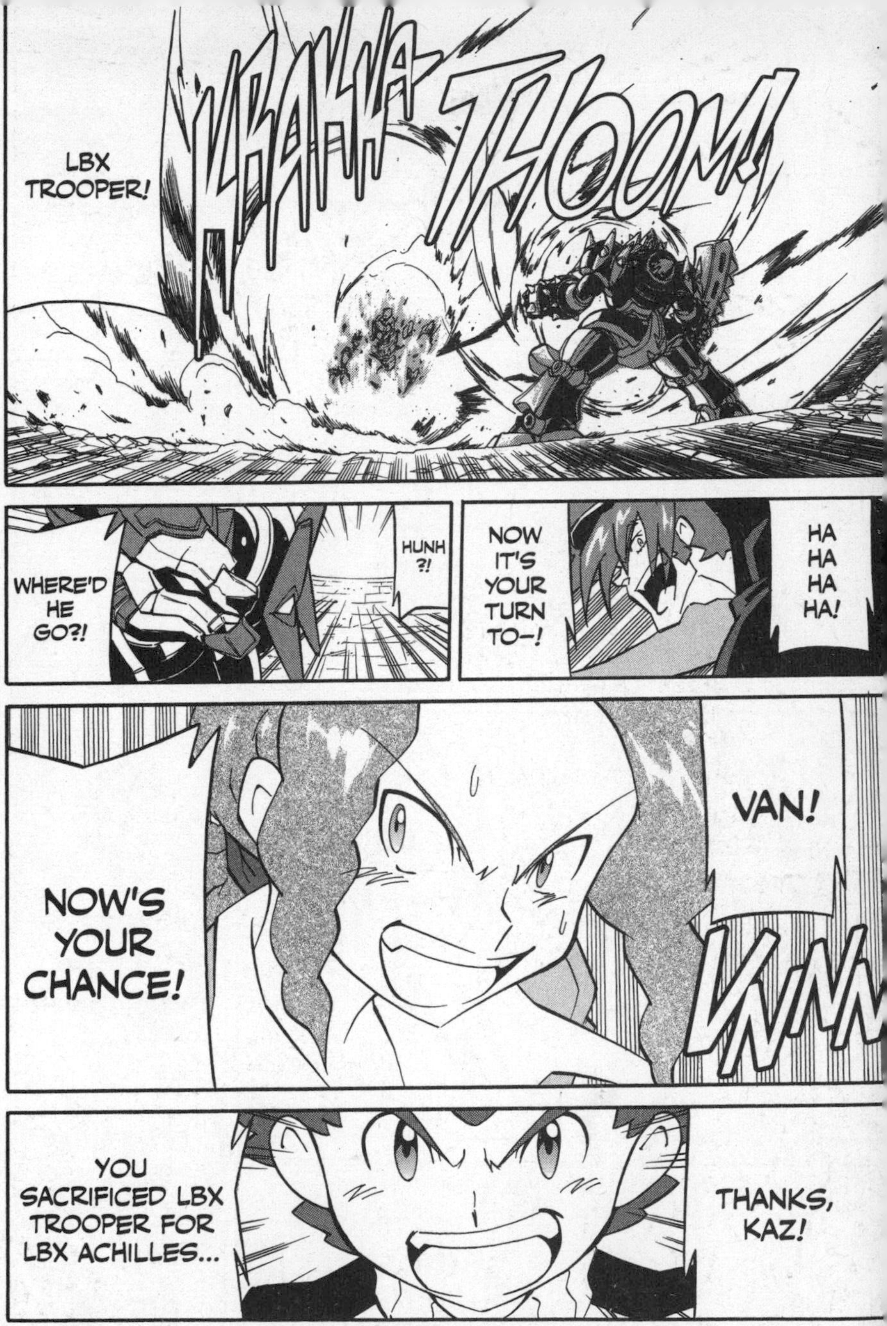

KRAKA THOOM!
LBX TROOPER!
HA HA HA HA!
NOW IT'S YOUR TURN TO—!
HUNH ?!
WHERE'D HE GO?!
VAN!
VNN
NOW'S YOUR CHANCE!
THANKS, KAZ!
YOU SACRIFICED LBX TROOPER FOR LBX ACHILLES...

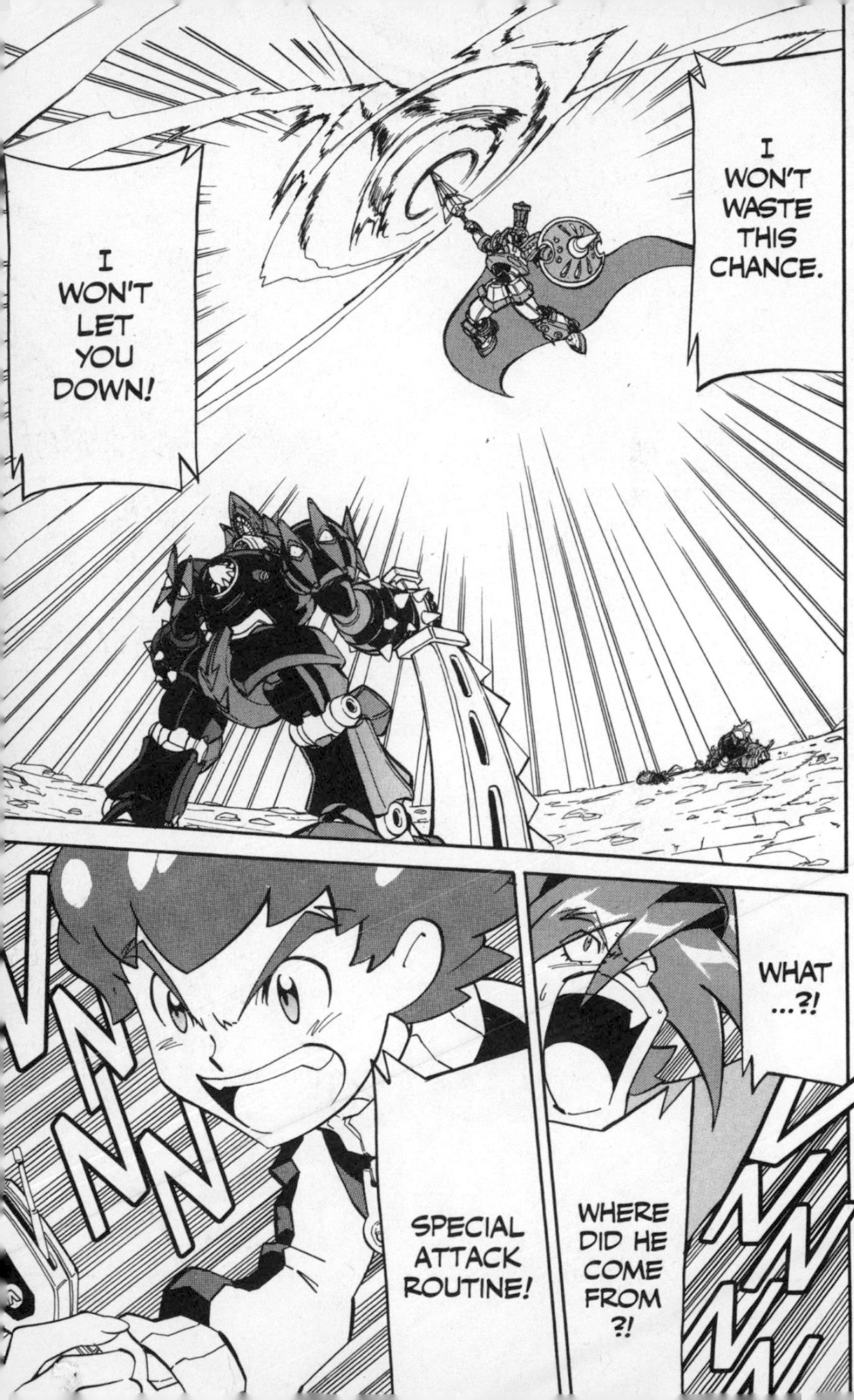
I WON'T WASTE THIS CHANCE.
I WON'T LET YOU DOWN!
WHAT ...?!
WHERE DID HE COME FROM ?!
SPECIAL ATTACK ROUTINE!

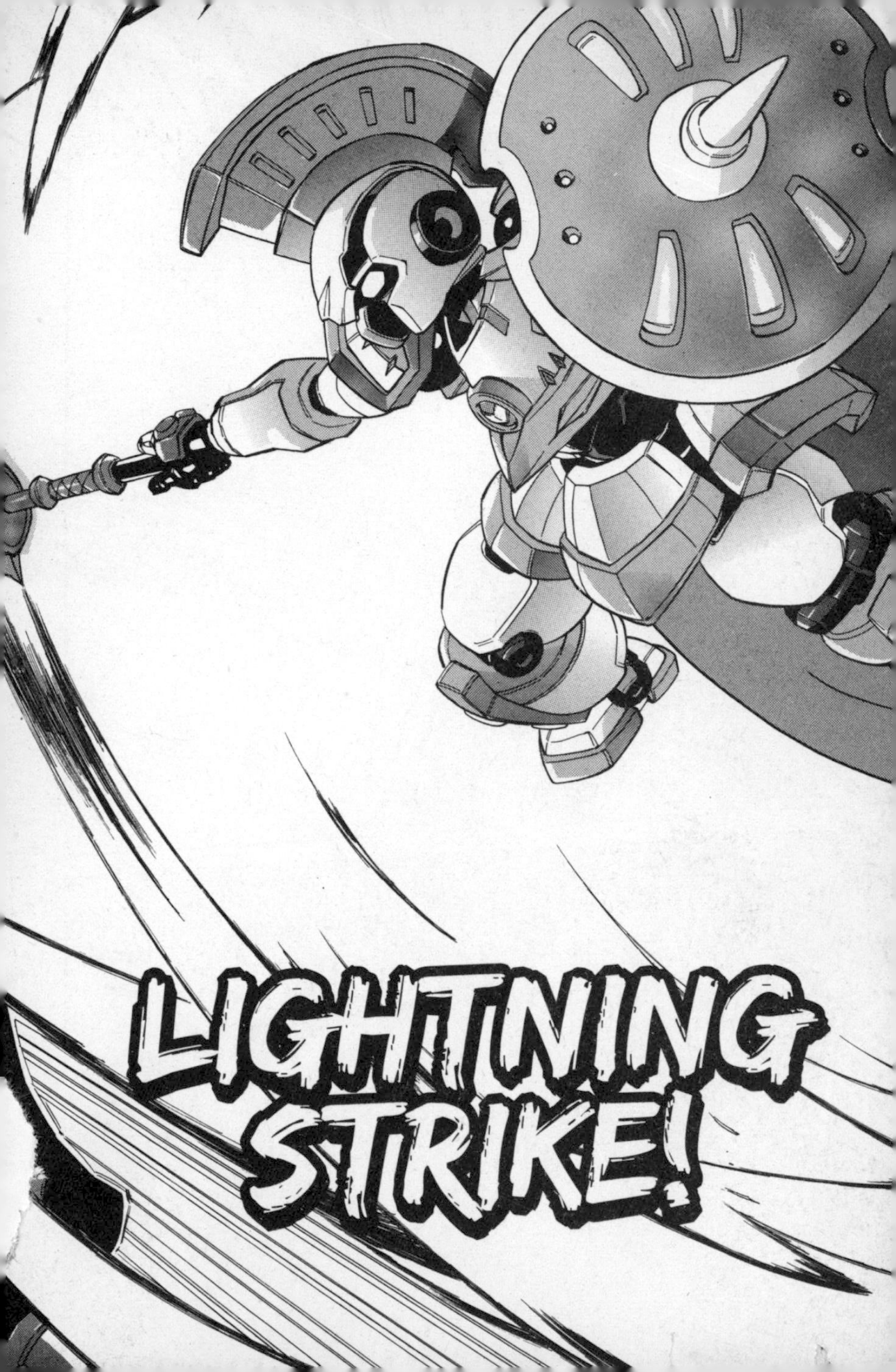
LIGHTNING STRIKE!

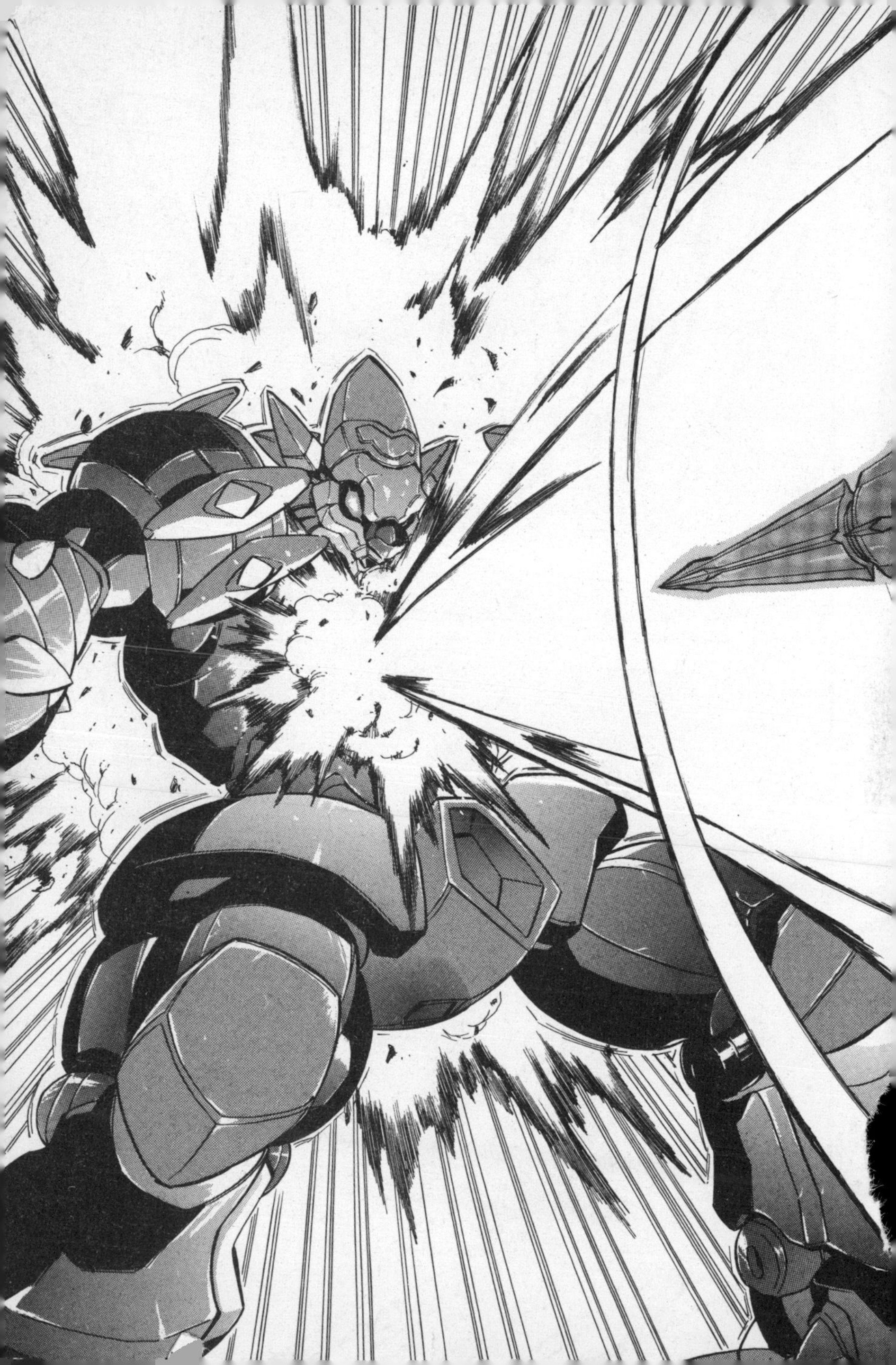

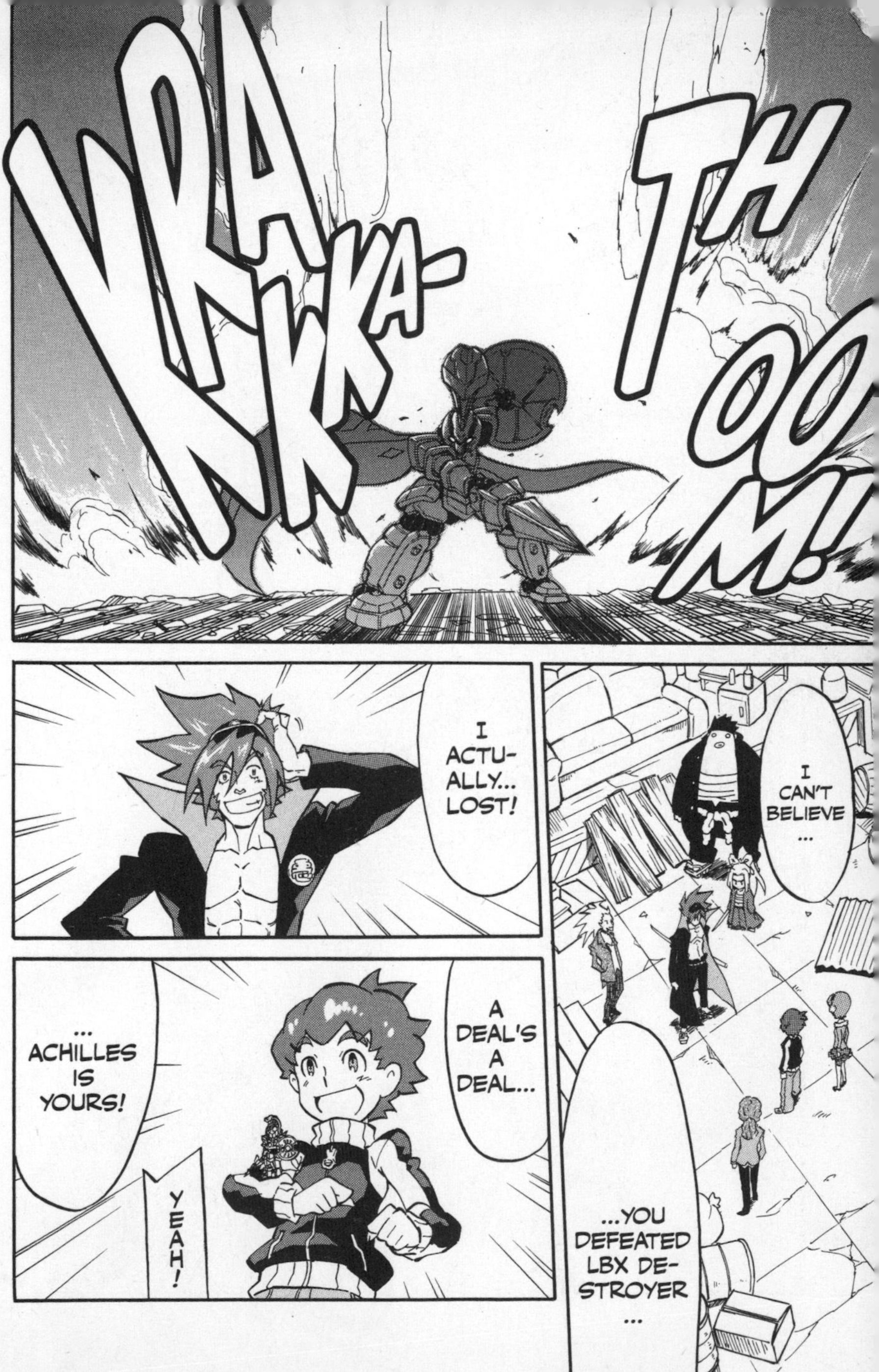
VRAKKA-THOOM!
I CAN'T BELIEVE...
...YOU DEFEATED LBX DESTROYER...
I ACTUALLY... LOST!
A DEAL'S A DEAL...
...ACHILLES IS YOURS!
YEAH!

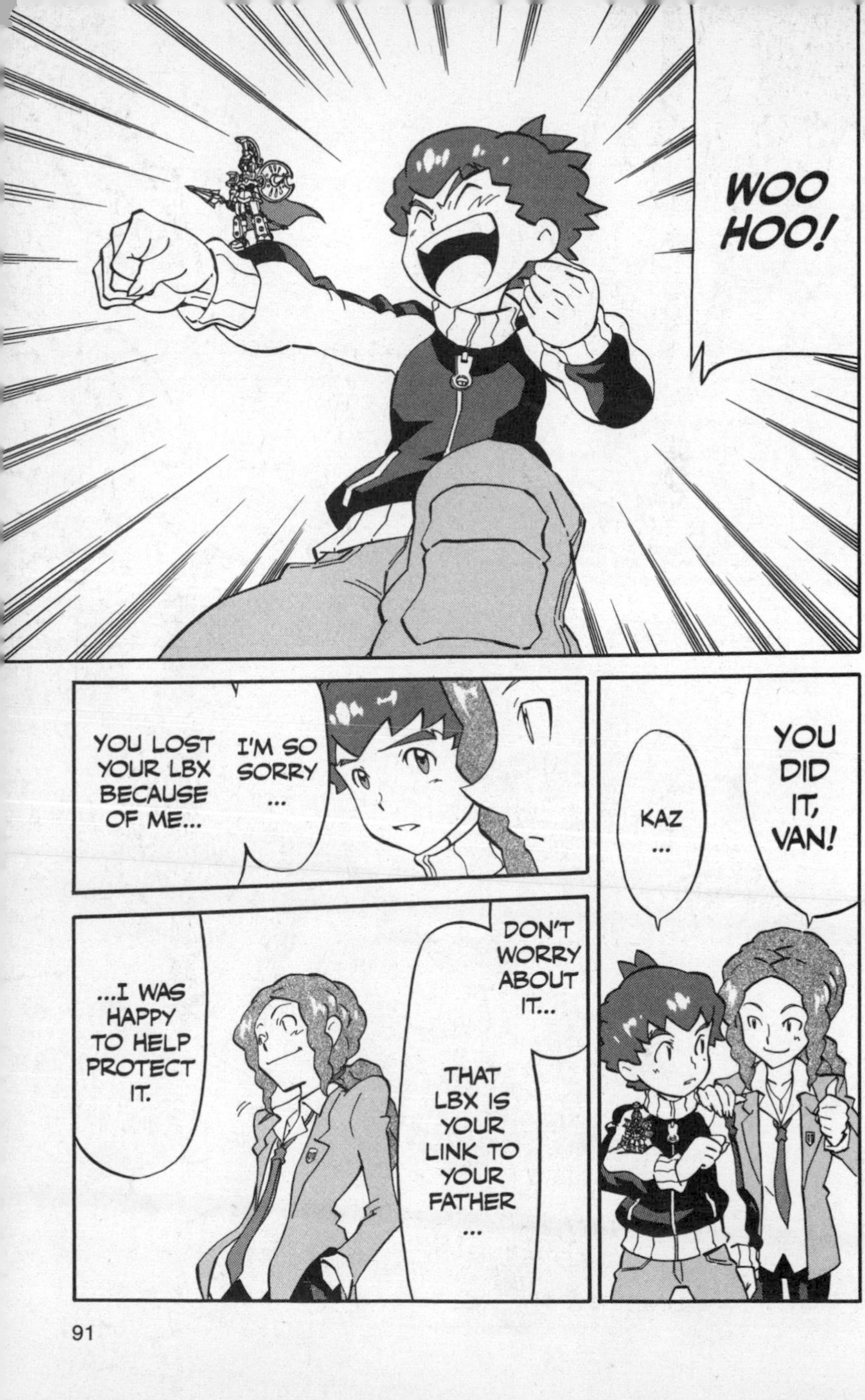
WOO HOO!
YOU DID IT, VAN!
KAZ ...
I'M SO SORRY ...
YOU LOST YOUR LBX BECAUSE OF ME...
DON'T WORRY ABOUT IT...
THAT LBX IS YOUR LINK TO YOUR FATHER ...
...I WAS HAPPY TO HELP PROTECT IT.

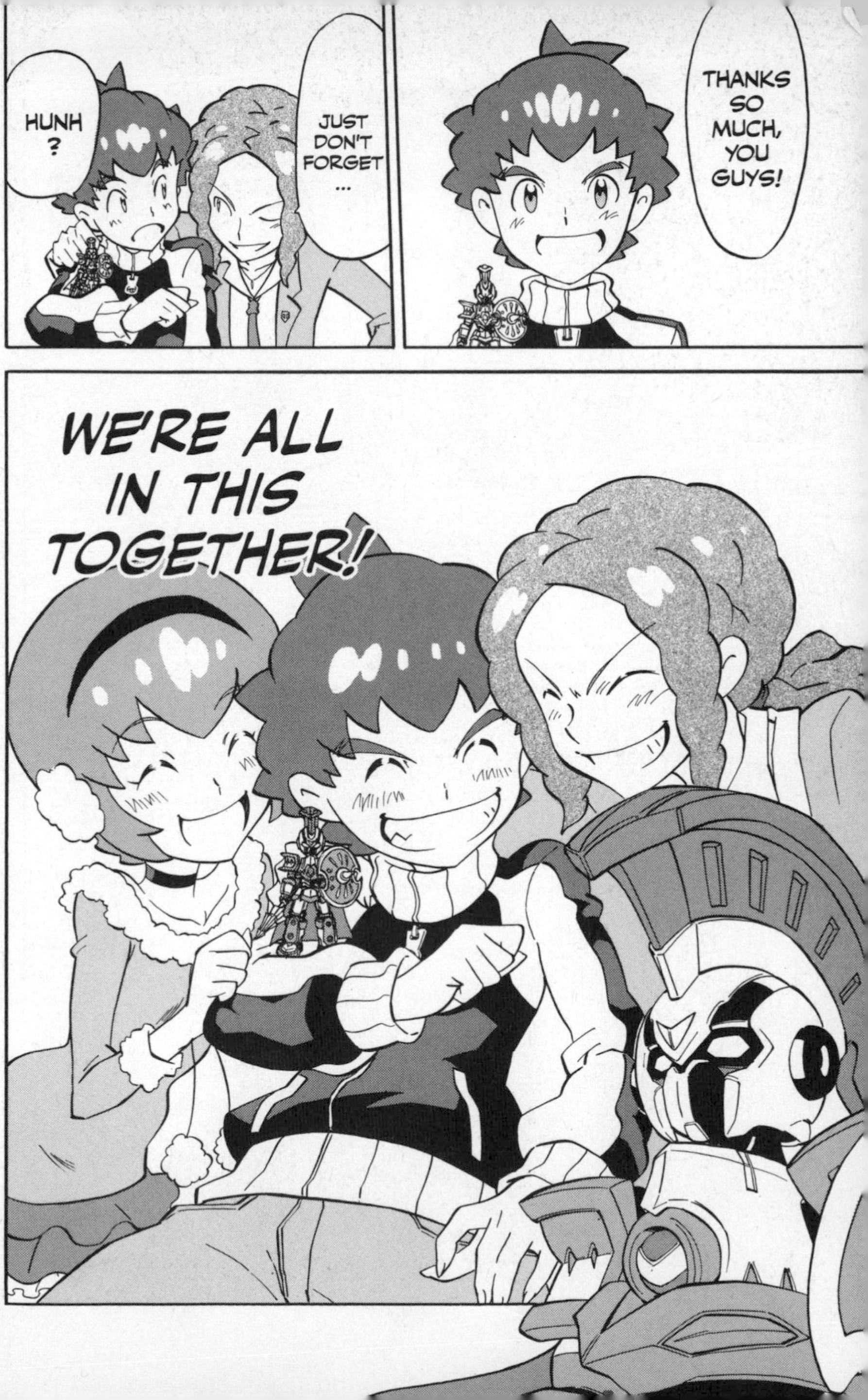
THANKS SO MUCH, YOU GUYS!
JUST DON'T FORGET...
HUNH?
WE'RE ALL IN THIS TOGETHER!

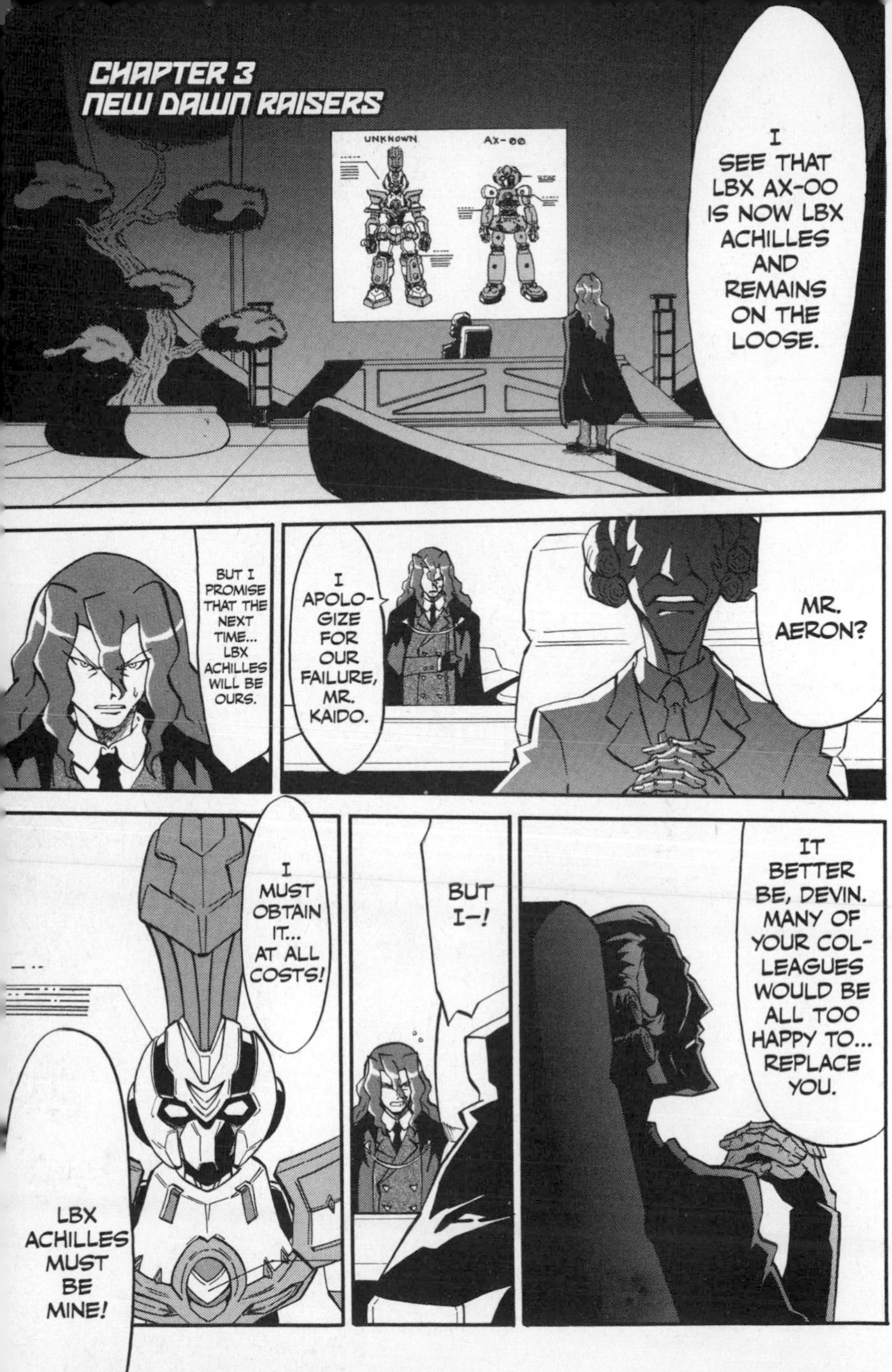
CHAPTER 3
NEW DAWN RAISERS
UNKNOWN
AX-00
I SEE THAT LBX AX-00 IS NOW LBX ACHILLES AND REMAINS ON THE LOOSE.
MR. AERON?
I APOLOGIZE FOR OUR FAILURE, MR. KAIDO.
BUT I PROMISE THAT THE NEXT TIME... LBX ACHILLES WILL BE OURS.
IT BETTER BE, DEVIN. MANY OF YOUR COLLEAGUES WOULD BE ALL TOO HAPPY TO... REPLACE YOU.
BUT I—!
I MUST OBTAIN IT... AT ALL COSTS!
LBX ACHILLES MUST BE MINE!

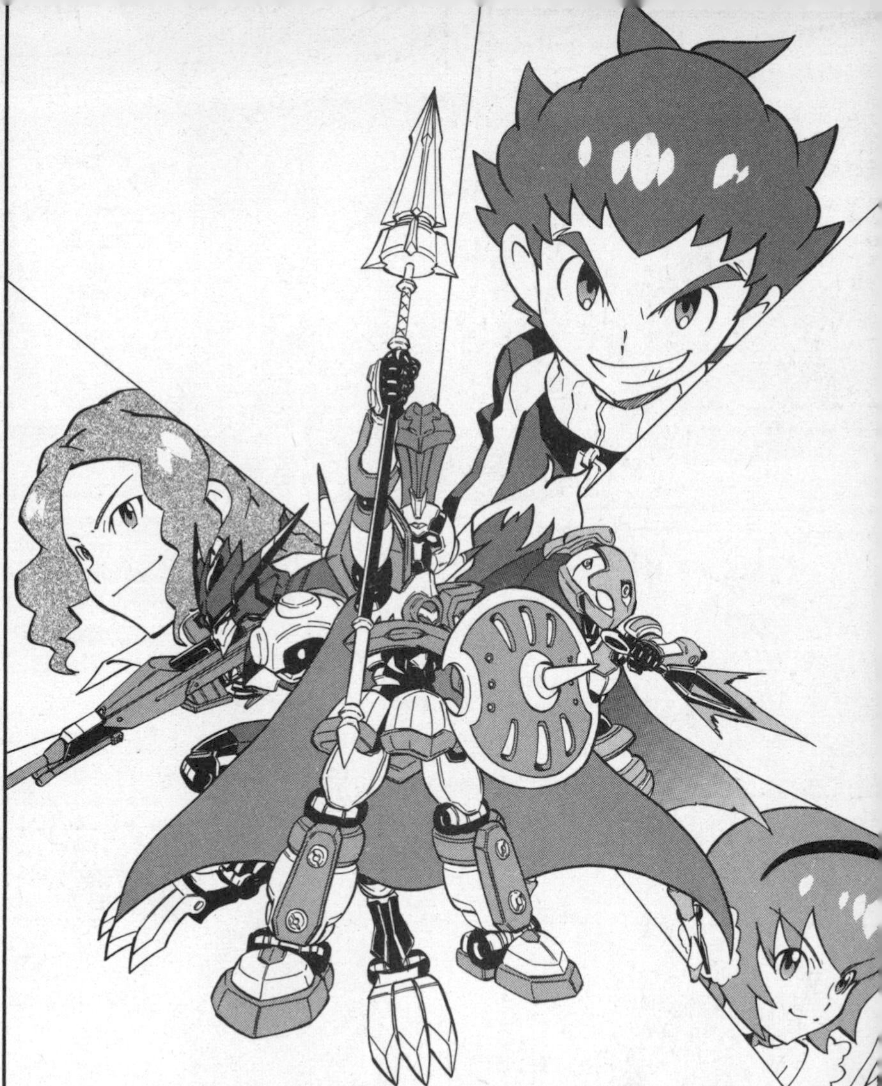

CHAPTER 3
NEW DAWN RAISERS

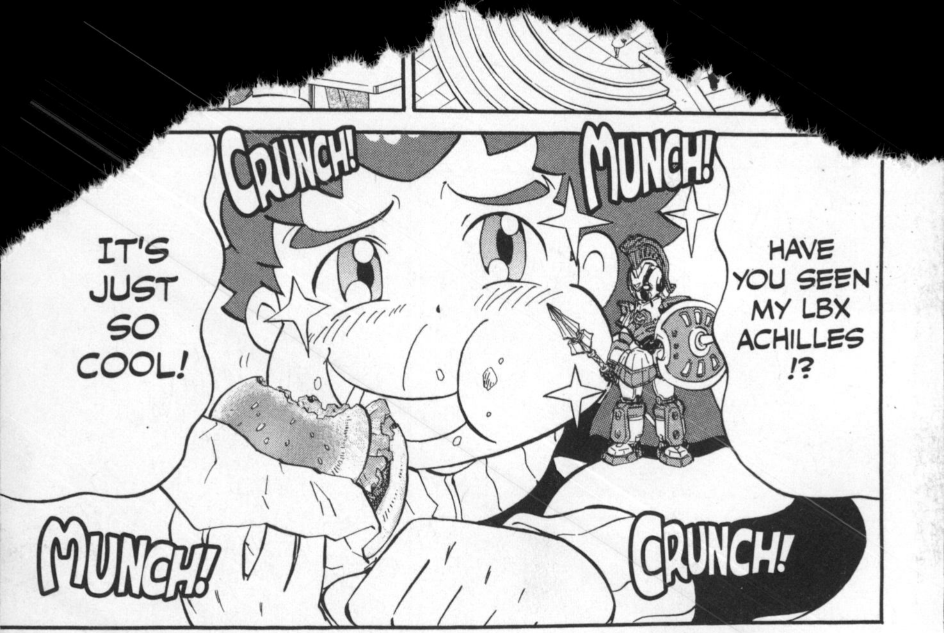
MUNCH!
HAVE YOU SEEN MY LBX ACHILLES !?
CRUNCH!
IT'S JUST SO COOL!
CRUNCH!
MUNCH!

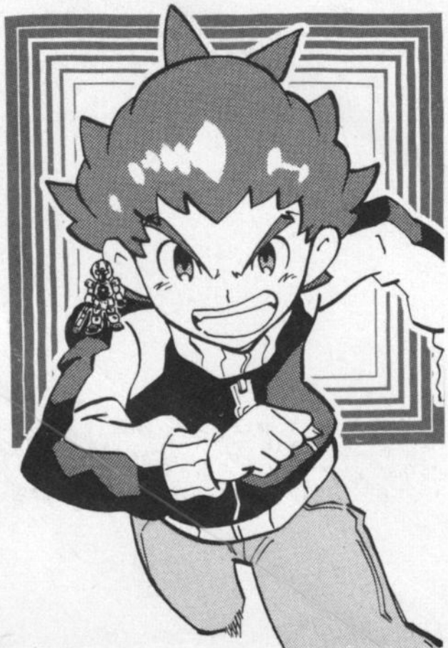

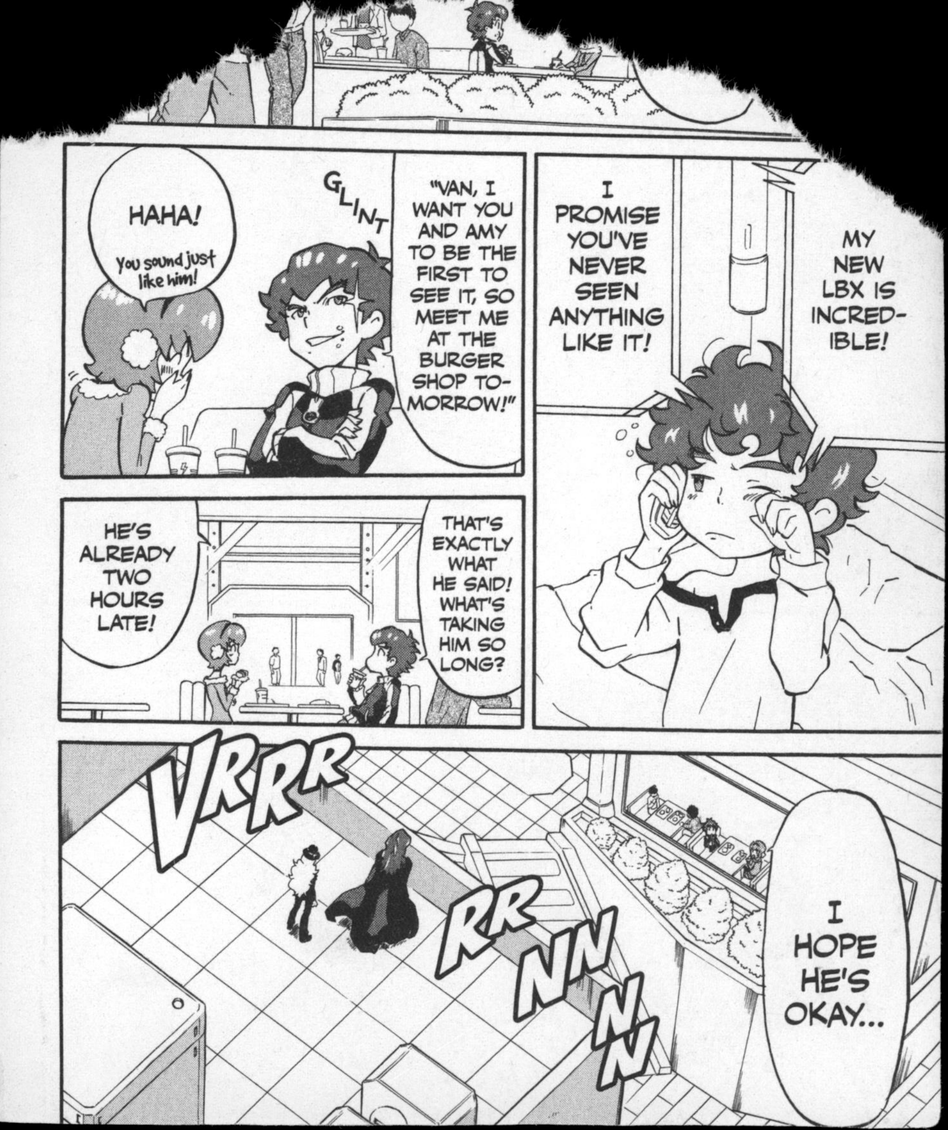
MY NEW LBX IS INCRED-IBLE!
I PROMISE YOU'VE NEVER SEEN ANYTHING LIKE IT!
"VAN, I WANT YOU AND AMY TO BE THE FIRST TO SEE IT, SO MEET ME AT THE BURGER SHOP TO-MORROW!"
GLINT
HAHA!
You sound just like him!
THAT'S EXACTLY WHAT HE SAID! WHAT'S TAKING HIM SO LONG?
HE'S ALREADY TWO HOURS LATE!
I HOPE HE'S OKAY...
VRRRR
RRNNNNN

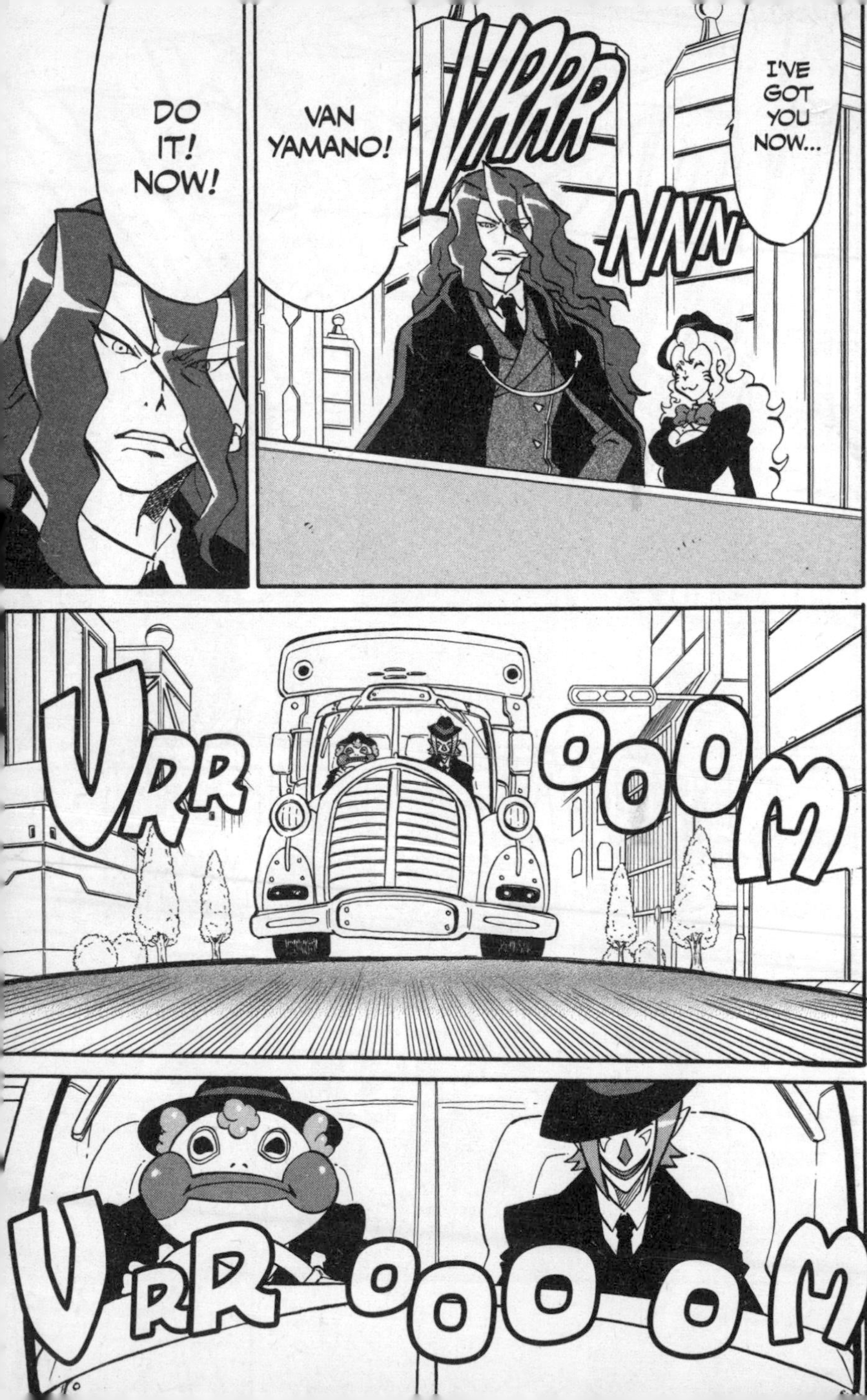
I'VE GOT YOU NOW...
VRRRNNN
VAN YAMANO!
DO IT! NOW!
VRROOOM
VRROOOOM

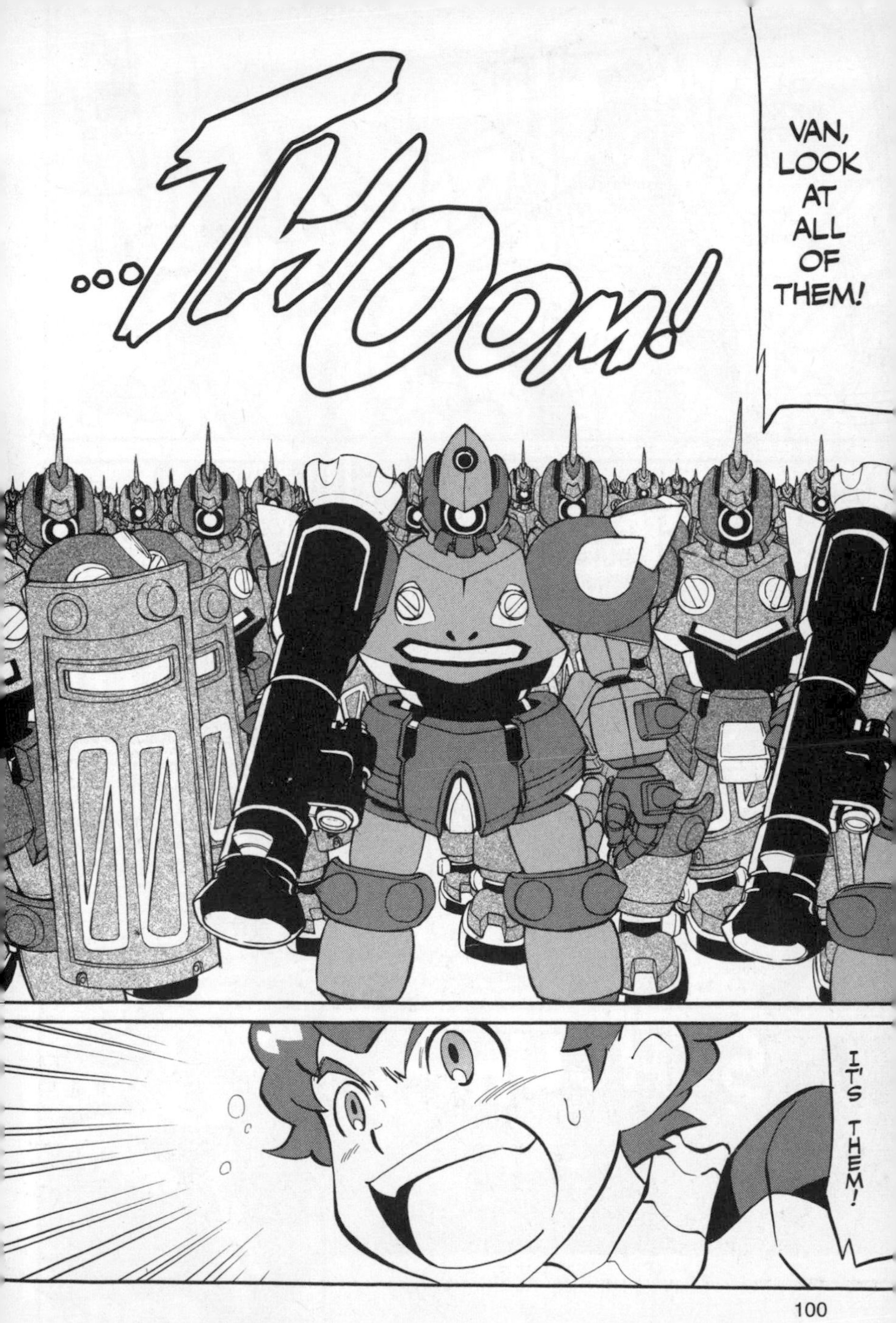
VAN, LOOK AT ALL OF THEM!
...THOOM!
IT'S THEM!

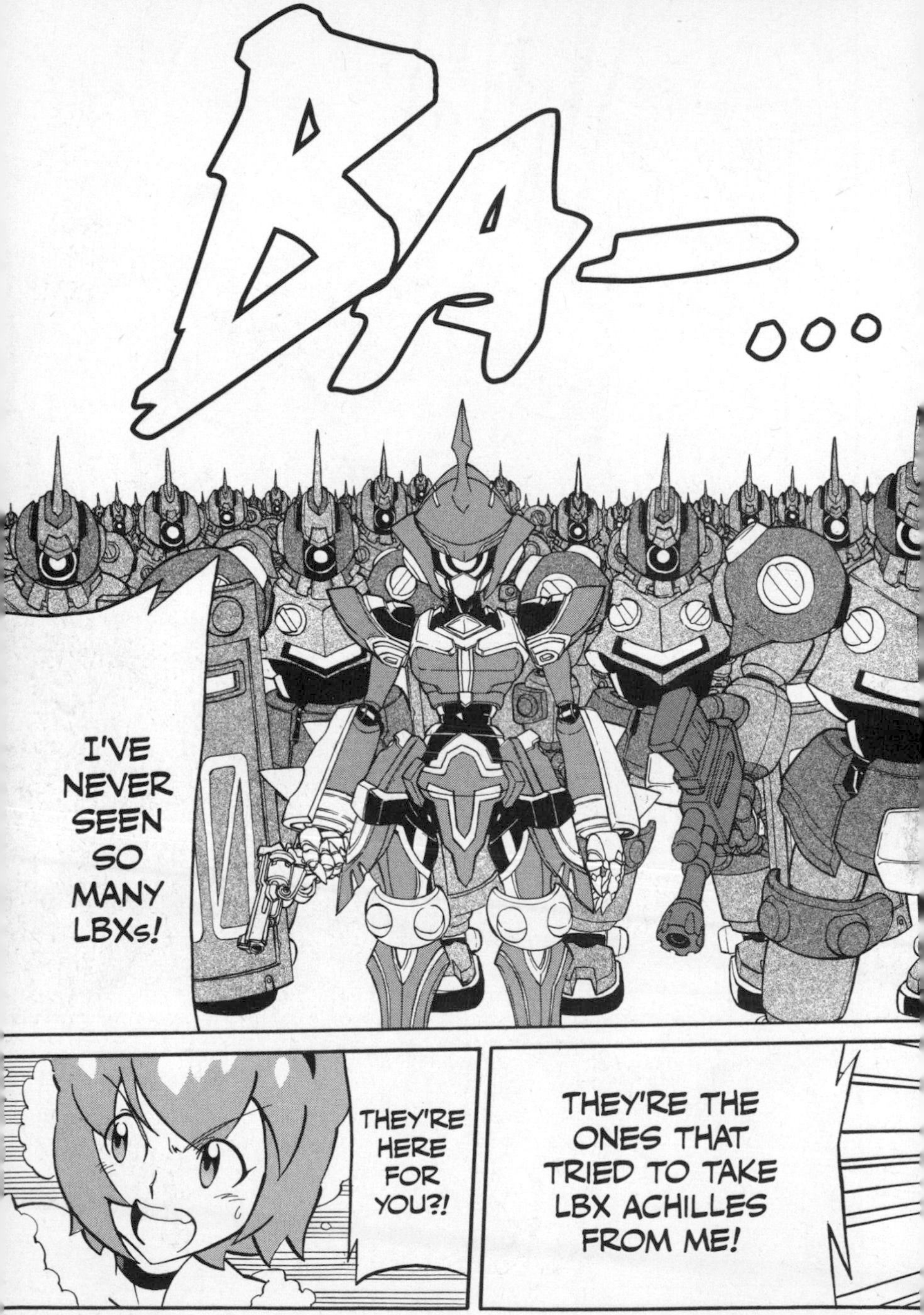
BA-...
I'VE NEVER SEEN SO MANY LBXs!
THEY'RE THE ONES THAT TRIED TO TAKE LBX ACHILLES FROM ME!
THEY'RE HERE FOR YOU?!

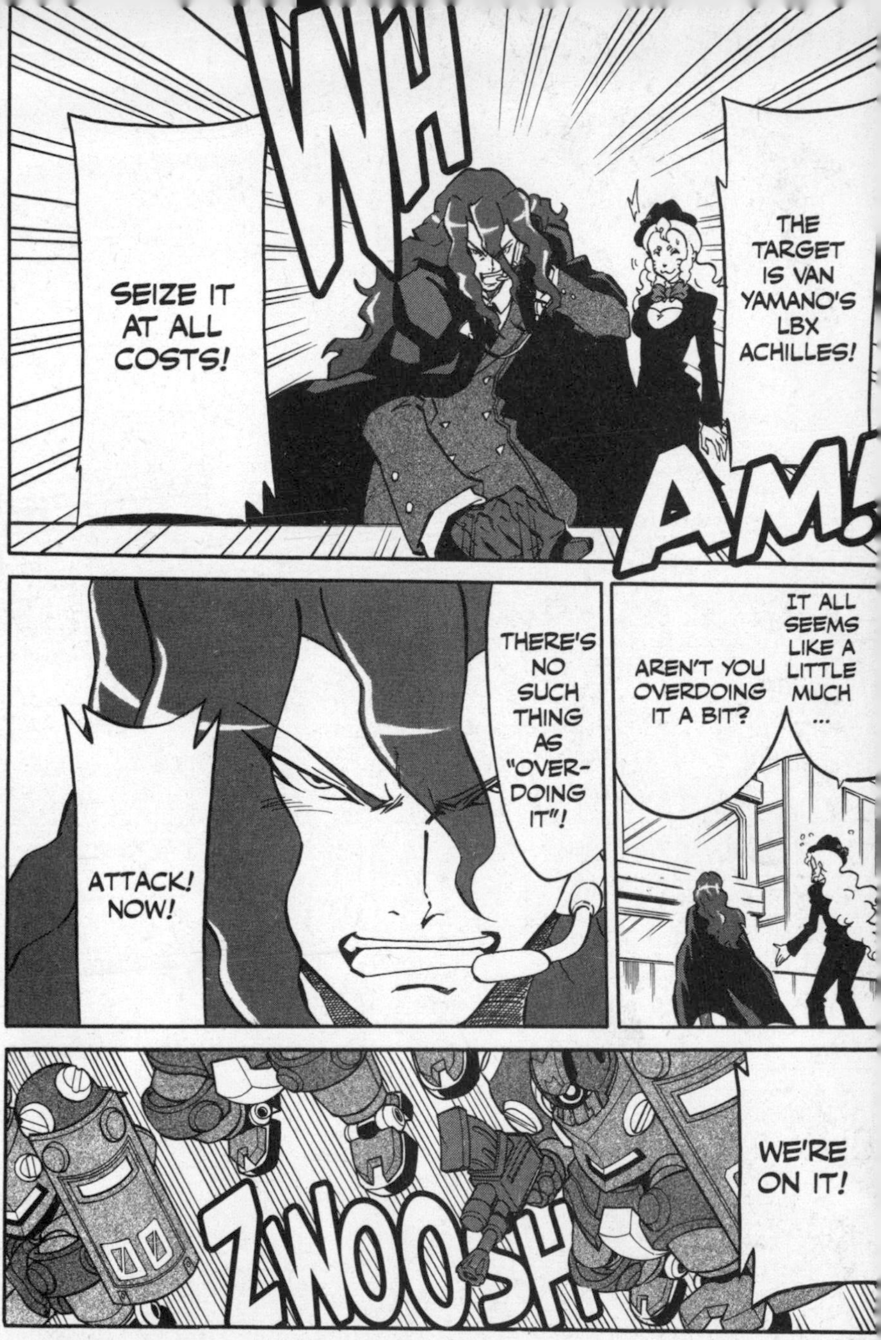
THE TARGET IS VAN YAMANO'S LBX ACHILLES!
WHAM!
SEIZE IT AT ALL COSTS!
IT ALL SEEMS LIKE A LITTLE MUCH ...
AREN'T YOU OVERDOING IT A BIT?
THERE'S NO SUCH THING AS "OVER-DOING IT"!
ATTACK! NOW!
WE'RE ON IT!
ZWOOSH!

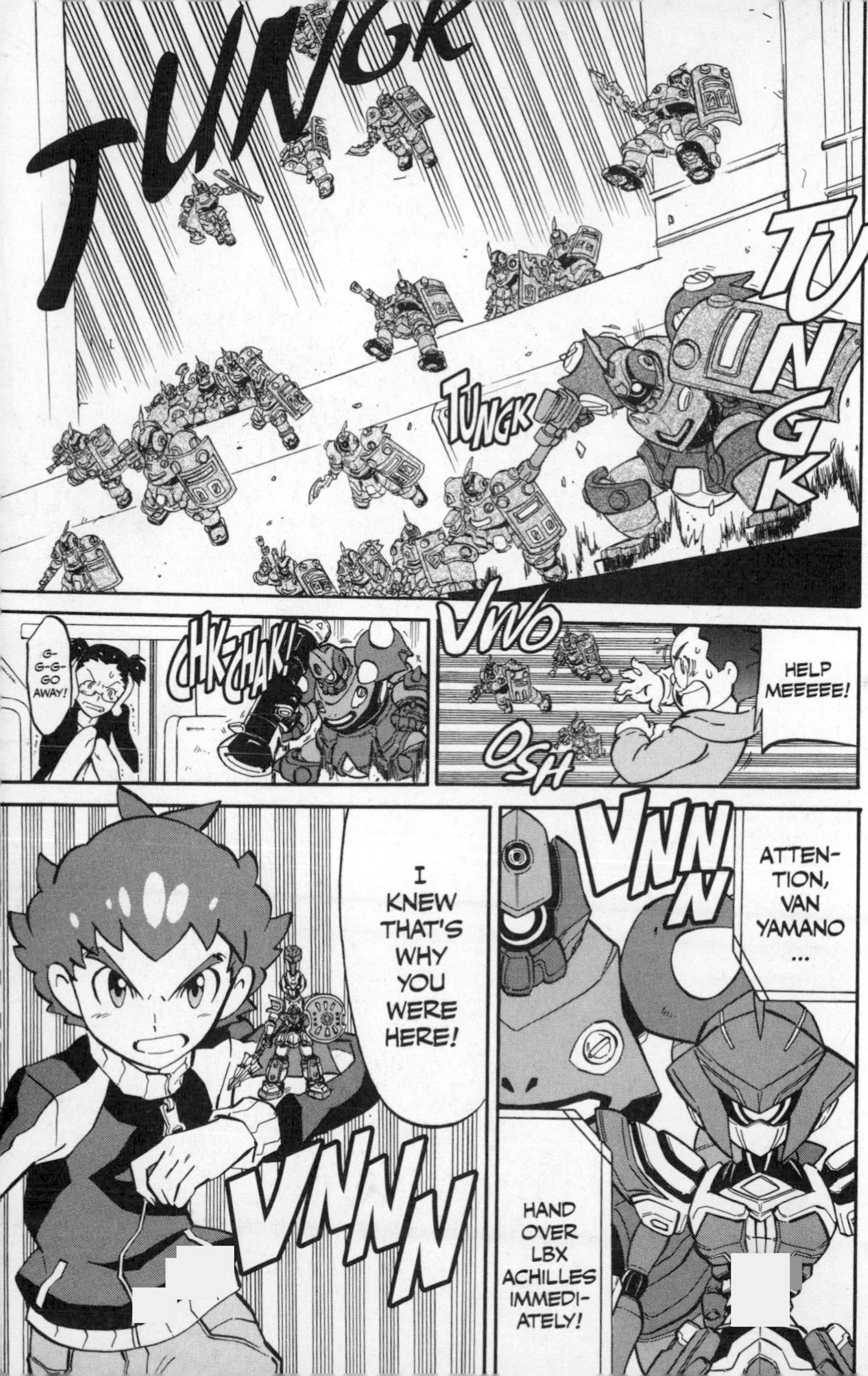
TUINGK
TUNGK
TUNGK
HELP MEEEEE!
VWOOSH
CHK-CHAK!
G-G-G-GO AWAY!
VNNN
ATTENTION, VAN YAMANO...
HAND OVER LBX ACHILLES IMMEDIATELY!
I KNEW THAT'S WHY YOU WERE HERE!
VNNNN

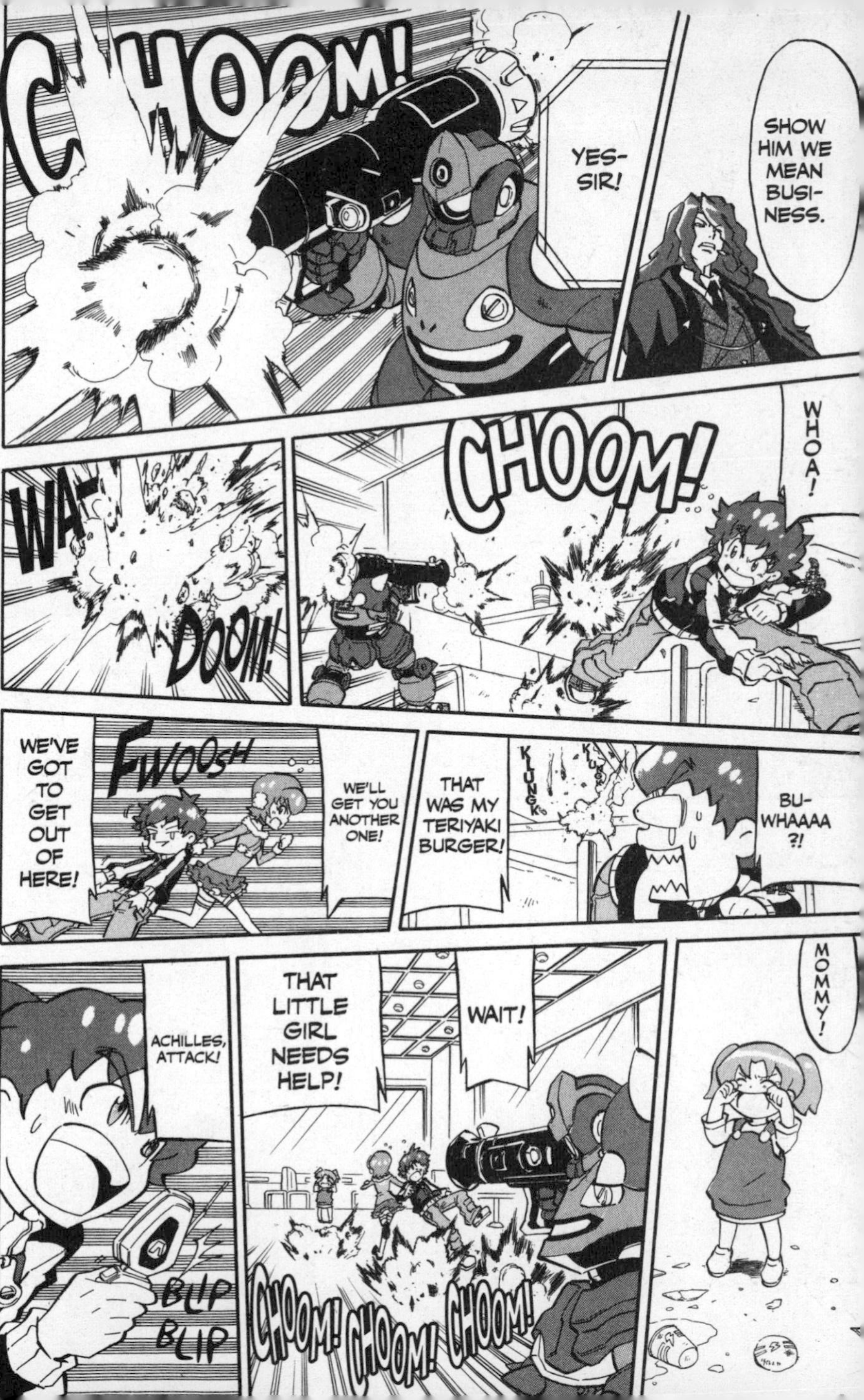
SHOW HIM WE MEAN BUSI- NESS.
YES- SIR!
CHOOM!
WHOA!
CHOOM!
WA-
DOOM!
BU- WHAAAA ?!
KLUNGK
KLUNGK
THAT WAS MY TERIYAKI BURGER!
WE'LL GET YOU ANOTHER ONE!
FWOOSH
WE'VE GOT TO GET OUT OF HERE!
MOMMY!
WAIT!
THAT LITTLE GIRL NEEDS HELP!
CHOOM! CHOOM! CHOOM!
ACHILLES, ATTACK!
BLIP BLIP

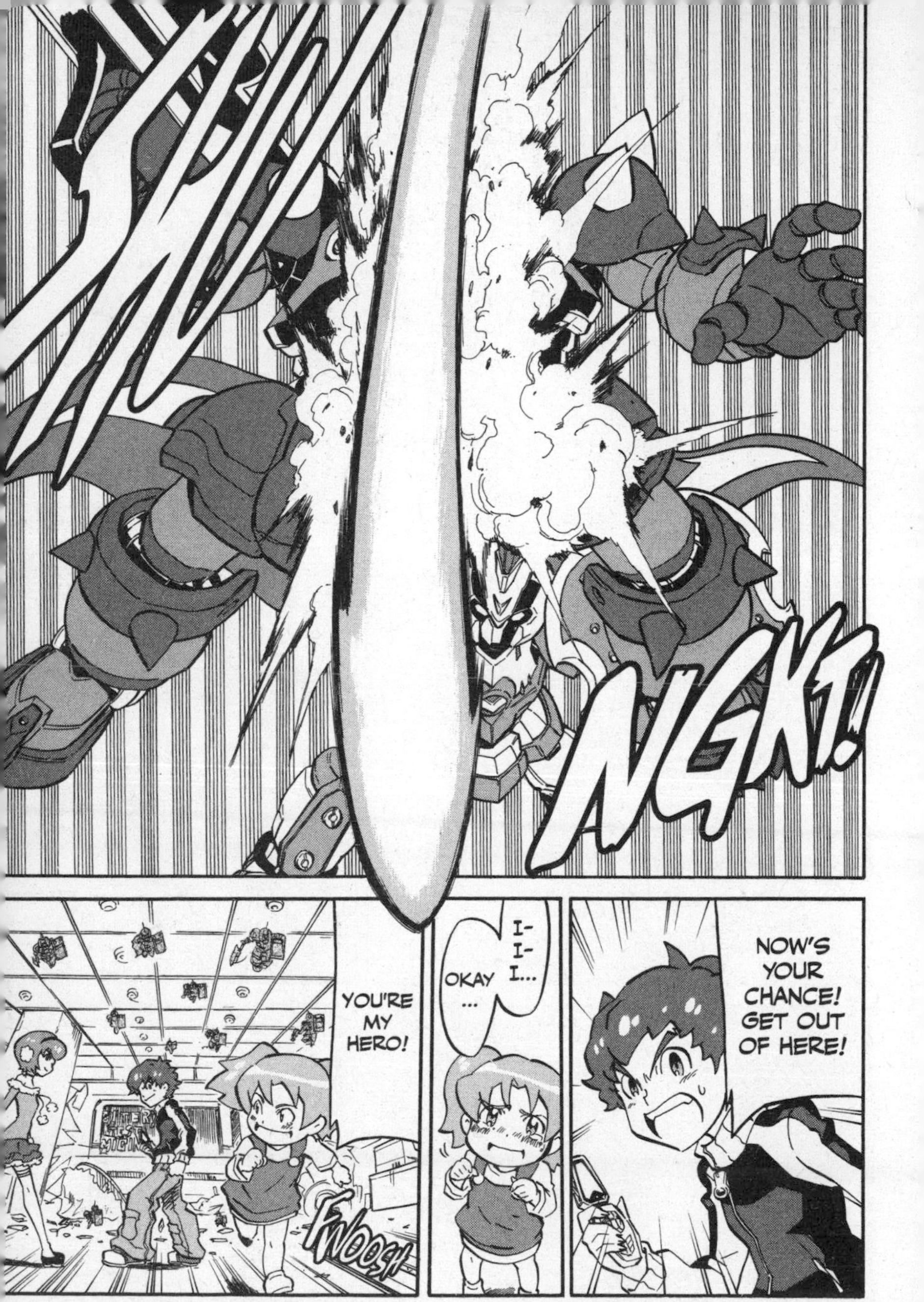
NGK!
NOW'S YOUR CHANCE! GET OUT OF HERE!
I- I- I...
OKAY ...
YOU'RE MY HERO!
FWOOSH

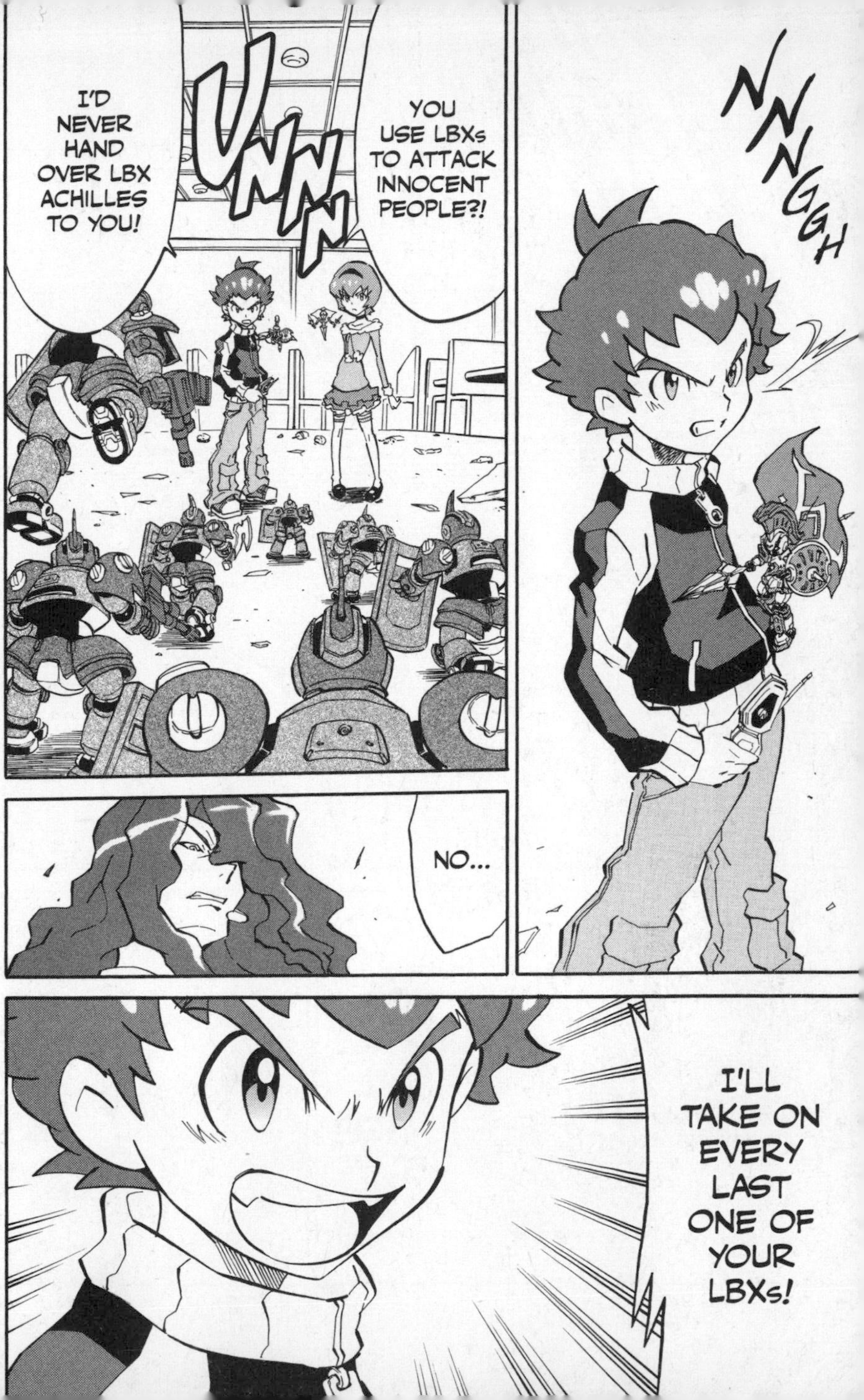
NNNGGH
YOU USE LBXs TO ATTACK INNOCENT PEOPLE?!
UNNN
I'D NEVER HAND OVER LBX ACHILLES TO YOU!
NO...
I'LL TAKE ON EVERY LAST ONE OF YOUR LBXs!

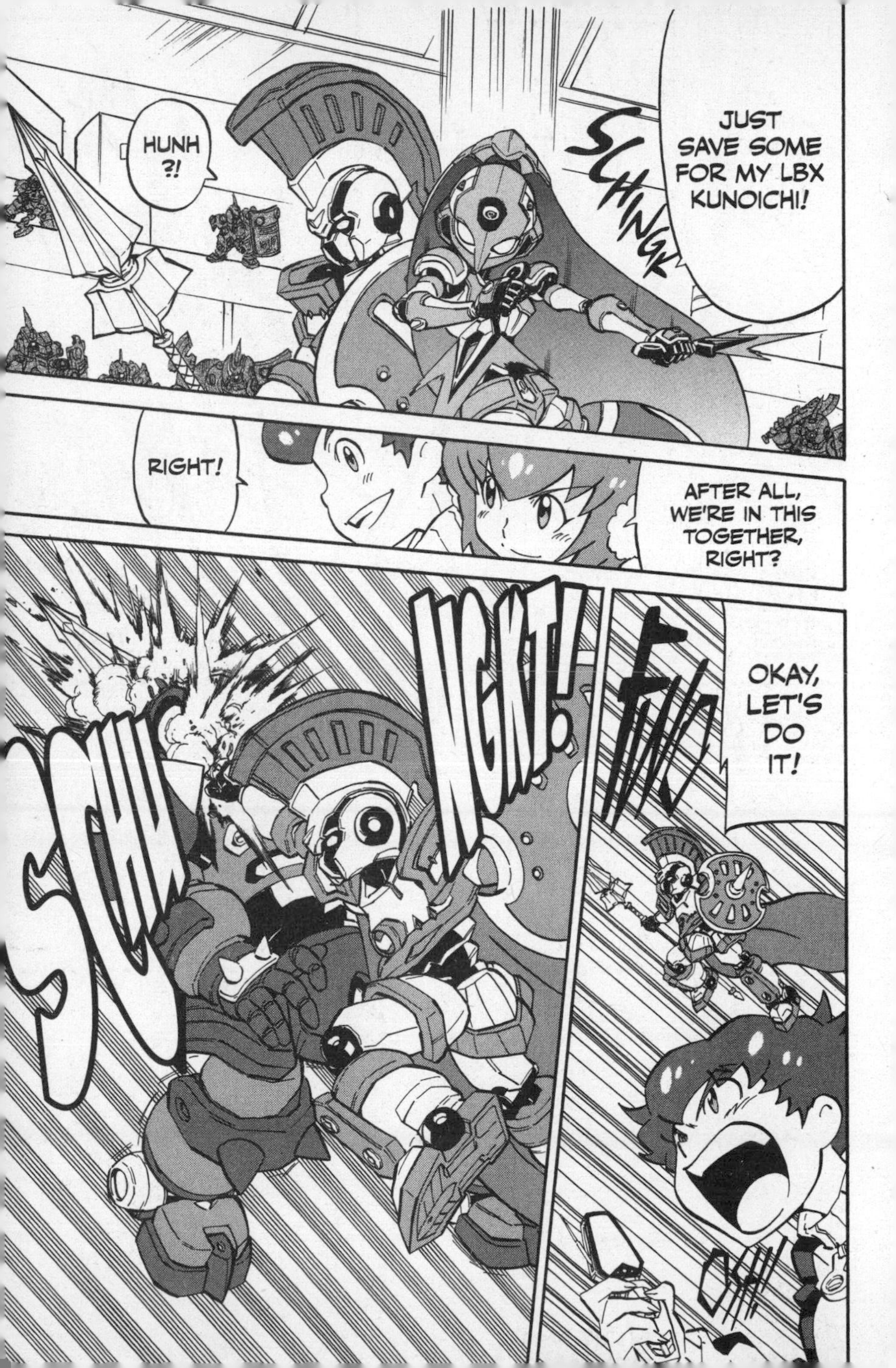
JUST SAVE SOME FOR MY LBX KUNOICHI!
SCHINGK
HUNH ?!
AFTER ALL, WE'RE IN THIS TOGETHER, RIGHT?
RIGHT!
OKAY, LET'S DO IT!
SCHU
NCKT!

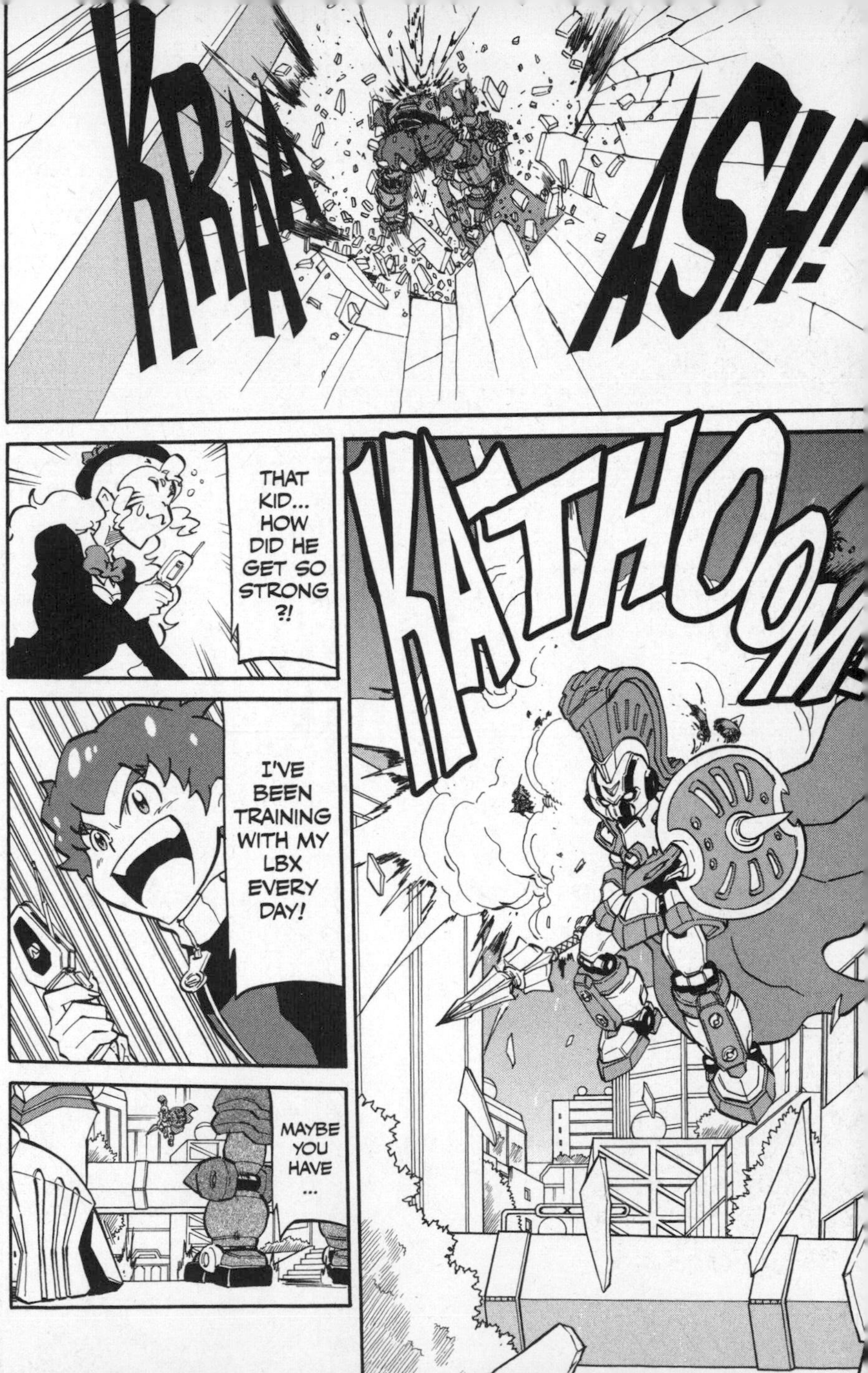
KRAAASH!
KATHOOM!
THAT KID... HOW DID HE GET SO STRONG?!
I'VE BEEN TRAINING WITH MY LBX EVERY DAY!
MAYBE YOU HAVE...

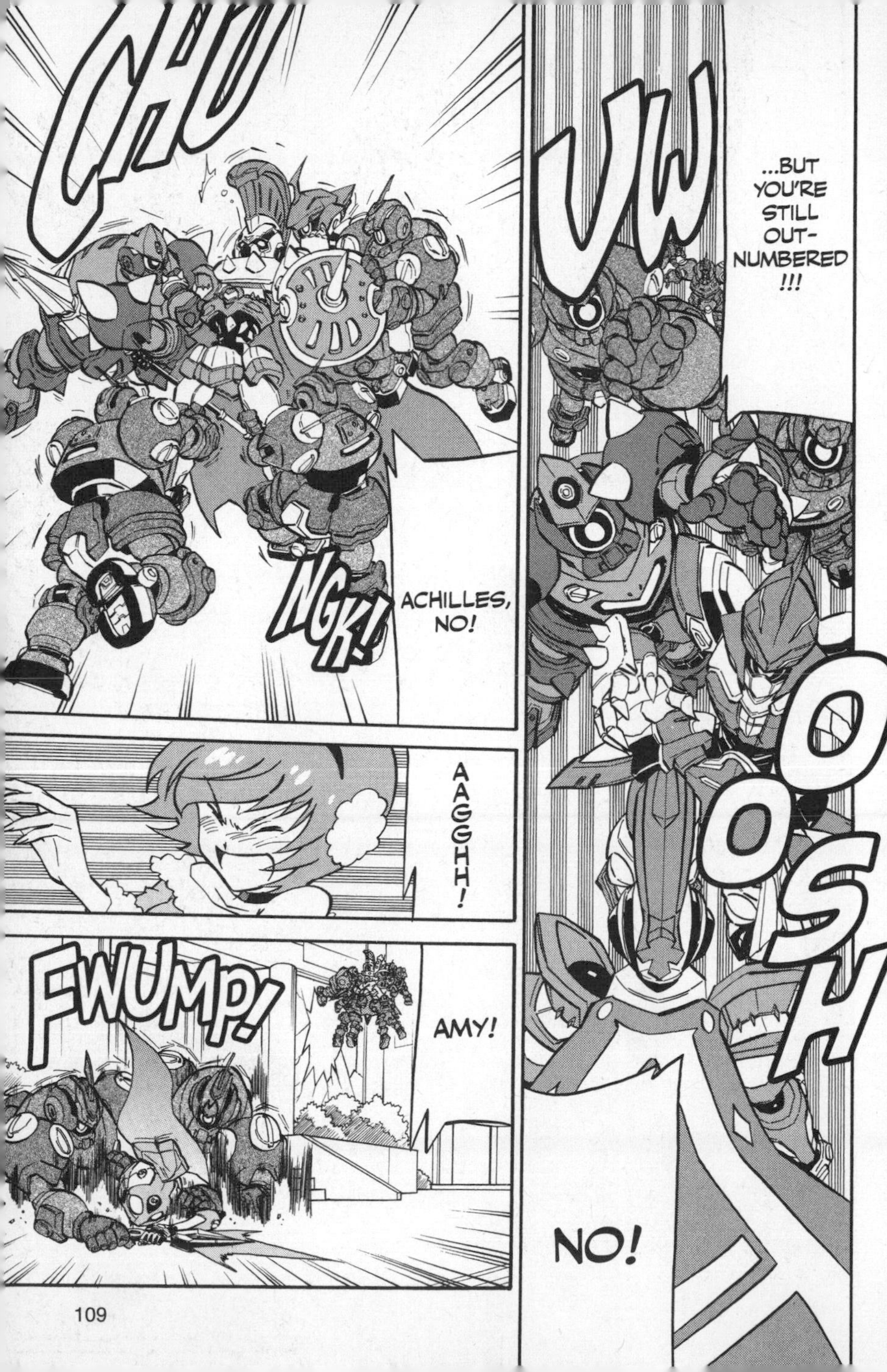
...BUT YOU'RE STILL OUT-NUMBERED!!!
OOSH
NO!
CHU
NGK!
ACHILLES, NO!
AAGGHH!
FWUMP!
AMY!

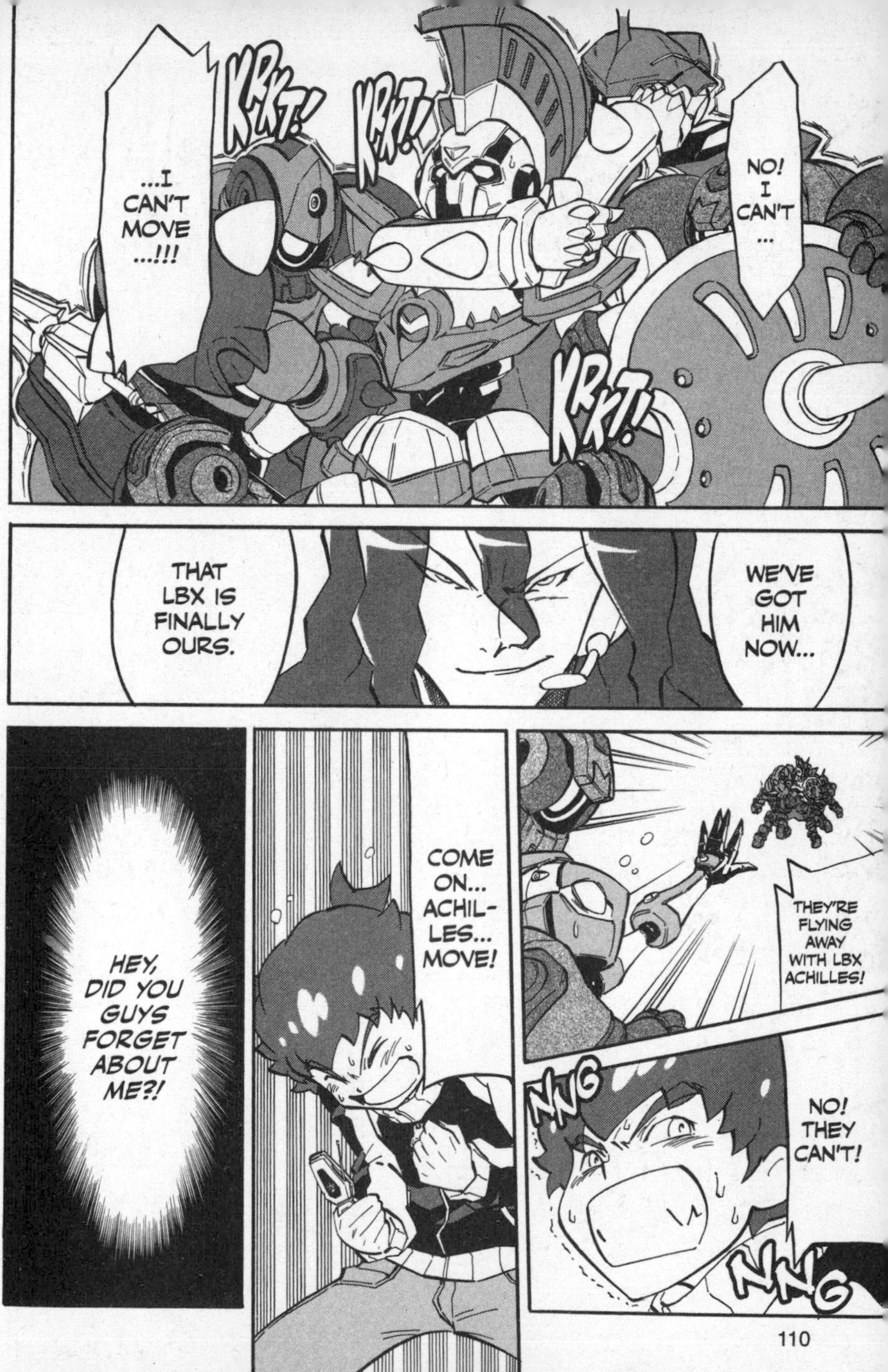
NO! I CAN'T ...
KRKT! KRKT!
...I CAN'T MOVE ...!!!
KRKT!
WE'VE GOT HIM NOW...
THAT LBX IS FINALLY OURS.
THEY'RE FLYING AWAY WITH LBX ACHILLES!
NNG
NO! THEY CAN'T!
NNG
COME ON... ACHIL-LES... MOVE!
HEY, DID YOU GUYS FORGET ABOUT ME?!

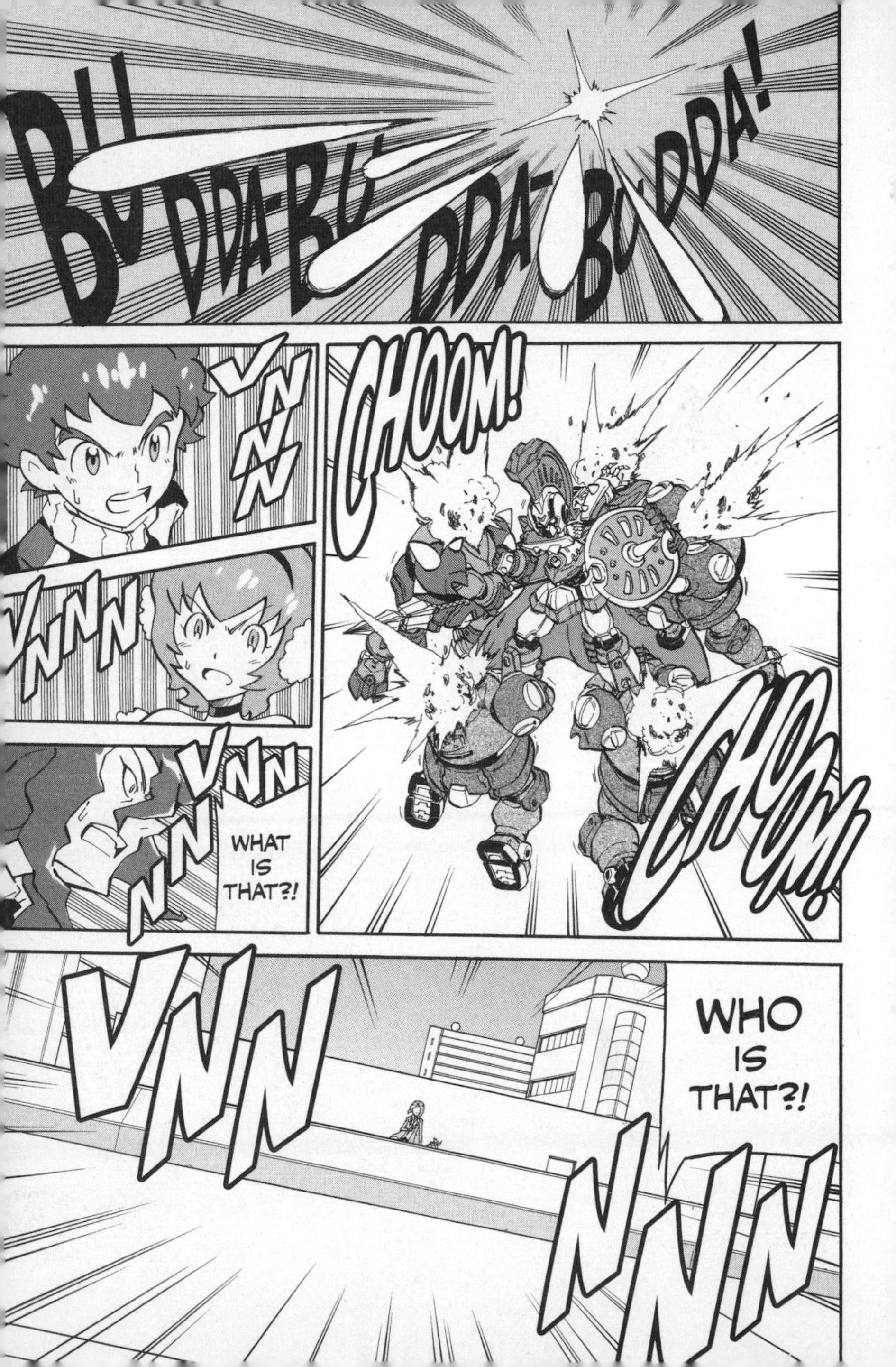
BUDDA-BUDDA-BUDDA-BUDDA!
CHOOM!
CHOOM!
VNNN
VNNN
VNN NNN
WHAT IS THAT?!
VNNN
WHO IS THAT?!
NNNN

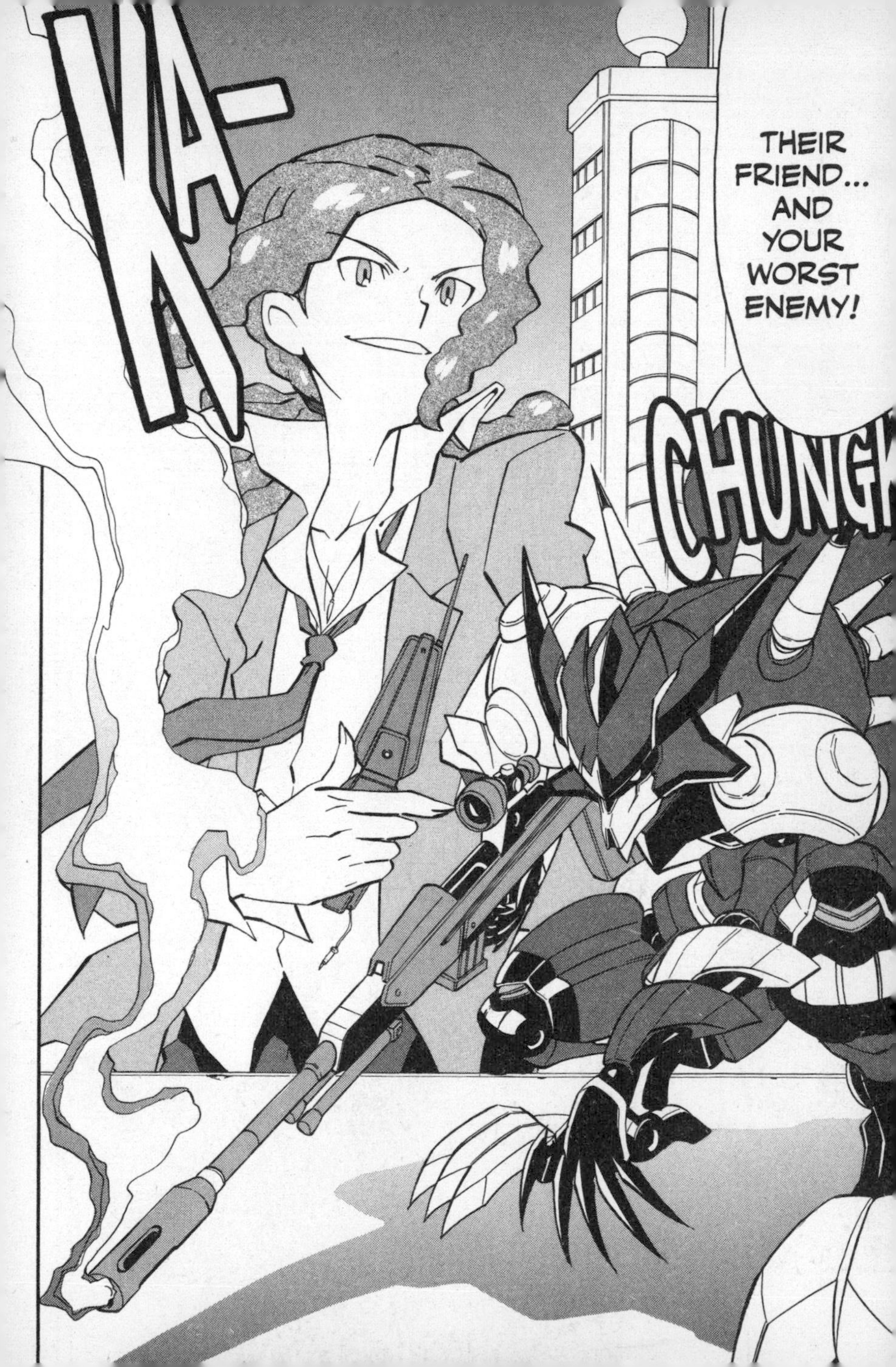
THEIR FRIEND... AND YOUR WORST ENEMY!
VA-
CHUNGK

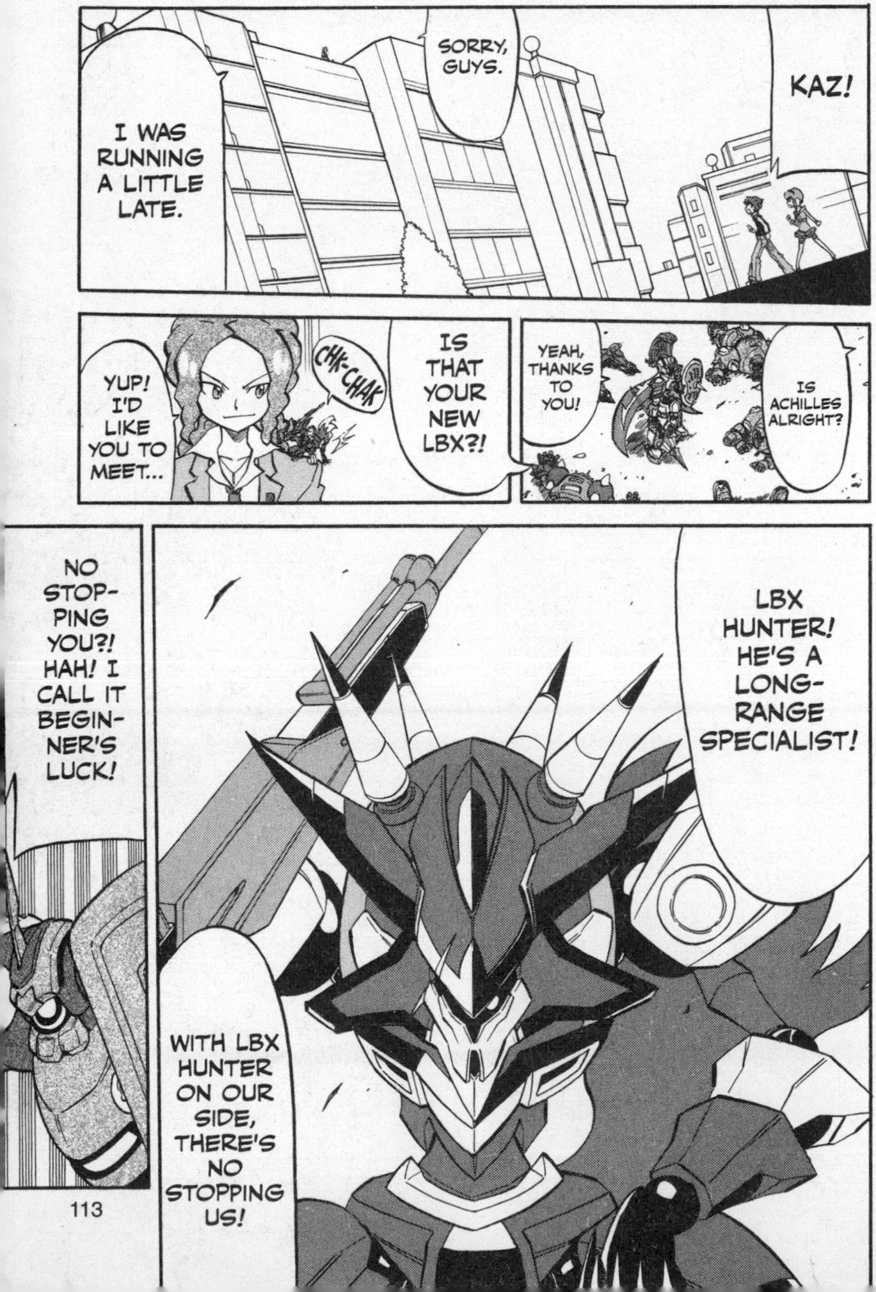
KAZ!
SORRY, GUYS.
I WAS RUNNING A LITTLE LATE.
IS ACHILLES ALRIGHT?
YEAH, THANKS TO YOU!
IS THAT YOUR NEW LBX?!
CHK-CHAK
YUP! I'D LIKE YOU TO MEET...
LBX HUNTER! HE'S A LONG-RANGE SPECIALIST!
WITH LBX HUNTER ON OUR SIDE, THERE'S NO STOPPING US!
NO STOPPING YOU?! HAH! I CALL IT BEGINNER'S LUCK!

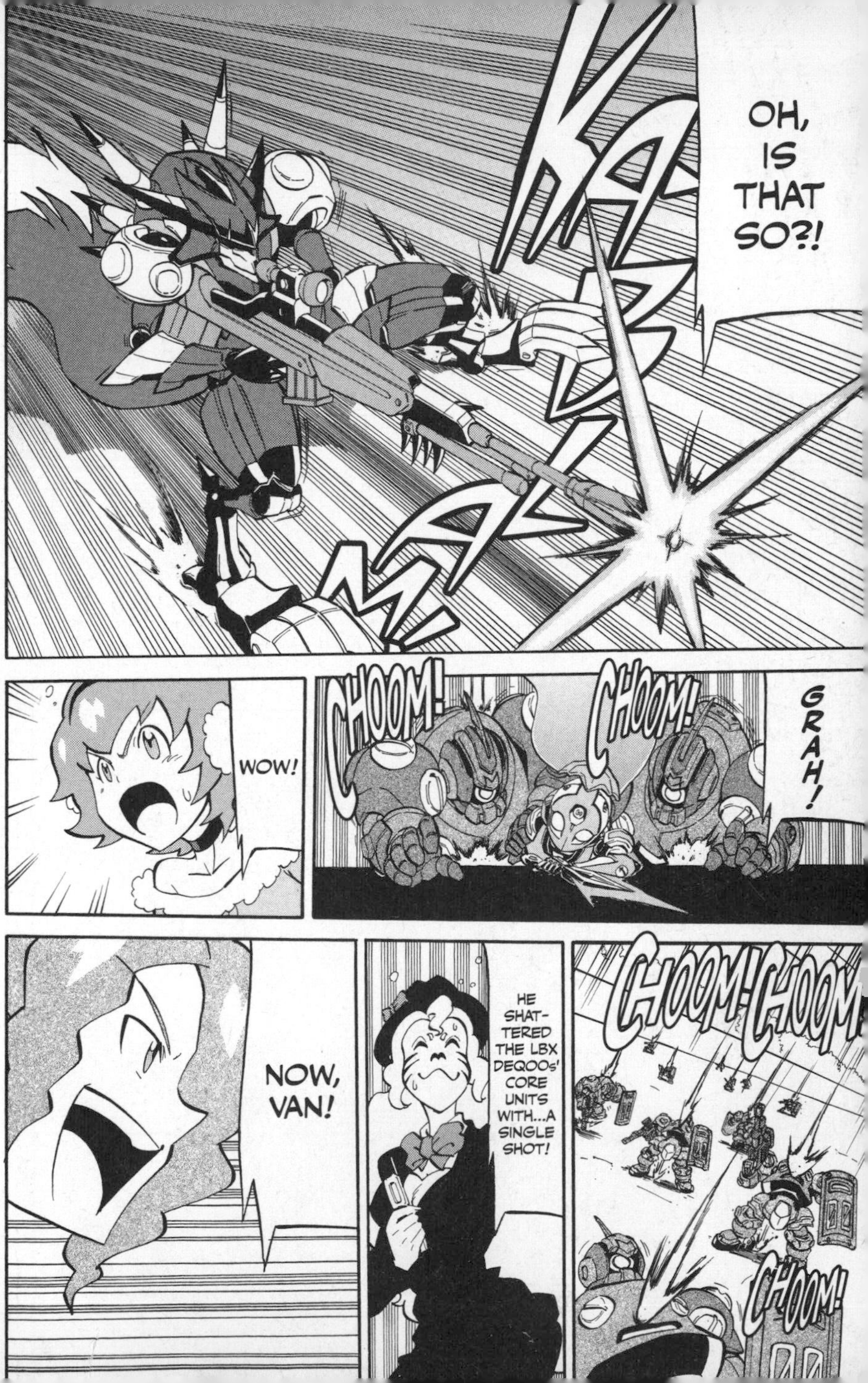

OH, IS THAT SO?!
GRAH!
CHOOM!
CHOOM!
WOW!
CHOOM-CHOOM!
CHOOM!
HE SHAT-TERED THE LBX DEQOOs' CORE UNITS WITH...A SINGLE SHOT!
NOW, VAN!

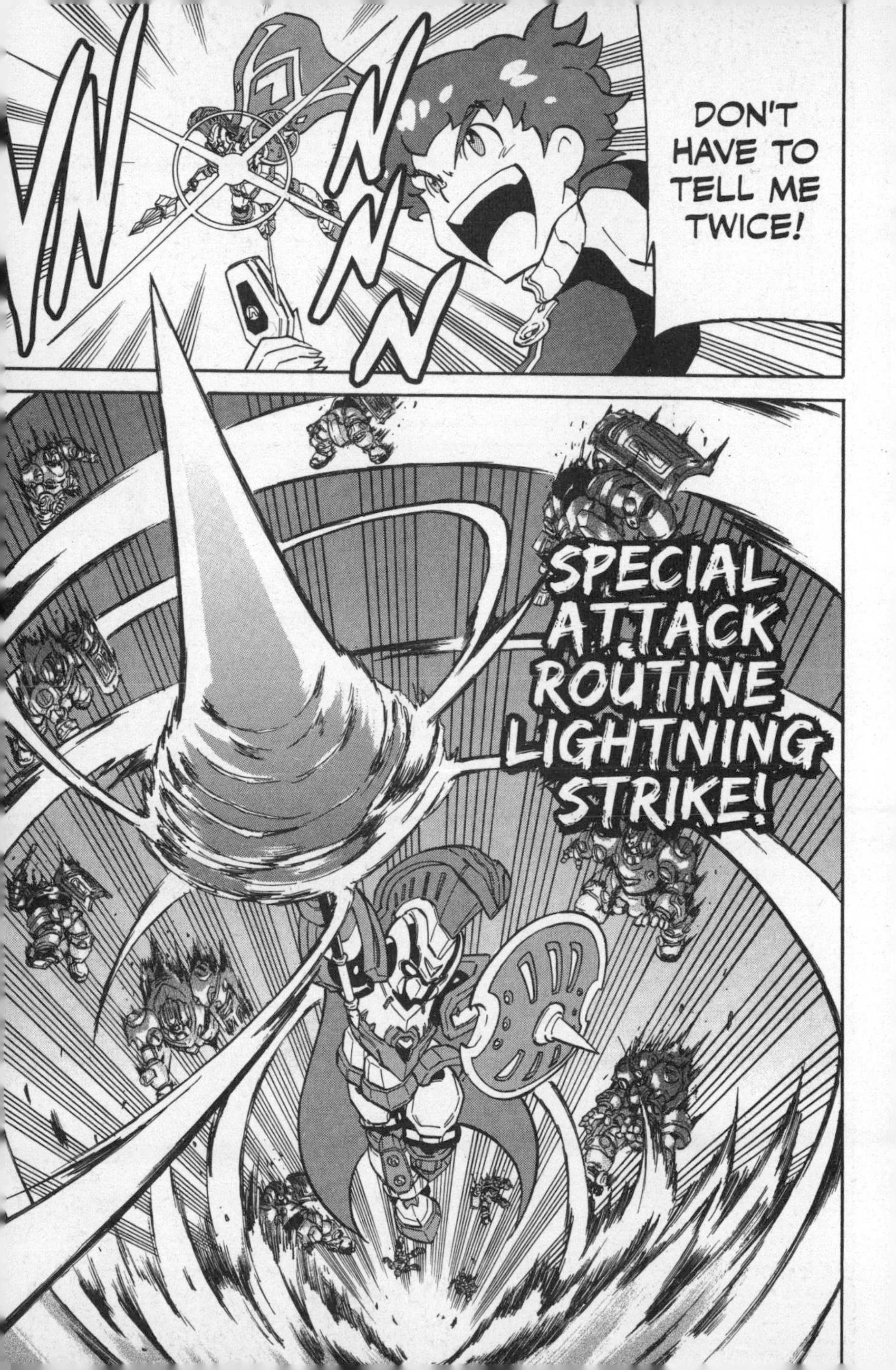
DON'T HAVE TO TELL ME TWICE!
SPECIAL ATTACK ROUTINE LIGHTNING STRIKE!

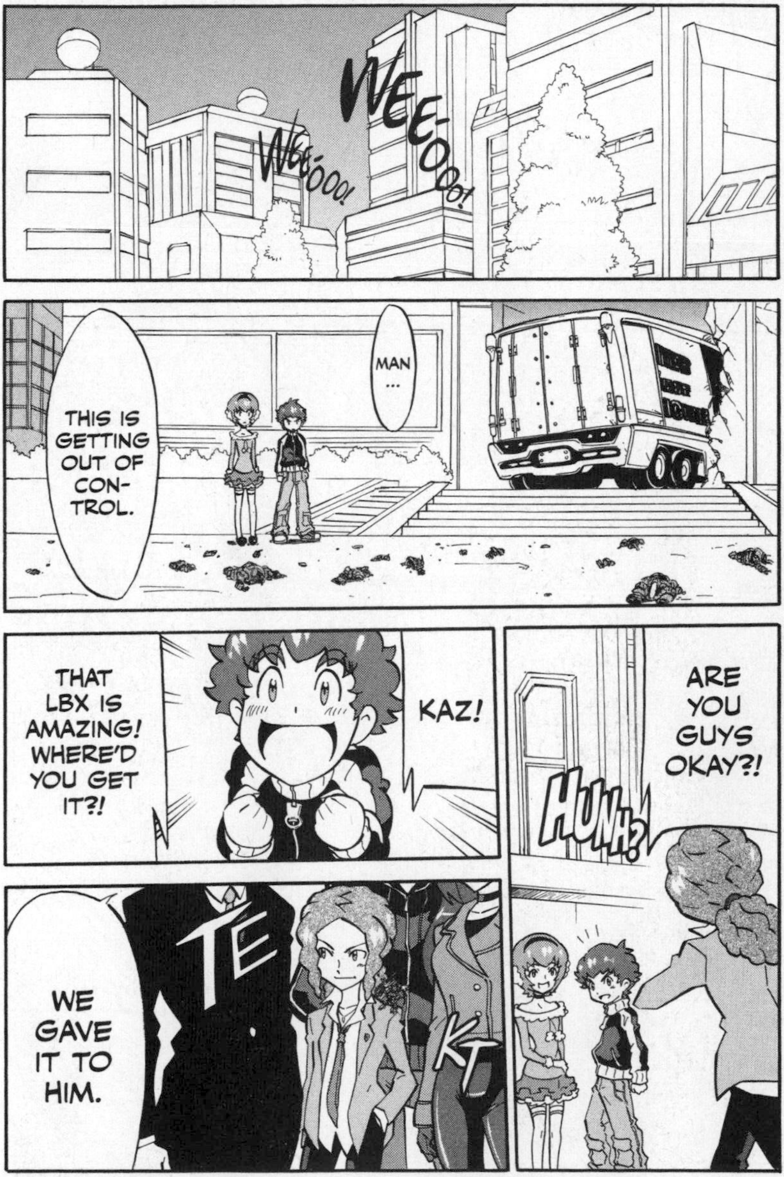
WEE-OOO!
WEE-OOO!
MAN ...
THIS IS GETTING OUT OF CON-TROL.
ARE YOU GUYS OKAY?!
HUNH?
KAZ!
THAT LBX IS AMAZING! WHERE'D YOU GET IT?!
TEKT
WE GAVE IT TO HIM.

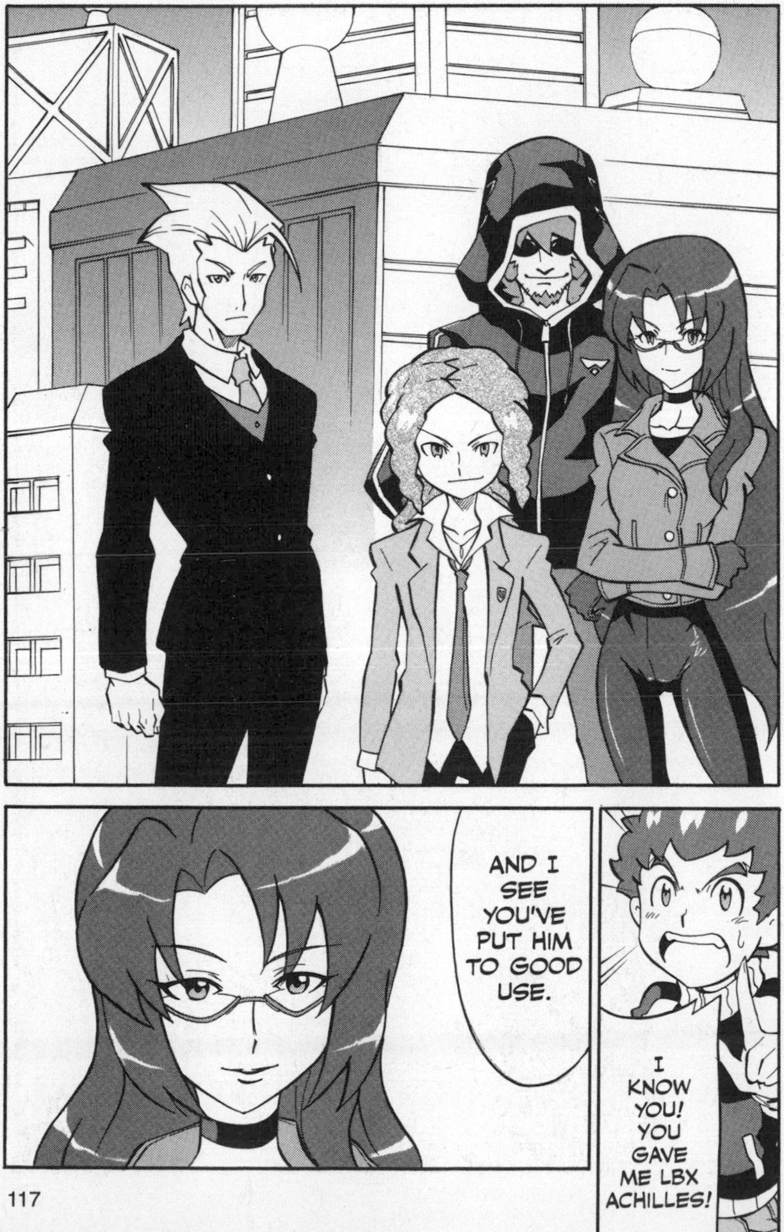
I KNOW YOU! YOU GAVE ME LBX ACHILLES!
AND I SEE YOU'VE PUT HIM TO GOOD USE.

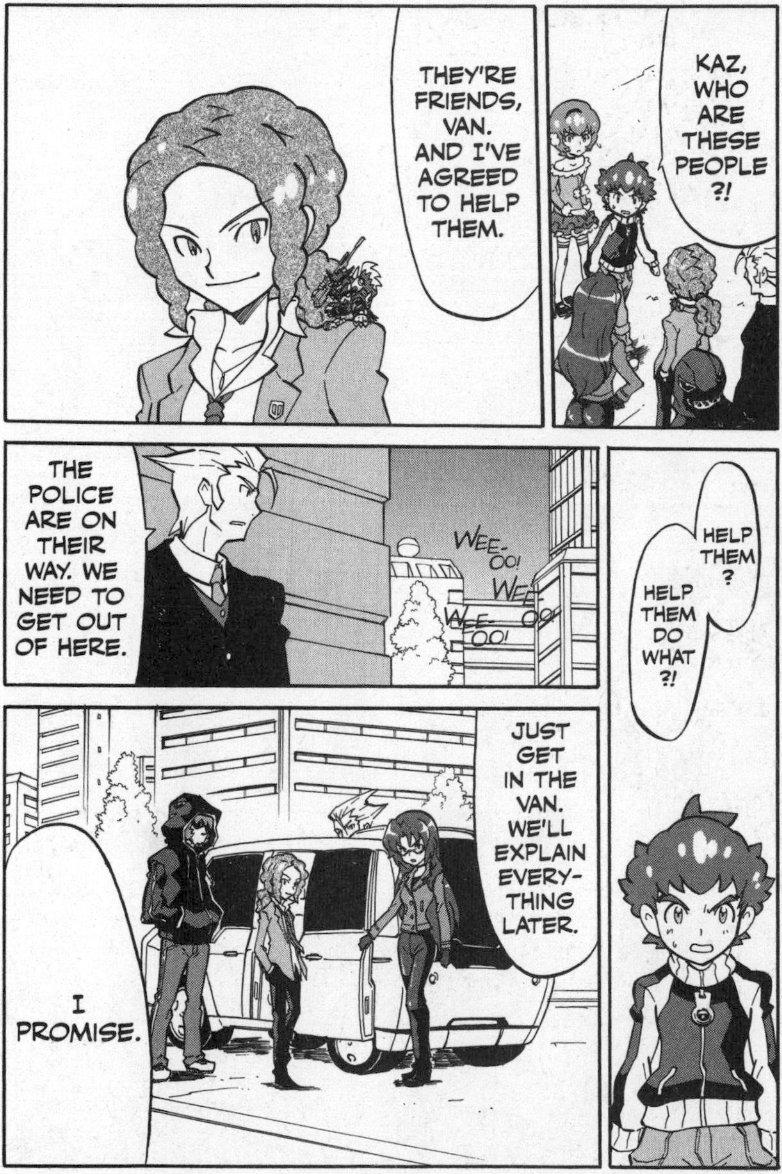
KAZ, WHO ARE THESE PEOPLE ?!
THEY'RE FRIENDS, VAN. AND I'VE AGREED TO HELP THEM.
HELP THEM ?
HELP THEM DO WHAT ?!
THE POLICE ARE ON THEIR WAY. WE NEED TO GET OUT OF HERE.
WEE-OO! WEE-OO! WEE-OO!
JUST GET IN THE VAN. WE'LL EXPLAIN EVERY-THING LATER.
I PROMISE.

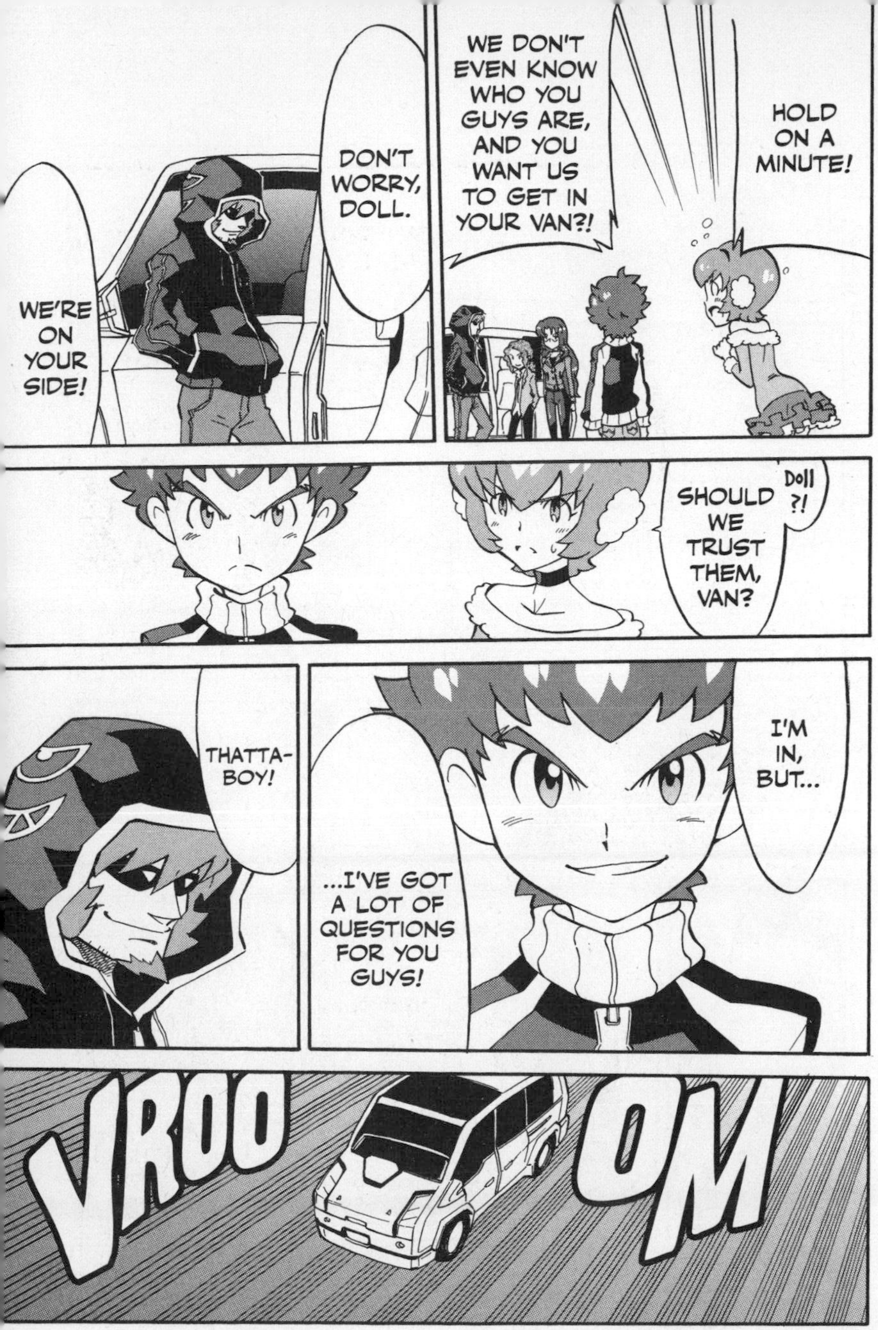
HOLD ON A MINUTE!
WE DON'T EVEN KNOW WHO YOU GUYS ARE, AND YOU WANT US TO GET IN YOUR VAN?!
DON'T WORRY, DOLL.
WE'RE ON YOUR SIDE!
Doll ?!
SHOULD WE TRUST THEM, VAN?
I'M IN, BUT...
...I'VE GOT A LOT OF QUESTIONS FOR YOU GUYS!
THATTA-BOY!
VROO OM

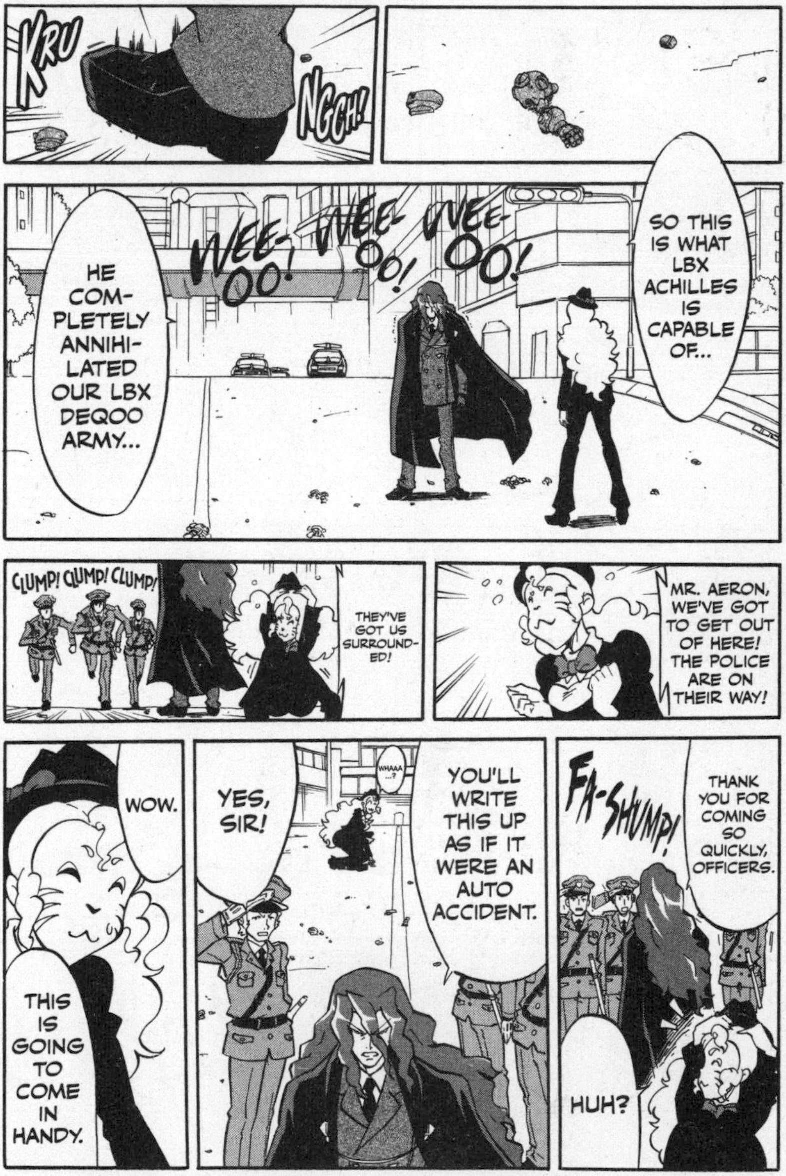
KRU
NGCH!
SO THIS IS WHAT LBX ACHILLES IS CAPABLE OF...
WEE-OO! WEE-OO! WEE-OO!
HE COMPLETELY ANNIHILATED OUR LBX DEQOO ARMY...
MR. AERON, WE'VE GOT TO GET OUT OF HERE! THE POLICE ARE ON THEIR WAY!
THEY'VE GOT US SURROUNDED!
CLUMP! CLUMP! CLUMP!
THANK YOU FOR COMING SO QUICKLY, OFFICERS.
FA-SHUMP!
HUH?
YOU'LL WRITE THIS UP AS IF IT WERE AN AUTO ACCIDENT.
WHAAA...?
YES, SIR!
WOW.
THIS IS GOING TO COME IN HANDY.

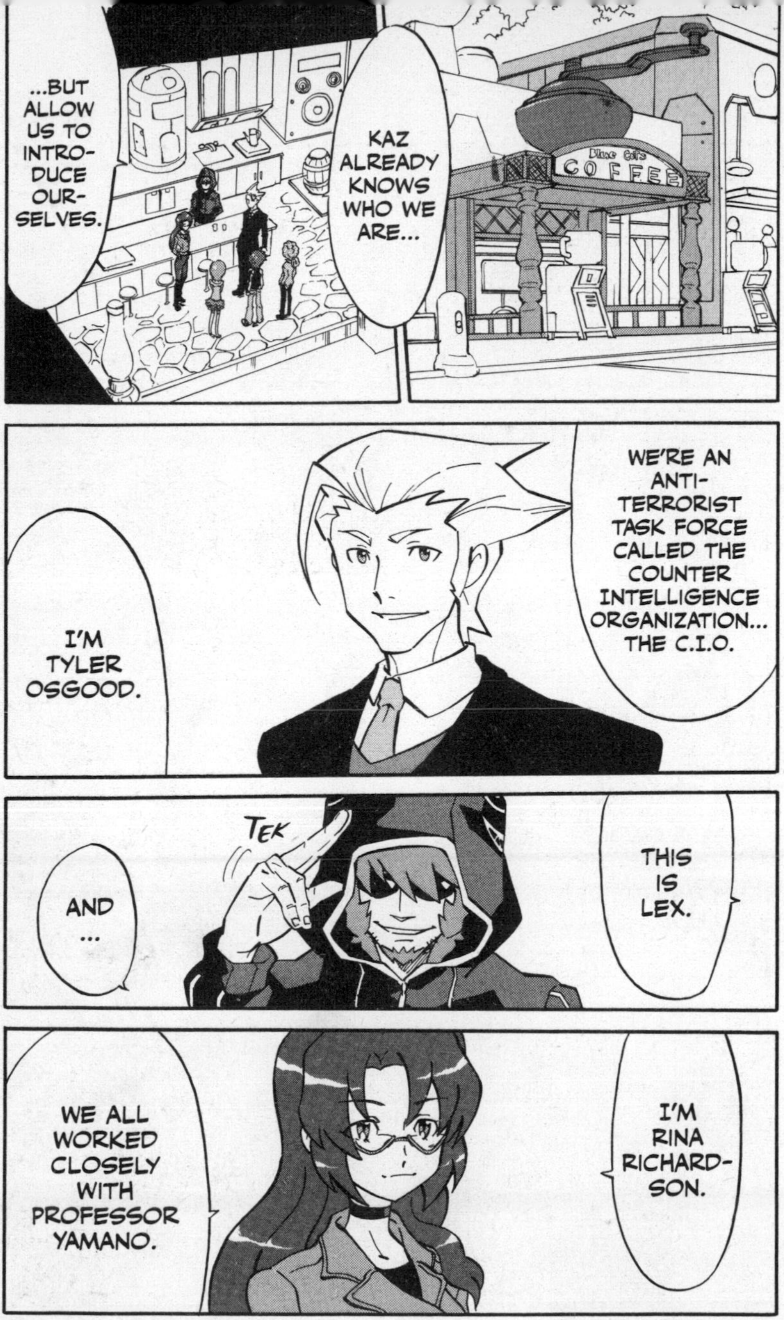
KAZ ALREADY KNOWS WHO WE ARE...
...BUT ALLOW US TO INTRODUCE OURSELVES.
WE'RE AN ANTI-TERRORIST TASK FORCE CALLED THE COUNTER INTELLIGENCE ORGANIZATION... THE C.I.O.
I'M TYLER OSGOOD.
THIS IS LEX.
TEK
AND ...
I'M RINA RICHARDSON.
WE ALL WORKED CLOSELY WITH PROFESSOR YAMANO.

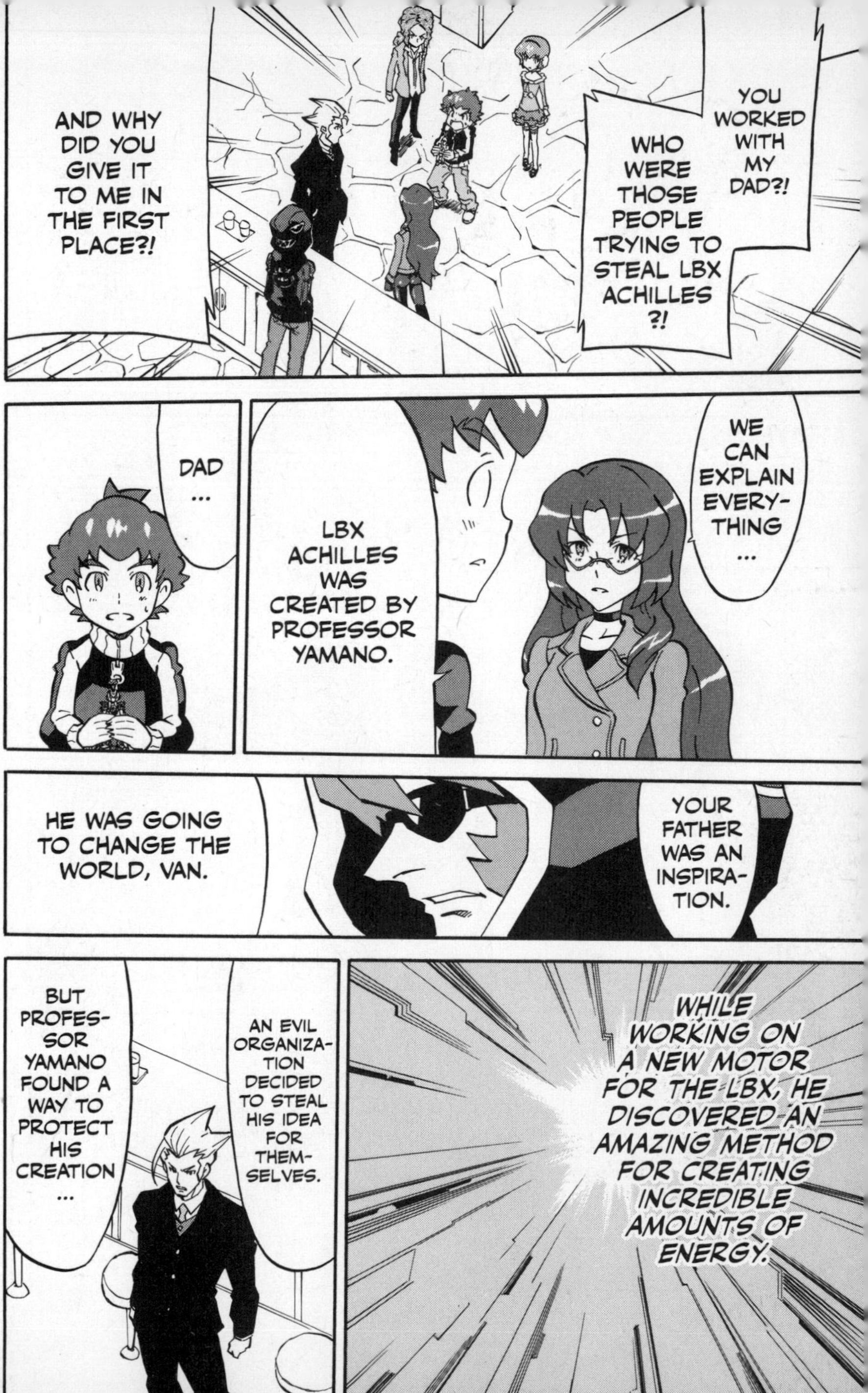
YOU WORKED WITH MY DAD?!
WHO WERE THOSE PEOPLE TRYING TO STEAL LBX ACHILLES ?!
AND WHY DID YOU GIVE IT TO ME IN THE FIRST PLACE?!
WE CAN EXPLAIN EVERY-THING ...
LBX ACHILLES WAS CREATED BY PROFESSOR YAMANO.
DAD ...
YOUR FATHER WAS AN INSPIRA-TION.
HE WAS GOING TO CHANGE THE WORLD, VAN.
WHILE WORKING ON A NEW MOTOR FOR THE LBX, HE DISCOVERED AN AMAZING METHOD FOR CREATING INCREDIBLE AMOUNTS OF ENERGY.
AN EVIL ORGANIZA-TION DECIDED TO STEAL HIS IDEA FOR THEM-SELVES.
BUT PROFES-SOR YAMANO FOUND A WAY TO PROTECT HIS CREATION ...

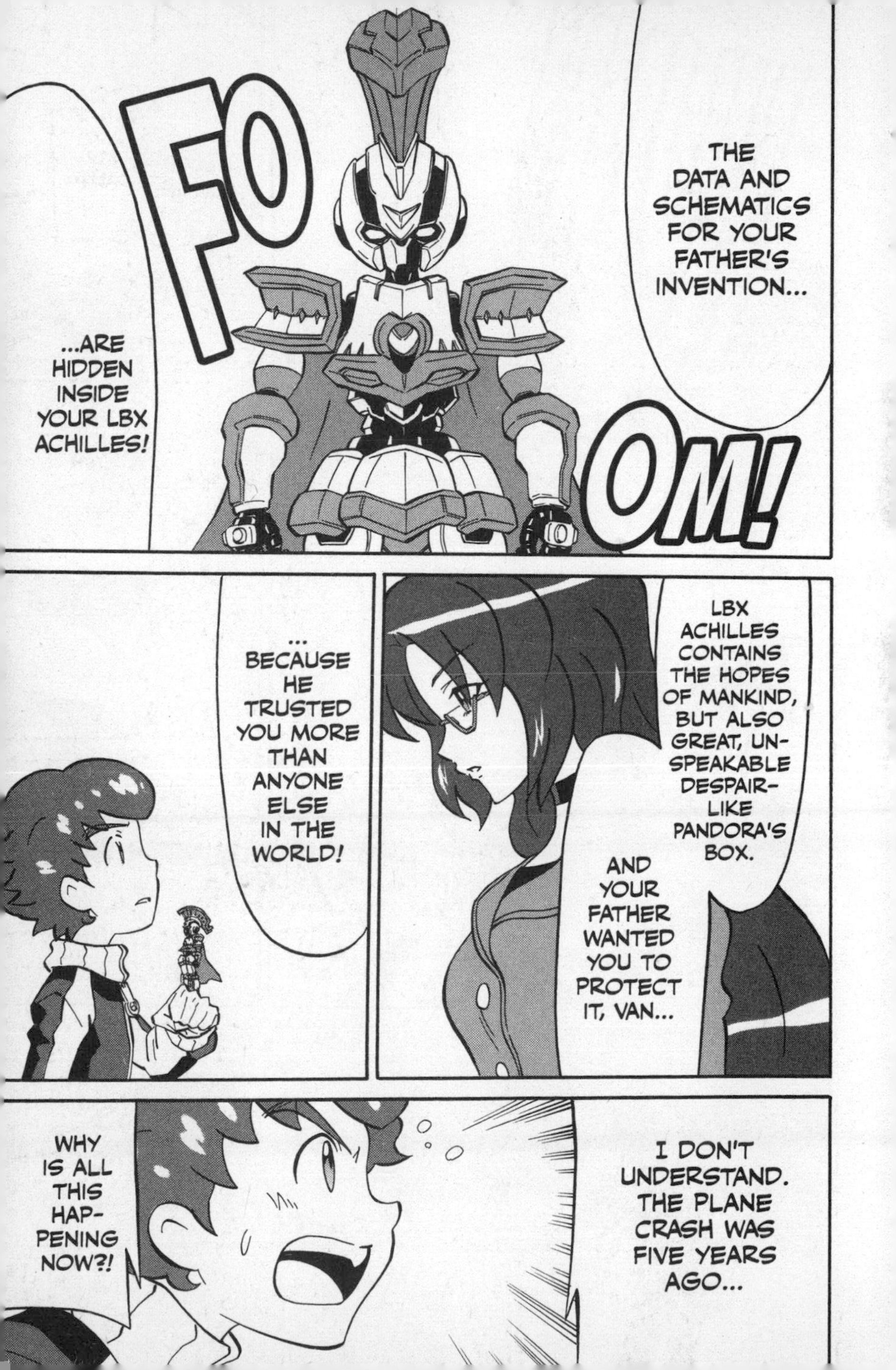
THE DATA AND SCHEMATICS FOR YOUR FATHER'S INVENTION...
FOOM!
...ARE HIDDEN INSIDE YOUR LBX ACHILLES!
LBX ACHILLES CONTAINS THE HOPES OF MANKIND, BUT ALSO GREAT, UN-SPEAKABLE DESPAIR-LIKE PANDORA'S BOX.
AND YOUR FATHER WANTED YOU TO PROTECT IT, VAN...
... BECAUSE HE TRUSTED YOU MORE THAN ANYONE ELSE IN THE WORLD!
I DON'T UNDERSTAND. THE PLANE CRASH WAS FIVE YEARS AGO...
WHY IS ALL THIS HAP-PENING NOW?!

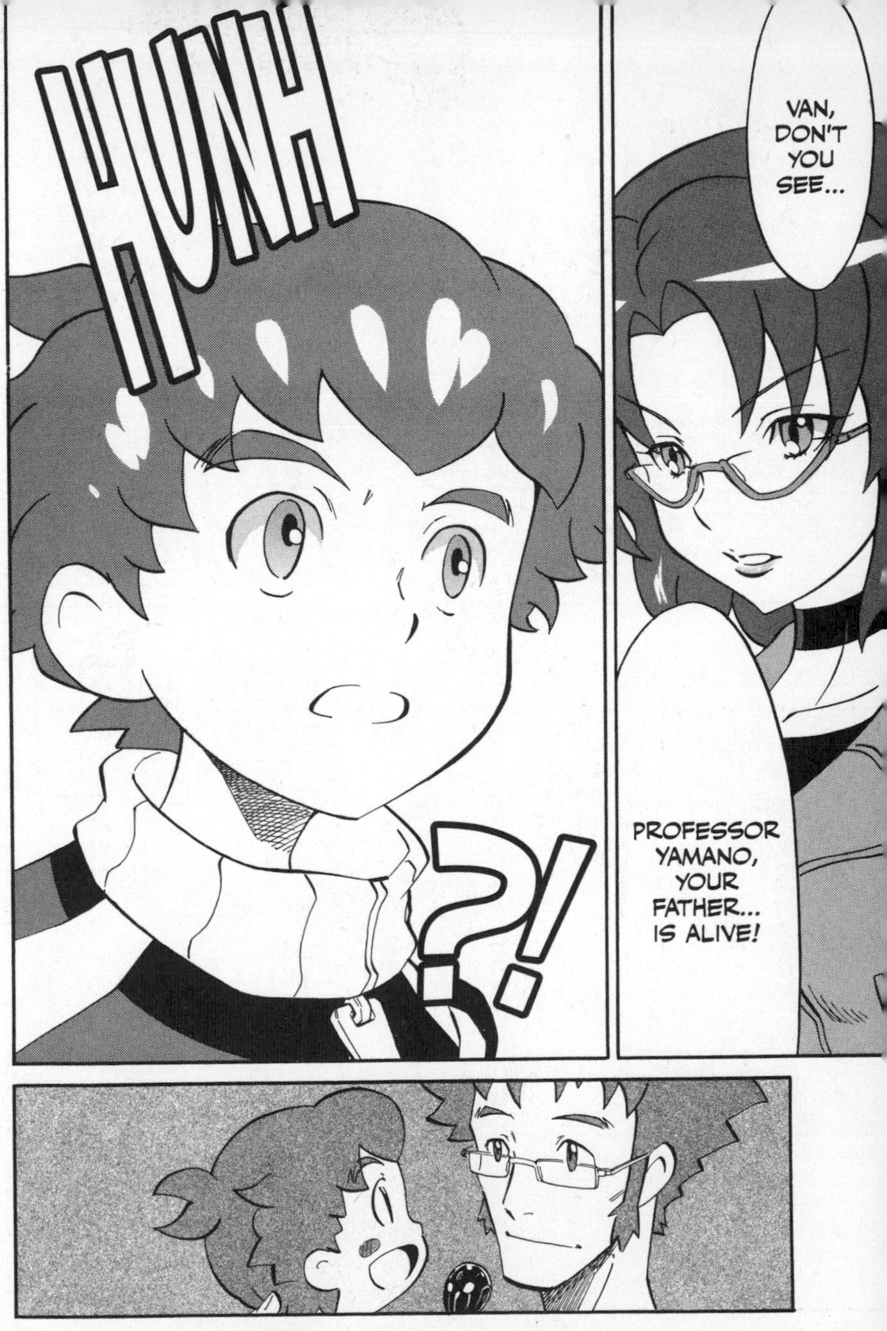
VAN, DON'T YOU SEE...
PROFESSOR YAMANO, YOUR FATHER... IS ALIVE!
HUNH
?!

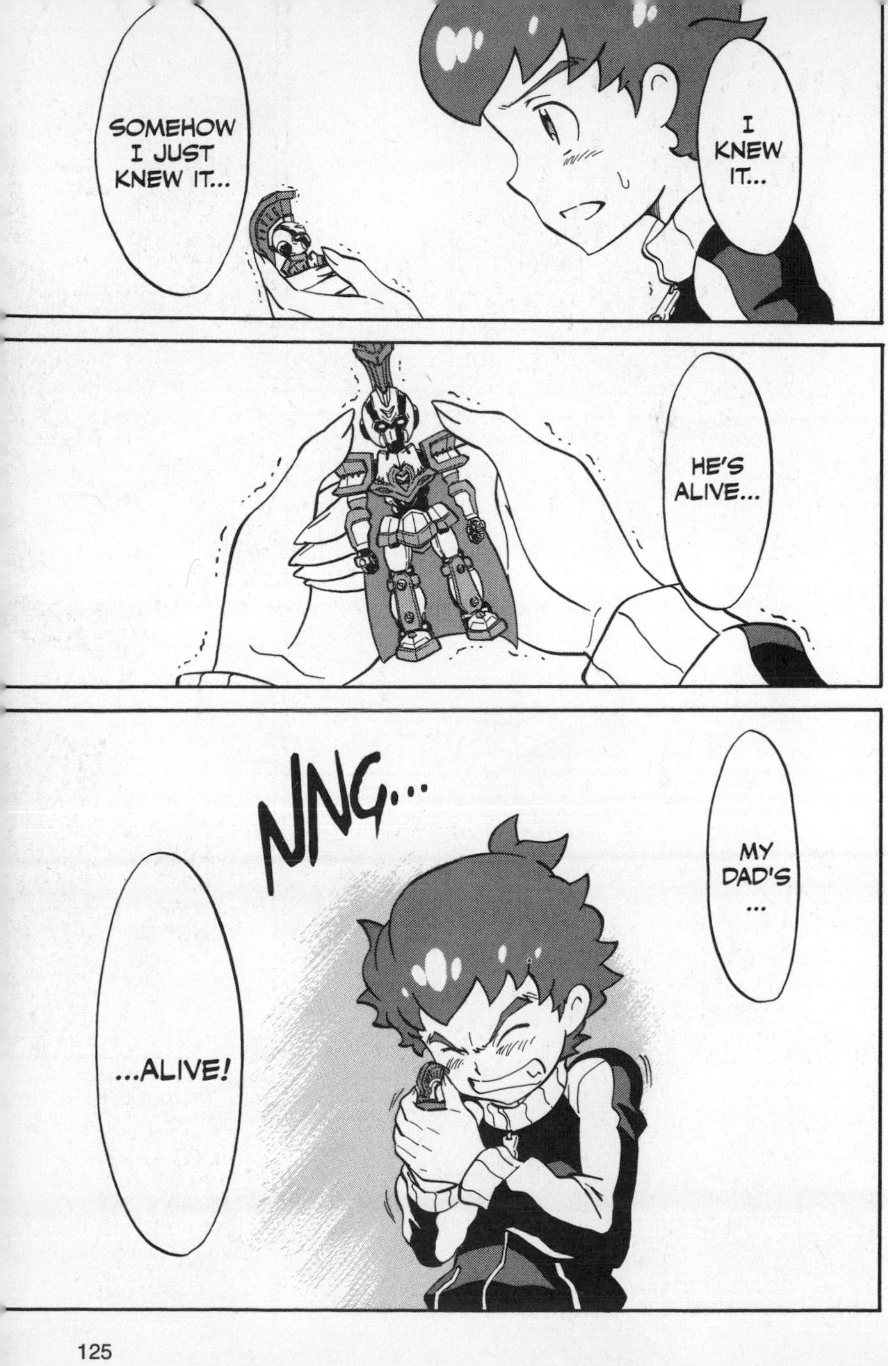
I KNEW IT...
SOMEHOW I JUST KNEW IT...
HE'S ALIVE...
MY DAD'S ...
NNG...
...ALIVE!

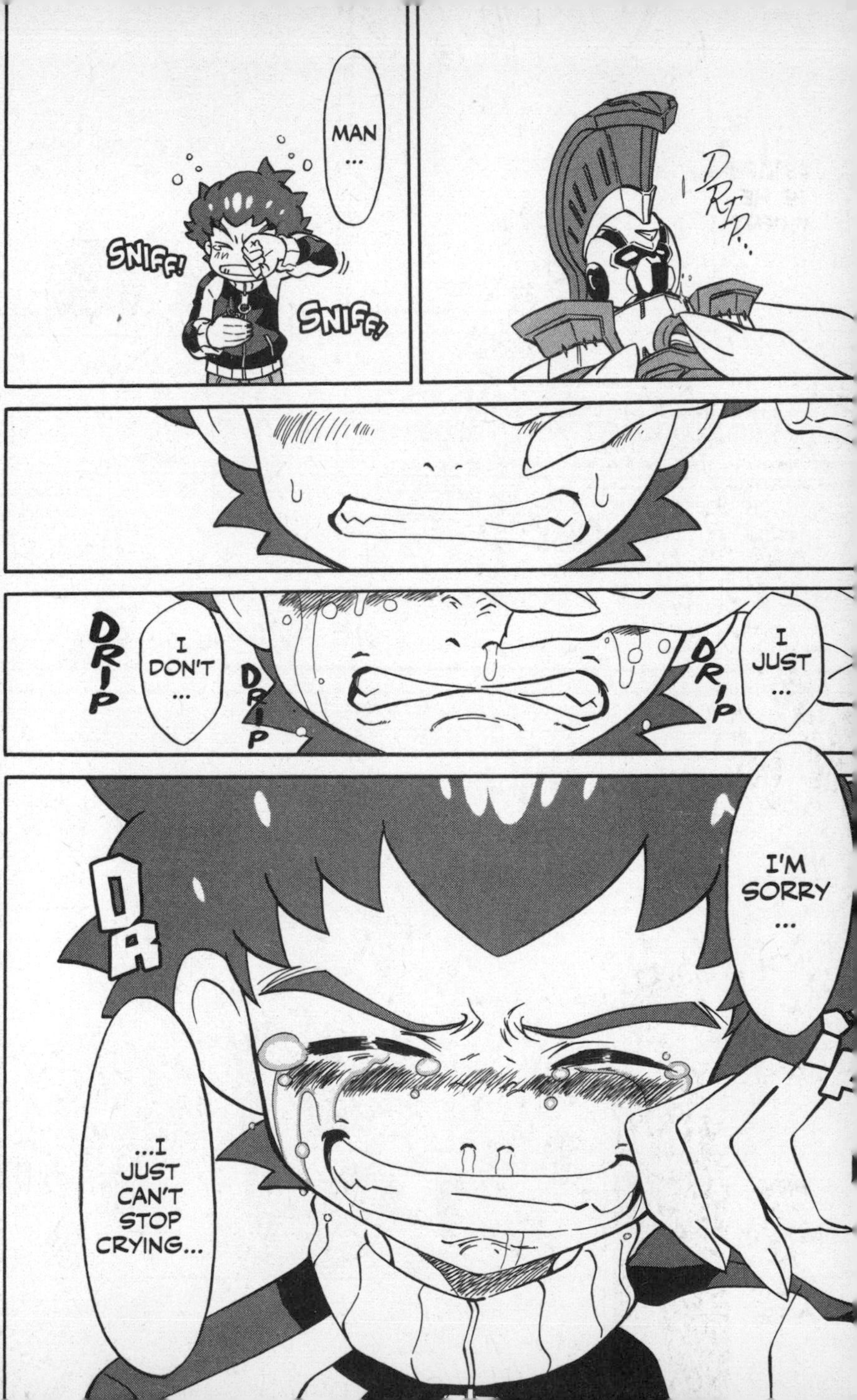
DRIP...
MAN...
SNIFF!
SNIFF!
I JUST...
DRIP
DRIP
I DON'T...
DRIP
I'M SORRY...
DR
...I JUST CAN'T STOP CRYING...

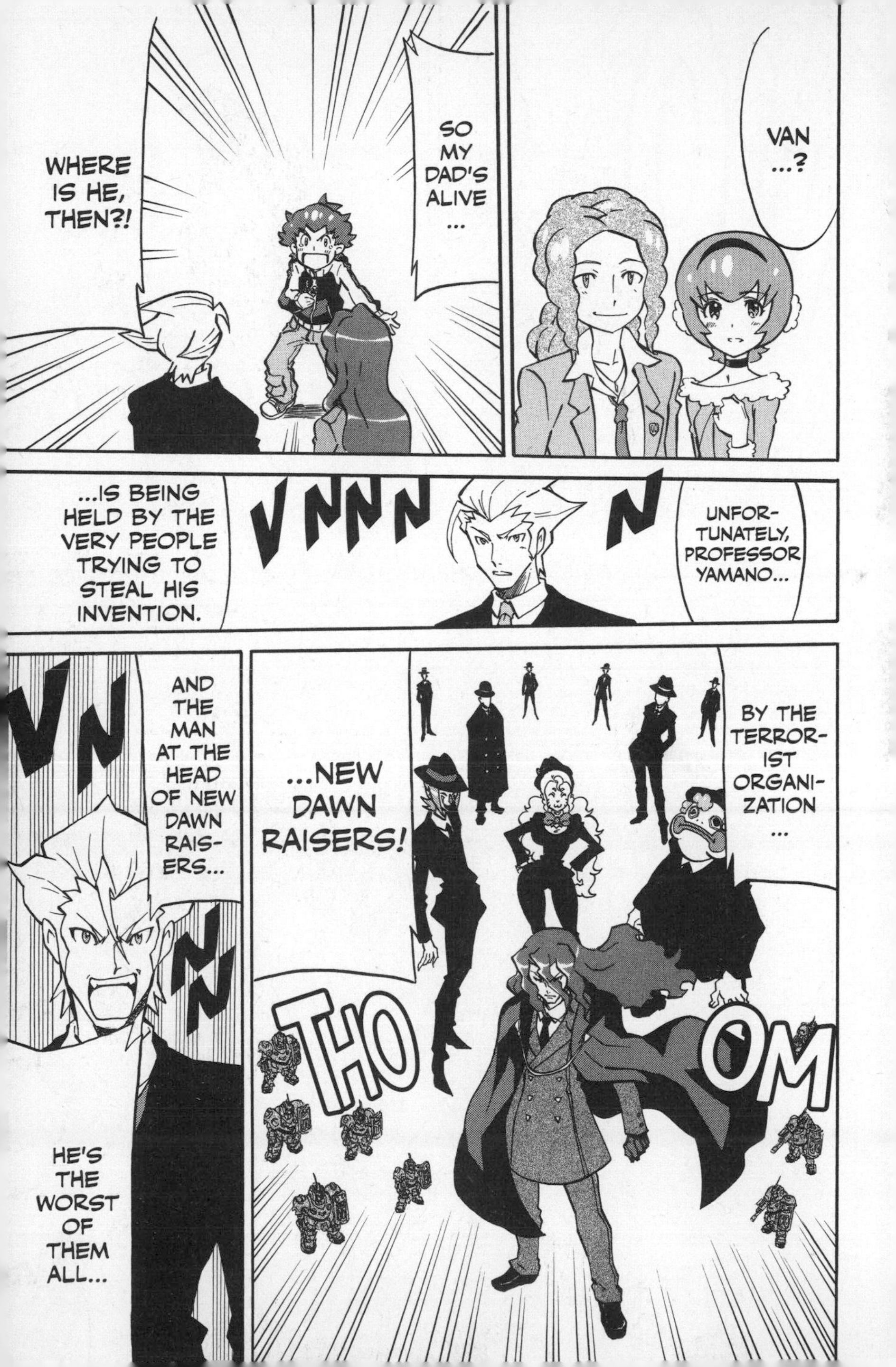
VAN ...?
SO MY DAD'S ALIVE ...
WHERE IS HE, THEN?!
UNFORTUNATELY, PROFESSOR YAMANO...
VNNNN
...IS BEING HELD BY THE VERY PEOPLE TRYING TO STEAL HIS INVENTION.
BY THE TERRORIST ORGANIZATION ...
...NEW DAWN RAISERS!
THOOM
AND THE MAN AT THE HEAD OF NEW DAWN RAISERS...
VNNN
HE'S THE WORST OF THEM ALL...

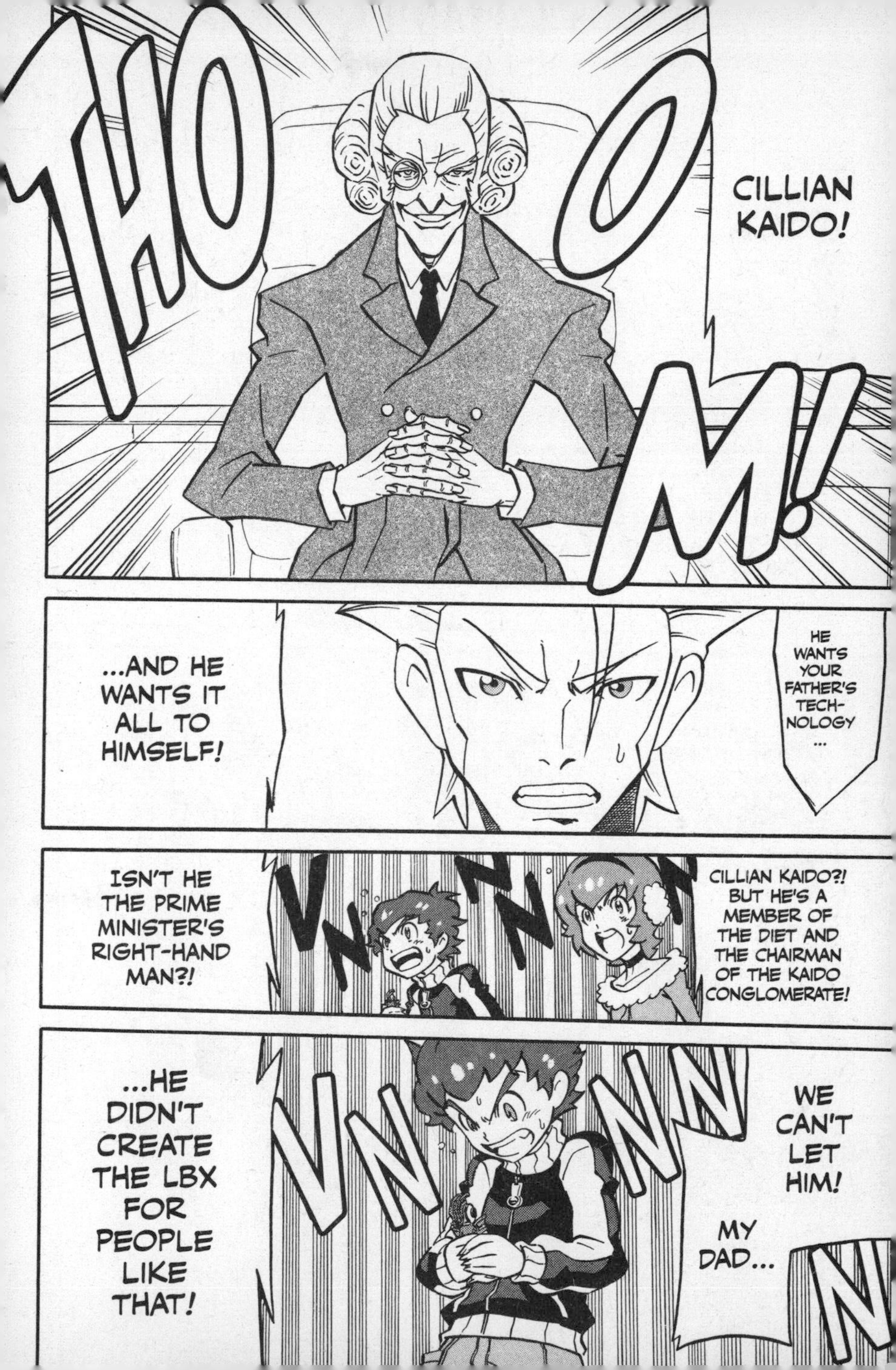
CILLIAN KAIDO!
THOOOM!
HE WANTS YOUR FATHER'S TECH-NOLOGY ...
...AND HE WANTS IT ALL TO HIMSELF!
CILLIAN KAIDO?! BUT HE'S A MEMBER OF THE DIET AND THE CHAIRMAN OF THE KAIDO CONGLOMERATE!
ISN'T HE THE PRIME MINISTER'S RIGHT-HAND MAN?!
WE CAN'T LET HIM!
MY DAD...
...HE DIDN'T CREATE THE LBX FOR PEOPLE LIKE THAT!

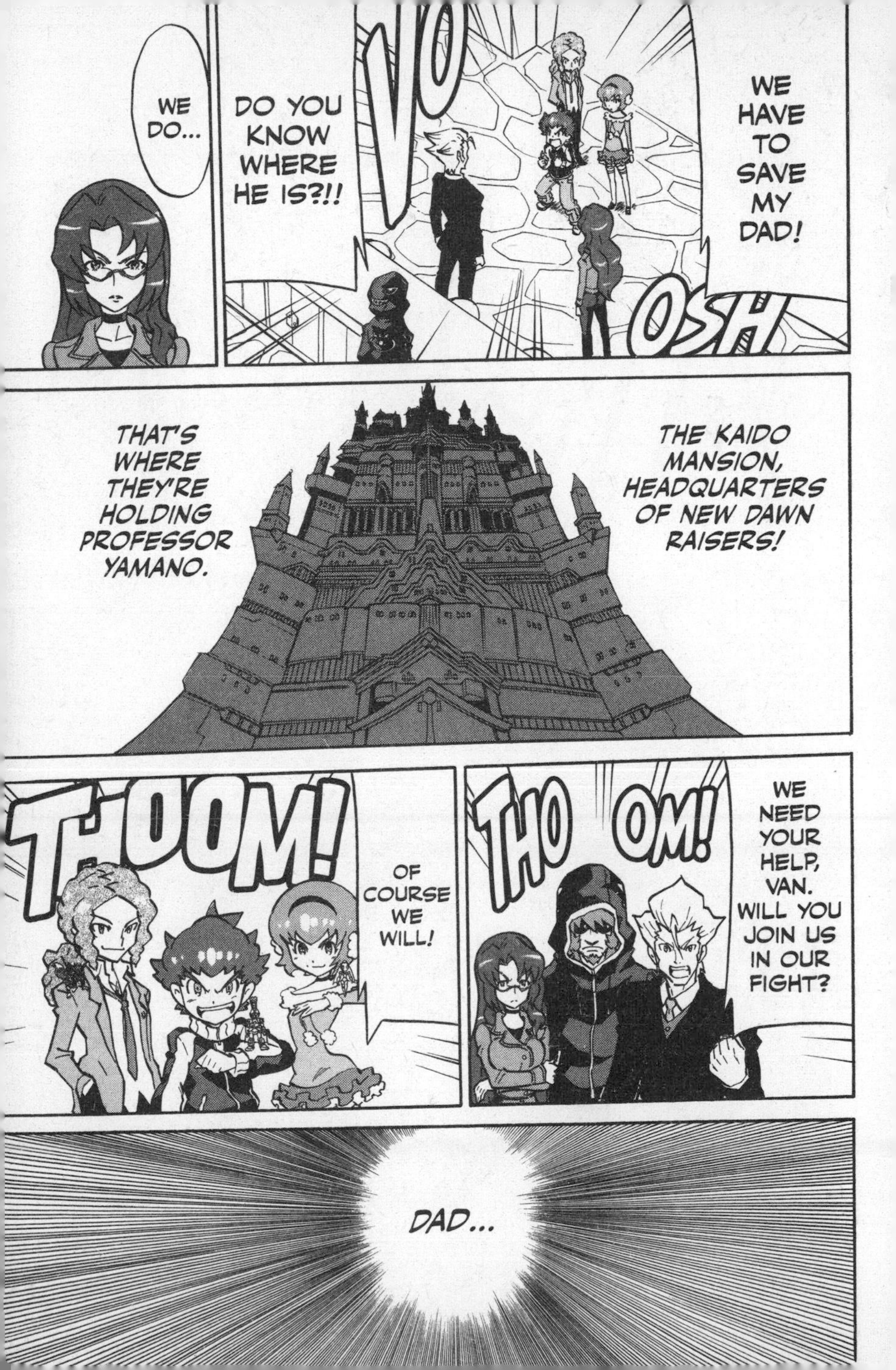

WE HAVE TO SAVE MY DAD!
VO
OSH
DO YOU KNOW WHERE HE IS?!!
WE DO...
THE KAIDO MANSION, HEADQUARTERS OF NEW DAWN RAISERS!
THAT'S WHERE THEY'RE HOLDING PROFESSOR YAMANO.
WE NEED YOUR HELP, VAN. WILL YOU JOIN US IN OUR FIGHT?
THO
OM!
OF COURSE WE WILL!
THOOM!
DAD...

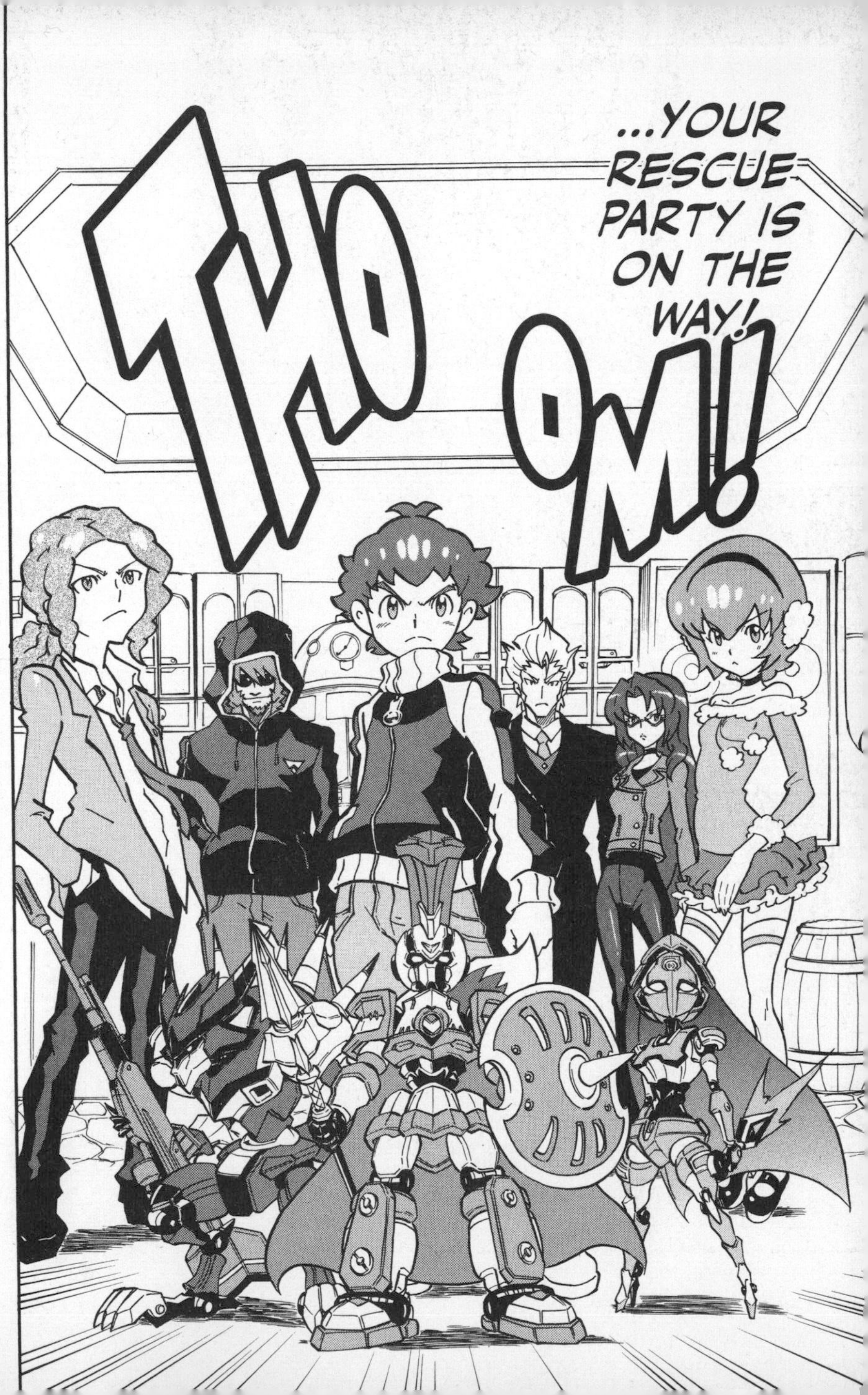
...YOUR RESCUE PARTY IS ON THE WAY!
THOOM!

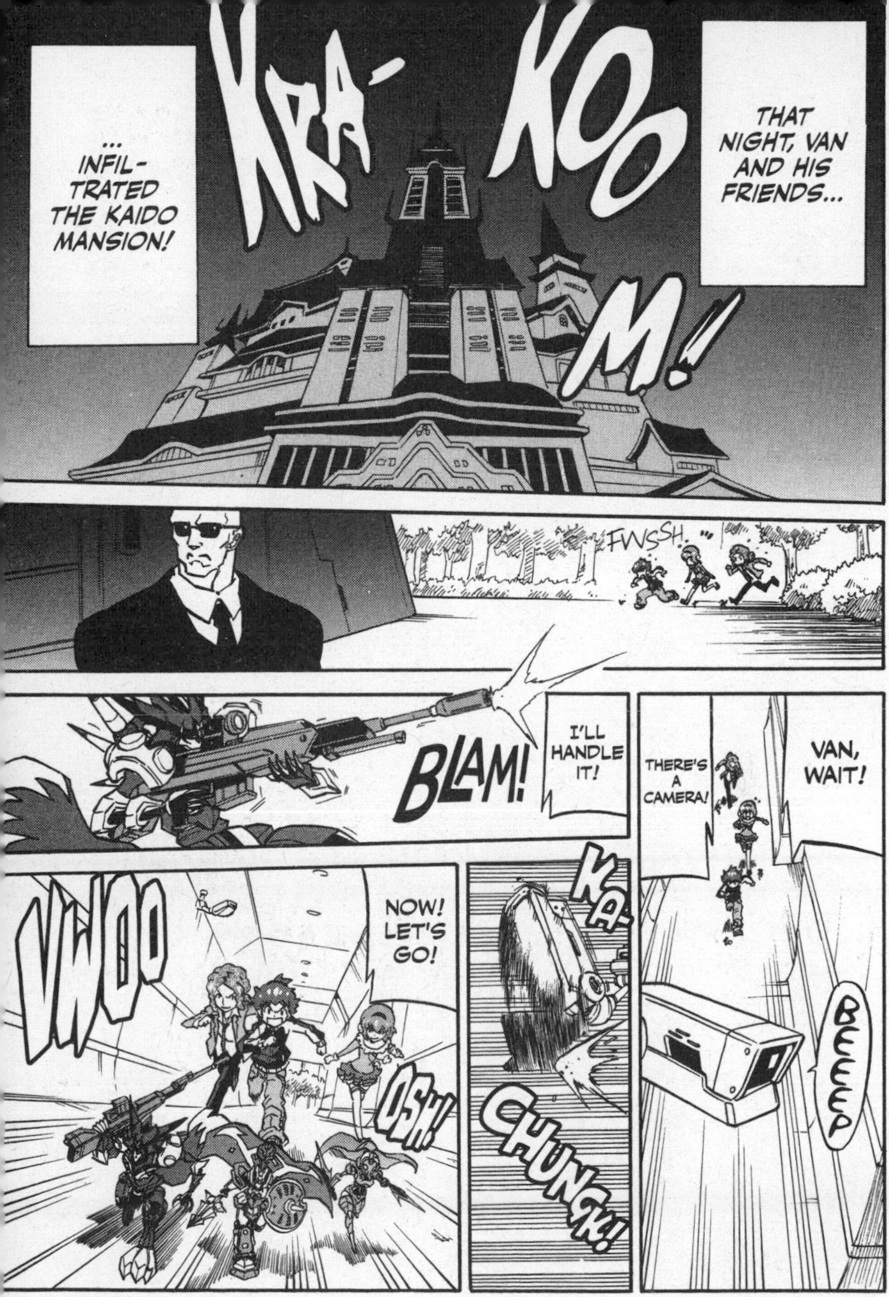
THAT NIGHT, VAN AND HIS FRIENDS...
KRA-KOOM!
...INFIL-TRATED THE KAIDO MANSION!
FWSSH
VAN, WAIT!
THERE'S A CAMERA!
BEEEP
I'LL HANDLE IT!
BLAM!
KA-CHUNCK!
NOW! LET'S GO!
VWOO
OSH!

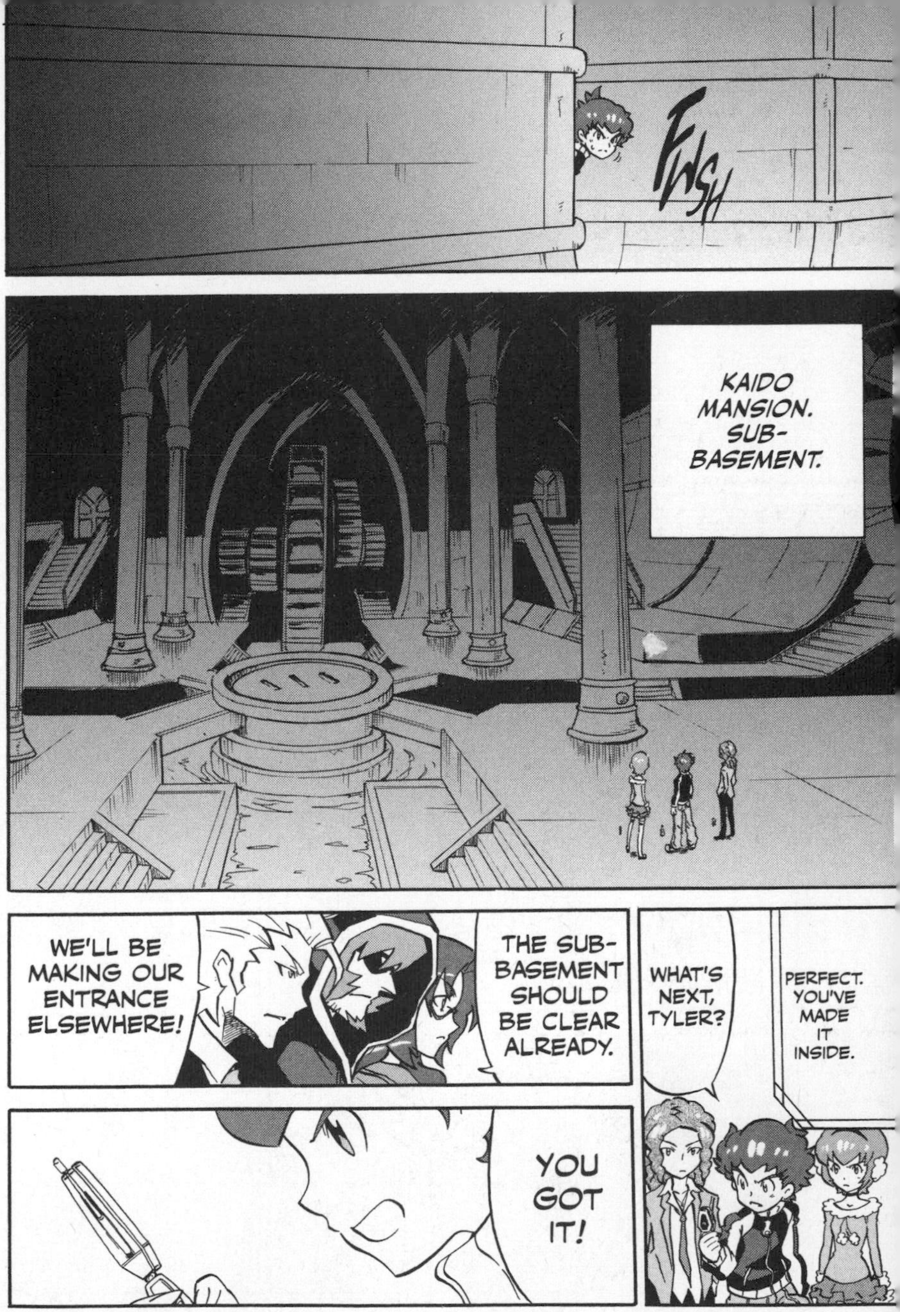
FWSH
KAIDO MANSION. SUB-BASEMENT.
PERFECT. YOU'VE MADE IT INSIDE.
WHAT'S NEXT, TYLER?
THE SUB-BASEMENT SHOULD BE CLEAR ALREADY.
WE'LL BE MAKING OUR ENTRANCE ELSEWHERE!
YOU GOT IT!

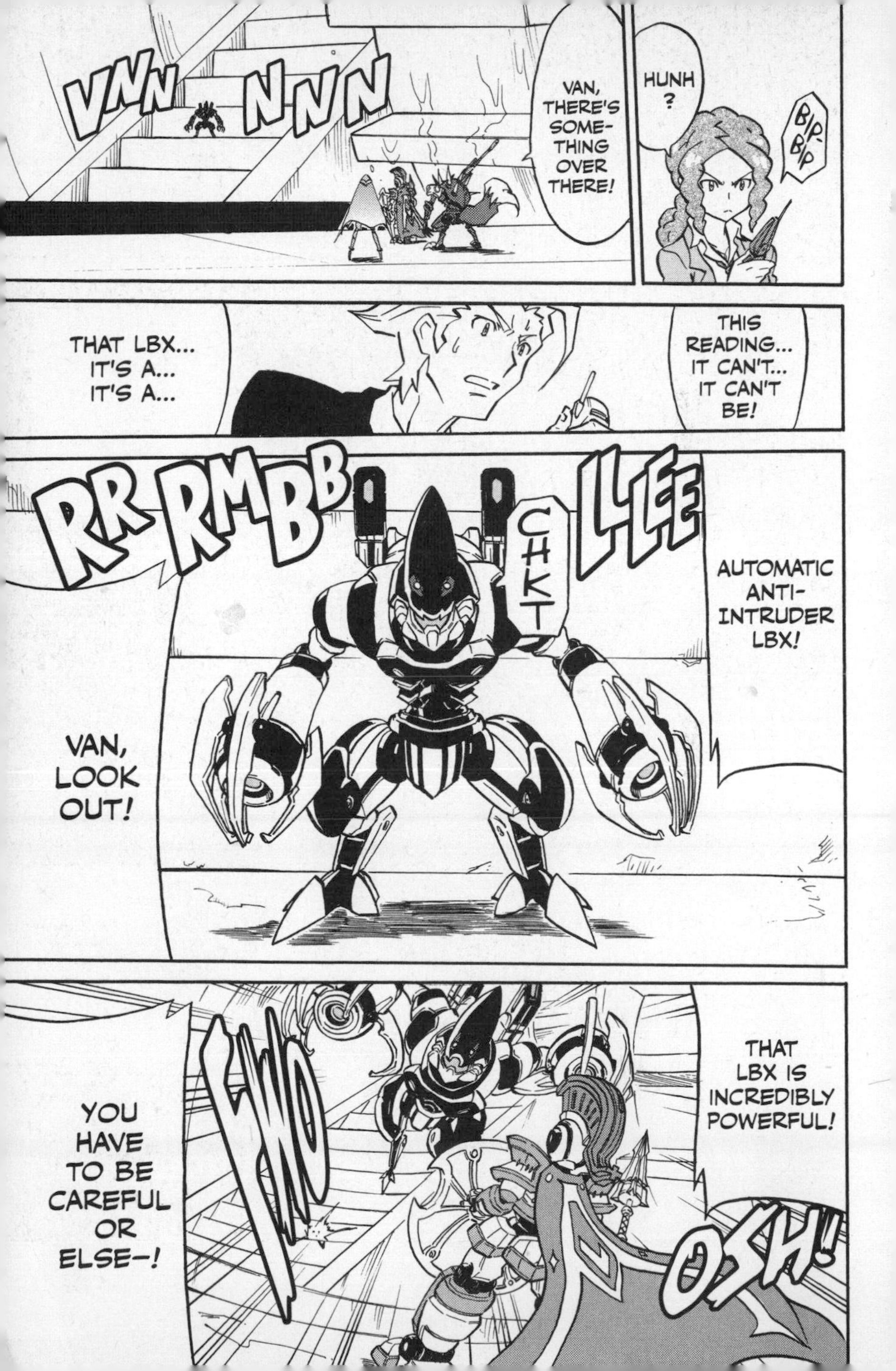
HUNH?
BIP-BIP
VAN, THERE'S SOMETHING OVER THERE!
VNN NNN
THIS READING... IT CAN'T... IT CAN'T BE!
THAT LBX... IT'S A... IT'S A...
AUTOMATIC ANTI-INTRUDER LBX!
RRRMBBLLEE
CHKT
VAN, LOOK OUT!
THAT LBX IS INCREDIBLY POWERFUL!
SWO
OSH!
YOU HAVE TO BE CAREFUL OR ELSE—!

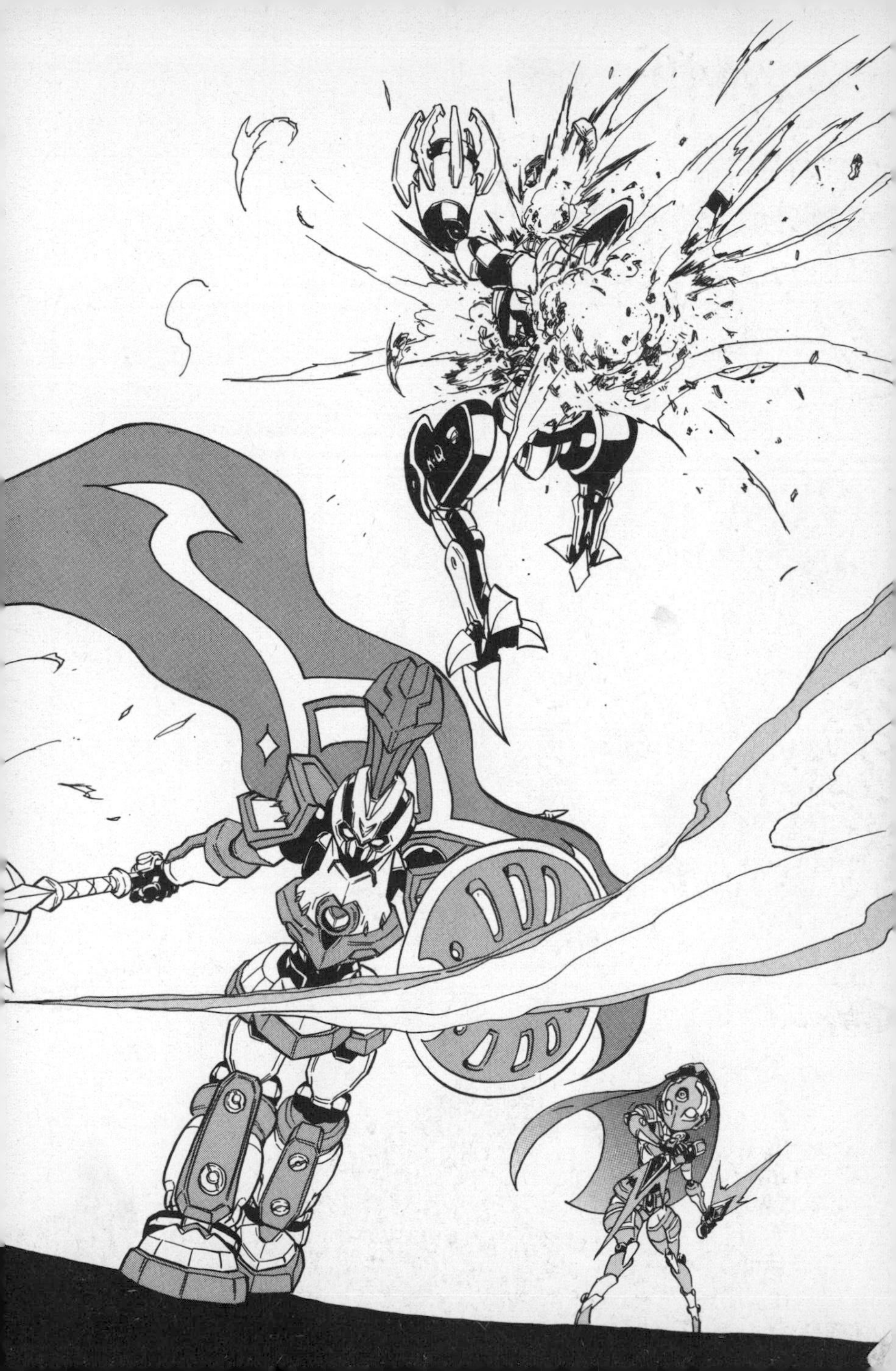

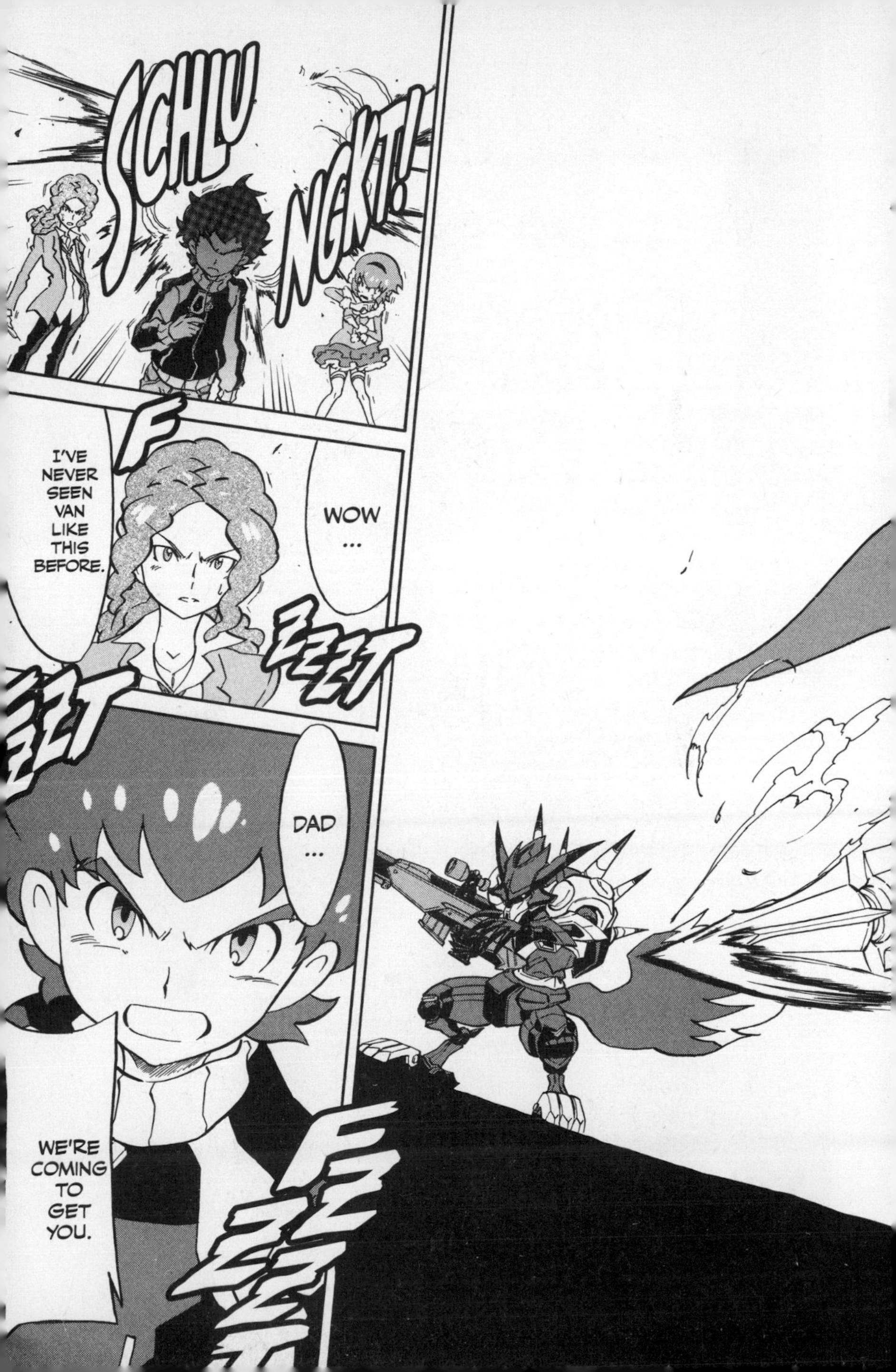
SCHLUNGKT!
WOW...
I'VE NEVER SEEN VAN LIKE THIS BEFORE.
ZZZT
ZZZT
DAD...
WE'RE COMING TO GET YOU.

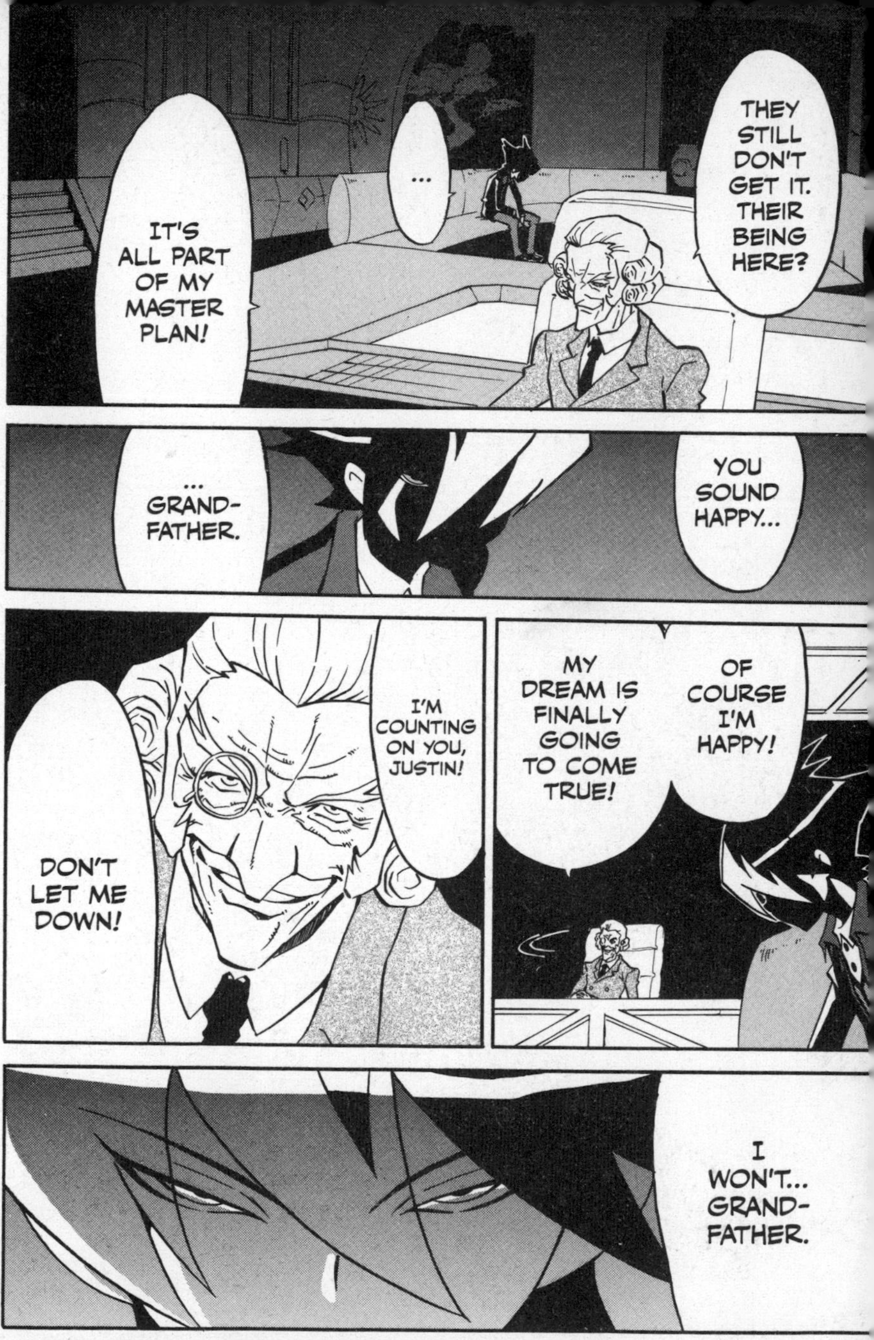
THEY STILL DON'T GET IT. THEIR BEING HERE?
...
IT'S ALL PART OF MY MASTER PLAN!
YOU SOUND HAPPY...
... GRAND-FATHER.
OF COURSE I'M HAPPY!
MY DREAM IS FINALLY GOING TO COME TRUE!
I'M COUNTING ON YOU, JUSTIN!
DON'T LET ME DOWN!
I WON'T... GRAND-FATHER.

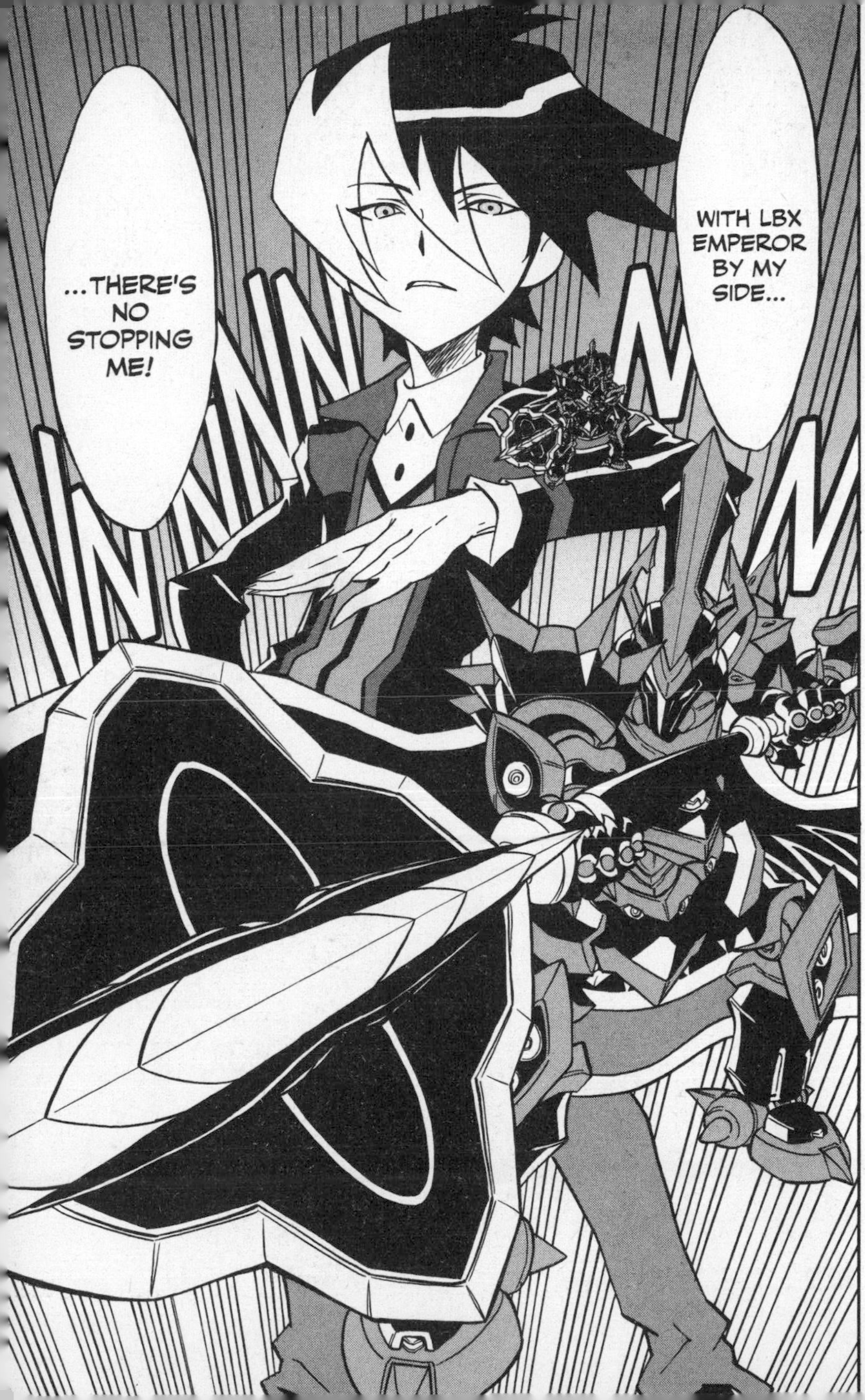
WITH LBX EMPEROR BY MY SIDE...
...THERE'S NO STOPPING ME!

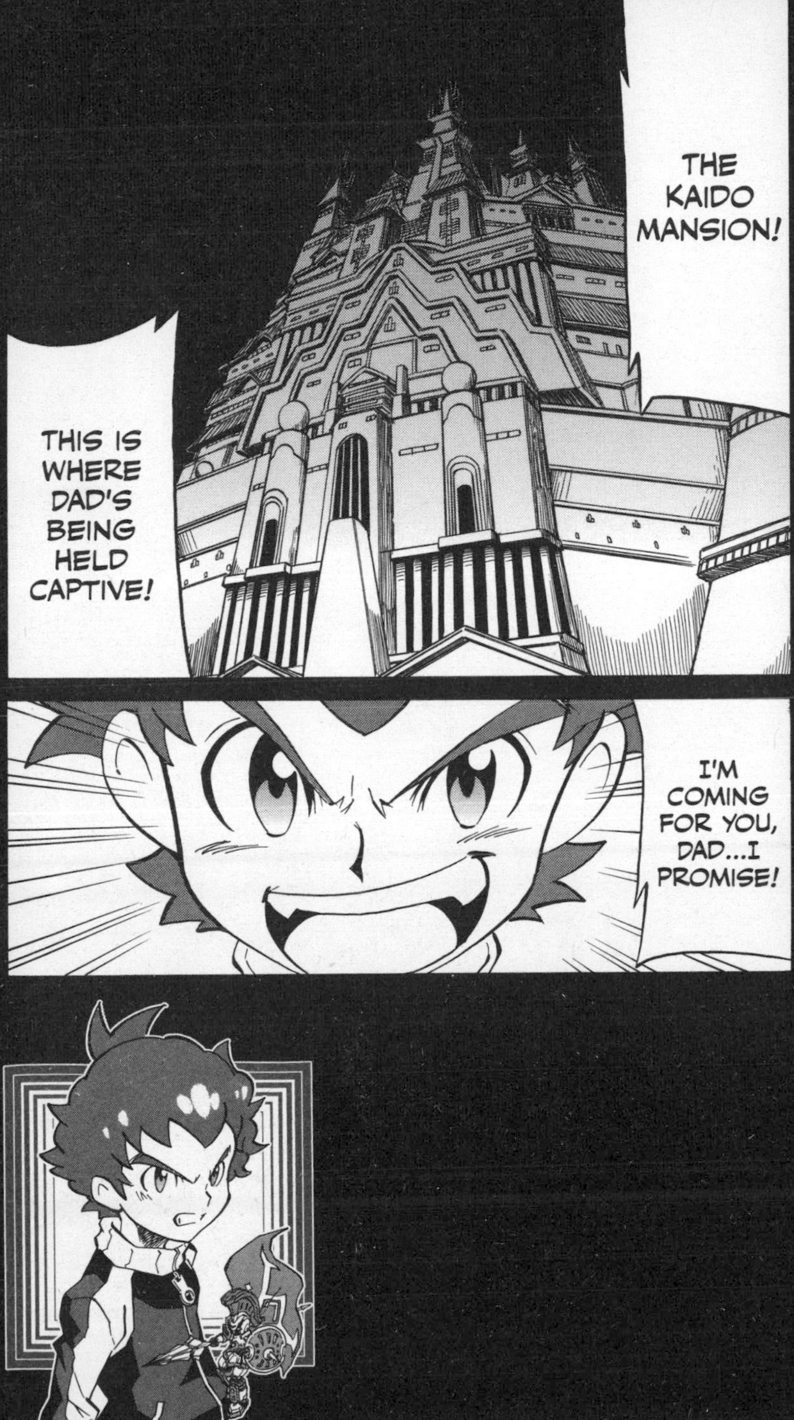
THE KAIDO MANSION!
THIS IS WHERE DAD'S BEING HELD CAPTIVE!
I'M COMING FOR YOU, DAD...I PROMISE!

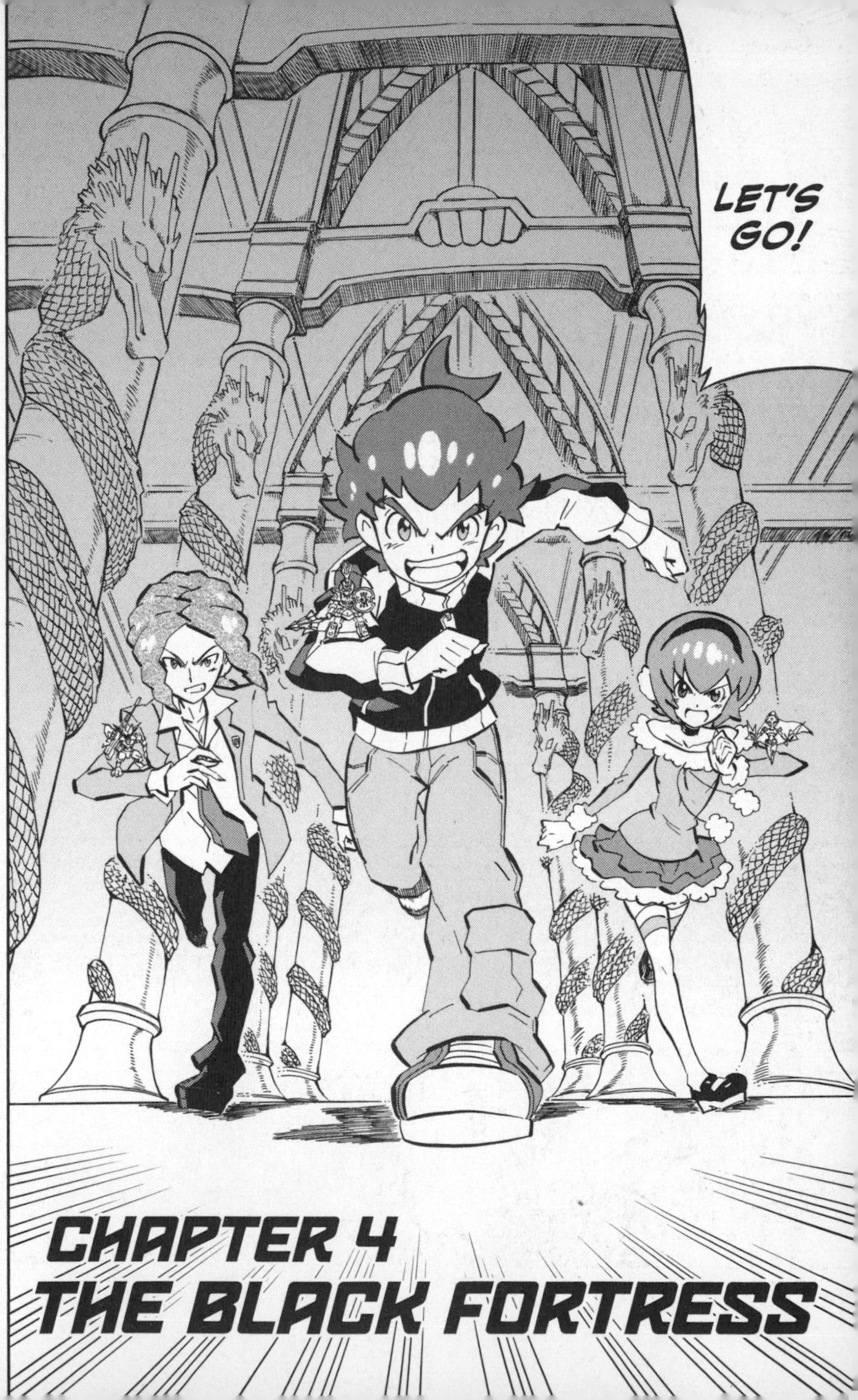
LET'S GO!
CHAPTER 4
THE BLACK FORTRESS

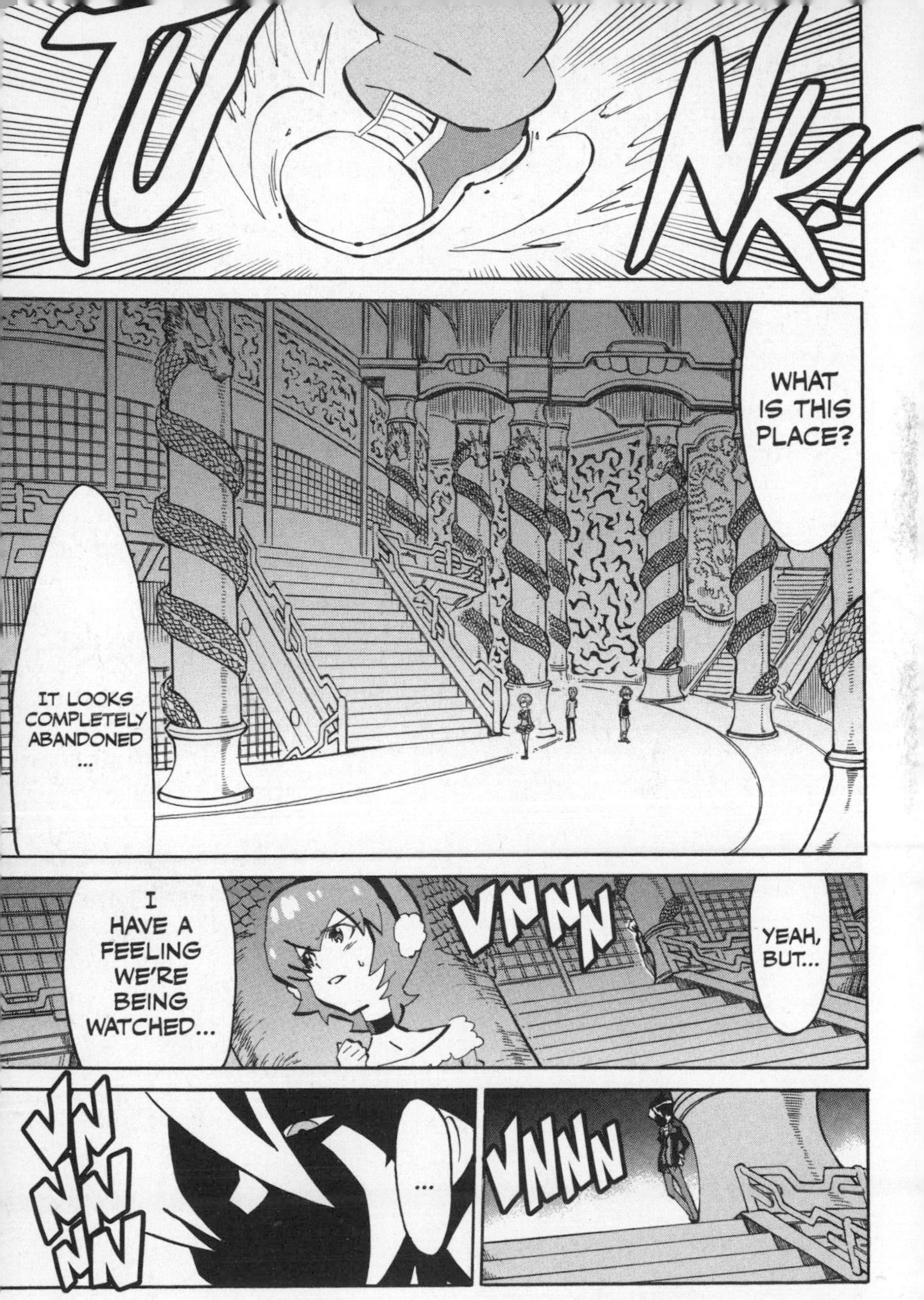
TU NK!!
WHAT IS THIS PLACE?
IT LOOKS COMPLETELY ABANDONED ...
YEAH, BUT...
VNNN
I HAVE A FEELING WE'RE BEING WATCHED...
VNNN
...
VNNNNN

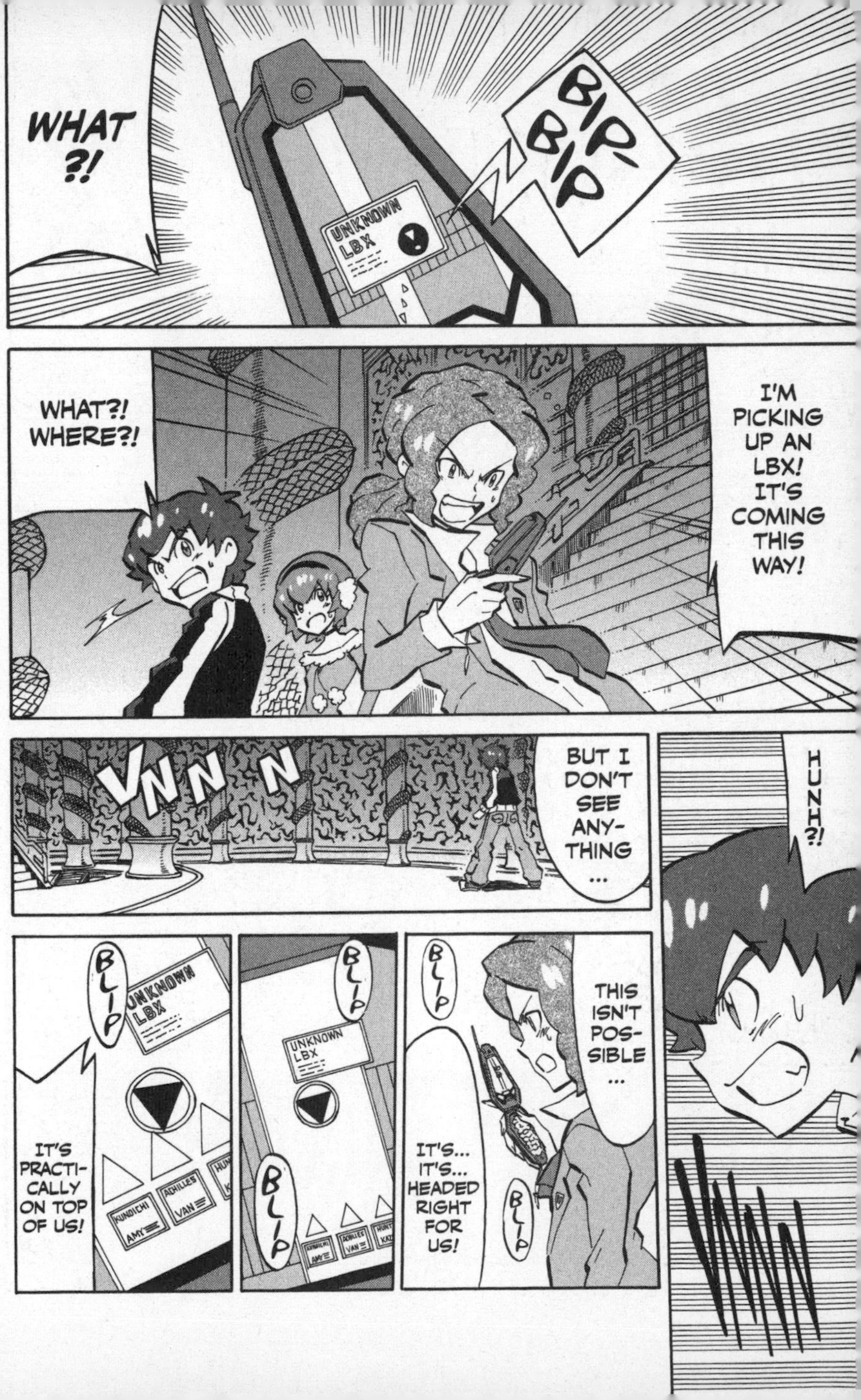
BIP-BIP-BIP
UNKNOWN LBX
WHAT ?!
I'M PICKING UP AN LBX! IT'S COMING THIS WAY!
WHAT?! WHERE?!
HUNH?!
VNNN
BUT I DON'T SEE ANY-THING ...
VNN N
BLIP
THIS ISN'T POS-SIBLE ...
IT'S... IT'S... HEADED RIGHT FOR US!
BLIP
BLIP
UNKNOWN LBX
BLIP
KUNOICHI AMY
ACHILLES VAN
BLIP
UNKNOWN LBX
KUNOICHI AMY
ACHILLES VAN
IT'S PRACTI-CALLY ON TOP OF US!

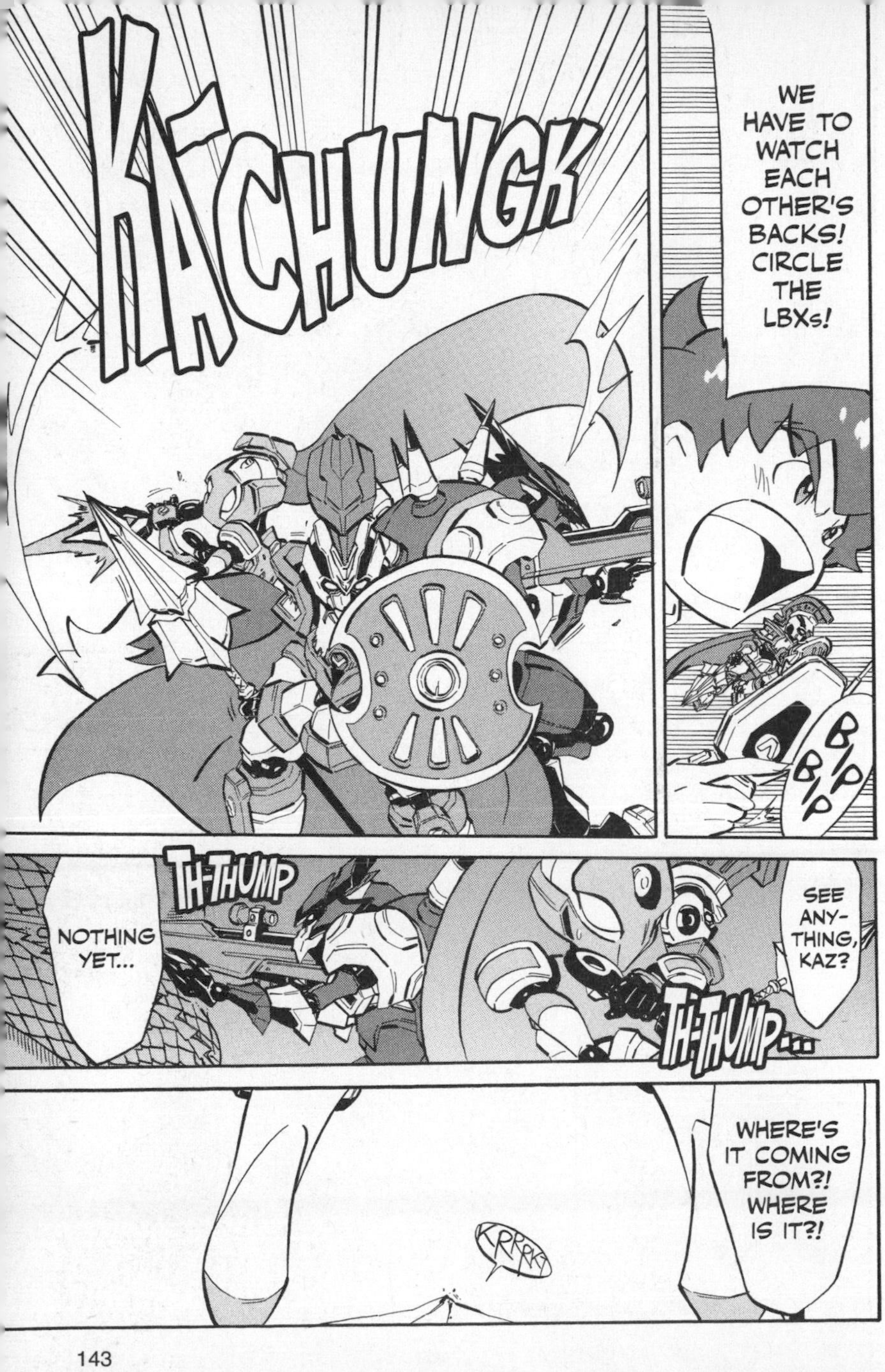
WE HAVE TO WATCH EACH OTHER'S BACKS! CIRCLE THE LBXs!
BIP BIP
KACHUNGK
SEE ANY-THING, KAZ?
TH-THUMP...
TH-THUMP
NOTHING YET...
WHERE'S IT COMING FROM?! WHERE IS IT?!
KRRRK

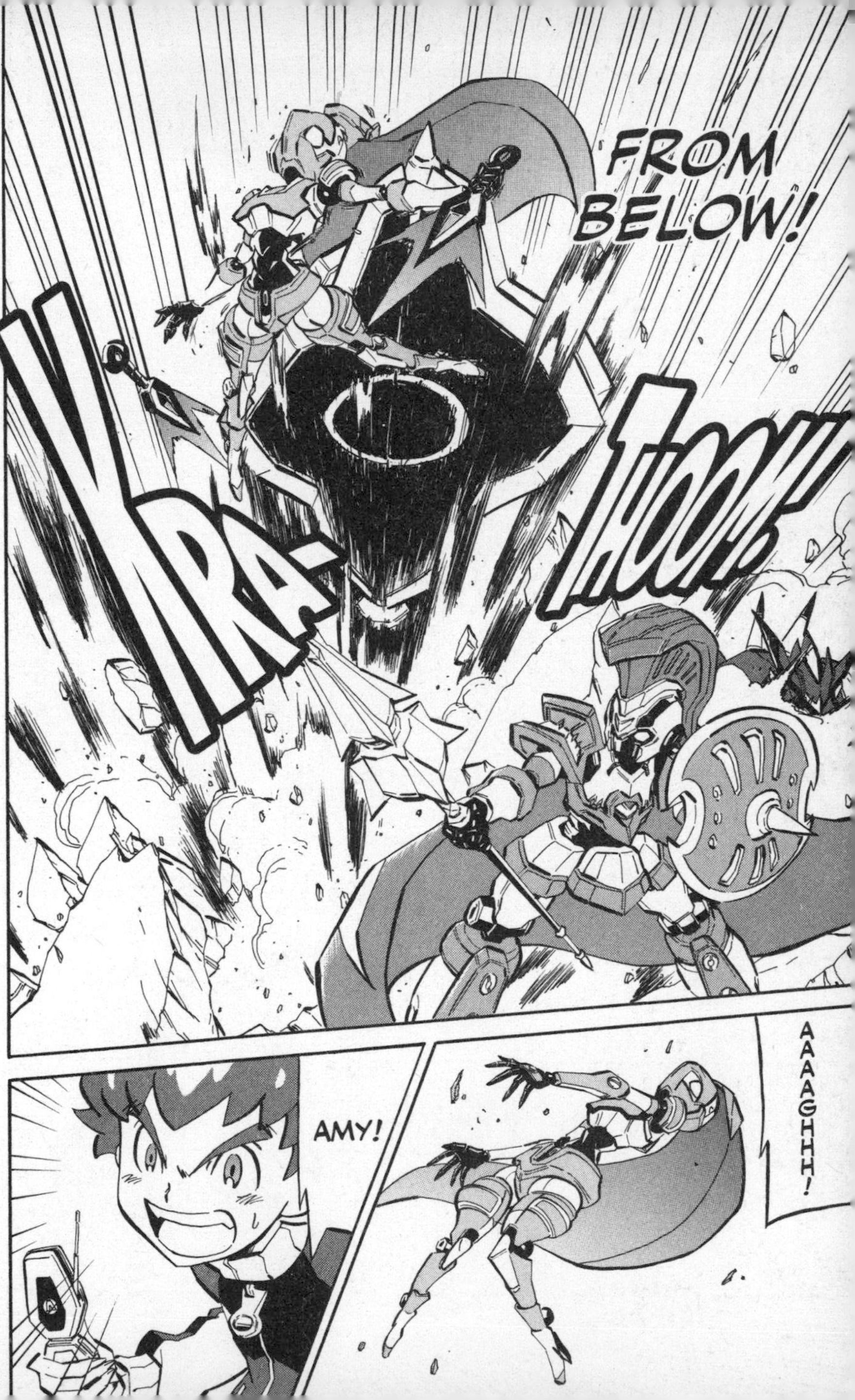
FROM BELOW!
VRRA-
THOOM!
AAAAGHHH!
AMY!

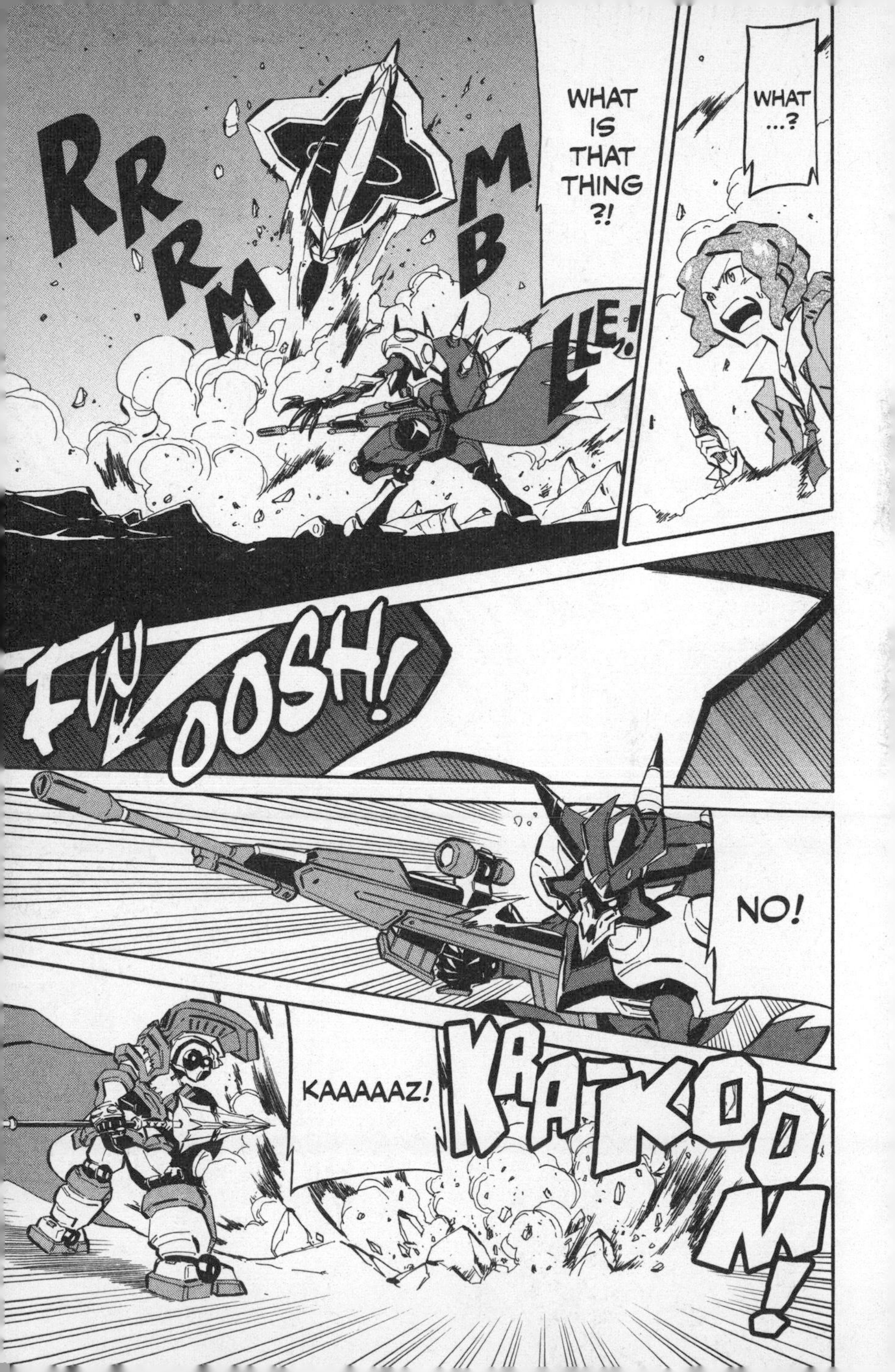
WHAT ...?
WHAT IS THAT THING?!
RRRMMMBLLE!!
FWOOSH!
NO!
KAAAAAZ!
KRA-KOOOM!

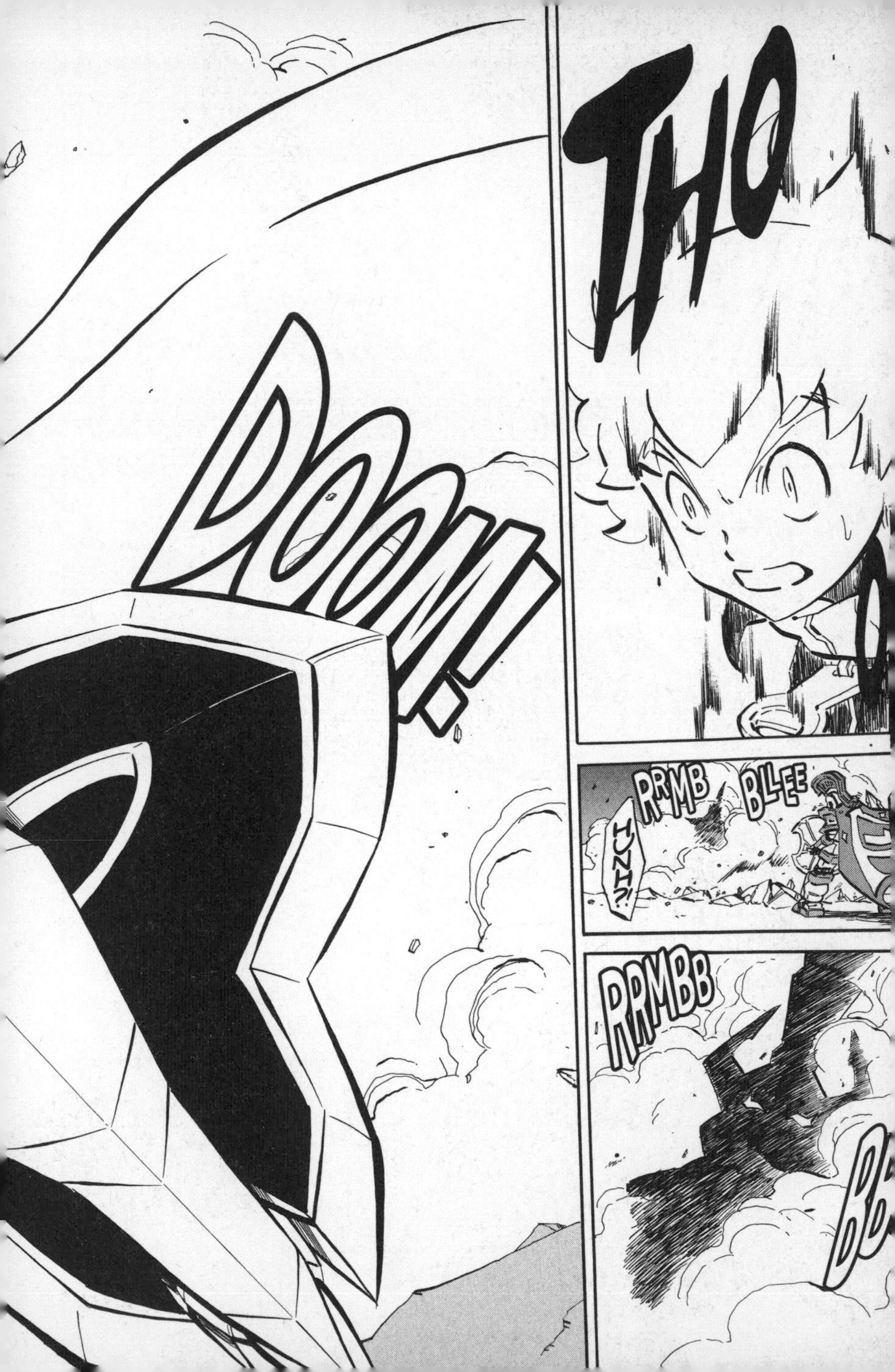
THO
RRMB
BLLEE
HUNH?!
RRMBB
BE
DOOOM!

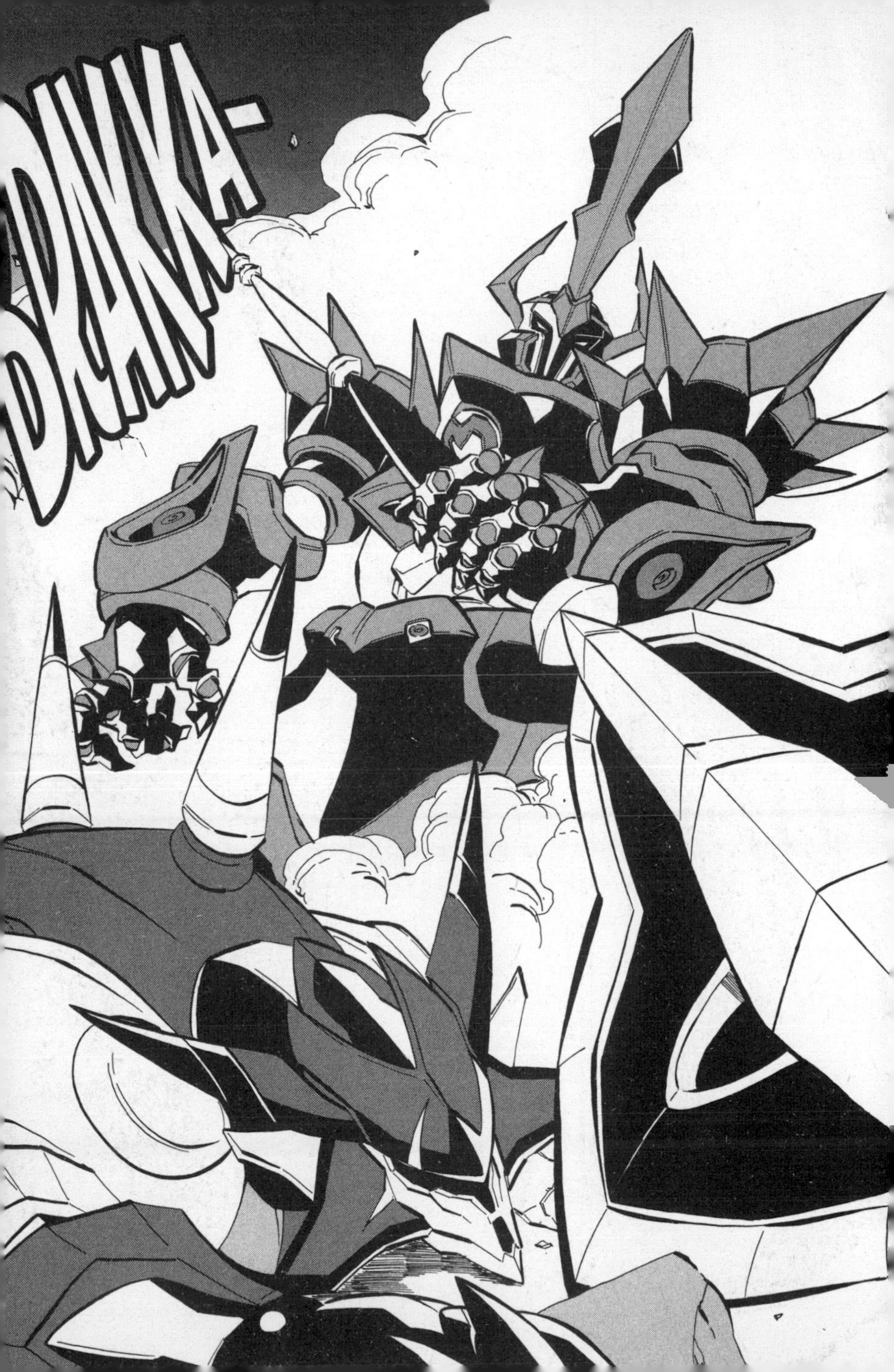
DANKA-

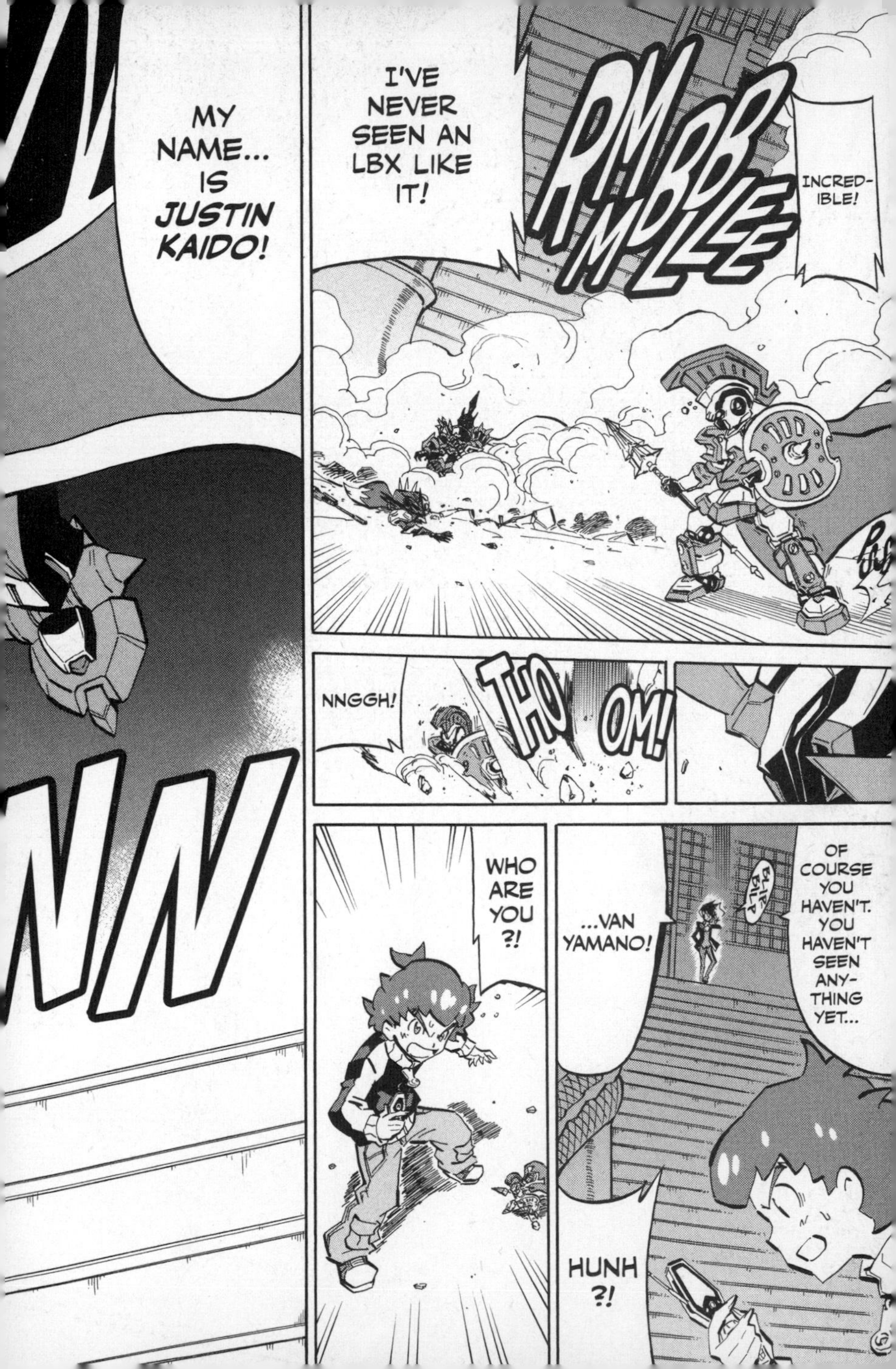
INCRED-IBLE!
I'VE NEVER SEEN AN LBX LIKE IT!
THOOM!
NNGGH!
OF COURSE YOU HAVEN'T. YOU HAVEN'T SEEN ANY-THING YET...
BLIP BLIP
...VAN YAMANO!
HUNH?!
WHO ARE YOU?!
MY NAME... IS JUSTIN KAIDO!

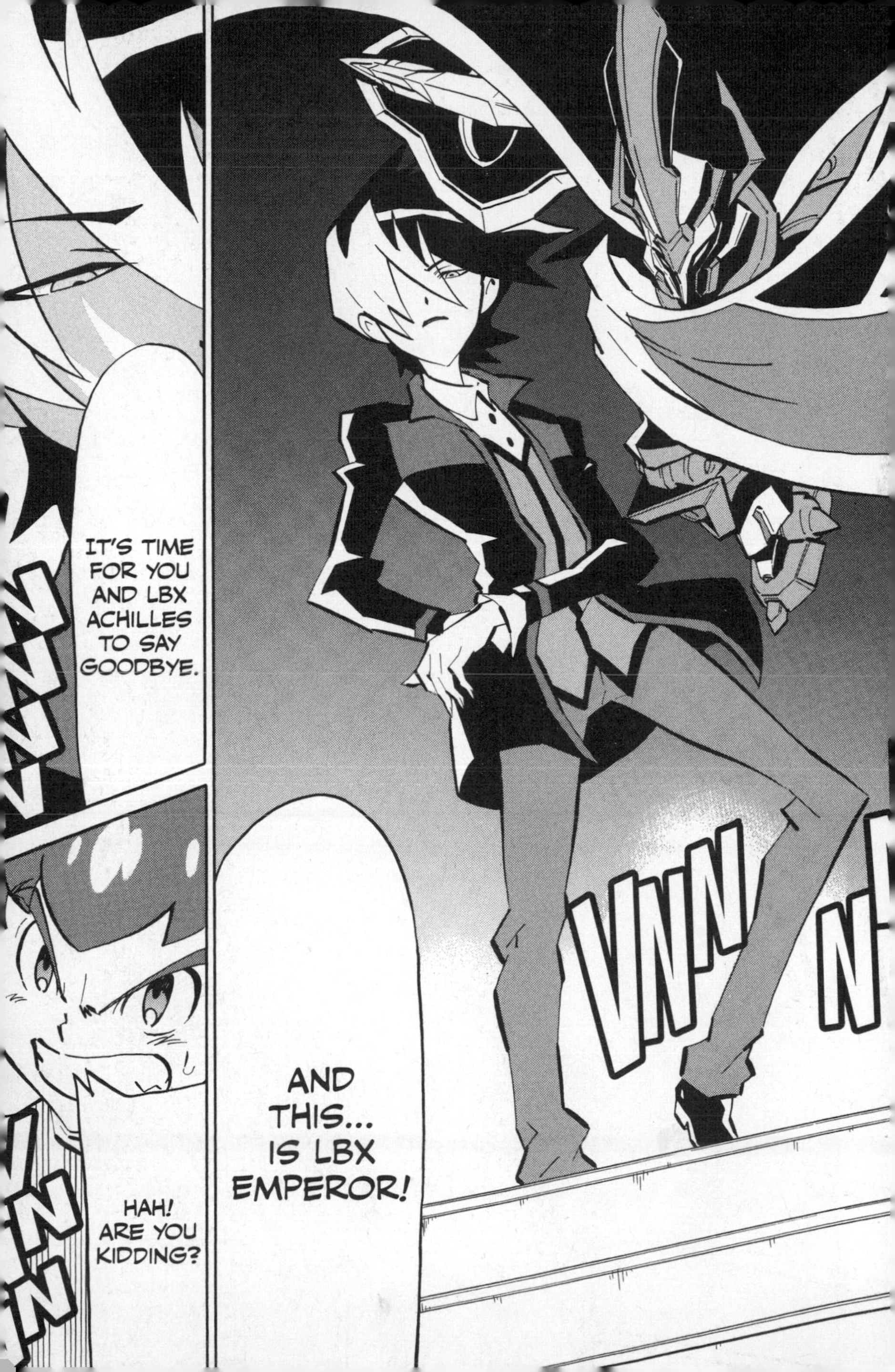
AND THIS... IS LBX EMPEROR!
VNNN
IT'S TIME FOR YOU AND LBX ACHILLES TO SAY GOODBYE.
HAH! ARE YOU KIDDING?

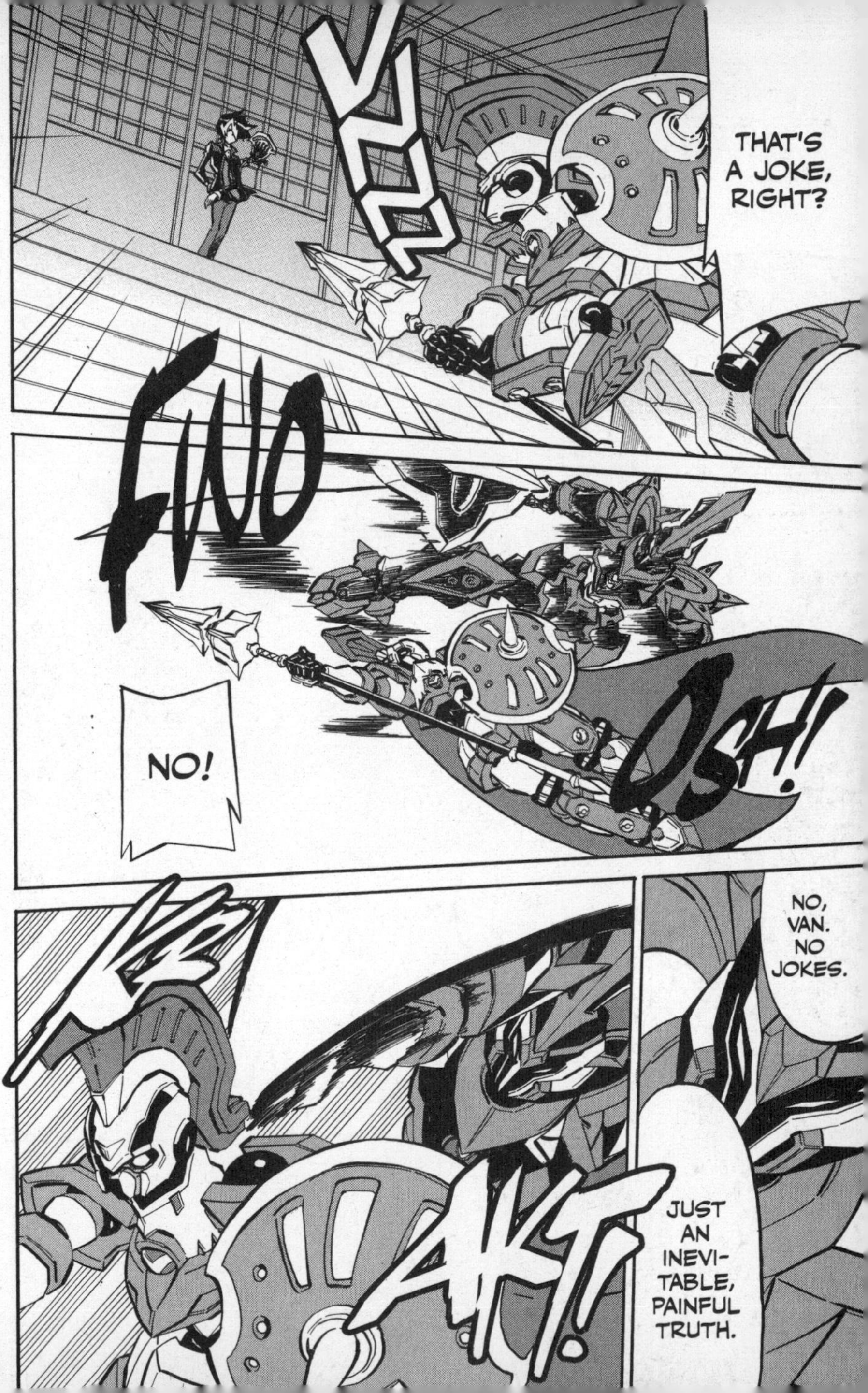
THAT'S A JOKE, RIGHT?
FWO
OSH!
NO!
NO, VAN. NO JOKES.
JUST AN INEVI-TABLE, PAINFUL TRUTH.

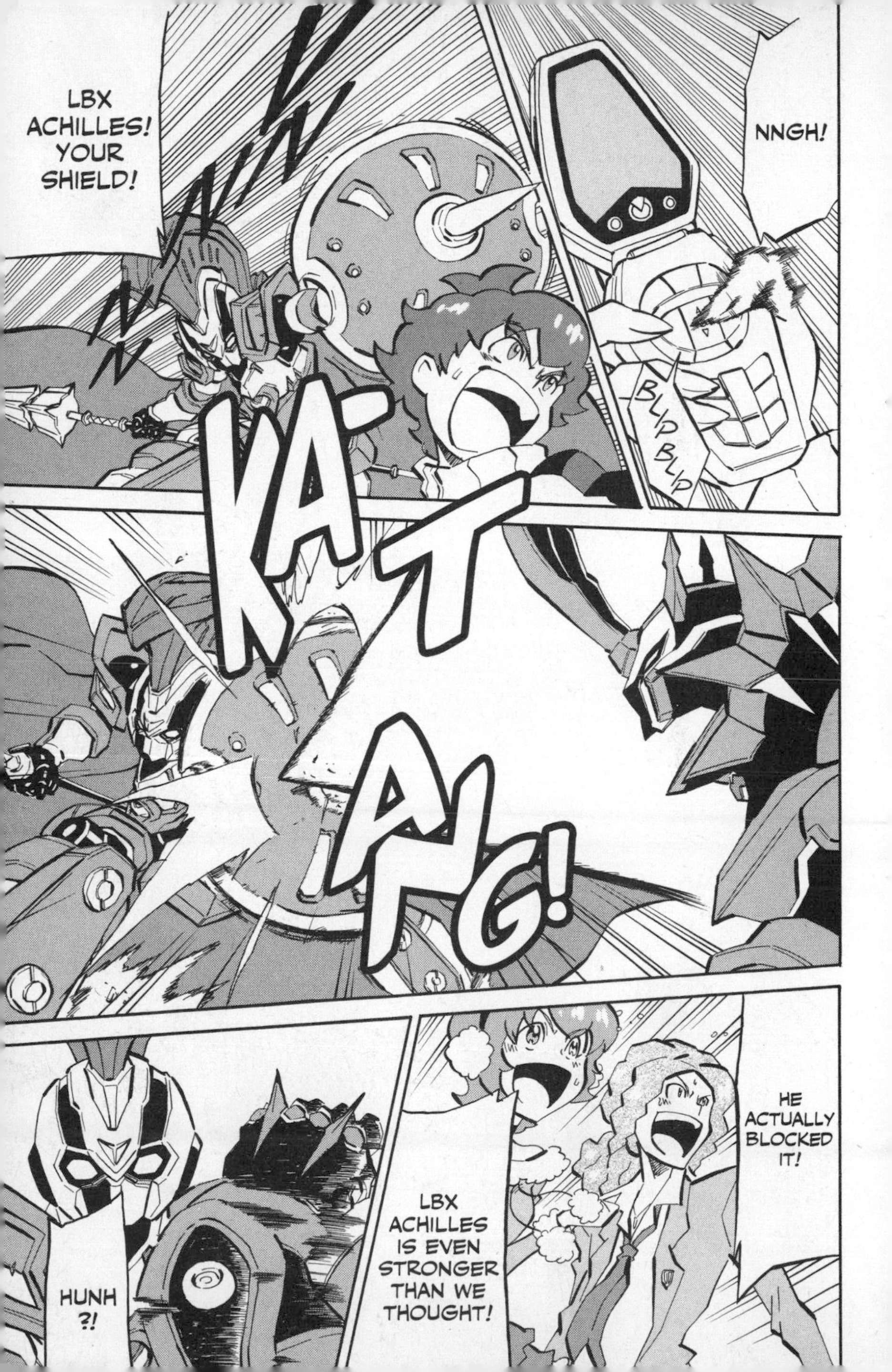
NNGH!
BLIP BLIP BLIP
LBX ACHILLES! YOUR SHIELD!
KATANG!
HE ACTUALLY BLOCKED IT!
LBX ACHILLES IS EVEN STRONGER THAN WE THOUGHT!
HUNH ?!

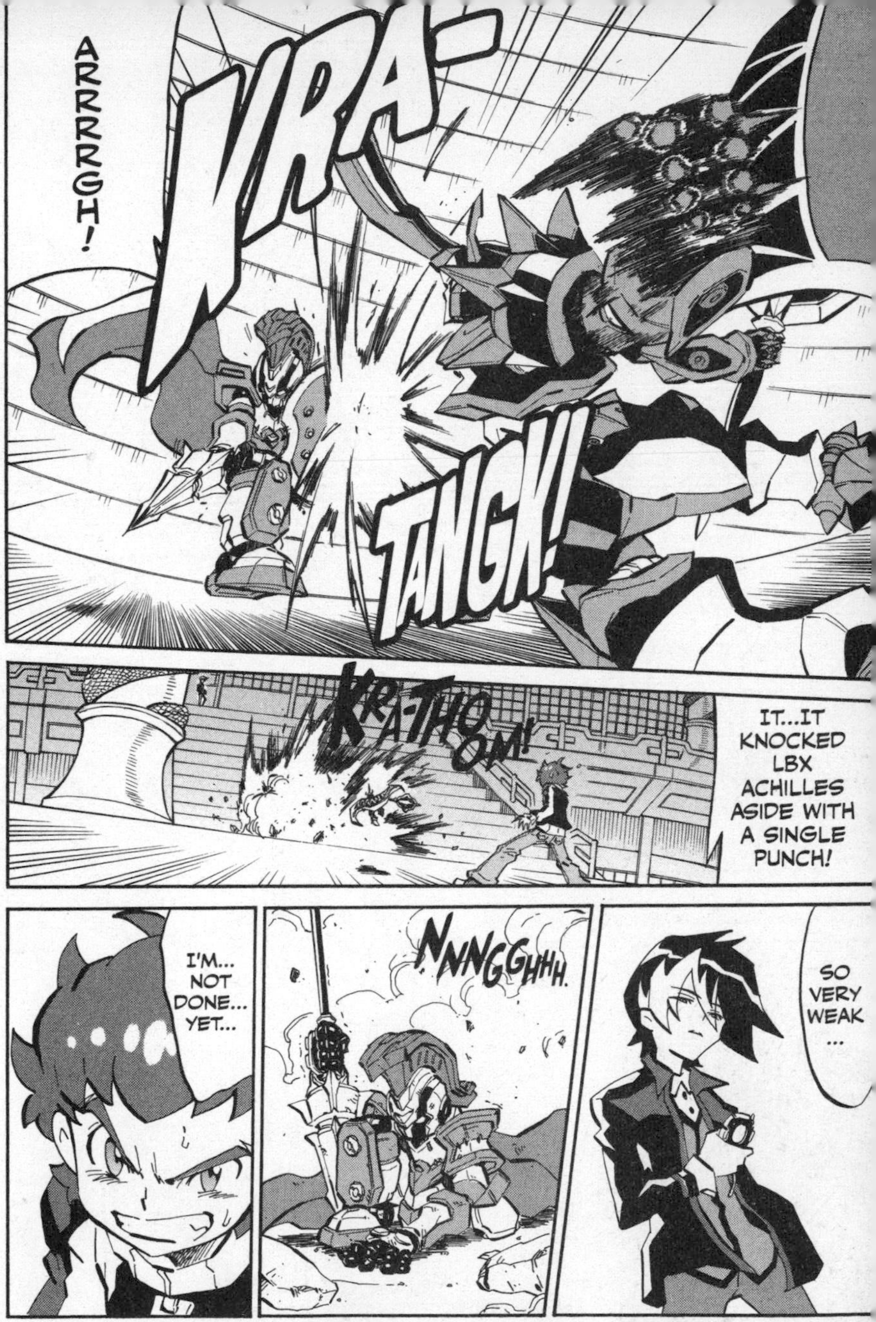
VRA-
ARRRRGH!
TANGK!!
IT...IT KNOCKED LBX ACHILLES ASIDE WITH A SINGLE PUNCH!
KRA-THOOM!
SO VERY WEAK ...
NNNGGHHH.
I'M... NOT DONE... YET...

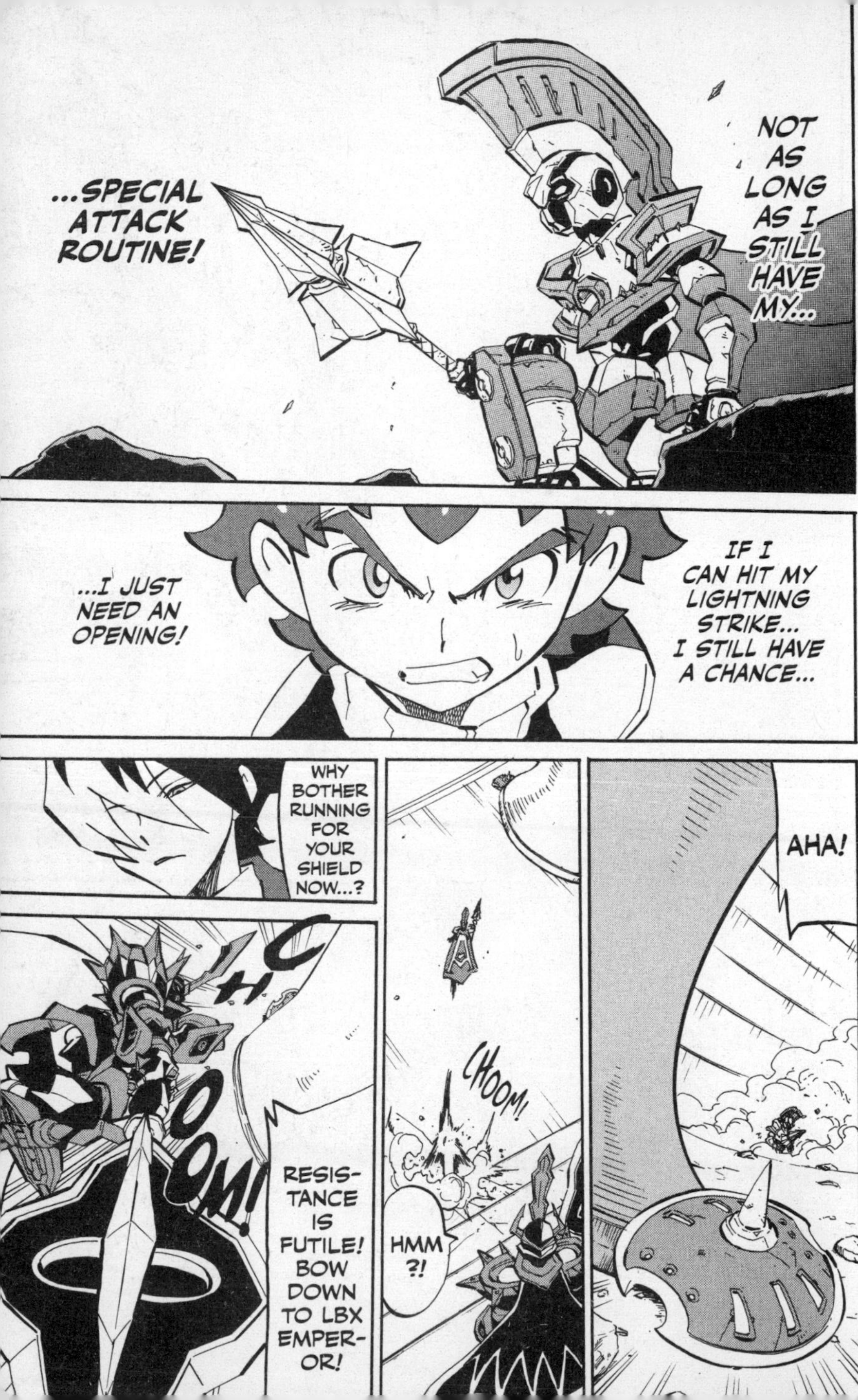
NOT AS LONG AS I STILL HAVE MY...
...SPECIAL ATTACK ROUTINE!
IF I CAN HIT MY LIGHTNING STRIKE... I STILL HAVE A CHANCE...
...I JUST NEED AN OPENING!
AHA!
CHOOM!
HMM ?!
WHY BOTHER RUNNING FOR YOUR SHIELD NOW...?
RESIS-TANCE IS FUTILE! BOW DOWN TO LBX EMPER-OR!

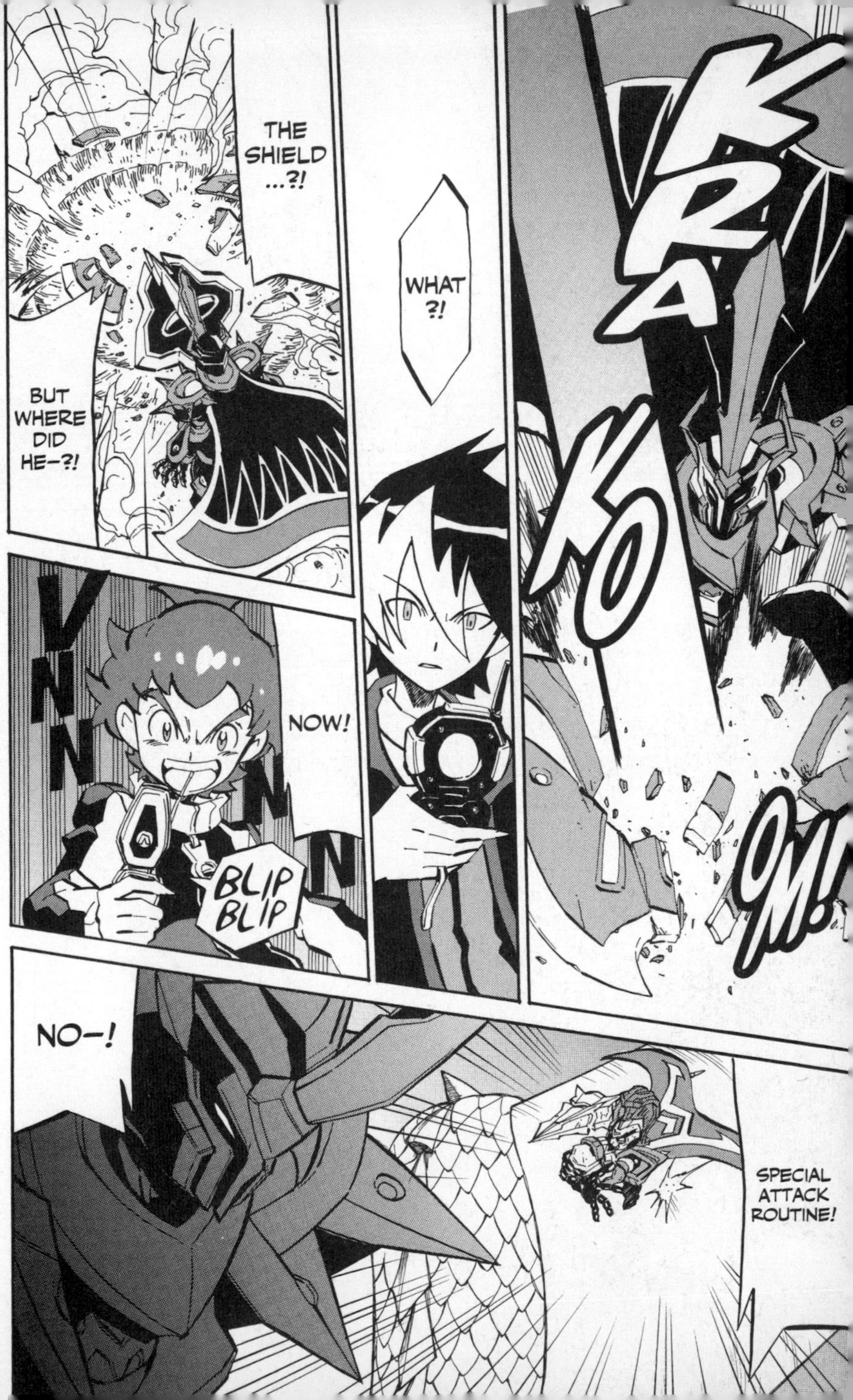
KRAKOOM!
WHAT?!
THE SHIELD...?!
BUT WHERE DID HE-?!
VNNNNN
NOW!
BLIP BLIP
SPECIAL ATTACK ROUTINE!
NO-!

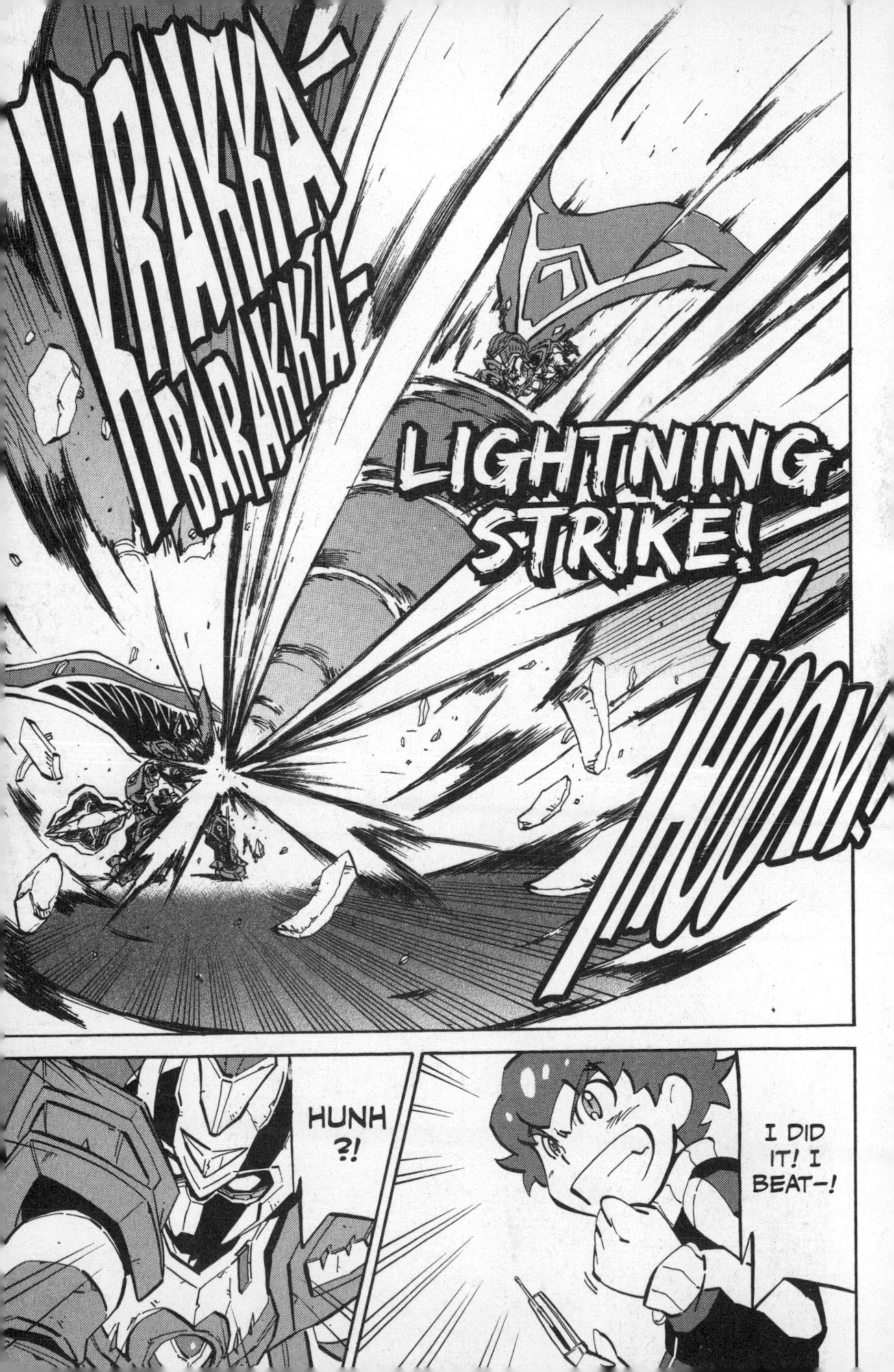
VRAKKA-
BARAKKA-
LIGHTNING-STRIKE!
I DID IT! I BEAT—!
HUNH ?!

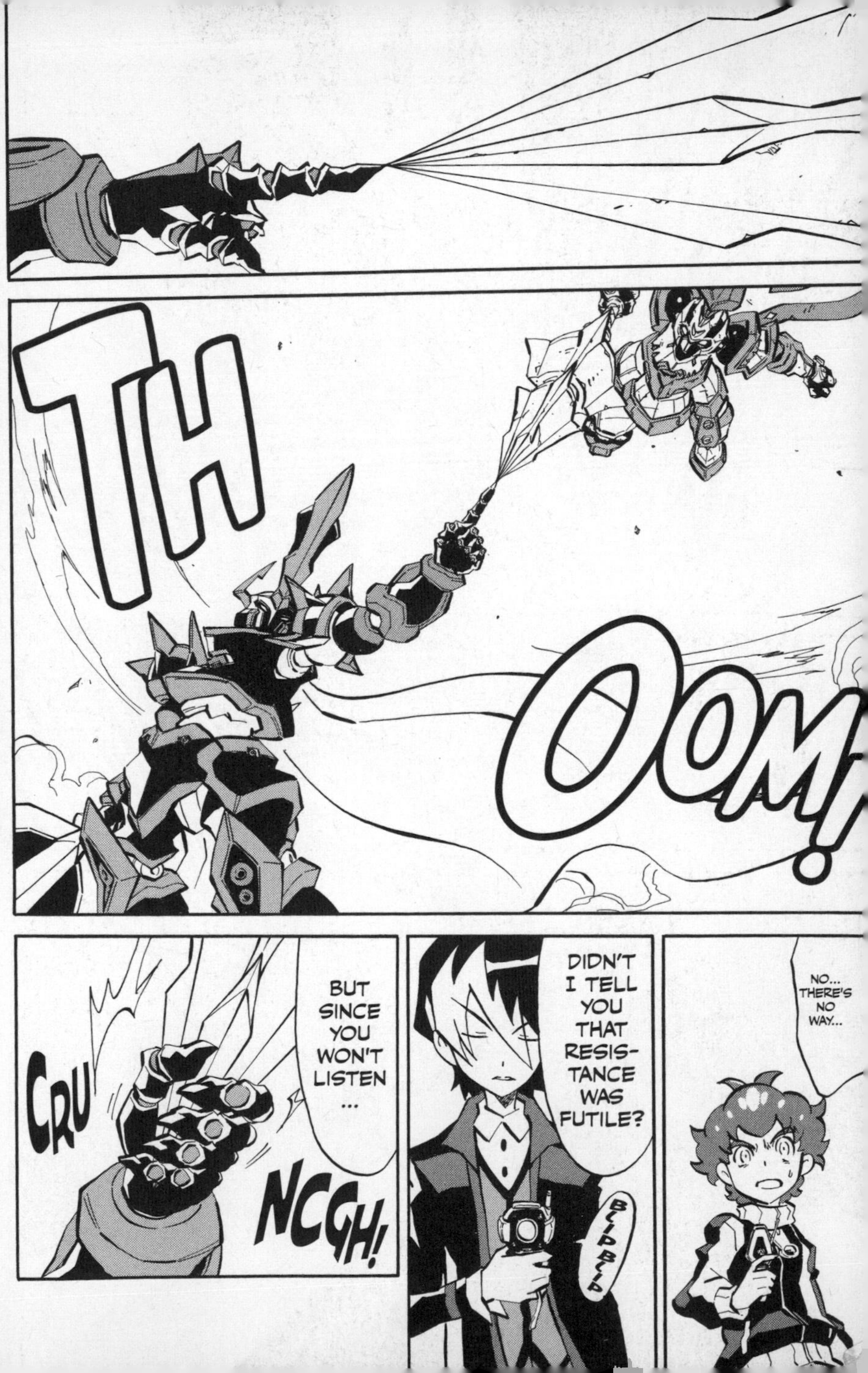
TH
OOM!
NO... THERE'S NO WAY...
DIDN'T I TELL YOU THAT RESIS-TANCE WAS FUTILE?
BLIPBLIP
BUT SINCE YOU WON'T LISTEN...
CRU
NCGH!

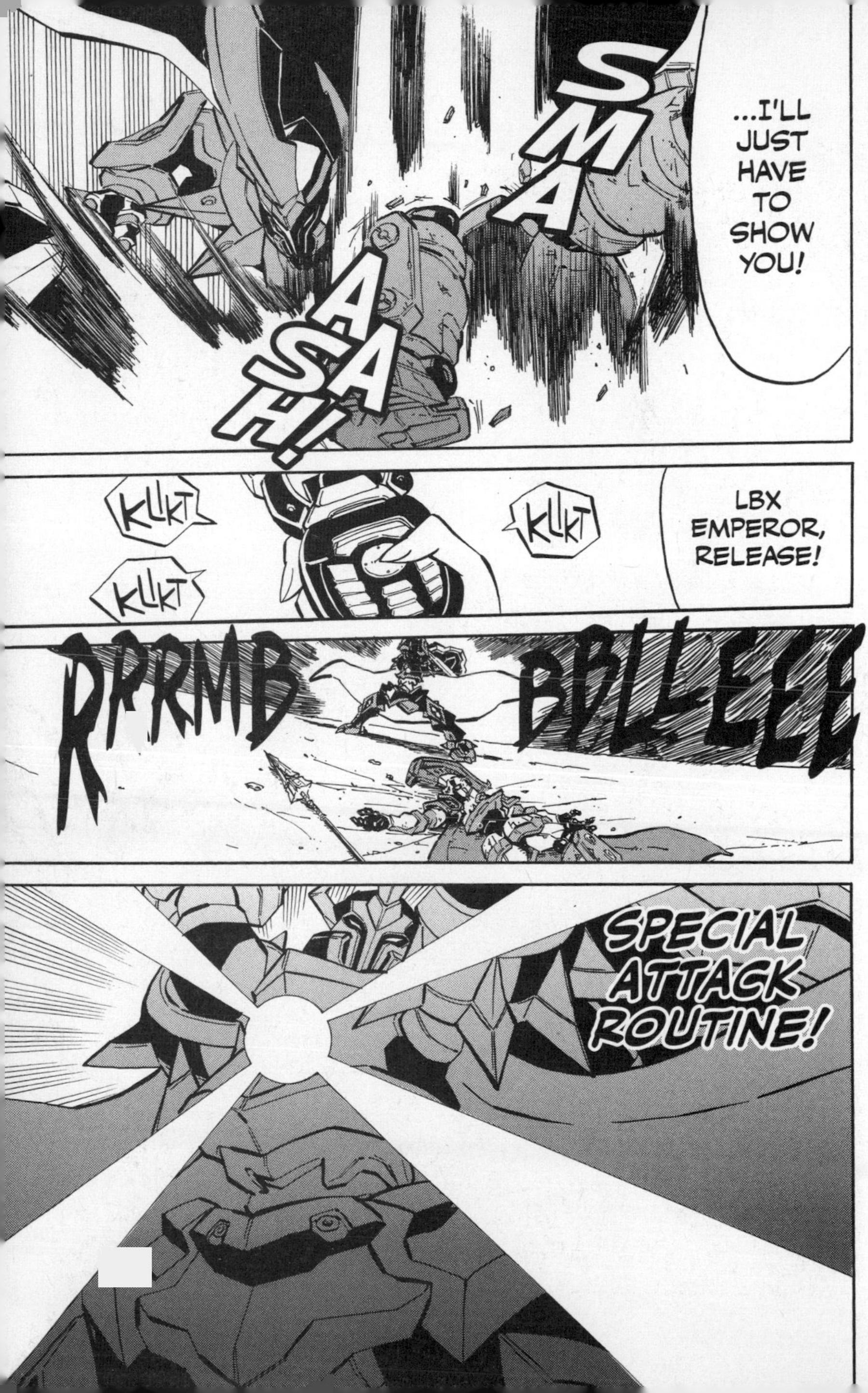
...I'LL JUST HAVE TO SHOW YOU!
SMAASH!
LBX EMPEROR, RELEASE!
KLIKT
KLIKT
KLIKT
BRLLEEE
RRRMB
SPECIAL ATTACK ROUTINE!

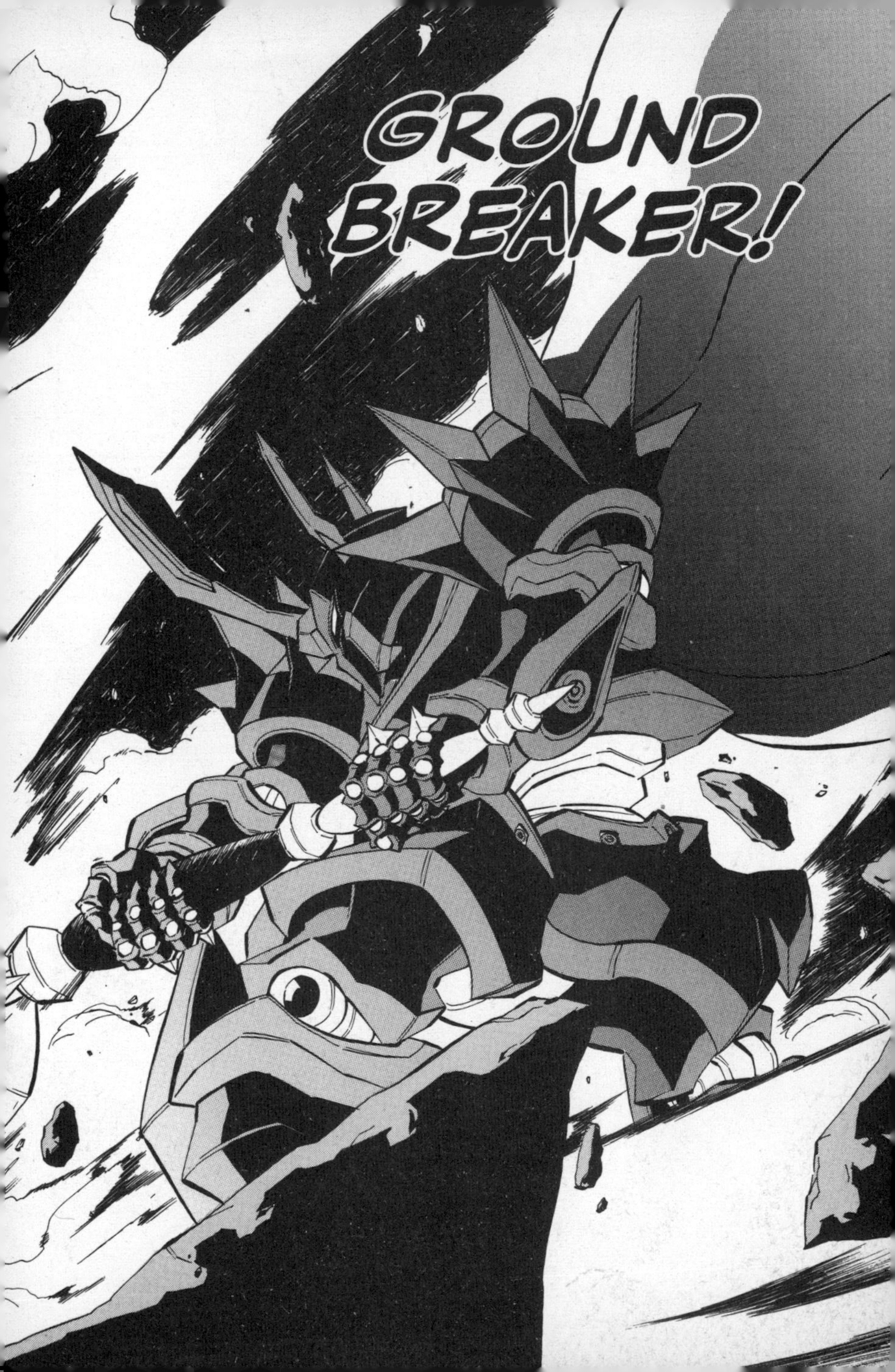
GROUND BREAKER!

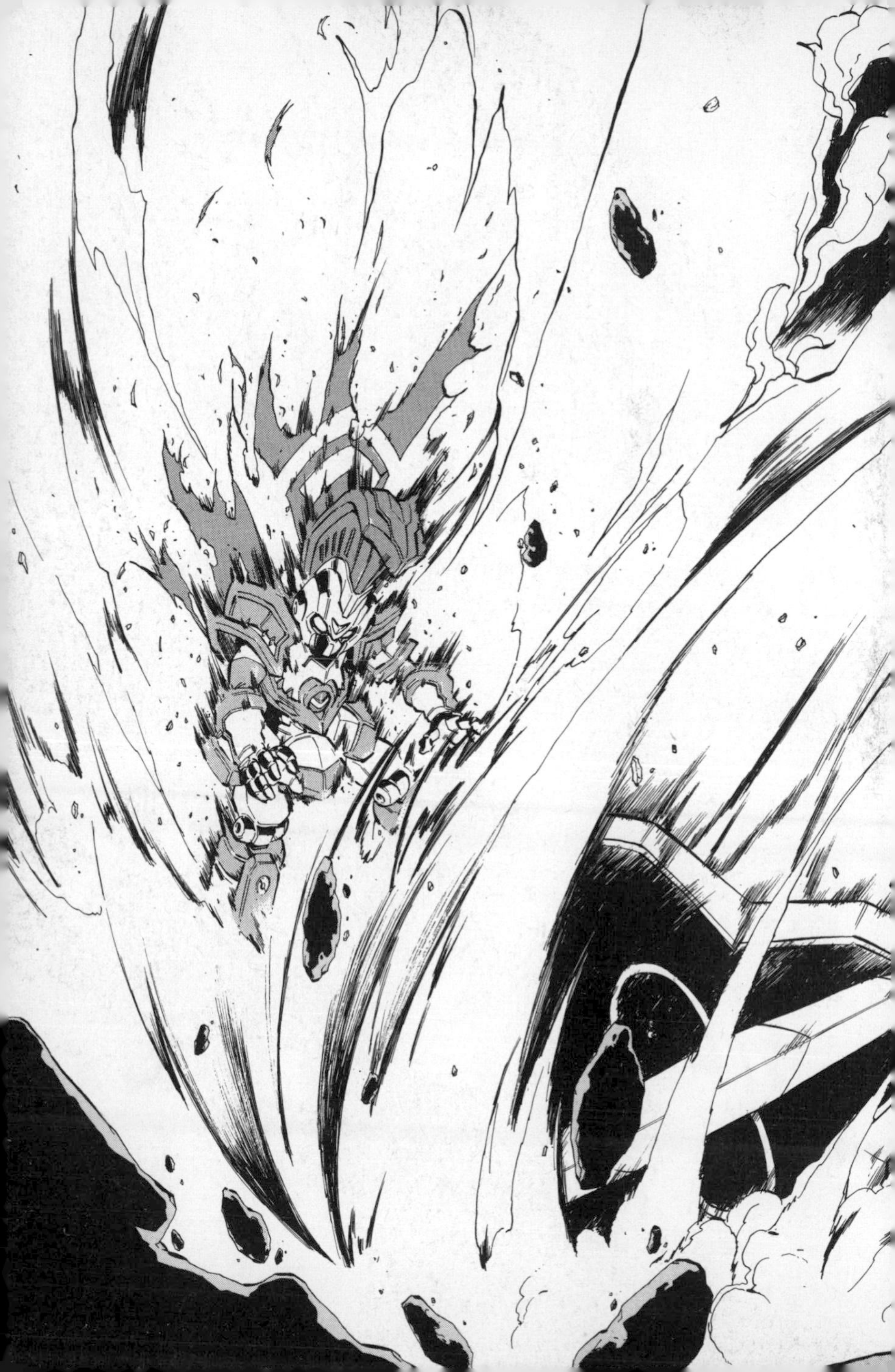

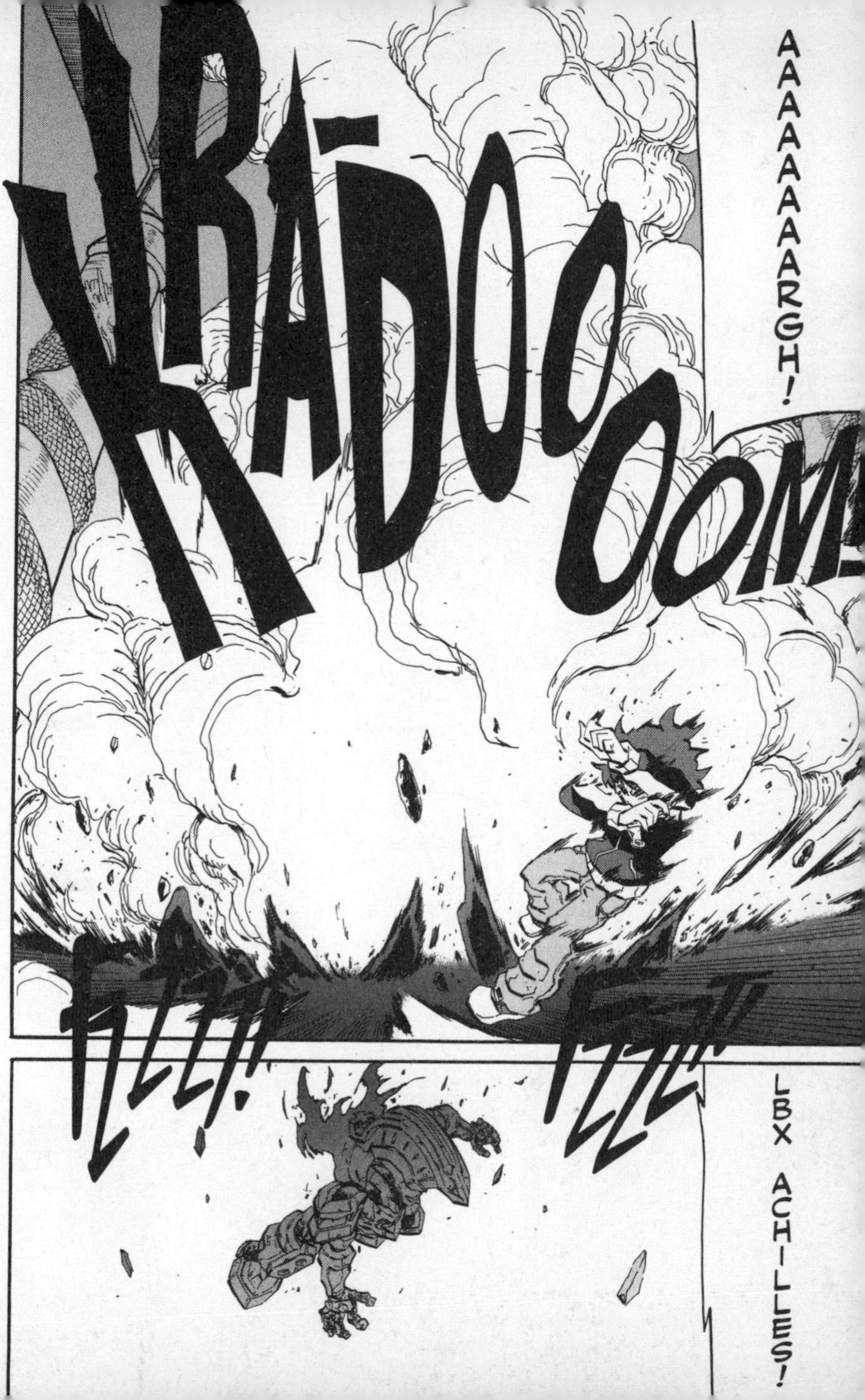
AAAAAAAAARGH!
KRA-DOOOOOM
FZZT!
FZZZ
LBX ACHILLES!

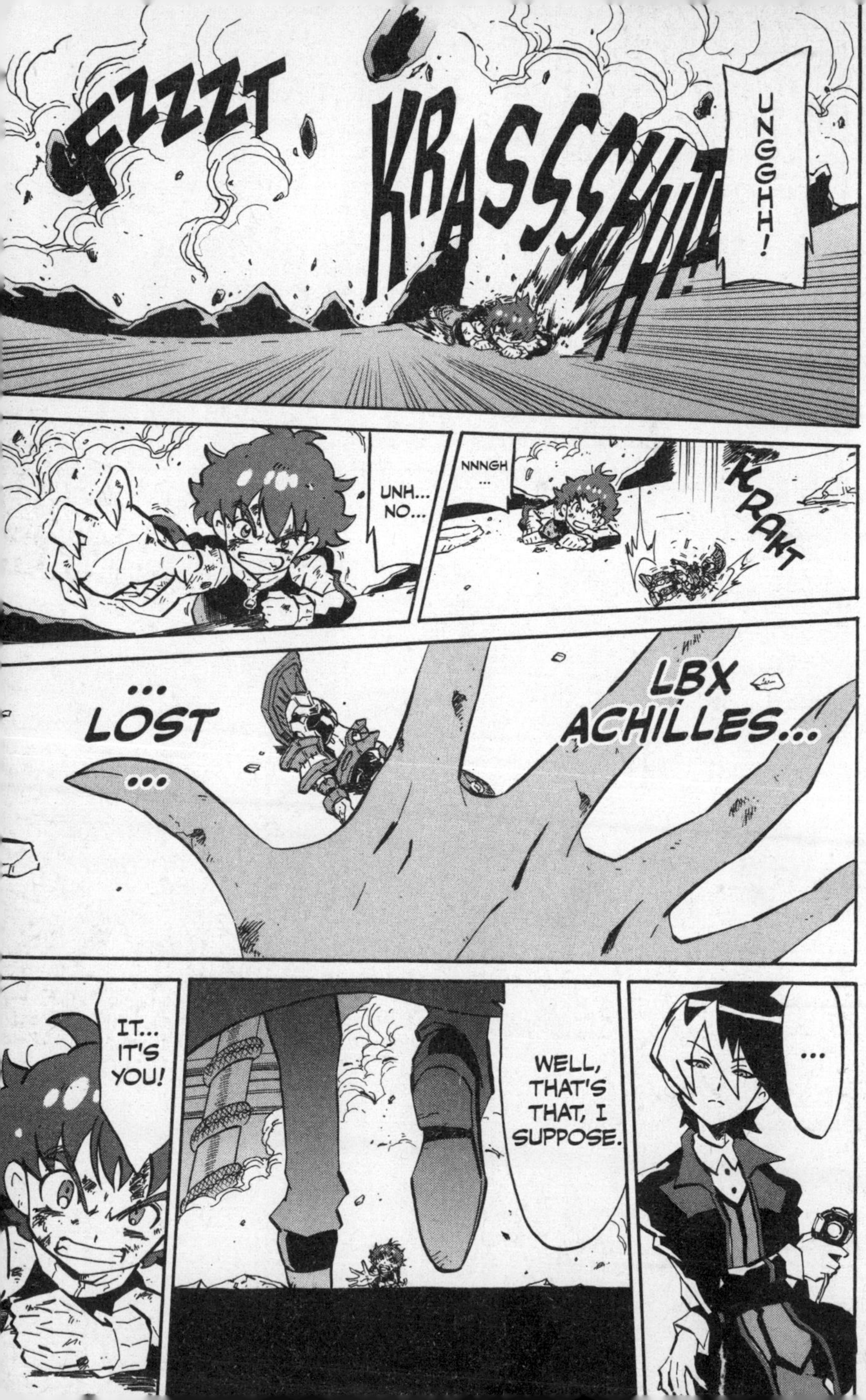
UNGGHH!
KRASSSHH!
FZZZZT
KRAKT
NNNGH...
UNH... NO...
LBX ACHILLES...
... LOST ...
...
WELL, THAT'S THAT, I SUPPOSE.
IT... IT'S YOU!

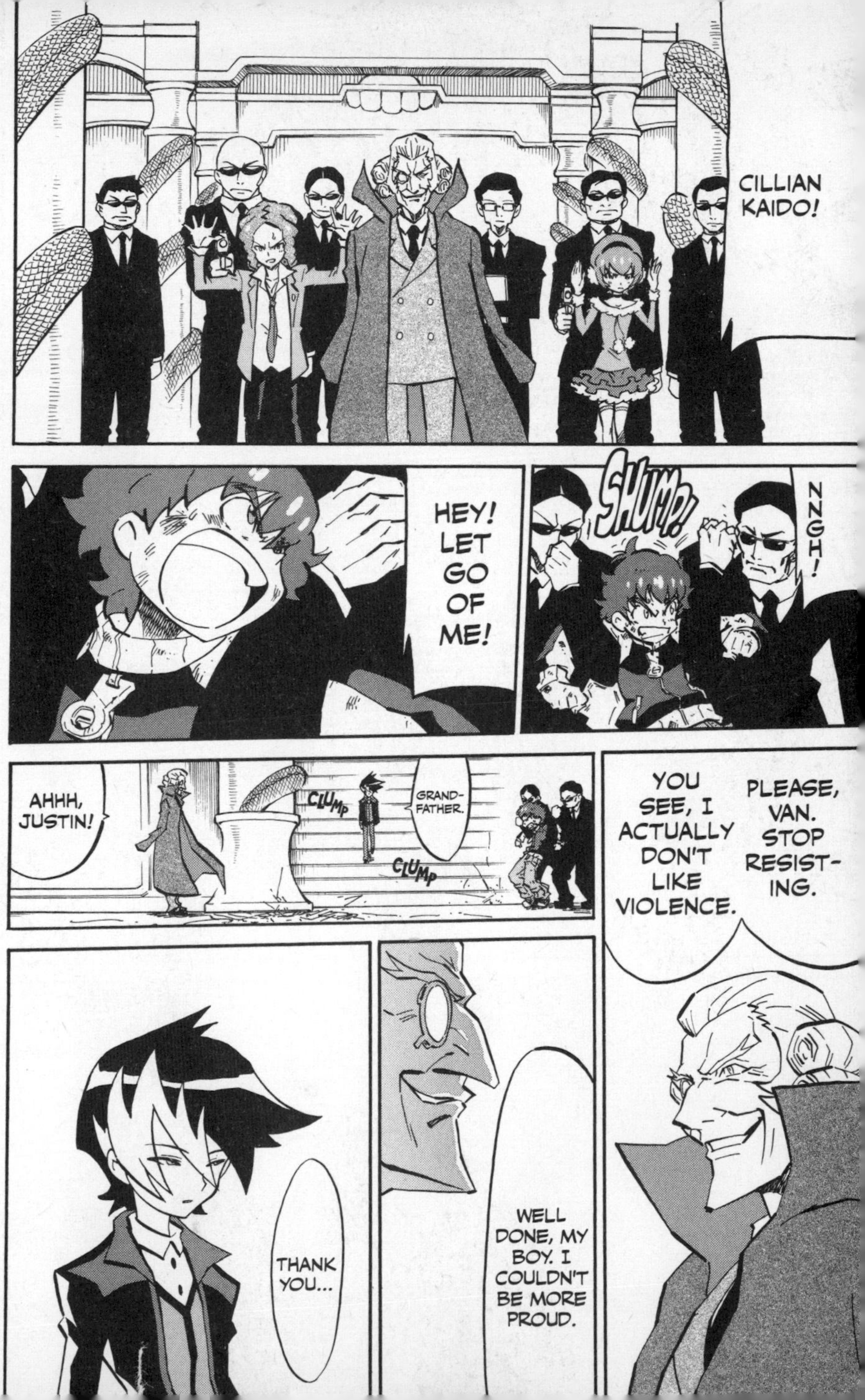

CILLIAN KAIDO!
NNGH!
SHUMP!
HEY! LET GO OF ME!
PLEASE, VAN. STOP RESIST-ING.
YOU SEE, I ACTUALLY DON'T LIKE VIOLENCE.
GRAND-FATHER.
CLUMP
AHHH, JUSTIN!
CLUMP
WELL DONE, MY BOY. I COULDN'T BE MORE PROUD.
THANK YOU...

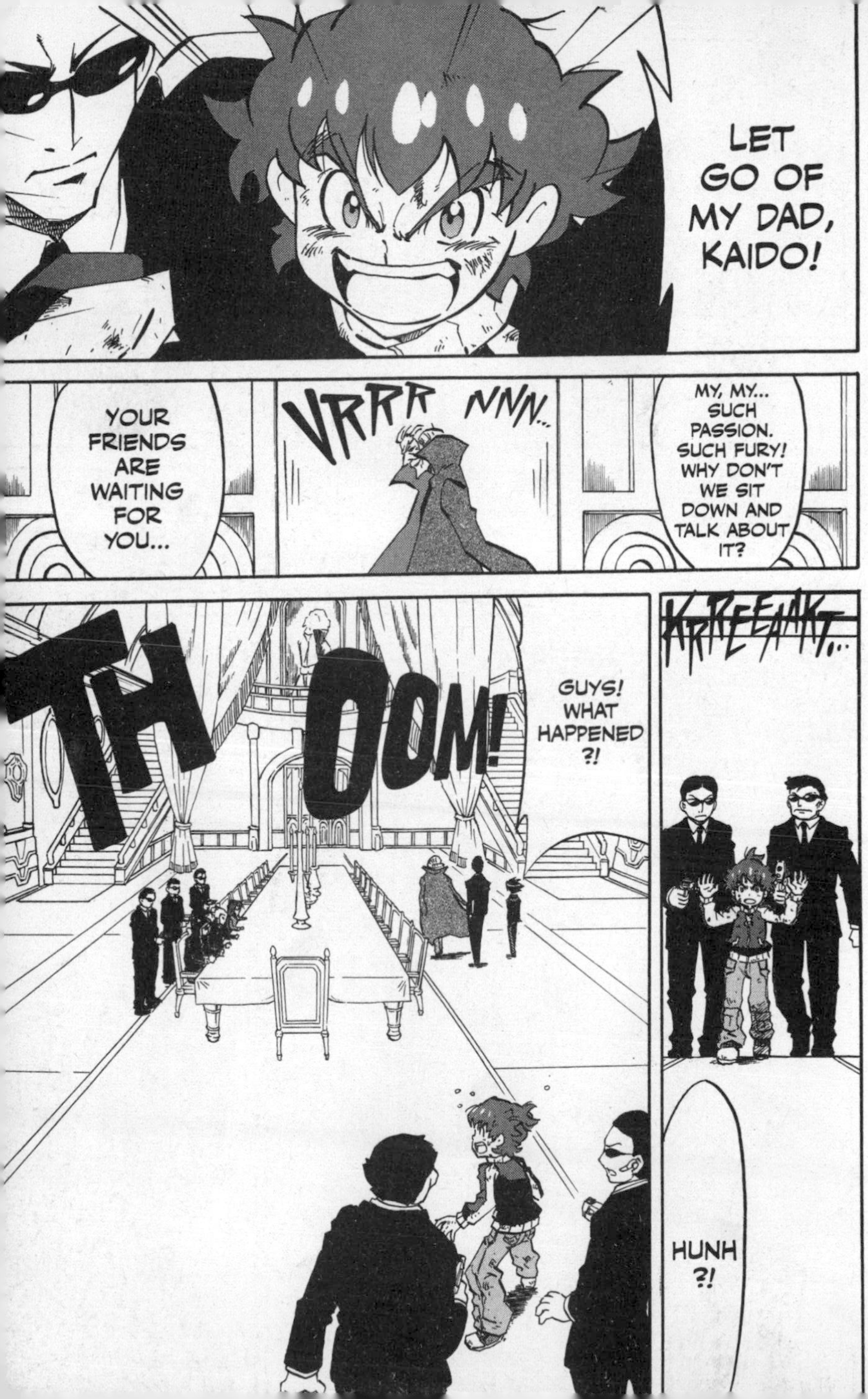
LET GO OF MY DAD, KAIDO!
MY, MY... SUCH PASSION. SUCH FURY! WHY DON'T WE SIT DOWN AND TALK ABOUT IT?
VRRR NNN...
YOUR FRIENDS ARE WAITING FOR YOU...
KRREEAAKT...
HUNH ?!
THOOM!
GUYS! WHAT HAPPENED ?!

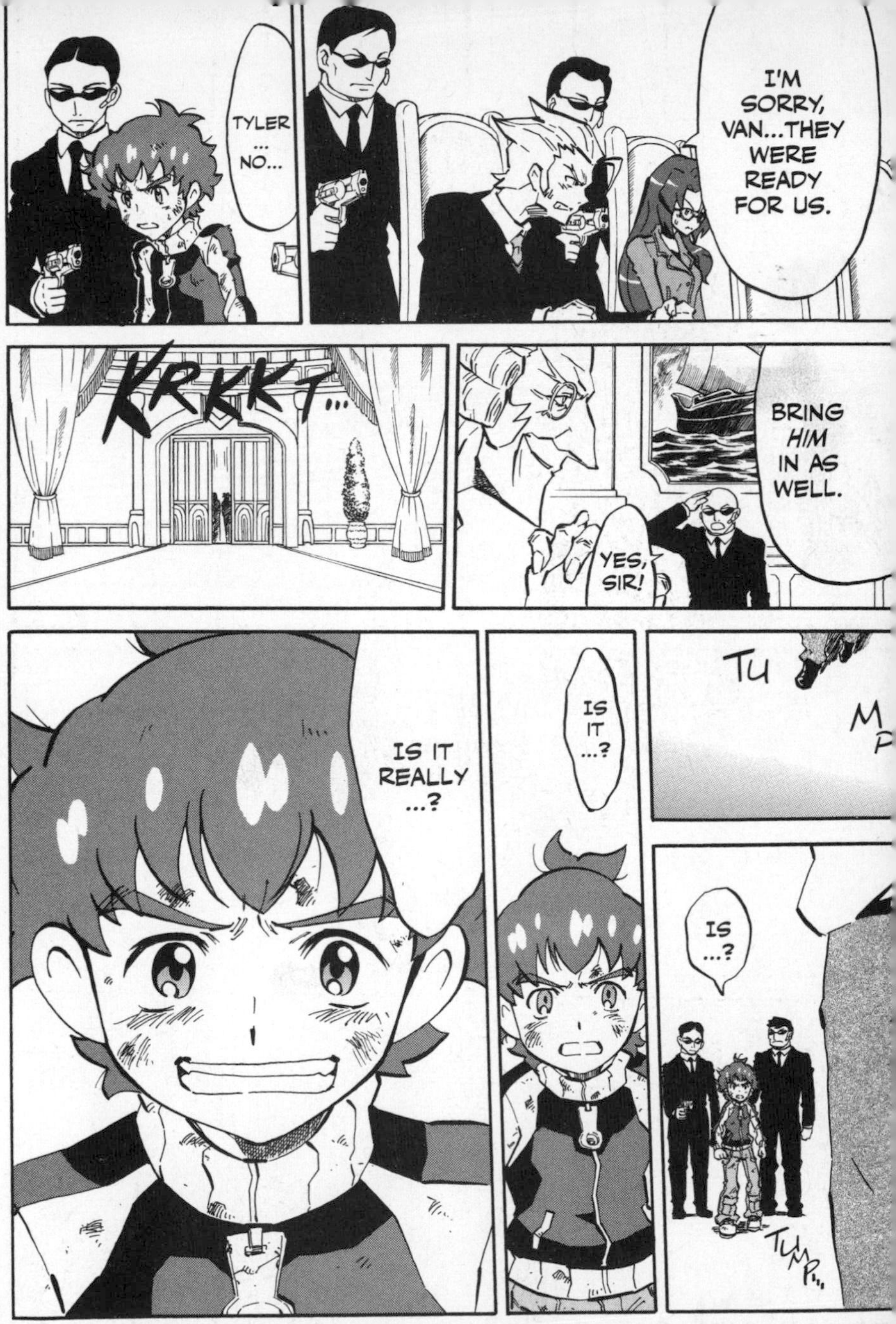
I'M SORRY, VAN...THEY WERE READY FOR US.
TYLER ... NO...
BRING HIM IN AS WELL.
YES, SIR!
KRRKKT...
TUMP
IS ...?
TUMP...
IS IT ...?
IS IT REALLY ...?

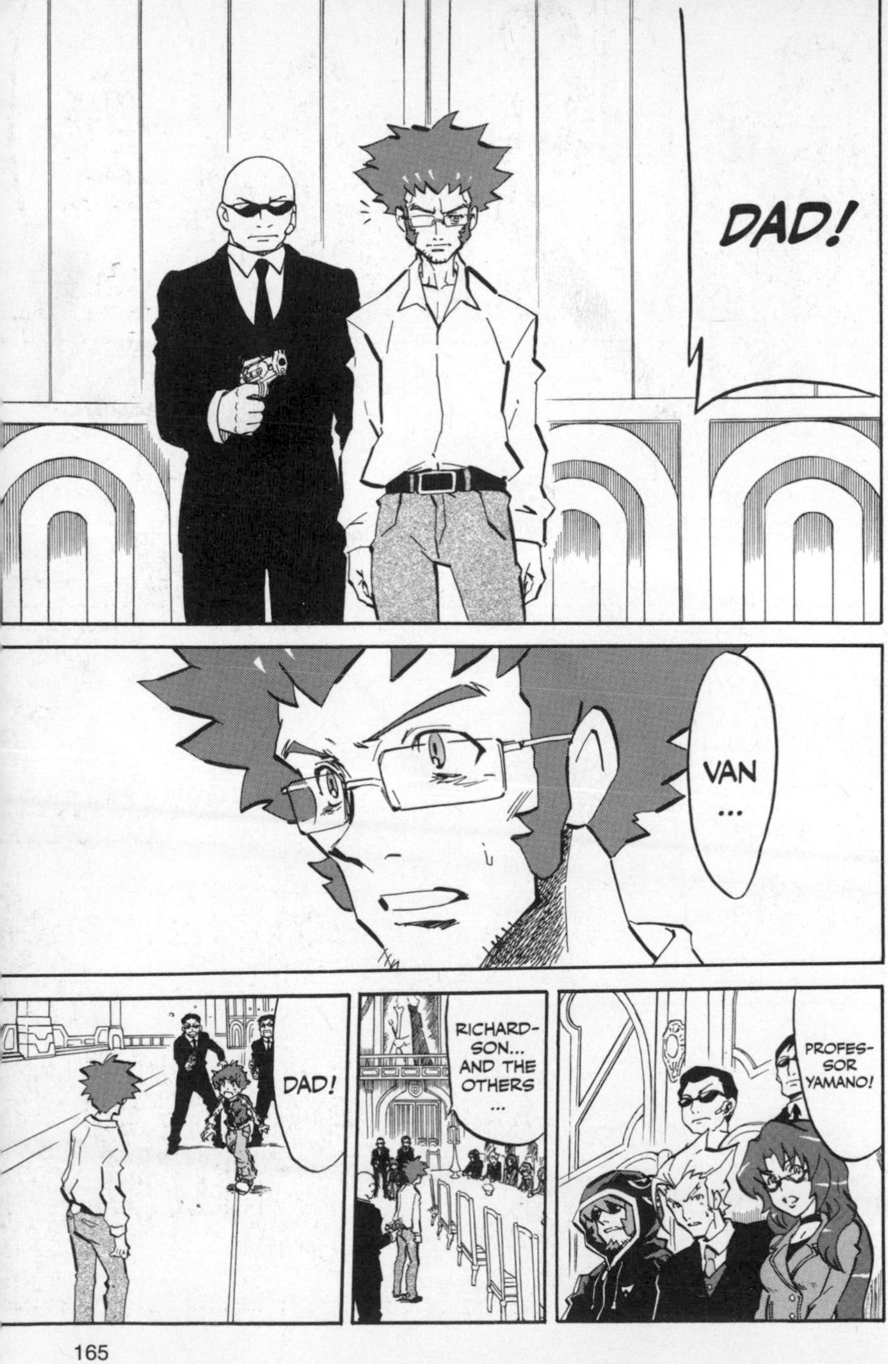
DAD!
VAN ...
PROFES-SOR YAMANO!
RICHARD-SON... AND THE OTHERS ...
DAD!

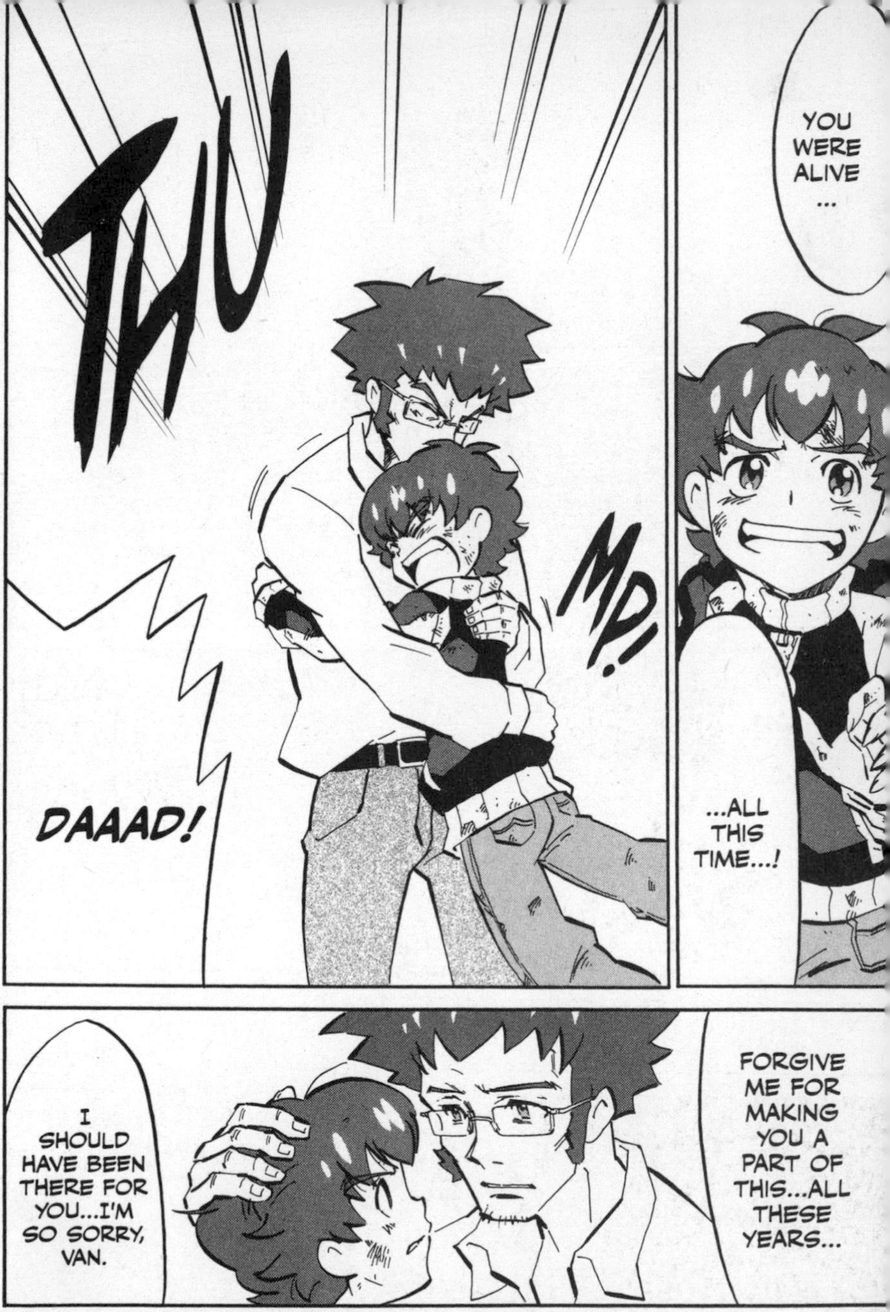
YOU WERE ALIVE ...
...ALL THIS TIME...!
THUMP!
DAAAD!
FORGIVE ME FOR MAKING YOU A PART OF THIS...ALL THESE YEARS...
I SHOULD HAVE BEEN THERE FOR YOU...I'M SO SORRY, VAN.

DAD, I'M SORRY ...

SORRY THAT I FAILED ...

...SORRY THAT I COULDN'T SAVE YOU FROM THIS PLACE.

VAN, I—

ENOUGH WITH THE SAPPY REUNION! IT'S GIVING ME A TOOTHACHE!

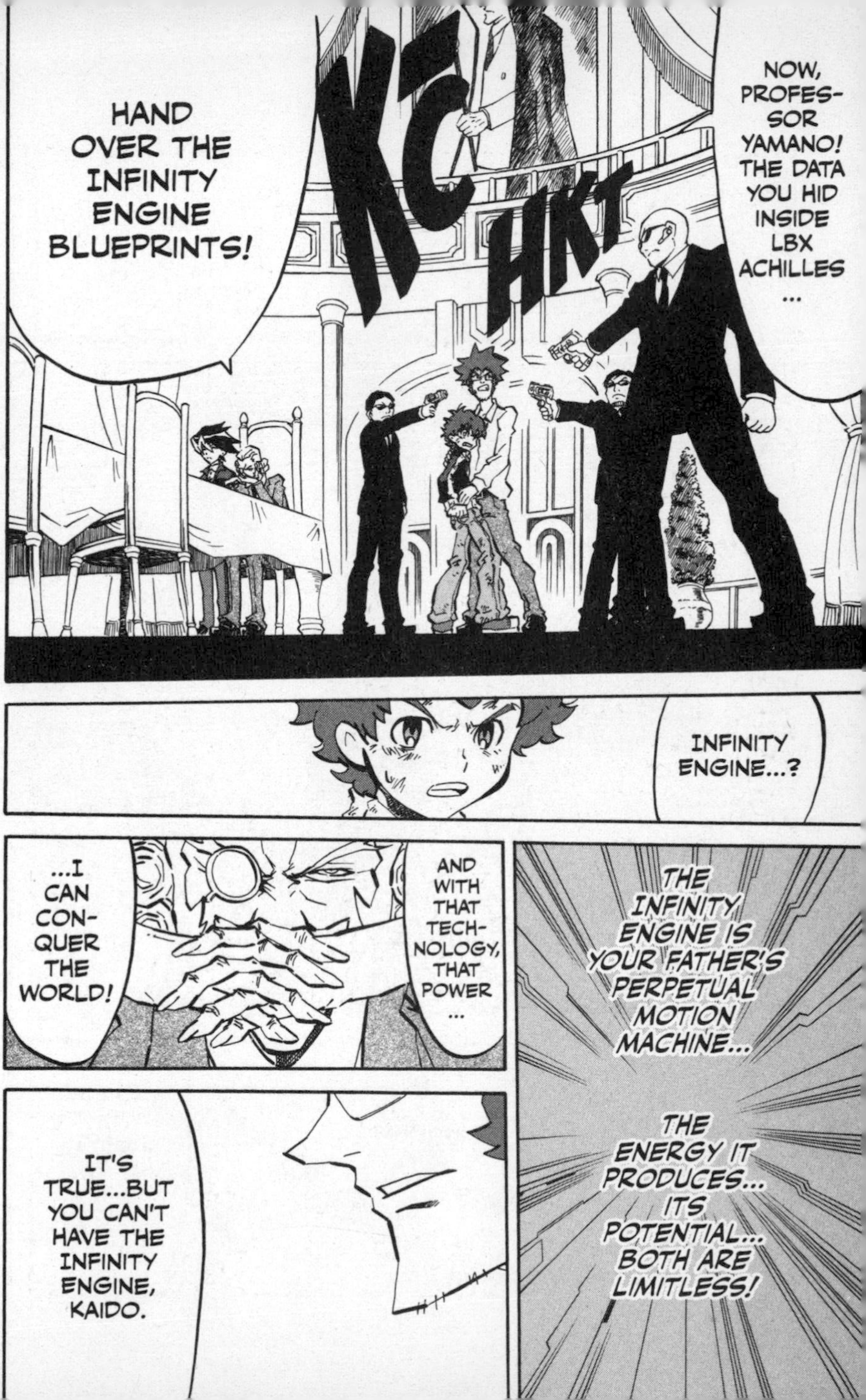
NOW, PROFES-SOR YAMANO! THE DATA YOU HID INSIDE LBX ACHILLES ...
KCHKT
HAND OVER THE INFINITY ENGINE BLUEPRINTS!
INFINITY ENGINE...?
THE INFINITY ENGINE IS YOUR FATHER'S PERPETUAL MOTION MACHINE...
THE ENERGY IT PRODUCES... ITS POTENTIAL... BOTH ARE LIMITLESS!
AND WITH THAT TECH-NOLOGY, THAT POWER ...
...I CAN CON-QUER THE WORLD!
IT'S TRUE...BUT YOU CAN'T HAVE THE INFINITY ENGINE, KAIDO.

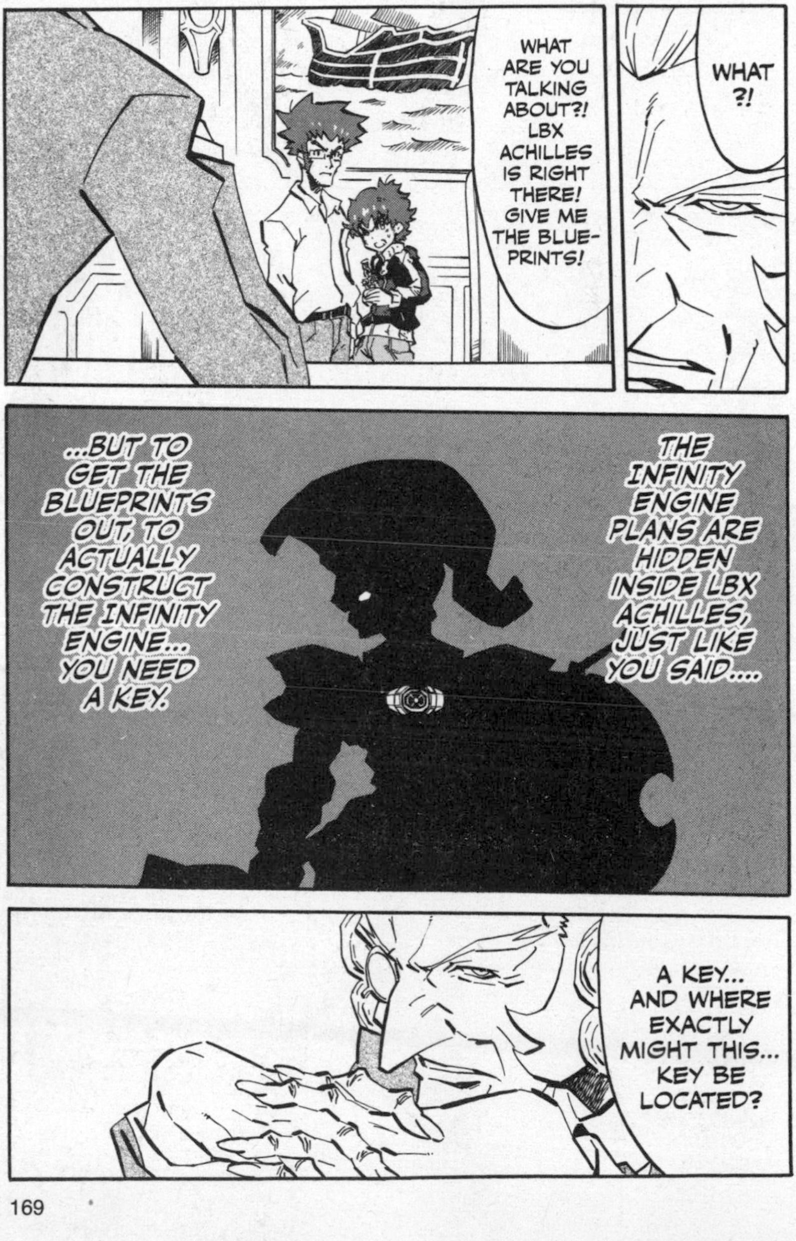
WHAT ?!
WHAT ARE YOU TALKING ABOUT?! LBX ACHILLES IS RIGHT THERE! GIVE ME THE BLUE-PRINTS!
THE INFINITY ENGINE PLANS ARE HIDDEN INSIDE LBX ACHILLES, JUST LIKE YOU SAID....
...BUT TO GET THE BLUEPRINTS OUT, TO ACTUALLY CONSTRUCT THE INFINITY ENGINE... YOU NEED A KEY.
A KEY... AND WHERE EXACTLY MIGHT THIS... KEY BE LOCATED?

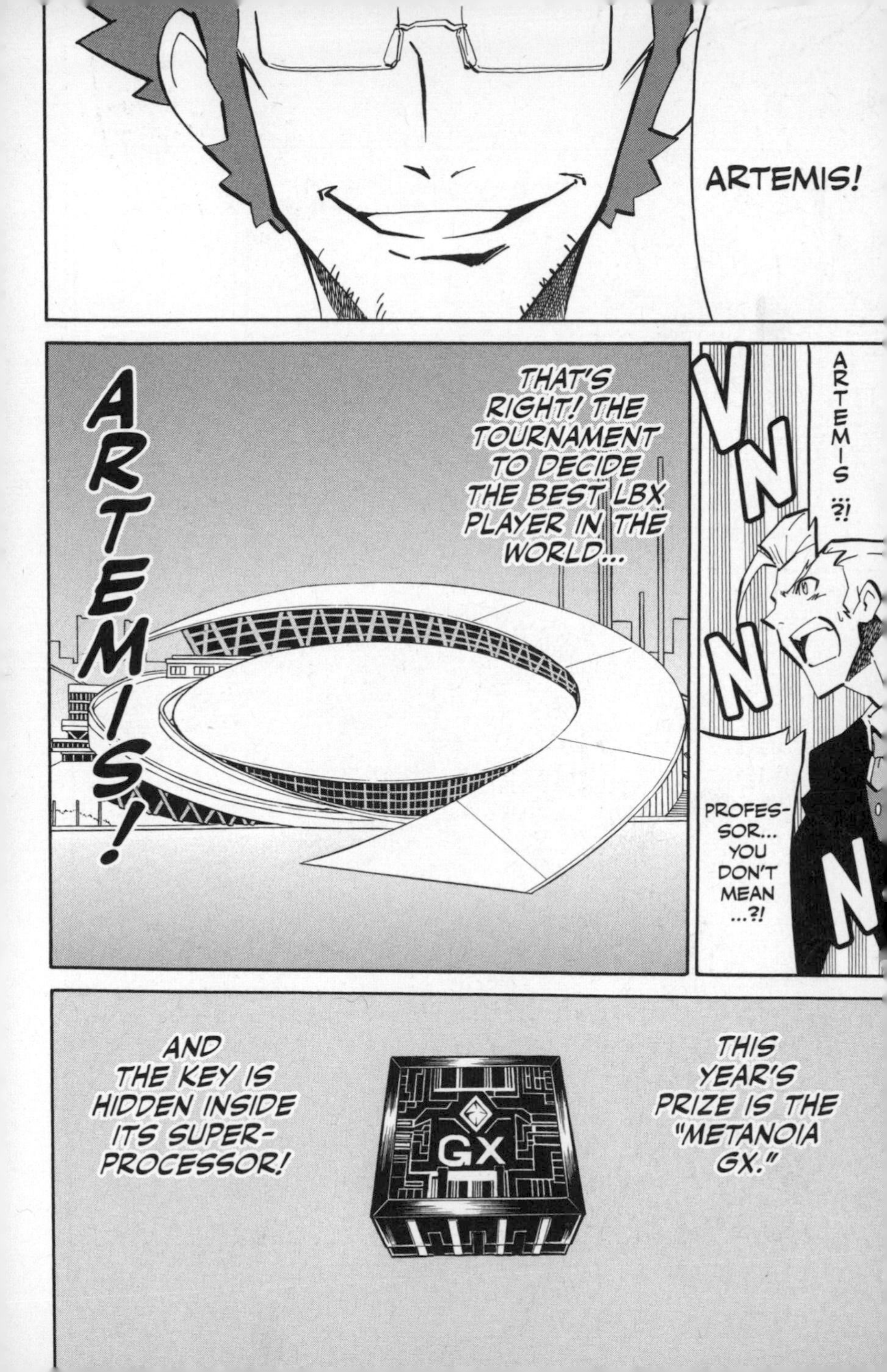
ARTEMIS!
ARTEMIS...?!
VNNNN
PROFESSOR... YOU DON'T MEAN ...?!
THAT'S RIGHT! THE TOURNAMENT TO DECIDE THE BEST LBX PLAYER IN THE WORLD...
ARTEMIS!
THIS YEAR'S PRIZE IS THE "METANOIA GX."
AND THE KEY IS HIDDEN INSIDE ITS SUPER-PROCESSOR!
GX

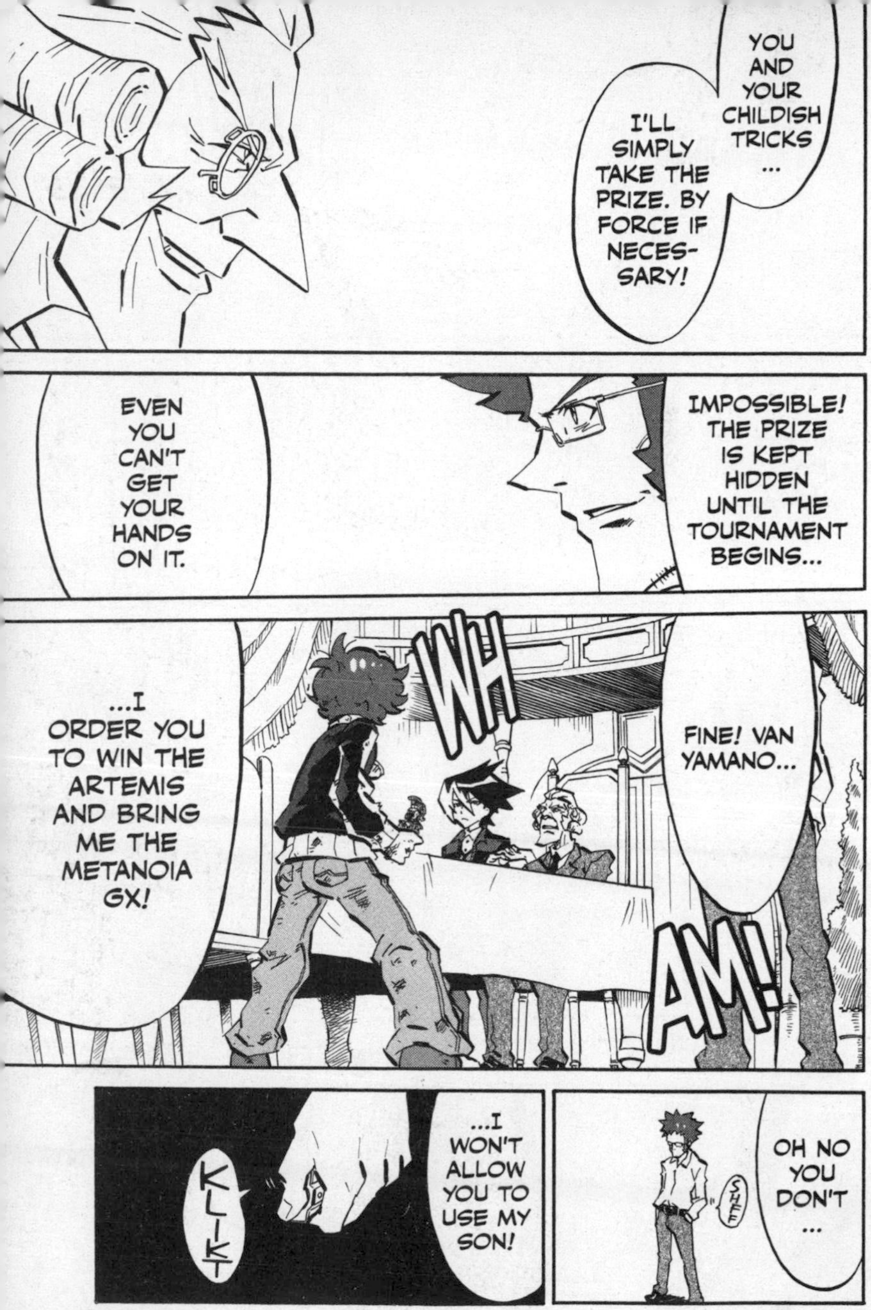
YOU AND YOUR CHILDISH TRICKS ...
I'LL SIMPLY TAKE THE PRIZE. BY FORCE IF NECES-SARY!
IMPOSSIBLE! THE PRIZE IS KEPT HIDDEN UNTIL THE TOURNAMENT BEGINS...
EVEN YOU CAN'T GET YOUR HANDS ON IT.
FINE! VAN YAMANO...
WH
AM!
...I ORDER YOU TO WIN THE ARTEMIS AND BRING ME THE METANOIA GX!
OH NO YOU DON'T ...
SHFF
...I WON'T ALLOW YOU TO USE MY SON!
KLIKT

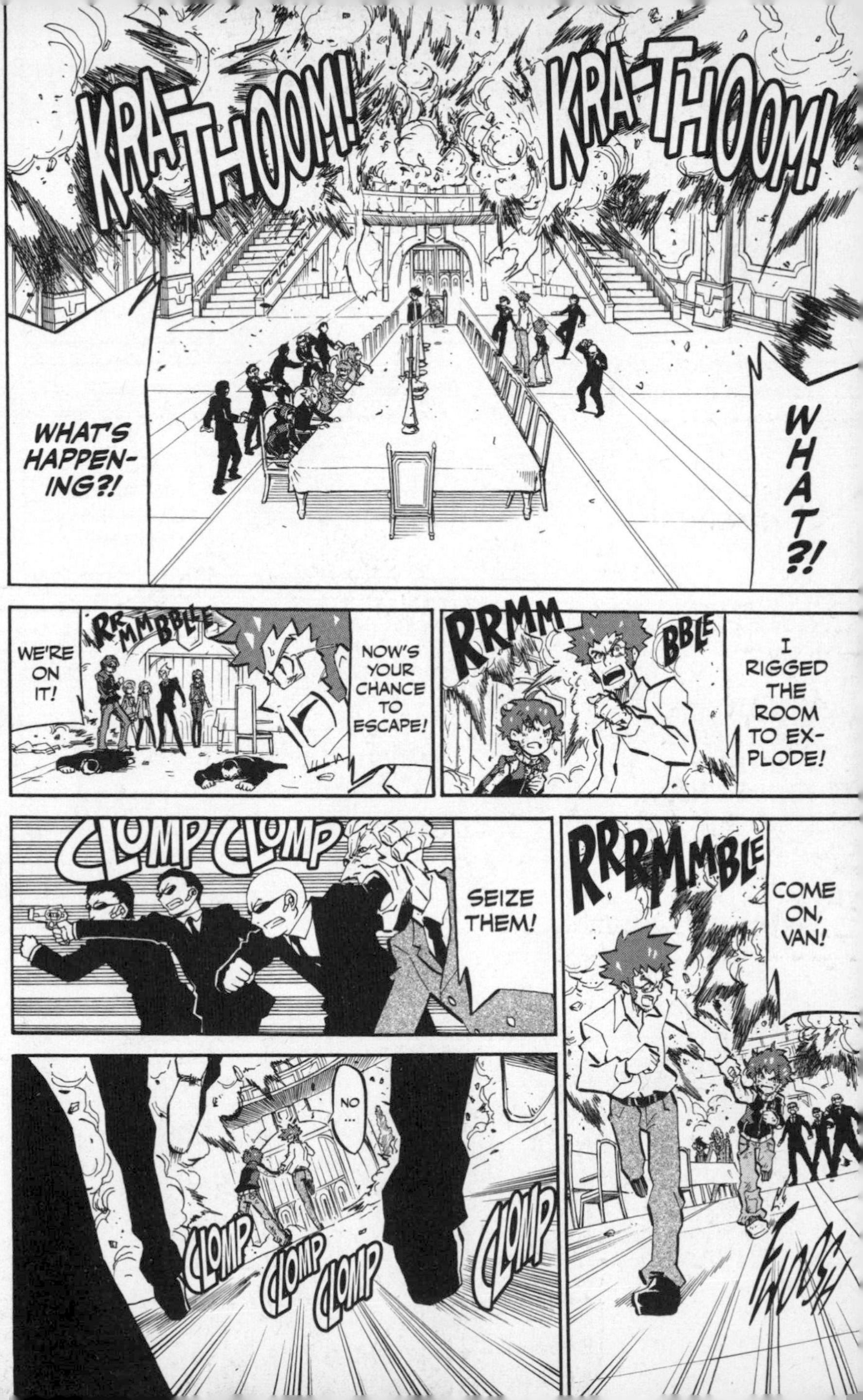
KRA-THOOM!
KRA-THOOM!
WHAT?!
WHAT'S HAPPEN-ING?!
RRMM BBLE
I RIGGED THE ROOM TO EX-PLODE!
NOW'S YOUR CHANCE TO ESCAPE!
RRMMBBLE
WE'RE ON IT!
RRRMMBLE
COME ON, VAN!
CLOMP CLOMP
SEIZE THEM!
NO ...
CLOMP
CLOMP
CLOMP
CLOMP

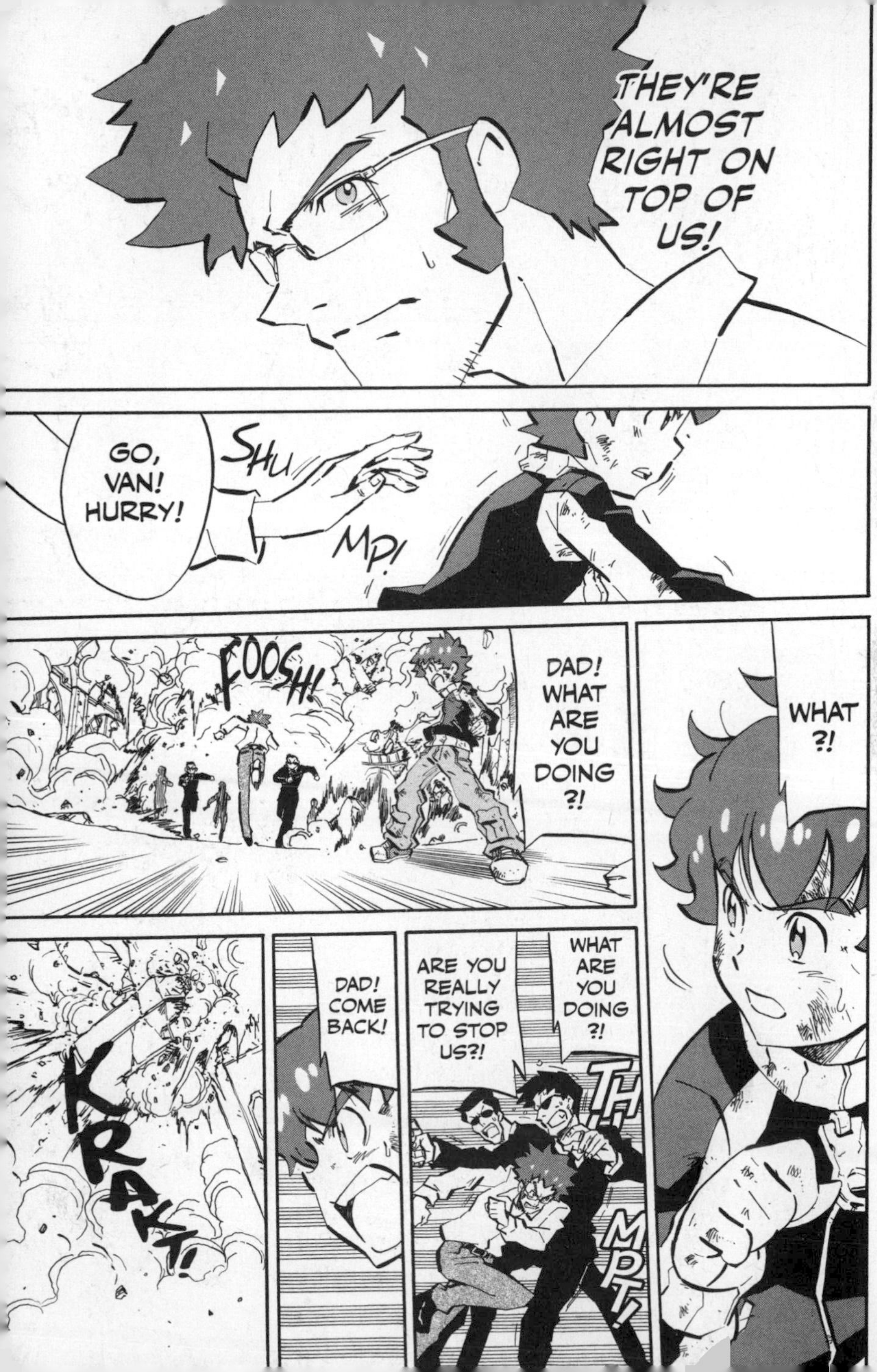
THEY'RE ALMOST RIGHT ON TOP OF US!
SHUMP!
GO, VAN! HURRY!
WHAT?!
DAD! WHAT ARE YOU DOING?!
FOOSH!
WHAT ARE YOU DOING?!
ARE YOU REALLY TRYING TO STOP US?!
THUMPT!
DAD! COME BACK!
KRAKT!

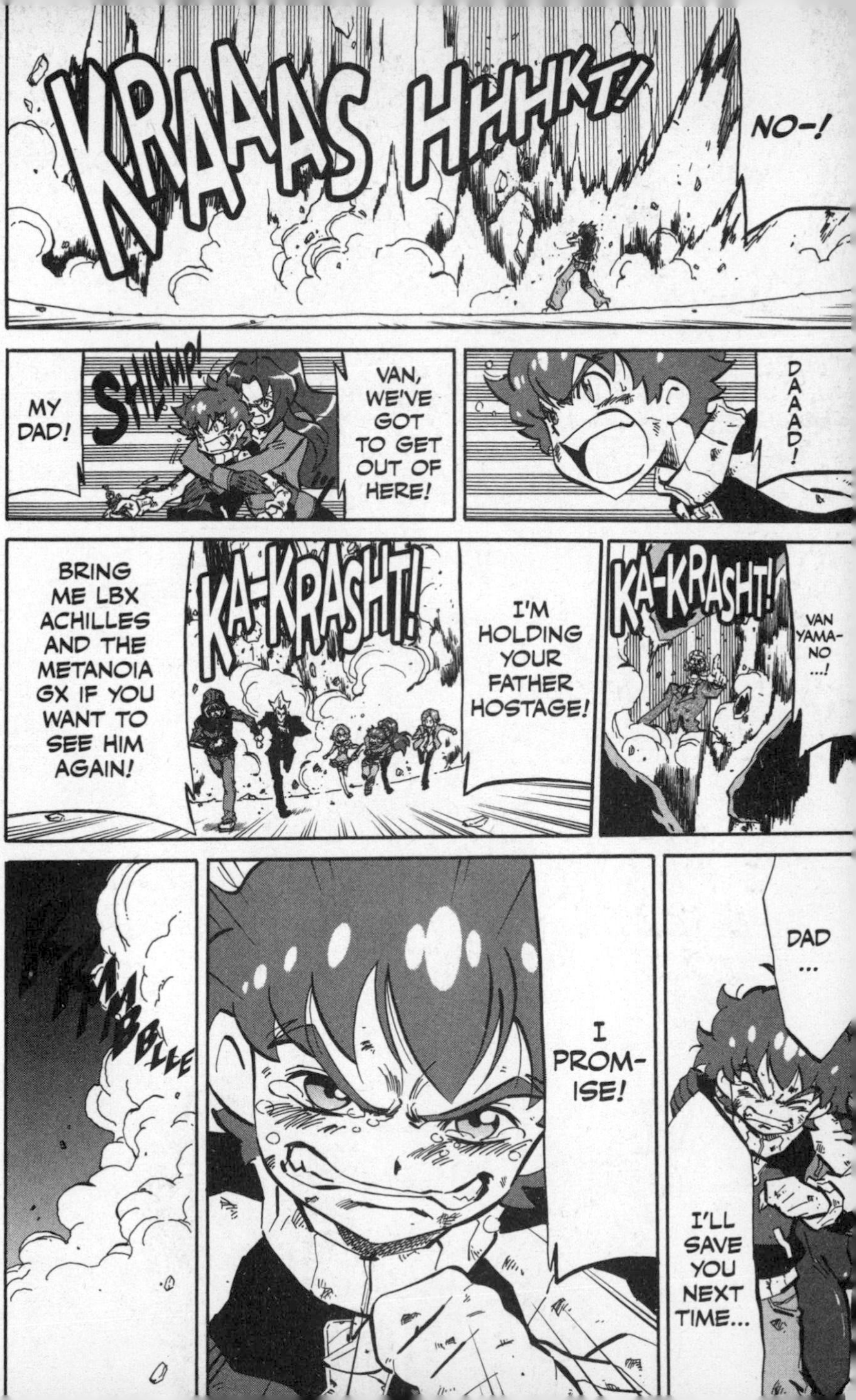
NO-!
KRAAAS HHHHKT!
DAAAAD!
VAN, WE'VE GOT TO GET OUT OF HERE!
SHLUMP!
MY DAD!
VAN YAMA-NO ...!
KA-KRASHT!
I'M HOLDING YOUR FATHER HOSTAGE!
KA-KRASHT!
BRING ME LBX ACHILLES AND THE METANOIA GX IF YOU WANT TO SEE HIM AGAIN!
DAD ...
I'LL SAVE YOU NEXT TIME...
I PROM-ISE!

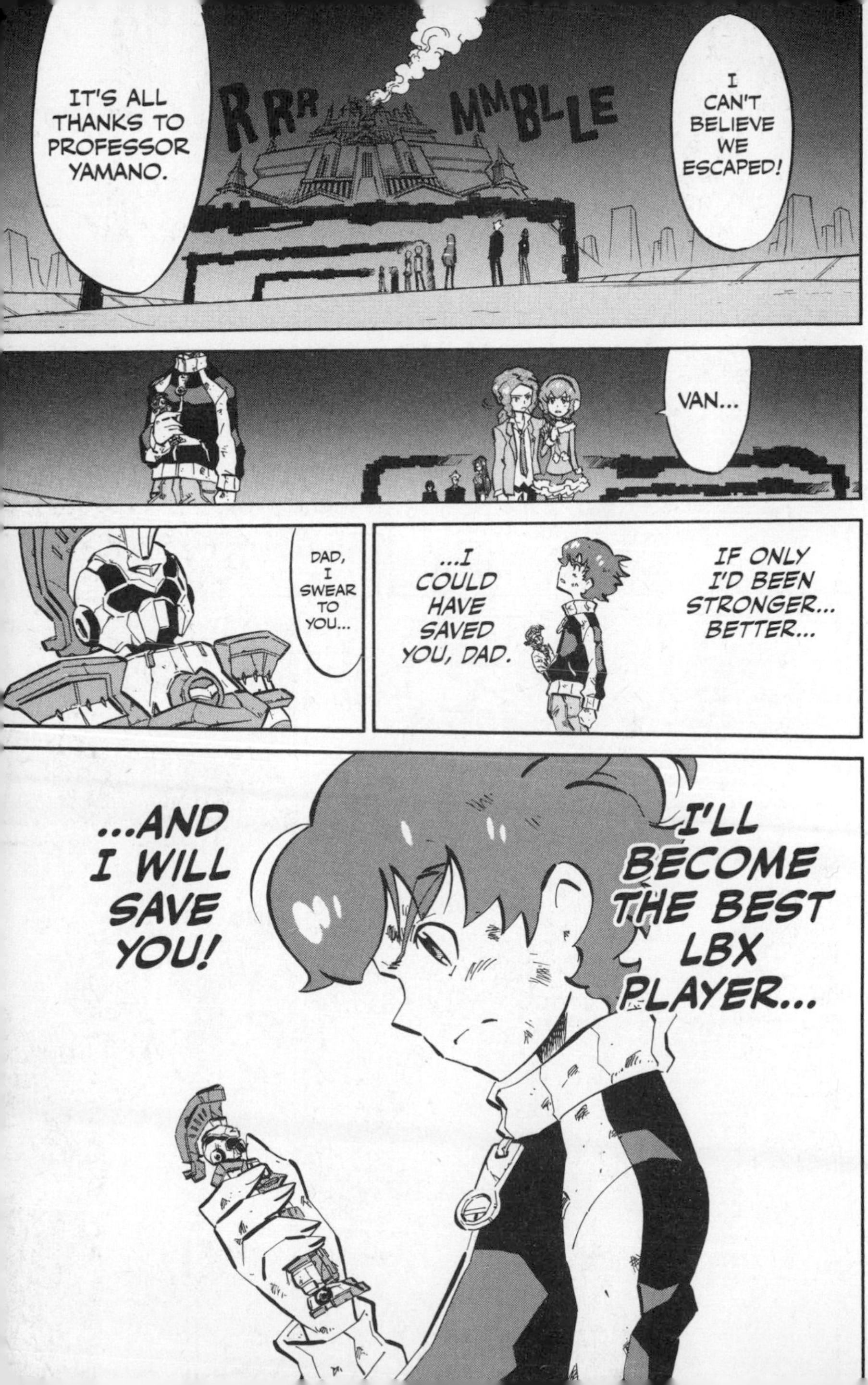
I CAN'T BELIEVE WE ESCAPED!
RRRMMBLLE
IT'S ALL THANKS TO PROFESSOR YAMANO.
VAN...
IF ONLY I'D BEEN STRONGER... BETTER...
...I COULD HAVE SAVED YOU, DAD.
DAD, I SWEAR TO YOU...
I'LL BECOME THE BEST LBX PLAYER...
...AND I WILL SAVE YOU!

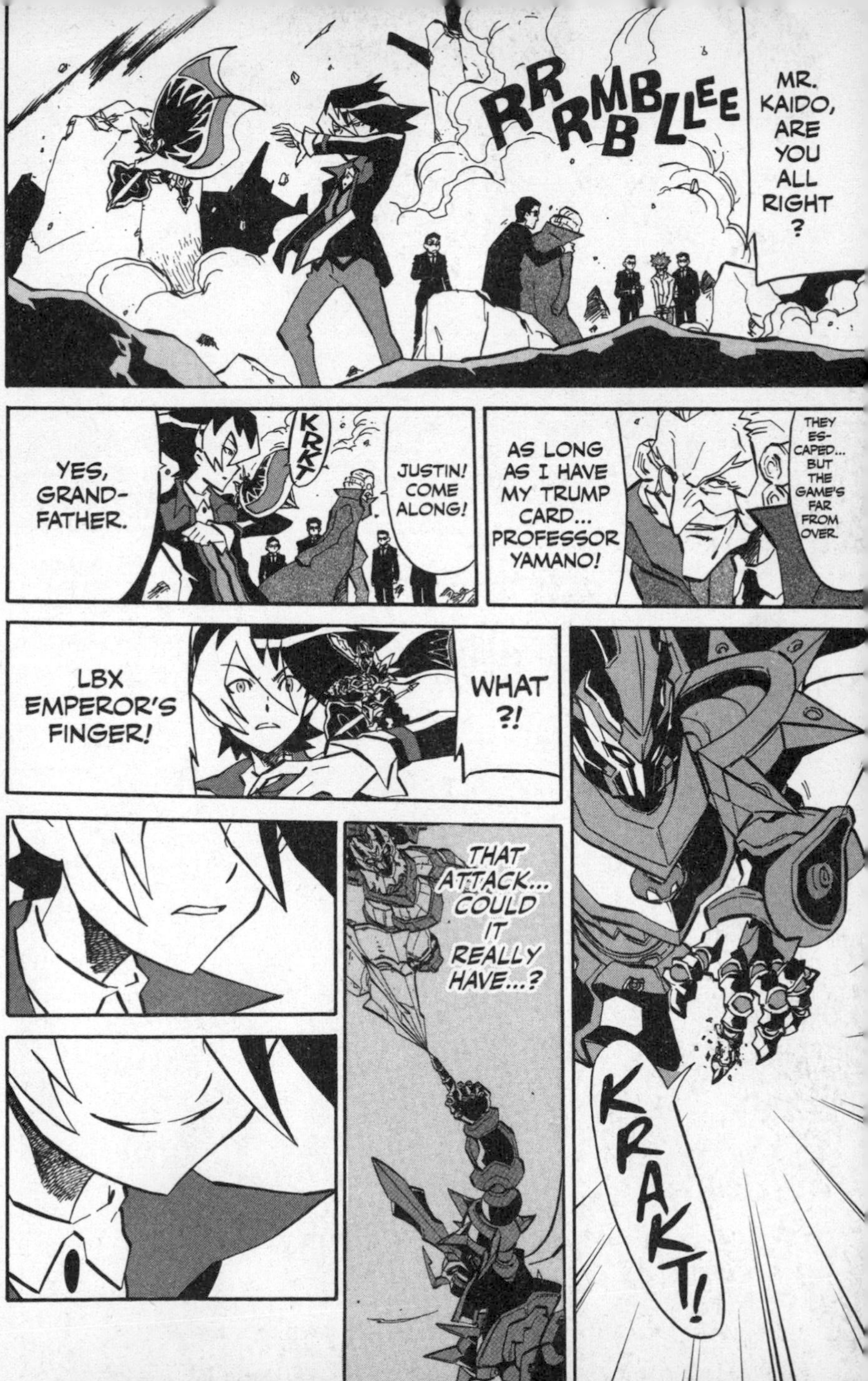
MR. KAIDO, ARE YOU ALL RIGHT?
RRRMBBLLEE
THEY ES-CAPED... BUT THE GAME'S FAR FROM OVER.
AS LONG AS I HAVE MY TRUMP CARD... PROFESSOR YAMANO!
JUSTIN! COME ALONG!
KRKT
YES, GRAND-FATHER.
KRAKT!
WHAT?!
LBX EMPEROR'S FINGER!
THAT ATTACK... COULD IT REALLY HAVE...?

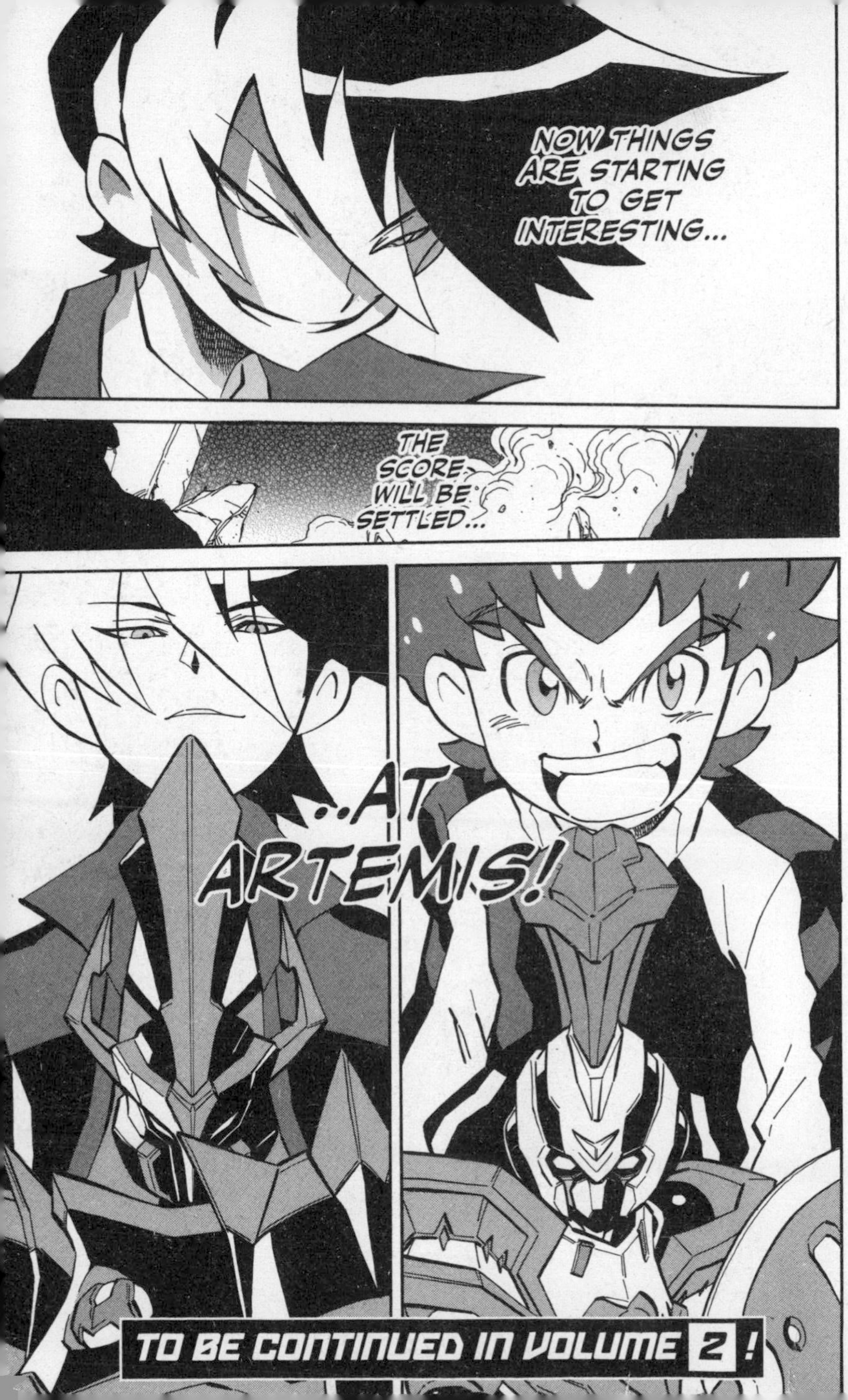
NOW THINGS ARE STARTING TO GET INTERESTING...
THE SCORE WILL BE SETTLED...
...AT ARTEMIS!
TO BE CONTINUED IN VOLUME 2 !

CHAPTER 0

LBX

LITTLE BATTLERS EXPERIENCE ™

NEW SERIES ANNOUNCEMENT

AS A SPECIAL BONUS, WE'VE INCLUDED THE ANNOUNCEMENT FROM THE JANUARY 2011 ISSUE OF *CORO CORO COMICS*! NOW YOU CAN FIND OUT HOW VAN AND LBX ACHILLES' FIERCE BATTLE BEGAN WITH CHAPTER 0 OF LBX!

*CONTAINS THE ORIGINAL STORY FROM *CORO CORO COMICS* MAGAZINE.

STARTING ON THE VERY NEXT PAGE!

HIDEAKI FUJII'S NEW SERIES!

SPECIAL ANNOUNCEMENT

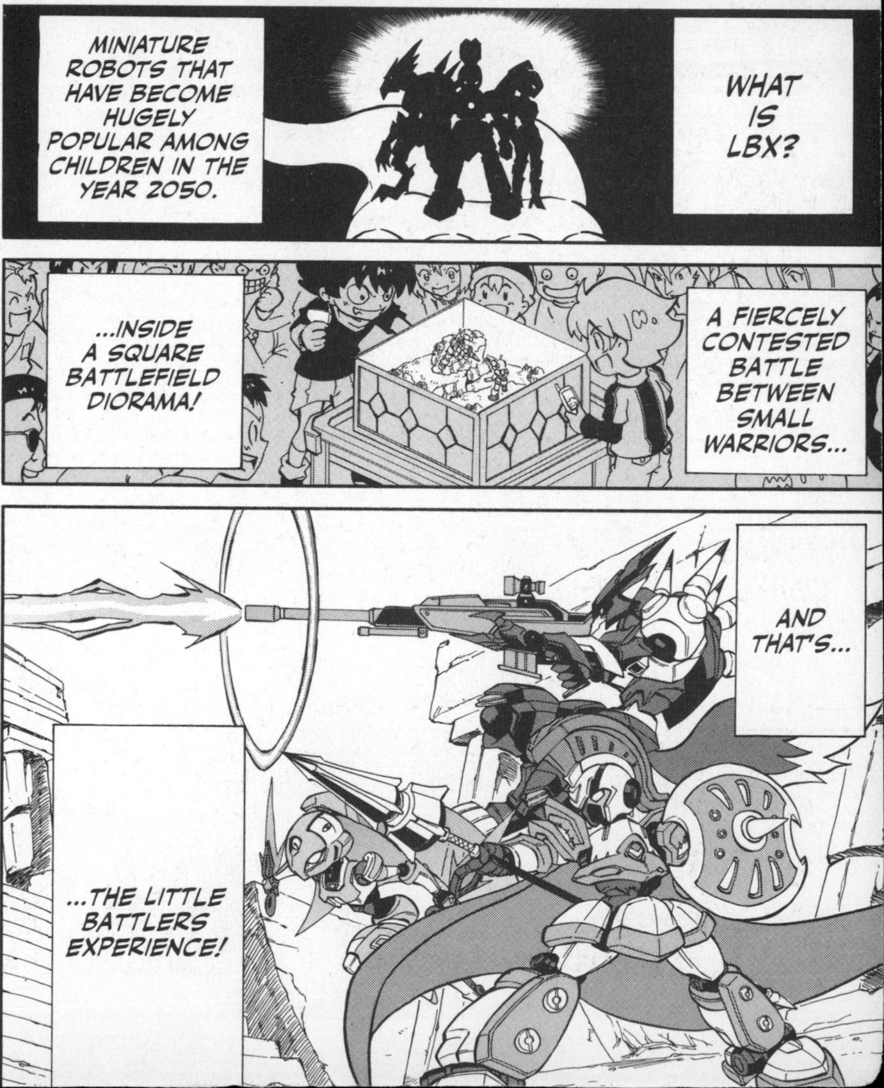
WHAT IS LBX?
MINIATURE ROBOTS THAT HAVE BECOME HUGELY POPULAR AMONG CHILDREN IN THE YEAR 2050.
A FIERCELY CONTESTED BATTLE BETWEEN SMALL WARRIORS...
...INSIDE A SQUARE BATTLEFIELD DIORAMA!
AND THAT'S...
...THE LITTLE BATTLERS EXPERIENCE!

LITTLE BATTLERS EXPERIENCE

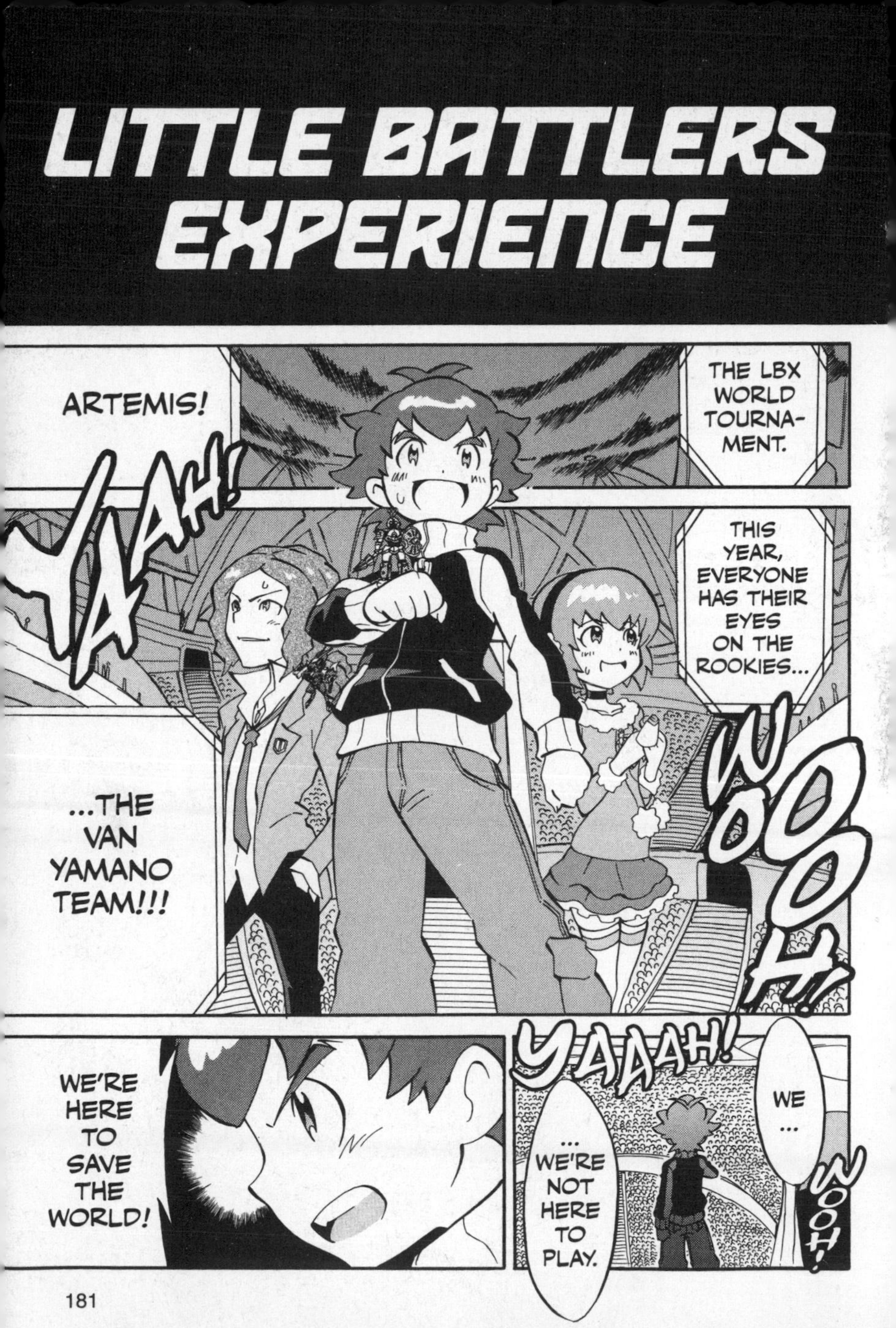
THE LBX WORLD TOURNAMENT.
ARTEMIS!
YAAH!
THIS YEAR, EVERYONE HAS THEIR EYES ON THE ROOKIES...
...THE VAN YAMANO TEAM!!!
WOOOOH!
YAAAH!
WE ...
... WE'RE NOT HERE TO PLAY.
WOOOH!
WE'RE HERE TO SAVE THE WORLD!

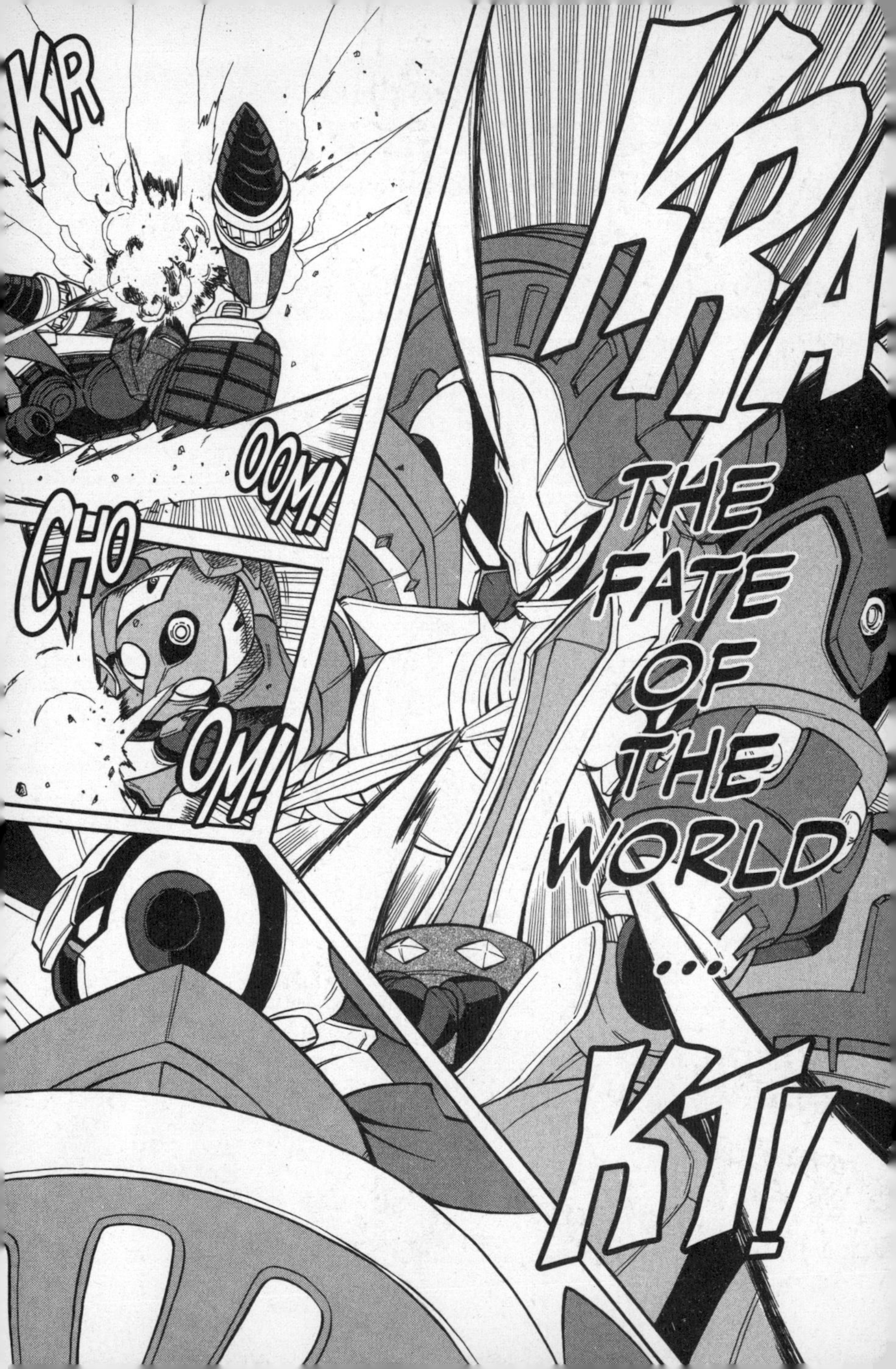

KRA
THE FATE OF THE WORLD
...
KT!
KR
OOM!
CHO
OM!

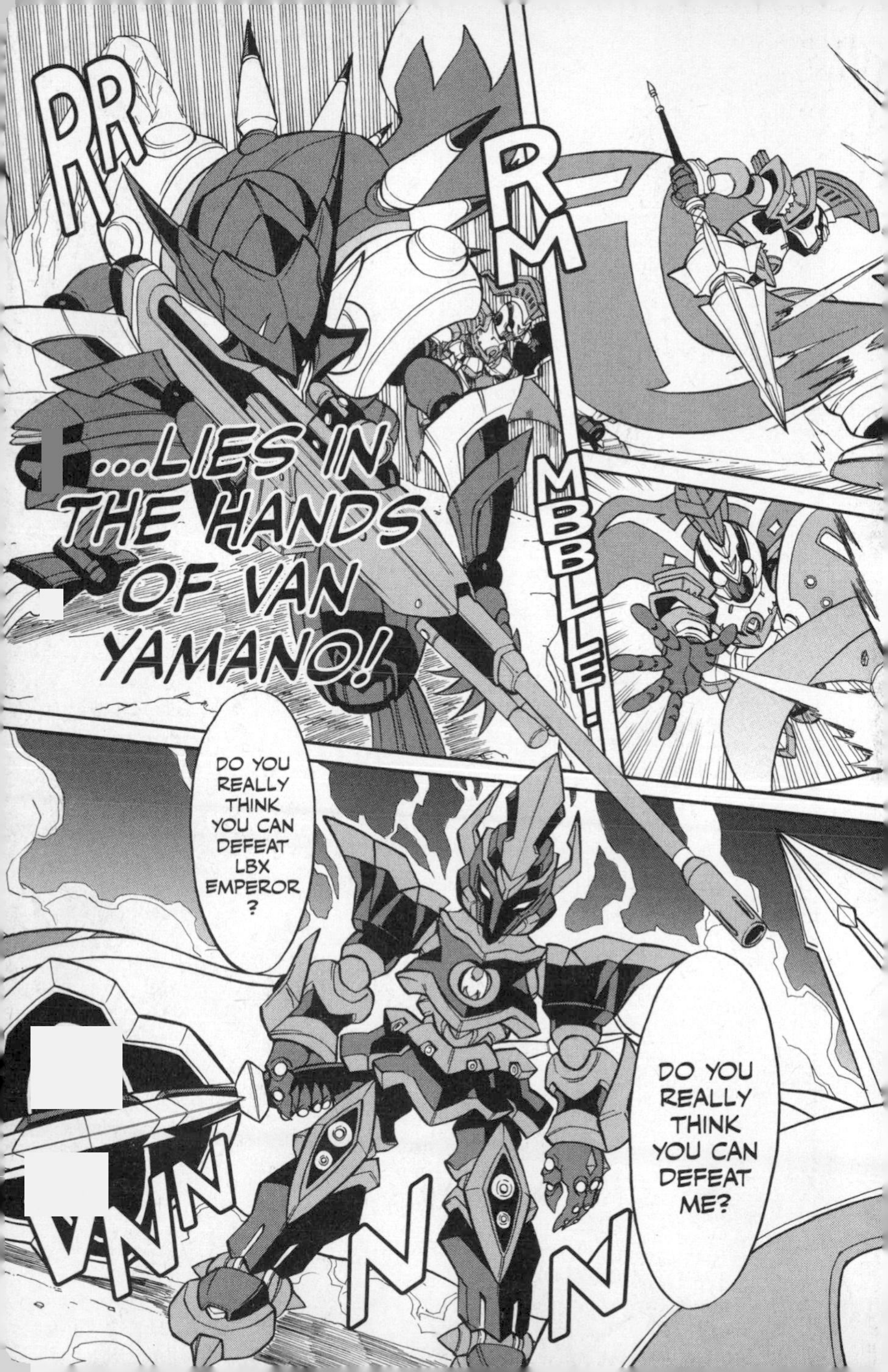
RR
RM
MBBLLE!
...LIES IN THE HANDS OF VAN YAMANO!
DO YOU REALLY THINK YOU CAN DEFEAT ME?
DO YOU REALLY THINK YOU CAN DEFEAT LBX EMPEROR?
VNN
N
N

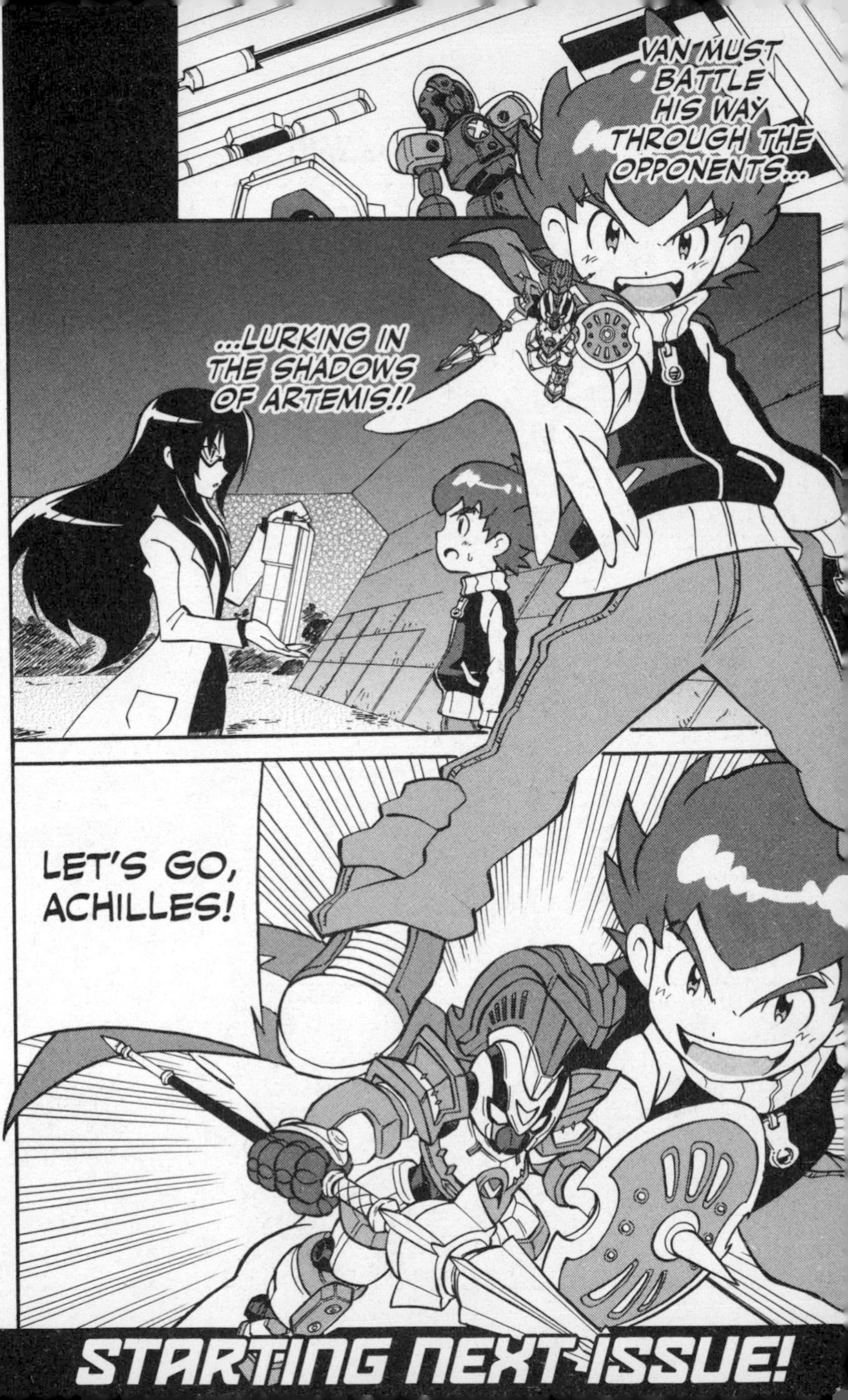
VAN MUST BATTLE HIS WAY THROUGH THE OPPONENTS...
...LURKING IN THE SHADOWS OF ARTEMIS!!
LET'S GO, ACHILLES!
STARTING NEXT ISSUE!

AFTERWORD

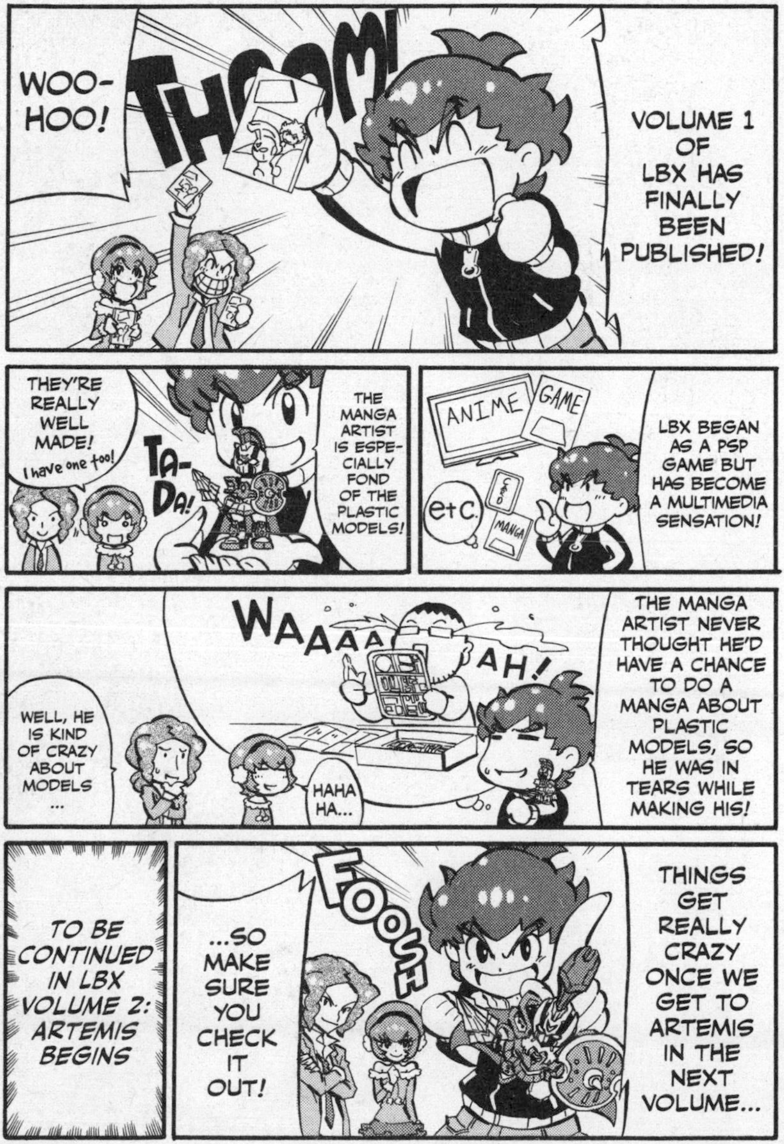
VOLUME 1 OF LBX HAS FINALLY BEEN PUBLISHED!
THOOM!
WOO-HOO!
LBX BEGAN AS A PSP GAME BUT HAS BECOME A MULTIMEDIA SENSATION!
ANIME
GAME
CARD
MANGA
etc.
THE MANGA ARTIST IS ESPECIALLY FOND OF THE PLASTIC MODELS!
TA-DA!
THEY'RE REALLY WELL MADE!
I have one too!
THE MANGA ARTIST NEVER THOUGHT HE'D HAVE A CHANCE TO DO A MANGA ABOUT PLASTIC MODELS, SO HE WAS IN TEARS WHILE MAKING HIS!
WAAAAAAH!
HAHA HA...
WELL, HE IS KIND OF CRAZY ABOUT MODELS ...
THINGS GET REALLY CRAZY ONCE WE GET TO ARTEMIS IN THE NEXT VOLUME...
FOOSH
...SO MAKE SURE YOU CHECK IT OUT!
TO BE CONTINUED IN LBX VOLUME 2: ARTEMIS BEGINS

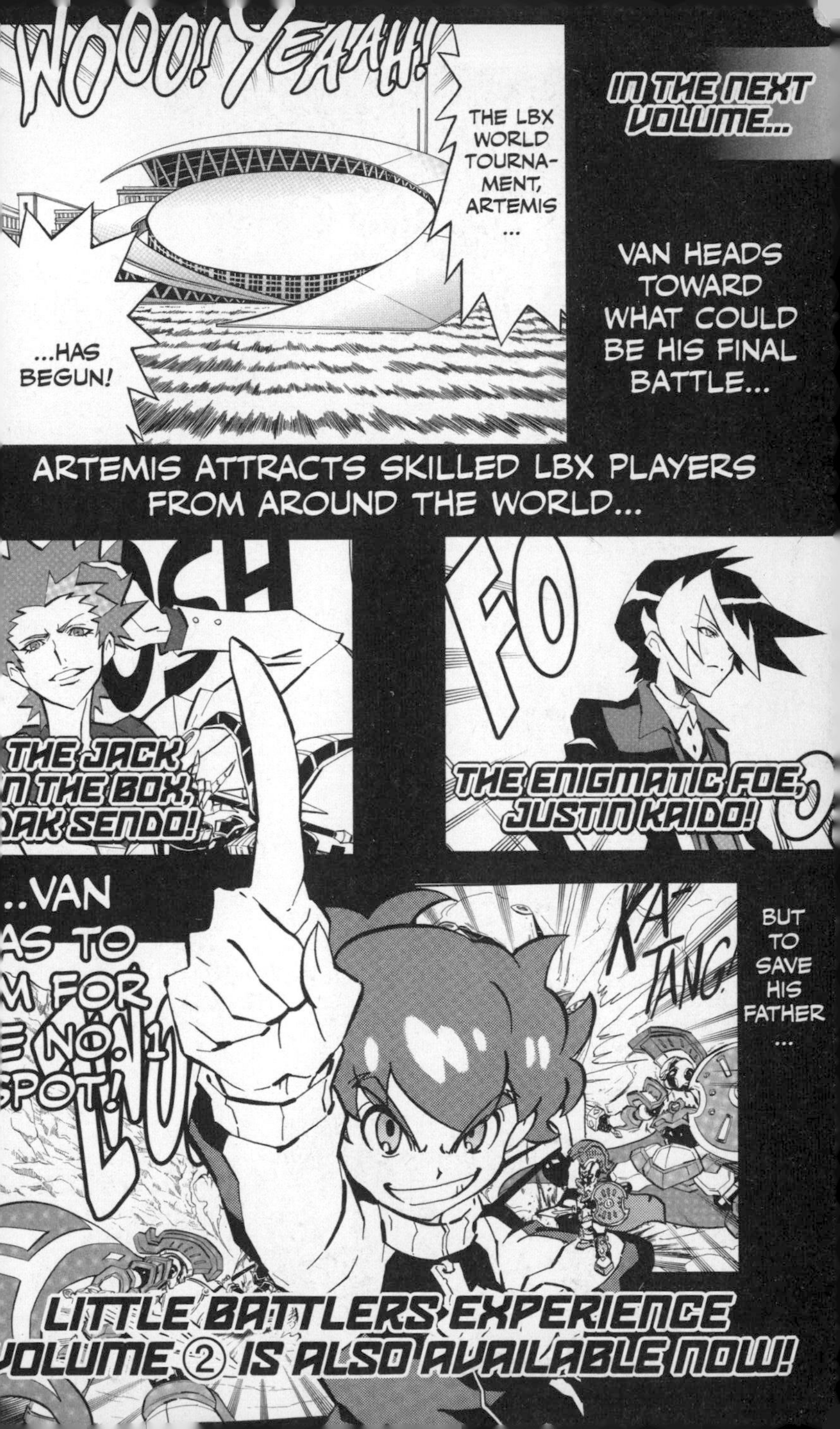
IN THE NEXT VOLUME...
VAN HEADS TOWARD WHAT COULD BE HIS FINAL BATTLE...
WOOO! YEAH!
THE LBX WORLD TOURNA-MENT, ARTEMIS ...
...HAS BEGUN!
ARTEMIS ATTRACTS SKILLED LBX PLAYERS FROM AROUND THE WORLD...
THE ENIGMATIC FOE, JUSTIN KAIDO!
THE JACK IN THE BOX, AK SENDO!
BUT TO SAVE HIS FATHER ...
KA-TANG!
..VAN AS TO M FOR E NO. 1 SPOT!
LITTLE BATTLERS EXPERIENCE VOLUME ② IS ALSO AVAILABLE NOW!

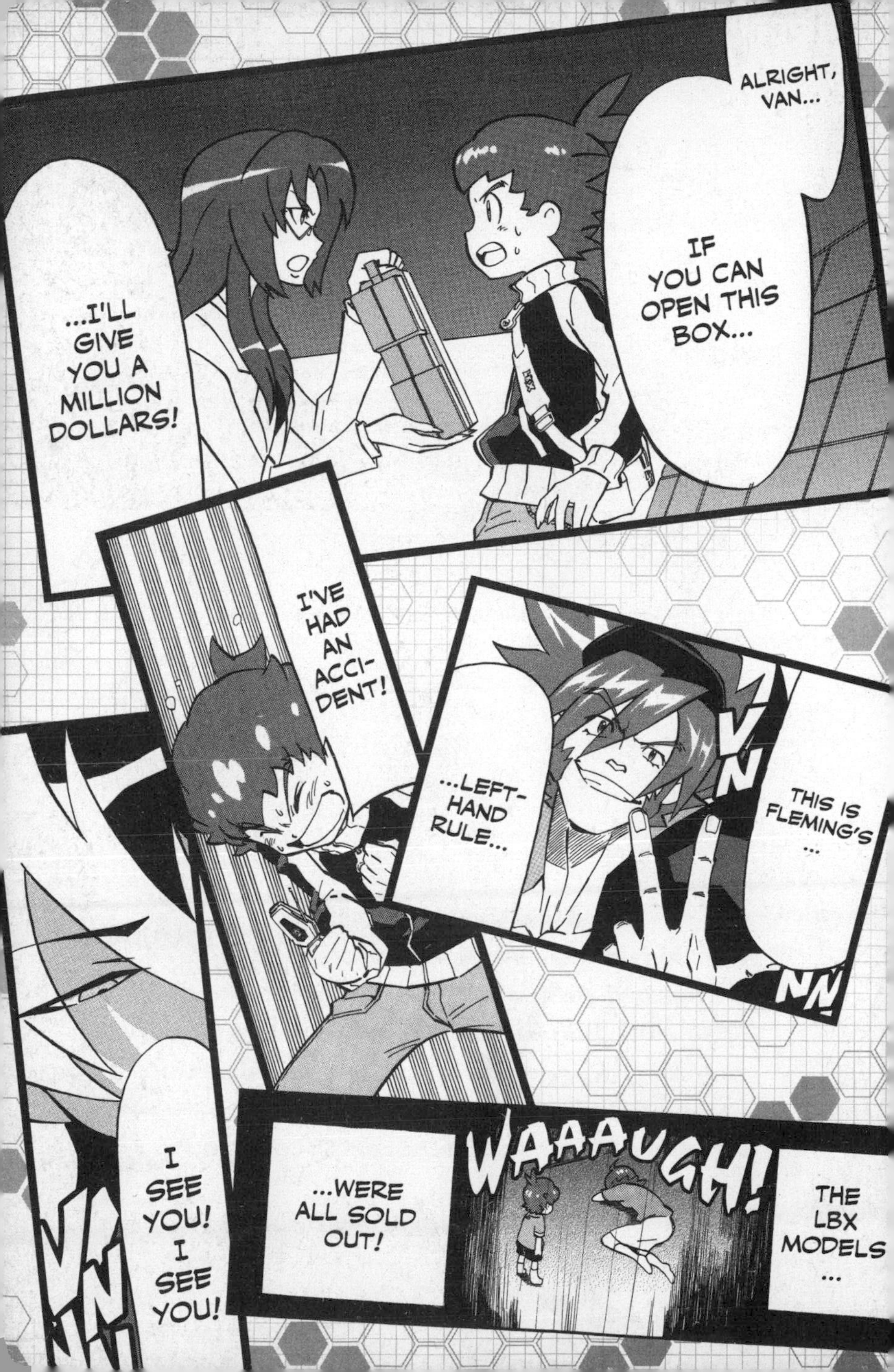
ALRIGHT, VAN...
IF YOU CAN OPEN THIS BOX...
...I'LL GIVE YOU A MILLION DOLLARS!
THIS IS FLEMING'S...
...LEFT-HAND RULE...
I'VE HAD AN ACCIDENT!
THE LBX MODELS...
WAAAUGH!
...WERE ALL SOLD OUT!
I SEE YOU! I SEE YOU!

VAN YAMANO AND ACHILLES' BATTLE BEGINS NOW!! GO
AND READ AHEAD INTO THE PAGES... WILL YOU FIND

HOPE? OR DESPAIR?
NOW! BATTLE START!!!

◆ Hideaki Fujii ◆

Hideaki Fujii was born on December 12, 1977,
in Miyazaki Prefecture. He made his debut in
2000 with *Shin Megami Tensei: Devil Children*
(*Monthly Comic BomBom*). His signature
works include *Battle Spirits: Breakthrough
Boy Bashin* and many others. Blood type A.

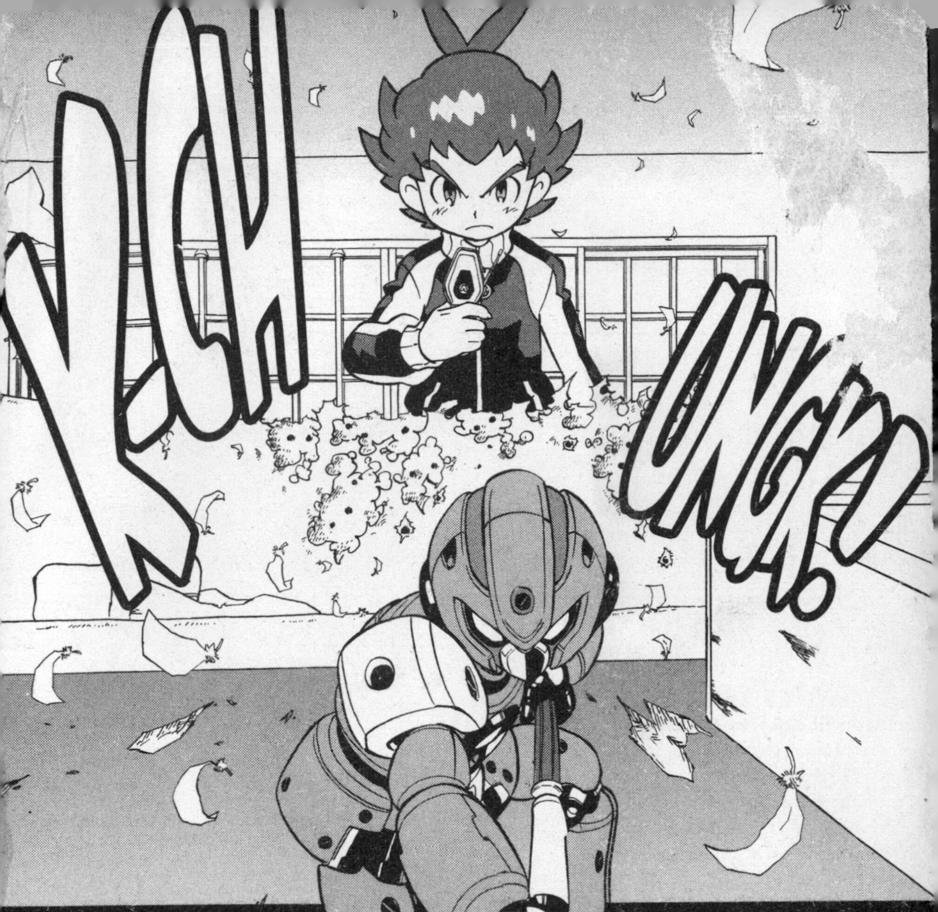

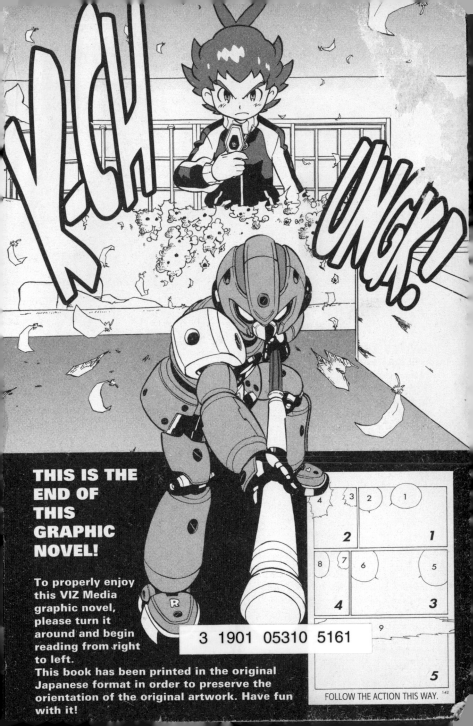

THIS IS THE END OF THIS GRAPHIC NOVEL!

To properly enjoy this VIZ Media graphic novel, please turn it around and begin reading from right to left.
This book has been printed in the original Japanese format in order to preserve the orientation of the original artwork. Have fun with it!

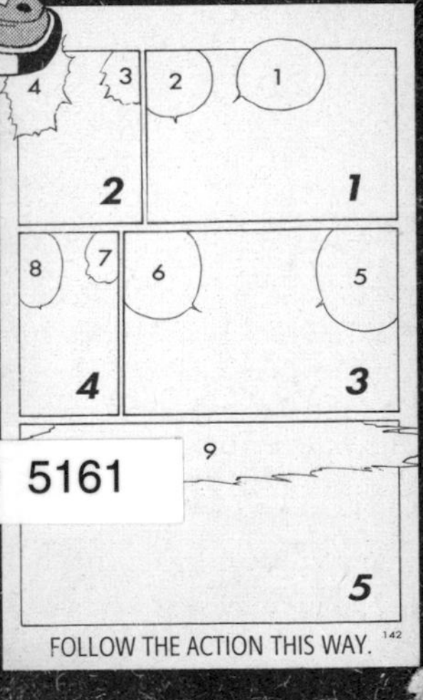
1
2
3
4
5
6
7
8
9
FOLLOW THE ACTION THIS WAY.